of tea....

**Praise for the Novels
of Katie MacAlister**

The Art of Stealing Time
A TIME THIEF NOVEL

"I highly recommend this book for the humor, the romance, and the wild ride it takes us on."
—Cocktails and Books

"[MacAlister is] still a brilliant writer, funny, fast, silly, and completely irreverent.... Her sassy wit and crazy characters will still entertain her fans."
—Bitten by Books

Time Thief
A TIME THIEF NOVEL

"If you enjoy a good murder mystery mixed with familial betrayal, the otherworld, and a romance, then this is the book for you."
—Dark Faerie Tales

"Silly, sassy, and salacious—Katie MacAlister ... gets up to her usual tricks in this comical paranormal romance."
—The Urban Book Thief

Sparks Fly
A NOVEL OF THE LIGHT DRAGONS

"Once again I was drawn into the wondrous world of this author's dragons and hated leaving once their story was told. I loved this visit and cannot wait for the next book to see just what new adventures lay in wait for these dragons."
—Love Romances & More

continued ...

"Fast-paced . . . an entertaining read and a fine addition to MacAlister's dragon series."—Bookshelf Bombshells

"Balanced by a well-organized plot and MacAlister's trademark humor." — *Publishers Weekly*

It's All Greek to Me

"This author delivers again with yet another steamy, sexy read with humorous situations, dialogue, and characters. The plot is fast-paced and fun, typical of MacAlister's novels. The characters are impossible not to like. The hiccups in their relationship only serve to make the reader root harder for them. The events range from amusing to steamy to serious. The reader can't be bored with MacAlister's novel." —Fresh Fiction

"A fun and sexy read." —The Season for Romance

"A wonderful, lighthearted romantic romp, as a kick-butt American Amazon and a hunky Greek find love. Filled with humor; fans will laugh with the zaniness of Harry meets Yacky." —*Midwest Book Review*

"Katie MacAlister sizzles with this upbeat and funny summer romance. . . . MacAlister's dialogue is fast-paced and entertaining. . . . Her characters are interesting and her heroes are always attractive/intriguing . . . a good, fun, fast summer read." —Books with Benefits

"Fabulous banter between the main characters. . . . Katie MacAlister's got a breezy, fun writing style that keeps me reading." —Book Binge

THE
IMPORTANCE OF
BEING ALICE

Katie MacAlister

A SIGNET BOOK

SIGNET
Published by the Penguin Group
Penguin Group (USA) LLC, 375 Hudson Street,
New York, New York 10014

USA | Canada | UK | Ireland | Australia | New Zealand | India | South Africa | China
penguin.com
A Penguin Random House Company

First published by Signet, an imprint of New American Library,
a division of Penguin Group (USA) LLC

First Printing, January 2015

 REGISTERED TRADEMARK — MARCA REGISTRADA

ISBN 978-0-451-47137-6

Printed in the United States of America
10   9   8   7   6   5   4   3   2   1

This book is dedicated to Janet Avants, because she inspired a group of us to form the Church of Jante, and also to her husband, Gary, because he rescues kittens and dogs. But mostly to Janet, because hello! How many people inspire their own Internet religion? Smooches to you both.

Chapter 1

Expense Account
  Item one: ten pounds
  Remarks: Brothers are the bane of my existence.

"El-eeee-uuut."

    "Oh lord, not that again."

"El-eeee-uuut. Phone home, El-eeee-uuut."

"There is nothing else on this earth that you can be doing at this exact moment but that?"

"El-eeee-uuut."

Elliott Edmond Richard Ainslie, eighth Baron Ainslie, and eldest brother to eleven mostly adopted siblings—mostly brothers, due to his mother's belief that boys were easier to raise than girls—donned a long-suffering expression and leaned back in his office chair. "Very funny, Bertie. Almost as funny as the first one thousand, two hundred and thirty-two times you blighted me with that movie quote, although I feel honor-bound to point out *yet again* that it was E.T. who wanted to phone home, and not the young lad who found him."

"Dude, you always say that, and I still don't see that it matters. I mean, Elliott would have wanted to phone home if he went up in the mother ship with E.T., wouldn't he?" Bertie, the youngest of his brothers, slumped into the armchair nearest Elliott's desk with the boneless grace of young men of seventeen.

"You're getting your alien movies mixed up again; the mother ship was in *Close Encounters*. What's set you off on this eighties movie binge anyway? I thought you were studying for your exams." Elliott eyed his laptop with longing. He really needed to get this book started if he was going to have it finished in time to join the family on their annual trek to visit the orphanage and school his mother endowed in Kenya.

"Whatev."

"Really, Bertie? *Whatev?* You can't even be bothered to add the last syllable?" Elliott shook his head. "If this is what time in America has done to you, I shall have to speak to Mum about letting you return there in the autumn."

Bertie clicked his tongue dismissively, swiveling in the chair until his legs hung over one arm. "Mum'll let me go no matter what you say. My family is there. It's my crib, you know?"

"Your family is from a small village two hundred miles outside of Nairobi," Elliott corrected him. "At least that's what the people at the orphanage told Mum when she adopted you, and I see no reason why they would confuse a small village in Africa with Brooklyn, New York. But never mind all that. Did you want something in particular, or have you just come to blight me on a whim?"

"Elliott!" a voice said sharply from the door.

Elliott sighed to himself. This was all he needed to utterly destroy the morning's chance at work.

"You will not be cruel to your brother! He is needful of our love and understanding in order to help him integrate into this family. If you abuse him like that, you will end up making him feel that he is a stranger in a strange land." Lady Ainslie bustled into the room, clutched Bertie to her substantial bosom, and shot a potent glare over his head at her eldest son.

"He's been a part of the family since he was two months old, Mum. If he feels like a stranger, it's because he's cultivating that emotion, and not due to any ill will on my part," Elliott couldn't help but point out.

"You must love *all* your brothers and sisters," his mother went on, smooshing poor Bertie's face into the aforementioned bosom. Elliott winced in sympathy when Bertie's arms flailed, indicating a lack of oxygen. "No matter what their origins, color, or cultural roots."

"I do love all my siblings, although I will admit to preferring those you and Papa adopted rather than the two related by blood."

"Yes, well, that's because your dear papa and I were first cousins," Lady Ainslie admitted, utterly ignoring the fact that she was smothering one of her beloved sons. "To be honest, we're lucky that your sister Jane's webbed toes are the worst that came out of that. But I digress. You must not pick on dear Bertie, or he will get a complex."

Elliott gave consideration to the fact that Bertie's wild gestures were now more feeble twitches than anything else. "I don't think that will be a problem if you continue to asphyxiate him like that."

"What? Oh." Lady Ainslie looked down, and with an annoyed click of her tongue released Bertie. He collapsed to the floor, gasping for air, his face, already dark due to his ancestry, now strangely mottled. "Silly boy should have said something. Now, what did I come to see you about?"

"I haven't the slightest idea. Is it something to do with the builders? They haven't rescheduled again, have they?"

"No, no, they're still coming on Monday as planned. It will be terribly inconvenient having them underfoot for the monthly Mothers Without Borders meeting, but I suppose it is necessary to have the work done."

"If you wish for the walls to remain upright, then yes," Elliott said mildly.

He'd worked and saved and scrimped until he had, after seven years, managed to accrue enough money to start the restoration of the seventeenth-century house he had inherited. Along with a lot of debts, he thought sourly to himself, not the least of which was a nearly crippling inheritance tax.

If only his father hadn't been such a poor financial planner. If only his mother hadn't spent her own modest fortune on endowing any number of charities in her late husband's name. It wasn't that Elliott was against supporting such worthy causes—he was as charitable as the next man, doing his part to end child hunger and abuse to animals and to provide homes for needy hedgehogs—but he couldn't help but wish that supporting his large family and money-sucking estate hadn't fallen so squarely on his shoulders.

He had to get this book done. Hell, he had to get the damned thing started. Without the money the book contracts brought in, he'd be sunk. They all would be in desperate straits, everyone from his spendthrift mother right down to Levar, the second-youngest brother, who was recovering from a very expensive operation to straighten one of his legs. "Is there something in particular you wanted to discuss with me? Because if you've just come to chat, I will have to beg off. I really must get this book under way if I'm to meet the deadline. Bertie, for god's sake, stop with the dramatics. You aren't dying."

"I saw spots," Bertie said, ceasing the fish-out-of-water noises in order to haul himself up to the chair. "I saw a light. I wanted to go into the light."

Elliott bit back the urge to say it was a shame he hadn't, because he truly did love all his brothers and sisters. Even impressionable, heedless Bertie, who had recently returned from a two-month visit to see distant family members who had long ago emigrated from the small village in Kenya to the U.S. "Right. What have I told you both about my office door?"

"When the door is shut, Elliott is working," they parroted in unison.

"And if I don't work . . . ?"

"We don't eat," they answered in unison.

"So why is it you're both here when this is my working time?"

"I need a tenner," Bertie said with an endearing grin.

Their mother looked askance. "You just had your allowance. What did you spend that on?"

"Girls," he answered, his grin growing. "Three of them. Triplets with golden hair, and golden skin, and knockers that would make you drool."

"Bertie!" Elliott said with a meaningful nod toward their mother.

"Oh, well," Lady Ainslie said, dismissing this evidence of teenage libido. "Young men should be interested in girls. Unless, of course, they're interested in boys, which is perfectly all right no matter what the Reverend Charles says, and if he thinks he's going to make an example of dear Gabrielle simply because she ran off with his poor downtrodden wife, well then, he simply needs to think again. The Ainslies have been a part of Ainston village since the Conqueror came over, and I shan't have him blackening our name now. That brings to mind the letter I intended on sending Charles after that scathing sermon he read last week, which was quite obviously pointed at me. Elliott, dear, have your secretary send a letter expressing my discontent, and threatening to cease our donations to the church if he doesn't stop writing sermons about women who raise their daughters to become wife-stealing lesbians."

Elliott sighed and looked at his watch. "I don't have a secretary, Mum."

"No?" She looked vaguely surprised. "You ought to, dear. You are a famous writer, after all. No one can kill off people quite like you do. Now, much as I would like to stay and chat, I really must go write an article for *The M'kula Times & Agricultural Review* regarding the upcoming celebration at the Lord Ainslie Memorial School of Animal Husbandry. I've been invited to speak at the opening of the new manure house next month, and I want to alert all our friends in Kenya to that worthy event. Do give your brother ten pounds. Young men always need ten pounds."

"And, speaking of that, have you given any thought to my suggestion?"

"What suggestion?" Her face darkened. "You're not still intending on committing that atrocity?"

"If by 'atrocity' you mean requiring that the members of this family find gainful employment elsewhere, then yes." He held up a hand to forestall the objection that he was certain she would make. "Mum, I have explained it at least three times: I cannot continue to support every single member of this family anymore. All those brothers and sisters are a drain on the estate, one that cannot continue unchecked."

"You are exaggerating the situation," she said dismissively. "They are your family. You owe them support."

"Emotional support, yes. Help where I can give it, of course. But the financial situation has made it quite clear that only those members of the family who actually work for the estate will continue to be employed. Everyone else is going to have to find a job elsewhere. We can't afford to support them simply because they are family."

"You are heartless and cruel!" his mother declared, one hand to her substantial bosom. "Your father would turn over in his grave if he knew how you were willing to disown all your siblings without so much as a thought for their welfare."

"I have had many thoughts for their welfare, but I am also responsible for the estate, and everyone employed by it, as well as the many tenant farmers. Mum, I'm sorry, but there's no other way. If I don't cut out the deadweight, we'll be foreclosed upon, and I don't think anyone wants to see that happen."

"But your brothers and sisters! What are they to do? How will they live?"

He smiled grimly. "Just like the rest of us. They'll have to get real jobs."

She gasped in horror. "You plan on throwing everyone to the wolves?"

"Hardly that. Dixon's job as the estate agent is quite secure—I couldn't do half the work he does. Gunner has employment elsewhere, so he doesn't come into the equation. Gabrielle is excellent at managing the tour guides and gift shop, so her job is safe. Assuming she comes back from wherever she ran off to. But the others will simply have to find jobs outside of the castle."

"You are not the man I thought you were," his mother said, giving him a look filled with righteous indignation. "I would wash my hands of you except I believe that one day your sanity will return to you. I just hope you haven't destroyed the family before that time."

With a dramatic flourish, she exited the room.

"One down," Elliott said with a sigh. He eyed his brother.

"This one will cost you a tenner," the little blighter had the nerve to say.

Elliott fought the urge to sigh again, and gave in to the roguish charm that won Bertie so much admiration from the local teenage female population. He dug a ten-pound note out of his wallet. "Mind this lasts longer than the last one I gave you. I'm not made—"

"—of money. I know, I know," Bertie said with a laugh. He tucked the cash away and gave Elliott a friendly buffet on the shoulder, saying, in a bizarre mix of British and American slang, "But you're the only one of us that has any dosh. Thanks, bro. You da man."

The door closed behind Bertie with a satisfying thud.

"Alone at—"

"Elliott, I remember now what it was I came to tell you before you began speaking so cruelly of all your helpless siblings," Lady Ainslie said, her head popping around the door just as Bertie left the room. "The man wishes to speak with you."

"Man?" Elliott ran over the mental list of men he knew who might show up at the castle and demand an audience. "What man? One of the builders?"

"No, no, the Irishman. The one you went to school with. He's on the phone for you."

"Patrick?" Elliott patted his pockets, realized that he didn't have his mobile phone, and followed after his mother as she disappeared down the dark corridor. "Mum, how often have I asked you not to answer my mobile phone?"

"But it was ringing, dear. And it might have been someone important."

When his mother turned right at the long galley, Elliott turned left and raced down the back stairs to the small room on the east side of the house that used to be known as the ladies' withdrawing room. In it was a comfortable, if eclectic, collection of furniture retrieved from the attics, and which made up the family's sitting room.

"Hullo?" He expected to see the phone turned off, but it was still active, and he could hear voices emitting from it. Picking it up, he said, "Patrick?"

"—and don't forget t'make an appointment with the agent. I want the condo sold no later than March. What? Elliott, is that you? Had t'send t'the back forty for you, did they?"

"Back forty what?" Elliott asked, confused.

"It's an American expression."

"Ah. To what do I owe the honor of this call? Oh, hell, that sounded rude. Ignore me—I'm in a foul mood. It's been a nightmare around here gearing up for some renovations, and I'm late getting started on a new book. Let me start again. Nice to hear from you, Patrick. How are you doing?"

Patrick laughed, and said something under his breath to his secretary about moving a meeting to the following week. "No need t'apologize. Your foul mood is why I'm calling. Your sister was talking about you the other day, and she suggested you be the one t'take the tickets, rather than my secretary trying to flog them on Craigslist."

Elliott sat in his favorite armchair, the one that was stained with decades of ink spilled by some long-dead literary ancestor. "My sister? Tickets? Craigslist? Christ, now I sound like a deranged parrot. Which sister, and what tickets are you talking about?"

"The tickets for my prewedding trip down a couple of rivers in Europe t'that city in Czechoslovakia. You know the place."

"Prague?"

"No, no, the other place. The one with that big bridge that gets all the attention."

Elliott thought. "Budapest?"

"Yes, that's the place. The river tour goes from Amsterdam t'Budapest."

"Budapest is Hungary, not the Czech Republic."

"Same difference," Patrick said with an airy lack of concern. "I've parted ways with Alice, so I don't need the tickets, and since your delicious sister swore it was bad juju for her t'take the place of an ex, she thought that you could do with the trip. Since I hear all hell is about t'break out at Ainslie Castle, that is, and of course, your straitened circumstances."

There was a tinge of satisfaction in Patrick's voice that Elliott ignored. Before he could respond, he heard someone yelling for him. No doubt it was yet another minor crisis. He sank down farther into the chair, asking, "Who's Alice?"

"My ex. It was past time t'let her go. You know my rule."

"Two years with any given woman, and not a single day more," Elliott said, making a face at nothing in particular. He'd always thought Patrick's method of conducting his romantic affairs particularly coldhearted.

"That's right. As a matter of fact, I broke that rule by sticking with Alice for three extra months, but where did that get me? She called me a bastard. She said that half the condo was hers. She claimed I misled her. Me! It would have been laughable if it wasn't so damned unpleasant. It was a sign, I tell you, Elliott, a sign that it doesn't do t'go against the rule. If you don't move on when you're supposed to, nothing good will come of it."

"I'll be sure to remind my sister of that," Elliott said smoothly. "Which sister will I be informing of your intentions two years hence? You've met all three of them over the years, although one wouldn't give a fig for you. At least not romantically speaking."

Patrick laughed again. "Don't be such a wet blanket. Who knows, Jane could be the one that breaks the rule. Regardless, I'll e-mail you the ticket information. Alice said she wouldn't go on the trip if I paid her to, so you'll have the cabin all t'yourself. Boat leaves next Monday. Don't worry about paying—it's no hardship to me, and I know you'll appreciate the largesse. You'll have a fortnight floating around rivers, which your sister says will give you peace and quiet you won't have at home. Regards t'Lady Ainslie. She sounds as distracted as ever. What's that? Yes, yes, I'll take that call. I'm done here. Elliott, must ring off. Your sister Jane and I are off t'Paris in the morning, and I have an important vendor from Australia on the line."

"Wait a moment, what—"

The connection ended, leaving Elliott to stare in confusion at his phone.

"Mum says the builder needs you. Something to do with wanting more money." Gunner paused and stared at Elliott. "You all right? You look even more harassed than usual."

"I just had an odd call from Patrick."

"Daft Irish bastard Patrick?" Gunner asked, coming into the room and setting down a duffel bag that had been slung over one shoulder.

"Yes, although he'd bloody your nose again if he heard you calling him that."

Gunner grinned. The first child adopted by the baron and baroness, he was a self-defined mutt of a man, with a mix of ethnicities that ranged from African to South Pacific, and even some Slavic. "He could try. I haven't seen him in . . . hell, eight years? Nine? What's he done now? Don't tell me he's found some new way to flaunt his wealth in front of you."

Elliott shook his head, then changed it to a nod. "He can't help it; he's got an inferiority complex when it comes to me. Actually, he's doing me a favor. I think." He explained about the cruise.

"Nice," Gunner said with a low whistle. "I wish I had mates who'd give me trips to the Continent like that."

Elliott eyed the scruffy duffel bag. "Aren't you leaving today for Spain?"

"Yes, but that's work. I'll be baking in the hot Spanish sun taking pictures of abandoned factories while you're swanning around on some cruise ship. The life of an industrial photographer is not a posh one. Not like that of writers."

"You know exactly how un-posh my life is," Elliott answered. "Did you know Jane was in the States? The last I heard she was in Ottawa working for an Internet firm."

"No, but it doesn't surprise me that Patrick managed to find and acquire her. He's been dying to hold a relationship with one of the girls over you ever since his balls dropped."

"I don't give a damn who he dates," Elliott protested.

"You and I know that, but Patrick clearly views it as a way of scoring against you. *You have a title and an aristocratic family that I can't ever have, so I'll bang your sister.* That sort of thing."

"A title that's bound by debts, and a family that's driving me insane before my time."

Gunner glanced at his watch. "Patrick will never see that. You going to take the tickets?"

"I don't know. It does make me feel a bit beholden to him—"

"Elliott! Come quick, Mum says the renovation man wants another check. Something about the cost of stone going up." Bertie appeared briefly in the doorway, jamming a motorcycle helmet on his head, clearly on his way out to spend the ten pounds. "Oh, and one of the hothouses is on fire, but it's the one with the aubergines, so no loss there. Later, brothers!"

"I like aubergines," Elliott started to say, but stopped when Gunner laughed aloud.

"Sounds like you'd best take Patrick's offer, El. You'll go mad if you have to stay here for the next few weeks."

"There are times when I wish a portal would open up

right here at my feet, one that would transport me to another place, one without demands for money I don't have, and time I can't waste. But reality persists in being unhelpful, and I always remain right where I am."

Gunner scooped up the duffel and slung the strap across his chest. "Two weeks, El. No phones, no distractions and endless interruptions, no demands for more checks . . . just the blissful lapping of water against the side of the ship, and the quiet of a cabin all to yourself."

"It does sound like heaven."

The distant sound of a fire truck reached their ears. Gunner gave his brother a friendly punch in the arm, and left, saying, "I'm off to Spain, followed by a jaunt to Portugal to photograph the inside of a partially collapsed mine. And possibly Bulgaria, if my employers can smuggle me into an old radium factory."

"That doesn't sound healthy."

Gunner shrugged. "There is an interested bidder on the property, but the Bulgarian government isn't too wild about letting people photograph it. If I can sneak in, then I'll get some shots. Otherwise, I will be home in a week."

Elliott waved absently, making a decision right then and there. He'd take the trip that Patrick offered. A cruise down Europe's most famous rivers couldn't be any more disruptive than home, after all.

Chapter 2

Diary of Alice Wood

New Diary Begins: Day One

"Tell me that you're not going to give in to the douche-canoe and let him ruin what will be a perfectly fabulous vacation. Tell me you're not going to do that, Alice."

I kicked at an empty cardboard box as I wandered from a minuscule kitchen to an equally minuscule bedroom, hopping and swearing when it turned out the box wasn't empty after all. "Son of a sea biscuit!"

"Chill, babe," came the slightly offended voice of one of my oldest friends. I jostled the phone in order to apologize and rub my hurting toes. "I was just expressing my opinion. You're a big girl. If you want to save up for a dream vacation for more than four years and then not take it, then that's your business."

"Sorry, Helen, I wasn't sea biscuiting you. I stubbed my toes on a box full of books."

"I thought you'd unpacked already?"

"I did some unpacking. Most of the stuff is in storage because this place is so tiny." I sank down on a worn futon, my spirits as flabby as the futon's stuffing. "Moving is hell."

"Yeah, well, I told you to fight the douche-canoe's dictates. You guys moved into that condo together, so it's just as much yours as it is his. He had no right to demand you vacate the premises just because he went mental and broke up with you."

I smiled sadly at my toes. It was really nice that Helen automatically took my side in the breakup of a two-year relationship, but I had a terrible feeling that the fault didn't totally lie at Patrick's door. "Unfortunately, he was the legal owner of the condo, and he was the one who made the payments on it, so I really don't have grounds to make any demands. Besides, I couldn't live there with him in a roommate capacity. That would be too awkward."

"I hear you. And I'm not saying you should; I'm simply saying you shouldn't be a doormat to his stupid whims. And that includes giving up your dream vacation. You said he isn't going on the trip, right?"

"His actual words were, 'I'd rather have my scrotum tattooed than spend a single day on vacation with you,' so that seems pretty clear that he's not going to use his tickets."

"There you go, then!" Helen's voice, normally warm and empathetic, took on a slightly tetchy quality when she covered the receiver and yelled a demand that her daughter be home in time for dinner. "Sorry, Edison is being unusually difficult. Where were we? Oh, yes, if Patrick stays home, then why shouldn't you go spend two glorious weeks on a fancy river cruise boat allowing the staff to bend over backward to make you feel like a princess?"

I shrugged even though no one was there to see it. "It just feels kind of callous. I mean, I'm devastated by Patrick's betrayal. One day we were fine, happy as little clams, and the next day he's insisting that we both need to move on—and, in my case, to take that literally."

"There's devastated, and then there's devastated," Helen said. "You paid for your share of the trip, Patrick isn't going, and you don't have a job to hold you back from taking two weeks off."

"That's another thing." I slumped back into the futon, wishing it would swallow me up. "I should be looking for a job. One that does not come with a handsome boss who will two years later kick you out of your home."

"Mmm, well, we can debate the wisdom of dating an employer later. Right now you need to pull yourself out of the self-pity pool, and pack up your swimsuit, a fancy dress, and some comfortable walking shoes, because Europe beckons. That's what your therapist said, yes?"

"Not really. She said I should keep a diary of all my emotions and thoughts and feelings about . . . well, basically everything, and then use that as discussion points in our sessions. I have to say, Helen, it's weird talking to a stranger about all that inner stuff going on."

"Weird good, or weird weird?"

"Weird good, I suppose. I'm going to start the diary today. She said it was very important to pick a day and make that your first day, so that all the emotional baggage crap is behind you, and you get a fresh start. So I thought I'd start today."

"Good for you. It's especially pertinent if you decide to take the trip you paid for, and which you'd be an idiot to throw away just because an asshat loses what few bits of intelligence he had."

Using my abused toes, I nudged aside a collection of mail that I had picked up from my former home, until the glossy brochure advertising a glorious two-week trip down the Danube, Main, and Rhine rivers lay exposed. I had to admit, the temptation to take the trip regardless of my unemployed state was great. "You don't think it looks like I'm desperate or anything, do you?"

"Desperate?"

"Yeah, you know, all single ladies go to Europe hoping to meet some handsome James Bond–cool European man who will sweep her off her feet with his delicious accent and expensive Italian shoes. And courtly old-world manners. The kind that holds chairs for women at casinos, and offers them lifts in tiny little sports cars that cost as much as a nice house. Although, I have to admit that would make for some great diary entries."

Helen's laugh rippled out of the phone. "Honey, you haven't been to Europe lately if you think that's what the men there are like. I hate to disabuse your idea of old-world courtliness, but your average European guy isn't going to have expensive Italian shoes or a fancy sports car. So no, I don't think you will look desperate by taking the trip. On the contrary, I think it sends quite a firm statement to He Who Shall Not Be Named."

"You named him a minute ago," I couldn't help but point out.

"Stop harshing my mellow. Take the trip, enjoy having a fancy cabin all to yourself, meet a James Bond if you can—although usually his women don't end up well as I recall, so maybe go for someone whose job isn't quite so dangerous. Write all about it in your diary, and let Patrick suck on the idea that you're not in the least bit bothered by the fact that he's an idiot to let you go."

"Patrick was James Bondian when I first met him," I said forlornly. "It was at the benefit for the library, and all the women were gaga about him because he has that sexy Irish accent, and those blue eyes and black hair and, oh hell." Anger, never slow to start when I thought of my recent ex, fired up with an intensity that had me sitting up straight. "He really is a bastard through and through."

"Atta girl."

"He used me."

"Like a wet paper towel!"

I shoved aside some books until I dug out a small laptop. I would start the diary right then and there. "He charmed me and swept me off my feet and made me quit my nice job with the library to become his private secretary, and then he seduced me into moving in with him!"

"Man deserves to be hung up by his balls for that."

I stood up, shaking the laptop at nothing. "He made me think we were going to get married at the end of this trip! He had me look up the laws for Americans getting married in Budapest!"

"Ball-hanging is too good for him. He deserves something worse. Off with his head!"

"I will take that trip!" I yelled at the small living room filled with boxes that I had yet to unpack. "And I will enjoy myself! A lot! So much that he'll gnash his teeth and tear out that lovely black hair, and will crawl back begging me to forgive him."

"Which you won't do because you are a smart woman and won't throw yourself into yet another disastrous relationship without first thinking about whether the man is the one for you, right?"

Helen's voice was filled with caution, but my spirits were soaring, and I wasn't going to let anyone ground them again. I looked at the clock on the laptop, and made the decision. "Oh, how I will enjoy his crawling. Gotta run, babe. The plane leaves tomorrow morning, and I have no idea where my clothes are."

"You're not naked, are you?"

I smiled and put the laptop on the mound of books. "No, but I've been wearing the same pair of sweatpants and tee since I moved three days ago, and I think they could be technically classified as a new life-form. Love to the kiddo. I'll post pictures of the boat and things."

"Enjoy yourself, lovey. Have fun with cathartic writing and suchlike. But be careful, OK?"

"Yes, Mom," I said with another smile, touched by Helen's concern. She was always telling me to stop being quite so heedless when it came to life, but hard experience had proved more than once that you have to grab what you can because you never know when it will be taken away from you.

Like Patrick.

I shoved down that thought and allowed the burst of adrenaline to carry me through the next twenty-four hours, from the hassle of digging out appropriate clothing to wear, to borrowing a suitcase to stuff said clothing into, getting myself and my gigantic bag onto an airplane to Amsterdam, and, finally, starting this diary.

"My boat cruise goes through Holland, Germany, Austria, Slovakia, and Hungary," I told my seatmate as the occupants of the plane settled down to the long ten-hour trip from Portland, Oregon, to Amsterdam. "On three different rivers. See? Castles!"

The woman next to me, obviously on summer break from college, admired the glossy brochure. "*Manny van Bris: Tour Guide to the Nearly Famous.* Well, now. That looks like a lot of fun."

"The staterooms," I read to her from the brochure, "are equipped with every modern convenience, and are designed to delight the traveler in a home-away-from home atmosphere. And I'll have a cabin all to myself since . . . since my friend can't make it."

"It sounds lovely," the woman said, giving me a look that told me I was on the verge of becoming That Person on a plane, the one you didn't want to get stuck sitting next to. I gave her a big smile, and settled back into my seat, my fingers sliding over the glossy paper.

Helen was right — I was due a vacation after the dramafest my life had suddenly become. I just hoped Patrick would realize that I had taken the trip after all. I had contemplated leaving him a message in case he was unaware of how easily I had moved on, but decided that a policy of pretending he didn't exist was better.

Besides, if I posted lots of pictures on Facebook of all the fabulous fun I was having on my glamorous boat trip, mutual friends would be sure to point them out to him. I smiled at the thought and made a mental note to include lots of photos of whatever handsome men came within the range of my camera.

Those were my thoughts as I dragged my by now jet-lagged self through the Amsterdam airport, found a cab, and made my way out to where the river cruise boats were lined up, waiting to take that day's flock of passen-

gers on board. The ships—long and sleek and elegant—
were stacked two and three deep, with long lines of
people streaming on board. I hauled my wheeled bag past
a couple of especially elegant ships, mentally hugging myself with delight. I'd made the right choice to come on this
trip. It would definitely show Patrick that I was so over
him.

The delight of that thought faded to nothing the second I spotted my boat.

"Excuse me," I said, staring in horror as I snagged a
uniformed person bearing a clipboard. "I'm looking for
the Manny van Bris River Tours section of the pier. Can
you tell me where that is?"

The man turned and pointed at the boat that I was
still staring at. "That would be your ship, madam."

"No." I shook my head. "It can't be. See, I have a brochure. It shows the ship right here, and this is clearly not
the same boat as that … that … heap."

The man gave me a sympathetic look, murmured
something about hoping I enjoyed my holiday, and hurried off to tend his shiny new ship.

My gaze drifted along the narrow boat moored alongside the dock. A small gangway stretched across the few
feet of water to the dockside, rusted chains hanging mo-
rosely off the flimsy walkway. The ship itself had once
been painted red and white, but now was mostly rust and
white, with large bare patches where the paint had peeled
off. At the front of the upper deck—there were three
decks on the ship, according to the brochure, although I
now viewed that source of information with much
skepticism—a handful of plastic white lawn chairs sat.

"This is not the same ship," I said, looking at the brochure one more time. "This can't be right. I can't have

spent four grand on that. It looks like it would sink if I so much as sneezed on it!"

"Alice Wood?" I looked up at the person who had called my name. A shiny-faced woman of indeterminate years, but with poufy blond hair that bespoke someone in her sixties, bustled carefully across the gangway and over to me. In a voice with a BBC America sort of English accent, she said, "You are Alice Wood of Portland, Oregon, United States?"

"Yes, I'm Alice, but that is not the same ship as shown here." I held out the brochure and tapped it.

"The ship pictured in the advertisement is just a depiction, as is noted in the fine print," she said dismissively, grabbing the handle of my suitcase and wheeling it away from me, toward the gangway. "This is our flagship, the *Manny B*. It needs a few cosmetic touches, but I assure you that once you're on board, you'll find it very comfortable, very comfortable indeed. I haven't introduced myself, have I? I'm Tiffany Jones, the cruise concierge, and your friend away from home. Call on me for whatever you need. Come along, now, you are the last of our guests to arrive, and Captain Manny is most adamant about leaving before the other ships."

"Really?" I said, looking upward at the rusted side of the ship as I carefully walked across the gangway. The latter didn't feel any too sturdy underfoot, but at least I made it across without falling into the water, or chunks of the ship hurling themselves onto my head. "Why is that?"

"He likes to get the best position on shore, of course."

I looked at the ship. "Position? Aren't they all along the banks?"

"If you look behind you, you'll see that the latecomers

have to anchor alongside other ships rather than the shore. Captain Manny prefers to claim the premium spot since the other captains are such beasts about our company. Petty, quite petty, and so very cutting with their comments about our fleet. Now, this is my concierge desk. Do you have your passport? I'll just hold on to it for you so you won't be bothered by all the trivialities of border crossings. Here is your room key." She handed a small key to me as she continued rushing ahead. "Through here is the lower lounge. It's a bar, really, and although it's empty now, you'll find it's quite the jumping nightspot, as you Americans like to say. Your cabin is just up the stairs here, and down the corridor. Mind your step. To the left is the upper lounge, and a wee little library to the right, just there. Around the corner we go. You have the veranda cabin, so you'll be able to enjoy the pleasure of a firsthand view from your own deck chair while cruising down the rivers. We just ask that you not sit outside when the wind is from the north due to noxious fumes from the engines. Carbon monoxide poisoning can be so unpleasant, can it not? And here we are! Your deluxe veranda cabin awaits you. Do take your time unpacking. There will be an informal drinks and nibblies party promptly at four p.m. in the upper lounge. Dinner is at seven. You needn't dress for the first night out. Do feel free to tell me if you need anything."

My head was spinning by the time she hustled off down the narrow hallway.

"Alice, my dear," I said softly. "You are in Wonderland, which means that has to be the White Rabbit."

I watched until she disappeared, feeling like I'd been deposited in a whirlwind. I turned to consider the doors before me. There were three cabins on this level of the ship, but the blank doors told me nothing about what the next two weeks held for me.

"It may be Wonderland, but it's also on a river," I said to myself under my breath, using the key in the door, "so even if the ship *does* sink, you can swim to shore. Just relax and enjoy two blissful weeks of Europe unblighted by the presence of any egotistical, narcissistic, backstabbing men."

I entered the cabin, coming to an abrupt halt at the sight of a chestnut-haired man who was seated at a minuscule table, hunched over a laptop. The man looked up with a start and stared at me with an expression of surprise that was probably identical to the one plastered all over my face.

"Um . . . ," I said.

"Um?" he asked, a little frown pulling down his eyebrows. "Really? That's how you greet people? The laxity of customer service these days. Well, it's of no matter; as I told that chatty concierge, I do not need anything, and don't wish to be disturbed. I have a book to write, and I need quiet to do so."

What on earth was this arrogant man doing in my cabin? Judging by his comments, he had probably snuck in thinking it was empty and thus available to be used as his personal office.

He had one of those rich British accents that made me think of Stephen Fry at his most pompous, and although he certainly wasn't hard at all on the eyes, he was most definitely not what I wanted in the form of cabin accoutrements. "You can blame the 'um' on jet lag. I've been awake for over twenty-four hours, and frankly, I don't give a damn whether or not you wish to be disturbed. You're in my cabin, and I would appreciate you writing your book elsewhere."

"*Your* cabin?" he said, frowning even more.

I went out to the hallway and pulled my suitcase in, noticing then that there were two small bags stacked against the wall next to one of the two twin beds that dominated the small room.

"I beg to differ," the man said, observing me with what might have been alarm. "This is my cabin."

I held up my key. "Beta deck, room four. That's what it says on the door, and it's where Tiffany left me, so would you please mind finding yourself another place to write?"

He stood up slowly, his eyes—which I noticed were a particularly clear gray—roaming over me in a speculative, wholly impersonal way. I will admit that the woman in me was a bit annoyed about that. I might not be seeking male attention or appreciation, but dammit, he didn't have to look me over like I was a particularly uninspiring view. "Your name wouldn't happen to be Anise, would it?"

"Alice," I corrected. "Who are you?"

He started to answer, checked himself, then said hesitantly, "Elliott Ainslie." I was about to tell him that I was tired and would appreciate him vamoosing when he added, "You're Patrick's ex."

A chill ran down my back, curled around my side, and settled in my stomach with a sick feeling. "You know Patrick?"

He nodded. "We were at school together. It would appear that there has been a gross miscommunication. Patrick gave me his travel tickets saying that his ex-girlfriend had decided not to take the trip, and since he had more important things to do, he'd let me have his cabin."

"Our cabin," I said, righteously indignant about many things, but mostly that Patrick felt so little about a vacation that I had long anticipated that he had tossed it away on a pal. "We went in halfsies on the cabin."

"I see. No doubt you will wish to take that matter up with Patrick. I'm sure he will see the justice in having to reimburse you for the cost of a different cabin."

"Different cabin?" I plopped down on one of the beds, the one nearest the tiny bathroom. "I *have* a cabin. There's no reason for me to get another one."

"But I am already in possession of this one—"

"Yeah, and you didn't pay for it, did you? You said Patrick gave you the tickets. Well, I *did* pay, a lot of money, four grand to be exact, so if anyone is finding a new cabin, it's you, not me."

Oh, he didn't like that. "Now, see here, Miss . . . Miss . . ."

"Alice Wood."

"See here, Miss Wood." He strode the three steps over to where I sat like a limp bit of broccoli on the bed. "I recognize that the situation is not of your making— although Patrick was quite adamant that you had made clear your intention to not take the trip as planned—but neither is it of mine, and since I was in possession of the cabin first, it only makes sense for you to be the one to relocate. You haven't even unpacked."

I lay down on the bed, wincing a little at both the mattress's lumpiness and the fact that it was inclined at a slight angle. "My cabin. I paid for it, I'm staying. Besides, if you were a gentleman, you'd offer to find a new room."

He swore under his breath for a moment, stomped up and down the cabin (all five steps' worth of it), then marched out of the cabin muttering things that I felt it better not to strain to overhear.

I sat up, glancing over at his laptop, but before I could do more than wonder if he was in contact with Patrick, he reappeared, snatched up his laptop, and exited again, trailing dark looks at me.

At that point, exhaustion claimed me, making it hard to get my body moving. But my curiosity trumped jet lag, and had me opening the drawers of the low dresser that lined one wall. Shirts, pants, and assorted undergarments were folded with precision.

"The man who folded those socks," I said aloud, kneeling to pull open the bottom drawer, "is borderline anal. I've never seen clothing so tidy. Good lord, he even has a travel iron."

Voices outside the door heralded the return of the gray-eyed intruder. I knee-walked the two steps over to the door and opened it to find him arguing with Tiffany.

"—very sorry, sir, but as I've told you three times now, there simply are no other free cabins. We are sailing at capacity, and I should like to point out that Manny van Bris Tours cannot be held responsible for errors of this sort. It is simply not feasible for us to maintain unoccupied cabins on the off chance that one of our customers should suddenly break up with his partner and require separate accommodations. Or in your case, give his ticket to you. Your friend purchased shared occupancy of this cabin, and I'm afraid that you will simply have to deal with the situation as best you can."

Tiffany's head swiveled as she considered me for a brief moment. On my knees looking back at her, I felt every single minute of the twenty-four-plus hours I'd been traveling—wrinkled, unwashed, and so tired that most of my inhibitions had fallen asleep.

"This ship isn't at all like the pictures in the brochure," I told her. "The mattress is lumpy, too."

She was about to answer me, but Elliott interrupted. "There's got to be somewhere else I can sleep on the ship. I don't require much room, just somewhere to sit with my laptop, and a bed to stretch out on at night."

"You have a cabin, sir," she said, with a hard glance at me. "There are no other options."

"You could go stay in a hotel," I suggested.

"If you wish to disembark, you will need to do so in the next three minutes," Tiffany said curtly, snapping closed the portfolio she held in her hands. "We will be leaving immediately."

Elliott looked like he really wanted to let loose with a blue cloud of profanity, but I had to give it to him—he just flexed his jaw a couple of times, and swallowed his frustration down. He turned to me. "I don't suppose you would consider a hotel—"

"Nope. I don't have enough money for one, even if I did want to consider it. What about you?" I gave him the once-over. He was dressed casually, in a pair of dark pants and a plain white shirt. He didn't look like his financial status matched his upper-class accent.

A quick grimace passed over his face. "I prefer not to spend my resources on something as trivial as a vacation."

"Broke, too, huh?" I gave a little half shrug. "I hear ya on that. Had to max out my credit card in order to have some spending money, not that I have a lot of that, but you can't go to Europe without buying at least a few postcards and stuff, right? So, what are you going to do? Sleep in the lounge at night? I suppose I could let you use this room during the day when I'm not here, if you wanted to write—"

He brushed past me into the cabin. "Such thoughtfulness isn't necessary. As you heard, I am the rightful possessor of a ticket that entitles me to the use of one-half of this cabin, which means exactly one-half of the table, and one of the beds, are at my disposal. I opt to use them."

"You can't do that! We don't know each other!" I was scandalized at the thought of sharing so confined a space, so *intimate* a space, with a complete stranger. What was worse was the fact that a tiny little bit of me was also intrigued. Elliott was an unknown, a conundrum just waiting for me to figure him out. And if there was anything I loved, it was a deep, intricate puzzle.

"I'm sure we can work out a rota for usage of the cabin during the day." He eyed me coolly as he set his laptop back onto the tiny round table, taking care, I noted, not to use more than half of the available space.

"But you're a man! We'll have to sleep together, and despite whatever horrible things Patrick has told you about me, I am not a ho."

"Pardon?"

"Ho. Player."

He just stared at me.

I sighed and slapped one hand on my thigh in irritation. "Woman of loose moral values."

"Ah. I have no doubt your morals are of the highest quality." He sat back down at his laptop and tapped a few keys.

I waited for a minute, then said, "Aren't you going to reassure me that Patrick didn't say bad things to you about me?"

"Why should I do that?" He spoke without even looking up from the screen.

I thigh-slapped again. "Because it's the polite thing to do! Here am I, all angsty and fragile emotionally speaking, and it's your duty as a gentleman and decent human being who cares about his fellow humans to make me feel better."

"Technically, I'm a nobleman, not a gentleman."

That wasn't at all what I was expecting him to say. I stood, my body wearily protesting activity after such a long day, and stared down at where he sat. "What is that supposed to mean?"

"Hmm?" He looked up at last, the slight frown back between his eyebrows. "It means that I have a title. Noblemen are usually considered gentlemen, but the reverse cannot be said."

I outright stared at him. Mouth slightly ajar, hands on hips, eyes bugging out slightly . . . the whole nine yards. "You're a prince or something? Like British royalty?"

"I am not a member of the British royal family, no. But I am the eighth Baron Ainslie."

"Holy crap!"

"Quite." He looked back at his computer and commenced typing.

I sat down on the edge of his bed, looking at him with amazement. He frowned at me until I moved over to the chair at the table. I couldn't seem to stop staring at him, my brain turning around and around the fact that a real live British aristocrat was sitting in front of me, in my cabin, a space that evidently would be occupied by us both for the next two weeks.

"My ancestors fought in the Revolutionary War," was the only thing I could think of to say.

He paused his typing, a startled expression on his face. "I'm sorry, that was probably the jet lag speaking." I knew I was long past the point where I had any verbal barriers to keep from blurting out any random thought that passed through my head, but I didn't care. "It's true, though. I had my family traced, and it turns out I have all sorts of grandfathers and uncles and cousins who fought you guys. Probably *your* ancestors," I added, in case he missed the pertinent point of the conversation.

"I wouldn't doubt that at all. The Ainslies were a very bloodthirsty people a few centuries ago." He typed a few words, then looked up. "Are you planning on talking the entire fortnight it will take to get to Budapest?"

"Fortnight." A little giggle slipped out. I was definitely loopy from lack of sleep. "That's such a British word. I watch a lot of BBC America."

He sighed, and closed the lid of the laptop. "Why don't you get some sleep? You look as if you're about to fall over, and your eyelids keep closing."

I blinked at him a couple of times, waiting for a synapse or two to fire in my brain. Now that I was safely ensconced on the boat, the last dregs of my energy seemed to evaporate into nothing. I felt as boneless as a Chicken McNugget. "What, go to bed right here in front of you?" I shook my head. There was something I had wanted to say, some point of importance. . . . "Oh, I remember. Sleeping. That's important. We have to have some rules if we're going to sleep together."

"I would take umbrage with the phrase you've chosen, but I can see it would completely escape your notice. What rules do you have?"

"No trying to get busy with me." I gave him an owlish look. "And don't say the thought would never so much as cross your mind, because you already hurt my feelings by not denying that Patrick said mean things to you about me, and if I thought that I repulsed you to the point where you would rather take a bath in scalding hot acid than try to get it on with me, then I would cry. A lot."

"Isn't the 'scalding hot' qualifier a bit redundant? An acid bath would be sufficiently horrible so as to make the temperature immaterial."

I stared at him again. It was all I could do to process the words he spoke. "You're really not going to give up even one thing, one itty-bitty word of comfort that would make me feel better about having to share my romantic cabin in romantic Europe with a total stranger, are you?"

"I'm told I don't snore," he said after a moment's thought.

"That's it," I said, standing up, my brain pretty much shutting down with exhaustion. "I'm going to jump in the river. You're welcome to my half of the cabin. Enjoy my clothes and my books and my secret stash of chocolate, as well."

He spoke just as I reached the door. "I speak with Patrick on average twice a year, and then most of our conversation takes the form of catching up with fellow schoolmates, and inquiries about my family, of which there are a great number. Despite what you may think, Patrick told me nothing other than he had found someone new, and his trip with you was off."

I wrapped my arms around myself and slumped against the door, his words hurting me in ways I doubt he could imagine.

I weighed the option of the river with the idea of flying home to my small, attic apartment, still and quiet and filled with unpacked boxes. An empty lifetime of grief stretched before me, one in which I had no place to be, friends who were busy with their own lives, and no real reason for going on. Neither of those possibilities held any charm, which left me with the only other choice.

I'd room with a stranger. A handsome, titled, English stranger who clearly didn't like me, and who wasn't the man who was supposed to be there.

"Fine," I said, collapsing fully clothed onto the bed. I lifted my head to glare at him. "But if I so much as catch you peeking at me when I'm sleeping, I'll smash your laptop right over your head."

One of his eyebrows lifted as he returned to his work. "You'd fit in very well with the early Ainslies."

"In your dreams, Baron."

I was asleep before the last word left my lips, but in my head, it was a perfect exit line.

Chapter 3

Diary of Alice Wood

Day One (yes, again)

I decided that yesterday doesn't count as day one, what with the horrible surprise that Patrick had given away his ticket. Given it away just like it was a minor little vacation, and not one that was supposed to end in our marriage.

However, all that is over. Today is fresh-start day, number two, but we won't focus on that, because Therapist Nora says that it's a drain on psychic energies to allow negativity to take over one's thoughts. Or something along those lines—I have to admit to tuning out when she goes into her psychic energy spiel.

"Day One," I said aloud when I woke up almost twelve hours later. I was still lying on top of the bed, fully clothed, although evidently my new roomie had taken pity on me and draped a blanket over me. I looked around the small cabin, saying aloud, "He's not here. Huh. I wonder if I snored him out of the room."

"Not quite, although you did snore." Elliott emerged from a minuscule bathroom that I vaguely remembered visiting in the middle of the night. "You appeared to be extremely tired. I assume you are feeling much better, and will be leaving the cabin shortly?"

"Subtlety isn't your forte, is it?" I asked as I took off my shoes and socks, and used them to gesture at his laptop, already open and running on the tiny table. "What sort of man works on his vacation?"

"One who is more interested in the quiet offered by an empty cabin," he said, his gaze drifting over to frown at the explosion of clothes that poured out of my travel bag. I remembered his travel iron and neat socks, and smiled to myself. I wasn't an overly messy person, but tiredness the night before, and a natural tendency to get distracted easily, had left my side of the room far from tidy.

I tossed my dirty socks and shoes on the ground next to my bag, and knelt down to dig out a light dress and clean underwear. "Like I said, not strong on the subtlety. What is it, exactly, that you plan on doing once I'm out of the cabin? Because I'll know if you touched my things."

He looked shocked. "I beg your pardon?"

I waved a pair of undies at him. "If you have some sort of lingerie fetish, I'll know." I thought a moment, and tucked my shoes into my bag. "Or feet fetish. My stuff is off-limits, OK? I don't want to have to keep locking my bag, but I will if I have to."

Elliott's shoulders stiffened. "If you were a man, I'd take offense with the suggestion that I have any desire to either fondle or steal your belongings."

"If I were a man, I'd have a problem with the fact that I had packed lingerie."

He stared at me in incomprehension.

"It was a little joke." I gave him a doubtful look, then continued. "What sort of books do you write?"

He sighed the sigh of a martyred man. "Fiction. And since I know it will be your next question, yes, I am published. I write espionage novels featuring a deaf former spy named Liam."

"Wow, that sounds . . . intense. Is espionage just an interest, or are you a former spy, too?"

"I'd tell you, but then I'd have to kill you."

I stared in horror at him. Was he serious, or just pulling my leg? He didn't look like he was joking, but then, some people had great deadpan delivery of lines like that.

No, he was joking. He had to be joking. He was a baron, after all. He couldn't be a baron and a spy. Could he?

"As it is, I am very late on a book, and since my family's activities ensure my home is less than conducive to productivity of any kind, I accepted Patrick's offer of two weeks in which to write unmolested." He gave me a stern look. "Despite the snoring, and the fact that you were evidently raised without such things as wardrobes, bureaus, or other devices intended to store clothes outside of a suitcase, I anticipate getting a good chunk of this book finished by the time we arrive in Budapest."

"I was supposed to get married in Budapest," I said sadly, thinking about all the work I'd done arranging with the U.S. embassy to have the marriage in Hungary.

The expression on his face was almost comical in its surprise. "I am not looking for a wife."

"Ha ha," I told him, grabbing my cosmetic bag and

clean clothes. "Ha ha ha. Like I'd ever consider marrying a man who has Patrick for a friend. Oh, it is to laugh."

"Good." He looked back at his laptop. "Just so we understand each other."

"There's nothing on this earth that could convince me to marry a man who obviously holds with all sorts of outdated notions of nobility, and has a gorgeous upper-crust accent, and a bad habit of treating people like they're servants even though they paid for half the room," I said without a care for grammar or proper pronoun usage, annoyed that he had dismissed me so completely. "I'm going to take a shower, and then have some breakfast, and then yes, you can have the cabin all to yourself. Europe, Mr. Lord Elliott, is out there, and I have no intention of missing it."

"It's Lord Ainslie, actually. Elliott, eighth Baron Ainslie of Ainslie Castle, if you want to be exact. The honorific is *my lord*."

"Power to the people! Up with the masses! *Vive la révolution!*" I said dramatically, flinging open the door to the bathroom. The warm air, vaguely piney and woodsy in scent, wrapped around me. "Day One calls!"

"That's from the French Revolution, not American. And it's technically day two," he called after me. "You missed dinner, last night, which was, according to the literature provided, the first official day of the tour."

"The day one reference was for my diary. I'm keeping one," I said, pausing. "My therapist, Nora, says that it's good for your chakras to quantify your emotions, so that you don't get blocked up." I waved a vague hand around my torso. "You know, chakra-wise."

A horrified expression crawled across his face. "You're not one of those New Age followers, are you? I should warn you that I have a strong aversion to incense and smudged sage."

"I'm not, actually, but my therapist is, and since she was free via the local mental health clinic, which I was forced to access due to the fact that Patrick betrayed me and kicked me out of the condo we shared, and generally acted like a complete asshat, I'm stuck with whatever sort of therapist I can get."

Elliott looked away quickly, and I realized that just because I had reason to be mean to Patrick, he didn't.

"Sorry. I shouldn't have bad-mouthed your friend like that. I'm sure if you're not female, and he doesn't ask you to live with him, and then later cancel a planned prewedding trip down various romantic rivers ending up in a wedding in Budapest, he's nice enough."

I thought for a moment he wasn't going to respond, but just as I decided to leave him to his muse, he said, "Actually, I've always thought he was a bit of an arse. At least so far as his attitude toward women goes."

"Really? Well, I guess it's good to know I'm not alone in one thing. Regardless, I should be out of your hair soon."

The thought struck me, as I went about my daily ablutions, that Elliott had awfully nice hair for a man who'd take someone else's ticket. It wasn't long, but had a small curl to it that made you think about running your fingers through it.

"Not that I have any intention of doing so," I told my reflection in the steamy mirror. "Even if I was looking for a man, and I'm certainly not that stupid, he would be off the table. He's friend to a rat bastard."

It was just a shame, too. How many bona fide lords does a girl meet? And how many of them have BBC voices, and nice faces, and curly hair that looks soft and silky and utterly gropeworthy?

"Especially since he realizes that Patrick is a boob," I told myself as I finished drying my hair, and turned first one way, then the other to make sure that my first real day in Europe wouldn't be ruined by having the hem of my sundress tucked up into the back of my underwear. I grabbed a little cotton shrug, fluffed up my bosomage at the memory of Elliott's hair, and went back into the cabin proper. Elliott was working at his laptop.

"Are you going up for breakfast?"

"No."

He didn't bother to even look at me when he spoke, but I could see his chocolate brown eyebrows pulled together in irritation. No doubt he had the morning crankies. Well, there was one sure fix for that.

"I can bring you back something if you like. I gather breakfast is a buffet situation. What sorts of things do you like?"

"I don't need anything." His jaw tightened as he continued to type with dogged determination.

"I know everyone is different, metabolically speaking, but I've always found that I'm much more creative, and have much more oomph, if I eat breakfast. And it's no trouble to get you a plate of fruit and pastries, assuming they have that, and I can't imagine they wouldn't. A few carbs and some fruit should give you all the energy you need to write like the wind."

"What I need is solitude!"

"Jeez, I was just trying to be nice!"

I gathered up my travel wallet, a guidebook, and a wounded sense of martyrdom, and prepared to enjoy the first day of my new life.

"Forgive me, that was rude."

I stopped at the door, glancing back at him. He made a vague gesture of apology. "I didn't mean to snap at you that way."

"I get snappish when I'm hungry. Have you eaten yet?"

"No." It was clear he didn't want to admit it, but after a moment of his fingers twitching, he turned off the laptop, and stood up. "Perhaps you're correct. A few minutes' delay while I breakfast isn't going to hurt my output."

He followed after me as I left the cabin. As we made our way down the hall to the stairs leading to the upper level, I couldn't help but ask, "So, about your spy novels— are you a James Bond fan, too?"

"Not particularly. I took up writing fiction after translating a couple of books. I realized that there was more chance of financial success in writing novels than in translating them."

I relaxed. He had to be joking earlier about killing me. Translators didn't go around offing innocent tourists. "That's really interesting. How many languages do you speak?"

"Four other than English. I have a knack for languages."

"I am seriously envious right now," I said, trying not to dwell on the fact that three years of Spanish in school left me with little more than the ability to order off a Mexican restaurant menu. "Wait, you had a job? A regular job? But you're almost royalty."

"I'm a baron. That's the lowest level of peerage other than a baronet."

I waved a hand. "Pfft. You're Lord Ainslie of Ainslieville. You should spend your days wandering around your grounds and letting the peasants tug their forelocks at you, and all that kind of stuff."

"The town is actually called Ainston, and most of its residents would burst out laughing if you told them to tug their forelocks."

"A proud, simple people, eh?"

"Proud and fiercely independent, yes."

A sudden thought struck me as we climbed the stairs. "Do you get to do that droit thing?"

"What droit thing?"

We emerged into a smallish sitting area dotted with several round tables that were identical to the one in our cabin. To the right was a door with a sign informing all that the dining room was open for meal service.

"That thing where the lord of the land gets to sleep with all the newly married women." I eyed him. I could just imagine all those lusty brides ogling him and hopping into his bed in order to get their motors started. So to speak.

He gave me a look that spoke volumes. "*Droit du seigneur* is a myth, Alice. It didn't really exist."

"It was in *Braveheart*!"

"As were a great many other events that bore no resemblance to what actually took place during William Wallace's life. What is it with you Americans and your fascination with men in kilts?" He shook his head, holding open the door for me to enter the dining room.

"You just said it—men in kilts. Mmrowr. Oooh, nice buffet."

But as I picked up an empty plate to fill, I was stopped by a piercing voice.

"And there is our last missing couple," Tiffany said

from across the dining room. Five square tables filled the room, leaving only one side free for the buffet offerings. "Mr. Ainslie, Miss Wood, I'd like to introduce you to the rest of your fellow passengers on this, the thirty-second cruise of Manny van Bris European Tours."

I paused in the act of scooping some melon onto the small plate, glancing over at where Elliott was wearing his martyred expression again. "Mr. Ainslie?" I said softly.

He grimaced. "It's easier that way. Less explaining to do."

"How egalitarian of you."

"This is Mr. Weekes, and his companion Mr. Sorensson," Tiffany said, moving to stand next to a table with two men in their late twenties.

"Anthony Weekes," the one with the dark hair and goatee said, giving us a little nod of the head. "This is comrade Dahl. He's from Norway." His buddy, a huge blond man of obvious Viking stock, murmured something polite, and continued to shovel vast quantities of rolls, potatoes, and eggs into his face.

The next table contained four Japanese girls of about sixteen. They wore matching blue and white school uniforms, and all giggled and bowed their heads when Tiffany said, "And here we have our group from Nagasaki. The girls won a radio contest being held in conjunction with our home-base twinned town, Edmund-upon-Dell. They are here with their two teachers, Miss ... er ..." Tiffany consulted her clipboard, frowned, and shook her head briefly. "Ms. Izumi and Ms. Megumi."

The two women in question sat at the next table and said in very precise English that it was their pleasure to meet us. The girls just giggled more, and whispered to one another, their eyes on Elliott.

Dammit, his curls caught their attention, too. Oh well. It was no concern of mine if the man got involved with underage schoolgirls. I smiled, and slipped a piece of ham onto my plate, ravenously wishing I could just dive facedown into the buffet.

"And last but in no way least are the delightful Ms. Arthur and Ms. Pennyworth. They are from England."

"Windsor," the one named Pennyworth said, giving us both a friendly smile. She looked to be in her mid-thirties, with a long oval face, and hair pulled down over her ears in a way that reminded me of medieval Madonnas. "I'm Laura. Deidre—she's my sister—we both work at an exclusive travel agency. That's why we're here, really—we always check on the tours that we sell."

"Isn't Windsor where the Queen's castle is?" I said, then looked over to Elliott. The look I received in return was quelling.

"Yes, Windsor Castle is there, but we don't deal with it," Laura said with a giggle. "Although Deidre has some terribly posh clients, don't you?"

My gaze slid over to the woman named Deidre, and immediately, the hairs on the back of my neck stood on end. Perhaps it was the predatory look in her eyes. Perhaps it was the long, scarlet fingernails that reminded me of dragon claws. Perhaps it was the way she was blatantly undressing Elliott with her eyes.

"Yeees," Deidre drawled, her gaze still firmly attached to Elliott. I had a feeling she was making a comment about her plans for him rather than answering her friend's question. As he moved to the buffet, she rose and strolled over to stand next to him, reaching at the same time he did for a glass. She gave a low, throaty chuckle, and leaned into him to say something.

I swear, if I had hackles, they would be standing on end by now.

"It's a pleasure to meet you all," I said, reminding myself that Elliott was not mine, and I didn't care if he decided to hook up with a slinky-hipped, scarlet-nailed hussy. It didn't matter to me in the least, I told myself as I took my plate over to the only free table and sat with my back to the buffet.

The throaty chuckle drifted over me again, this time followed by a short, deep laugh that had to be from Elliott.

Well, good riddance. Maybe he'd lighten up about shoving me out of the cabin every chance he got if he was busy hanging around Deidre. I kept my eyes on my plate, not wanting to appear at all interested when Elliott headed off to sit with the she-wolf.

The thump of a plate hitting the table made me jump. Elliott sat down across from me, his plate piled high with breakfast goodies.

"My apologies. I didn't mean to startle you."

"That's all right." I lowered my voice so just he could hear. "Although I'm surprised you didn't opt to eat that mountain of food with the Besom of Windsor."

He chewed a bit of egg before saying, "Besom?"

"It means hussy."

"I know what it means. I'm just surprised you do, as well."

I sat up straight and gave him back the quelling look he'd fired at me earlier. "It just so happens that I read a lot, and I collect odd words like 'besom.'"

He inclined his head in acknowledgment, then asked, "You wouldn't by any chance be referring to the brunette as a besom? A woman who I assume you have known approximately two minutes?"

"Oh, come on," I said, chomping noisily on a piece of toast. "Like you didn't notice the way she slunk over to where you were loading up your trough, and just happened to rub her breasts all over your arm."

That stopped his fork halfway to his mouth. He stared at me a second, then lowered it. "First of all, I resent you implying that I have taken an inordinate amount of food."

I looked pointedly at his plate.

"I am six foot four inches tall, and have large bones," he said in a somewhat huffy tone of voice. "I need a lot of food to sustain me, especially when I'm writing. All that brain energy has to come from somewhere."

"All right, I apologize for my cracks about the five gallons of food you are consuming. After all, I did persuade you to have breakfast, and you *are* a big guy. Big as in substantial, not chubby," I said quickly when he looked offended.

"And second . . ." He took a moment to breathe heavily through his nose. I bet he was counting to himself. "Second, I did not notice anyone slinking. The woman in question happens to be a very pleasant individual, who commented on the state of the ship, and how likely we were to sink. That is all. So if you could rein in your unwarranted jealousy, I believe the journey will be that much easier."

"Unwarranted jealousy!" It was my turn to be outraged. "I am not in any way, shape, or form jealous. I simply commented that Deidre clearly has her sights on you, and I was surprised you didn't give in to such obvious ogling and go sit with her so she can fawn on you, and probably touch your arm with those scarlet fingernails, and continue damn near stripping the clothes off of you with her eyes."

"Ogling me? Was she?" He looked interested and glanced over to where the two women were finishing their breakfast.

Deidre was waiting for that. She smiled a long, slow, very sultry smile at him, and completely ignored me.

"She couldn't be more obvious if she wrote her intentions on a neon sign," I said, giving a little smile and nod to Laura, who was looking vaguely embarrassed.

"I don't know about that, but I will say that I find it refreshing to find a woman who isn't coy about what she wants."

"Was that aimed at me?" I asked, shaking a piece of melon at him before popping it in my mouth, and saying around it, "Because I don't play games like that with people. I'm very straightforward."

"I wasn't aware that you had an interest in me of a sexual nature."

I swallowed down a big chunk of melon. "I don't!"

"Ah." He shoveled in another mouthful of eggs and ham. I had to give it to him—for a man who loaded up his plate, he had very nice table manners, and didn't make it obvious he was really packing it away.

I thought about telling him that I simply wanted to get along since we had to share a cabin, but decided that he'd just figure "the lady doth protest too much" like the woman in *Hamlet*. I bet barons all knew their Shakespeare inside and out.

Just then, Laura stopped next to our table. "Is this your first trip to Holland?" Laura asked in a conversational manner.

I dabbed off the toast crumbs. "It is. Actually, it's my first trip abroad, one that I've planned for almost two years, so I'm very excited to be here."

"And your boyfriend?" Laura asked, nodding at Elliott, who was at that moment sipping his coffee and wiping his fingers on his napkin, having finished the mountain of food.

"I'm not—," he started to say.

I shifted in my chair, inadvertently kicking him on the ankle.

He shot me a glare.

"Sorry—foot slipped." I gave him a wide, toothy smile, then turned back to Laura. "Is this your first time in Holland?"

"No, we try to visit a new place each summer, although occasionally we miss a year when Deidre has plans with her partner. I haven't been on the Rhine, though, and we're very much looking forward to seeing all the castles and cute little villages."

Behind me, Anthony Weekes snorted. "Comrade Dahl and I are here as part of a study. We received a grant."

"Really?" Laura asked. "A grant that allows you to take a cruise?"

"Yes." Anthony gave us all a somewhat smug smile. "It is important we experience the tour ourselves. We are studying tourists' encounters in Germany from an interdisciplinary perspective, using cultural analysis to detail how touristic formation is influenced by the human-environment relationships and subjectivities, and how the complex network of sociopolitical relations expands into a hero's quest phenomenological model."

No one said anything for a few moments. Other than

the Japanese schoolgirls, who giggled and whispered to one another.

"Oh," I said at last, feeling obligated to fill the silence. "That sounds . . . complicated."

"It is. Perhaps later we could interview you all about your multifaceted encounters with place-mythology and how you feel that the performative dimensions of your own individual spatialized identity are influenced by them."

"He's doing that on purpose, isn't he?" I whispered out of the side of my mouth.

"He is clearly an academic snob, if that's what you mean," Elliott answered.

"I hate people who talk over your head like that. And what's with the comrade thing?"

"I suspect he's trying very hard to be different. Or perhaps he's a dedicated Communist." Elliott folded his napkin and set it neatly to the side of his plate.

"Didn't that sort of thing go out with the end of the Cold War?"

"Some people work very hard to appear eccentric." He gave a little shrug. "Either way, I can't stay to analyze him. I have work to do."

Tiffany appeared seemingly out of nowhere. "We are due to have a briefing in ten minutes in the lounge regarding our arrival in Kinderdijk, but since Mr. Ainslie and Miss Wood have only just made it to breakfast, why don't I give you the information here? As those of you who have read the itinerary know, Kinderdijk is a UNESCO World Heritage site where you will find an absolutely fascinating collection of windmills open for exploration."

She went into an explanation of what flood management technologies we'd see by touring the site, but my attention was distracted when Anthony, who was taking his plates and coffee cup over to an area intended for dirty dishes, paused behind me and leaned down to ask, "Do you and comrade Elliott wish to skip the windmills and see the town with comrade Dahl and me?"

"Er . . ." I was a bit startled by both the fact that his mouth was almost touching my ear and that one of his hands casually rested on my shoulder. I didn't know if it was a European thing to be so touchy-feely, but the guy was definitely inside my personal space. "I kind of would like to see some windmills, to be honest. I mean, it's so very Holland, isn't it? But maybe Elliott would prefer touring other things."

"No," Elliott said, standing up. "Thank you, I have plans for the day."

"Your loss," Anthony said, returning to his partner. I rubbed my ear, chiding myself for my odd feeling of discomfort when it was clear that he was more interested in Elliott than me.

"You don't even want to see one little windmill?" I asked the latter man, feeling strangely deflated despite knowing that Elliott intended to stay on board the ship working.

"I've seen them before."

"But these are historic ones. I'd hate to think I was seeing all the good historic stuff and you weren't."

"I'm sure you will enjoy them despite my decision to remain behind," he said, giving me a little bow, which I found both charming and foreign. I don't think I'd ever seen a man bow before, but Elliott made it look like a perfectly natural way to take his leave.

"You are very lucky," a soft voice said as I took my plates over to the receptacle.

"In many ways, yes," I agreed, noting that Laura might have been speaking to me, but her eyes were on Elliott.

"He's really gorgeous."

I felt an odd sense of pride, as if Elliott's appearance had something to do with me. "He is that. And smart, too. He writes books about spies."

"Oooh, really." An odd speculative glint lit her eyes. She watched him leave the room, then asked, in her breathy soft voice, "I probably shouldn't ask this, but was he one, himself?"

"What, a spy?" I smiled. "He's a bit tall for a spy, isn't he? I mean, spies are supposed to blend in and not be noticeable. You'd have to be dead not to notice Elliott."

"And even then . . ." Deidre made a *mmrowr*ing noise as she passed us, following Elliott out of the room.

I sent a glare after her, but she didn't see it.

"You have to forgive Deidre," Laura said, a wry twist to her lips. "She just broke up with her latest partner, and is feeling a bit lonely."

It was on the tip of my tongue to say that I was in the exact same boat—literally!—but that same odd sense of pride that came from being Elliott's roomie had me clamping down on the words.

"I love Deidre very much, but I will admit that some-times she's a bit single-minded. Speaking of which, I'll just warn you that you might want to stay close to your boyfriend." Laura patted me on the arm, then followed after the others.

"An enigmatic man, comrade Elliott," Anthony said, strolling past me, Dahl in tow.

"You think so?" I watched them leave, wondering why he gave me such a weird vibe. It was clear he was *with* Dahl in all senses of the word, and yet, I could swear he was looking down my sundress earlier.

I shook my head at my fanciful thoughts. Residual jet lag was clearly muddling my thinking.

"Could you please pass along the information to Mr. Ainslie that the bus to take us to the windmills will leave in ten minutes?" Tiffany bustled by, pausing to call over her shoulder to me, "Please be sure to wear comfortable walking shoes."

The group of Japanese girls and their two teachers trotted past me, the older ladies giving me little nods of their heads before they hurried after their charges. In no time, I was left alone in the dining room, my mind turning over a strange new thought.

I'd seen a program on TV about how the British used to recruit spies, and it mentioned that a great percentage of them were recruited out of the big universities, the ones where the upper classes sent their sons and daughters.

People like barons. Elliott must have gone to one of those big universities. He was handy with languages, and knew several of them. He was obviously smart, and I was willing to bet would retain his calm under pressure.

In other words, the ideal makings of a spy. Had he been joking earlier when he'd said he would have to kill me if he told me the truth? Was it hyperbole or something more sinister?

Little goose bumps of sheer, unadulterated pleasure rippled up and down my arms when I hurried back to our cabin. There was nothing I loved more than a puzzle, and I anticipated a wonderful two weeks unraveling the mystery that surrounded Elliott.

The man himself looked up with a frown when I entered the cabin with a cheery wave. "You can stop glaring, because I'm just here for a second. We're all going to see the windmills. Historic ones, ones that are bound to be fascinating, but I won't press you to see them with us, since you said you had other things to do."

He grunted something incoherent. I stepped into the bathroom to make fast use of the toilet before sightseeing (who knew if windmills had facilities?), and when I came out again, he was writing, ignoring me when I gathered up my things. I had the worst urge to tell him to stop writing and come sightsee with the rest of us, but reminded myself that his welfare or happiness wasn't my business, and if he wanted solitude, then he could just have it.

I was halfway through the door when I looked back.

He looked so lonesome sitting all by himself, hunched over the small table, frowning slightly at the screen as he tapped on the keys.

He wants to be left alone, my inner sage advised. *Leave him be.*

He looks so sad, though. And lonely, and he's clearly one of those hidebound Englishmen who would sooner fall over dead than ask for any help. Or companionship, I told my sage. *Besides, I have to live with him for two weeks, so it won't hurt to extend the hand of friendship.*

You just like his plummy voice, the sage countered in a smug voice. *And you want to pry into his life to see if he is a spy or not.*

There is nothing wrong with ogling a man's voice from a distance or being interested in his life, I told her, and proceeded to drown out her reminder that I was still wholly and completely devastated by Patrick's betrayal by saying, "Hey, how about dinner?"

He looked up, his fingers momentarily stilled. "Pardon?"

"Dinner. Why don't we have dinner together? According to the cruise info, we're responsible for our own dinner today, so why don't we have it together?"

"I have to write," he said, casting covert glances at the laptop.

"You just got done telling me how you have to eat in order to keep your brain running, so you'll definitely need dinner by this evening."

"Work is more important than eating."

"Spoken like a true workaholic."

"I am nothing of the kind! I simply have a deadline I must meet."

"Uh-huh. And you'll work better with food, right? I mean, you feel better now after having breakfast, right? So why not prove me wrong and unwind tonight with a dinner out. It's the perfect opportunity to nail both birds with one stone." He started to object, but I added, "Come on, I won't even make you translate. Wait, do you speak Dutch?"

"I understand it tolerably well, yes."

"Well, don't worry, I won't let your brain so much as translate one little item. I got some restaurant recommendations off of Ricardo the pool guy at Patrick's condo, so we can go to one of them, have a bite, then go back to the ship and you can work your fingers to the bone if you like. OK?"

"Oooh, sounds intriguing."

I turned around, swearing silently to myself when Deidre oiled past me down the hall, a small day pack swinging from her perfectly manicured fingertips. "You won't mind if we join you for dinner, will you?"

I thought quickly. I very much did not want her to push her way into a dinner where I hoped to covertly pump Elliott for information about his possibly spy-laden past, but polite manners kept a refusal off my lips. "Not at all, although I have no idea when that will be, since Elliott is trying to get some work done. But if you're around when we decide to head out, you're welcome to come with us."

"I haven't actually said that I—"

"Oh, shoot, forgot something," I told Deidre, and, spinning around, reentered the room and closed the door behind me.

Elliott's eyebrows rose. "What did you forget?"

"Er . . . nothing. I just wanted a little privacy to plead with you. I really don't want to have dinner with Deidre, or even Laura for that matter, and I like *her*. I just thought it would be fun for us roomies to have dinner together."

"Why are you so obsessed with feeding me?" His eyes glittered in the morning sunlight, and I had a premonition that he was going to refuse the invitation. Since I'd had it up to my eyebrows with rejection from handsome, silver-tongued men, I went into full survival mode. I wanted to run away. I wanted to burst into tears. I wanted to hit Elliott over the head with something heavy.

I did none of those things, of course. I simply shrugged and turned to the door. "You know what? I don't care if you eat dinner or not. Do whatever you like. Life is too short to work yourself into a swivet over a stupid meal."

"I agree. And since you are so kind as to offer, I would be delighted to join you for dinner."

I looked over my shoulder at him. "You really are a horrible liar, aren't you? Oh, boy, that came out wrong. Lower your hackles, I simply meant that you don't tell polite lies well."

"I do not lie," he said in a low voice that was more a growl than anything else.

"Hey, I put the 'polite' qualifier in there; that makes it a compliment, not an insult. And I did mean it nicely, you know. My point is that you look like I just asked you to work with me at a smudged-sage stall during an Enya concert, and not out for a pleasant dining experience."

"If that is so, then I apologize," he said, evidently mollified. "You made a good point about breakfast, and as we have decided to share the cabin space, it makes sense that we do so as amicably as possible. Dinner together will allow us to learn each other's likes and dislikes more easily."

"Do you talk like that all the time?" I asked, a little in awe of the way words seemed to march off his lips in such a dignified, orderly manner. They always seemed to tumble out of my mouth and flop into an ungainly heap.

"In what manner?" he asked, his eyebrows rising in question.

"The kind that says you don't go out to dinner to have fun. That's it, isn't it?" I narrowed my gaze on him. He made a face that confirmed my suspicion. "What do you do to have fun? Wait, don't answer that!" I looked at my phone. The ten minutes were almost up.

"I have no intention of doing so."

"You can tell me later, over dinner. Shall we say seven? I'll meet you on the dock. Later, alligator!" I tucked my tour book into the small cross-body bag that held my various necessities, and dashed out of the cabin. The hall was blissfully empty of Deidres.

My spirits felt as ebullient as a cloud. For the first time in two weeks, I felt happy. Perhaps time spent with my new roommate wasn't going to be a chore after all.

Chapter 4

Expense Account
  Item one: fifteen euros
  Remarks: Hookah. I have no memory of this purchase.

"This day," Elliott said to a gull that sat on the railing of the cabin's minuscule deck and pecked in a desultory manner at a bit of bread it had scavenged up somewhere, "is one of the longest I've ever known. It should most definitely be seven o'clock by now, shouldn't it?"

The words spoken aloud shocked him into adding, "Not that I am looking forward to dinner with Alice, mind you. It's just that I've been in the cabin all day, and I've written the amount I set myself to write, and then some, and now I am hungry and thirsty and could do with a break. That's all very reasonable, isn't it, gull? It's not as if I've been wishing I could have gone with the others to see the windmills. I've seen windmills. Once you've seen four or five, you're really at the limit of wind-mill appreciation, and nothing further can be served by seeing more."

Except the fact that a little fresh air and exercise is good for the creative processes. And he might have been able to explain to Alice any signs that were in Dutch.

Guilt twinged at him when he thought of her. "I don't fancy her," he said, sitting down in a wobbly plastic chair and putting his feet up on the rusted railing. The gull, not in the least bit frightened of him, hopped along the rail-ing to peck hopefully at his shoes. "Oh, she's nice enough to look at. More than nice enough, quite pleasant, as a matter of fact. No, it's not that I couldn't fancy her given half the chance, but she's so . . ." He waved a hand in the air. The gull cocked his head and watched him, clearly expecting treats. ". . . so spontaneous. You didn't see, but she just asked me out to dinner as if I'd been hoping for it. Which I haven't. Hell, she was Patrick's girl! I'd never poach on a friend's girl. Although Patrick made it quite clear that he's done with her, so if I wanted to, it would be within my rights to do so."

He fell silent, absently watching the gull nibble on one shoelace. Why was he there, at that moment? Why hadn't he gone back home once he found the cabin was occu-pied? Why had he accepted Alice's dinner invitation when he had every intention of keeping her at arm's length?

Dammit, he didn't need a woman complicating his life, and he certainly didn't need a spontaneous, erratic woman who evidently acted on every whim, and who took so much joy in simple things.

"She's never been abroad," he informed the gull, who attempted to consume his shoelace despite the fact that it was attached to his shoe. "Look how excited she got about seeing a bunch of windmills—poor woman is desperate to soak up all the local color, and she's stuck with this motley group. I could have gone with them, could have shown her around, let her see the interesting side of Holland rather than a dry, uninteresting visit to a collection of moldy windmills. I could have gone with her today, and written during the night, while she was sleeping."

The memory of her snoring gently into her pillow the night before made him smile. She certainly had been exhausted, and although he had expected to find her presence in the cabin an irritation, it had been just the opposite—he had written late into the night, strangely comforted by the sounds of her sleeping just a few feet away.

"Right," he said, shaking his head and getting to his feet. The gull squawked its protest, and flapped its wings. "Those are borderline stalker thoughts. I refuse to be interested in her. She's on the rebound, and vulnerable, and it would be ungentlemanly to express any sort of carnal thoughts about her. I will simply accompany her to dinner, and then let her go her own way without my attentions."

He held on to such noble thoughts until the last few hours dragged past, most of which he spent writing. When he finally did escape his laptop that evening, he found himself on the dock watching as Alice hurried toward him. Her walnut-colored hair trailed after her like a banner, the gauzy material of her dress molding to her body with the gentle caresses of the wind. He suddenly wished he was that wind, then reminded himself of the fact that he wasn't interested in her, at least not in a physical way.

"Your Majesty!" she bellowed, waving her arm in the air in a manner guaranteed to attract attention. He sighed as several tourists, on the way to and from their own ships, paused to look curiously at him.

"She's deranged," he told the nearest group. They nodded and moved on.

"Are you hungry? I'm starved," Alice said, shoving a carrier bag at him, and pushing him forward. "Here, hold my souvenirs while I find the name of the place that Ricardo recommended. Hurry, or the others will see us and want to join in. I had a horrible time getting away from the group to get back here early. I thought Deidre was going to handcuff herself to me at one point, but I managed to get away. They were about to leave, though, so they'll be here any second. Boy, you missed a great trip. The windmills were awesome, and then Anthony and Dahl and I went into this itty-bitty little town where they wanted to check out a distillery that made some sort of special gin."

He looked closely at her. "And did you sample the special gin?"

"Nope. I don't like alcohol, as a rule. It doesn't work with my body chemistry, or something. It all tastes like rubbing alcohol to me." She gave him a blinding smile, then consulted a pocket notebook, riffling through the pages while she muttered to herself. "I know it's in here—I've written all the cool places I wanted to see in here for the last year, ever since I started planning the trip. Oh, here it is. Hang on—let me pull up a map. . . ." She tapped the screen of her mobile phone, turned around to stare at the town, then finally nodded and pointed. "This way! I hope you like exotic food. Ricardo says that this place—it's called Ladybug—has great Ethiopian food. I do love me some wat."

"What?"

"Wat. It's a stew, kind of spicy, but really yummy. The

Ethiopian place in my town serves it with this great flat bread called injera. You use the bread to scoop up bits of the wat, and eat it. Oh, but only use your right hand." Alice consulted her phone again, then led them down one of the streets that branched off from the dock. "I made the mistake of using my left hand once, and I thought the restaurant owner was going to have a conniption fit. Patrick got all bent out of shape when the guy told us to use only our right hands, but you know how he is—he doesn't like it when anyone tells him what to do."

She stopped so suddenly that Elliott, who was glancing around them with a bit of concern, bumped into her back.

"Sorry," she said at the same time he murmured an apology. She turned to face him, her lips held in a tight line. "Patrick is an ass, isn't he?"

Elliott frowned. What was this?

She put her hand on his arm, and it was then that he noticed the lines of strain around her eyes. Worse, it looked as if she was about to cry. "I mean, he just dumped me, totally out of the blue. Everything was fine, and then one day, he just said he'd had enough, and that I needed to move out. Only an ass would do that, right?"

"That's a very apt description of a man who would treat a woman in such a manner," he agreed, wondering a bit wildly what he could do to keep her from crying. He had a weakness against tears, especially women's tears, a weakness that horrified and repulsed him. As a result, he went to extraordinary lengths to avoid situations such as the one that was facing him now.

"You'd never treat someone that way, would you?" Alice asked with an audible sniff. Her eyes were definitely tearing up. Any moment now, one of the tears would break free, and then he'd be a goner. He had to distract her, and fast.

"A gull tried to eat my shoe earlier today. It was most amusing."

"I just know you wouldn't. You're too nice. Maybe it's because you're a lord, but I just know you wouldn't kick out a girlfriend without due cause."

A big fat tear trembled on her eyelashes. He had to reroute her train of thought immediately. What she needed was a shock to her system. He thought for an instant, then asked, "So, seal clubbing. As bad as whaling, or worse? What are your thoughts on the subject?"

"Especially when you were planning on marrying that girlfriend in Budapest."

Dammit, all his tactics were failing him! He had to act fast, or all would be lost. Desperately, he thought of subjects of conversation that might defuse the situation (satanic sacrifices? Global warming? An inquiry into her political beliefs?), but in the end, the pathetic little hiccup she gave that warned of imminent weeping drove him into doing the last thing he expected—he kissed her. He simply grasped her arms, pulled her up against him, and planted his mouth on hers.

Even while he was doing it, he was telling himself to keep it clinical, to stay at an emotional distance, and not to put any effort into the kiss. It was a distracting tactic, and nothing more.

Until she melted against him. Then the heady scent of sun-warmed woman teased him, sinking into his blood and triggering an instant reaction in the groin region. Worse, she put her arms around him and kissed him back, her mouth opening under his and allowing him to taste the warmth within. Sometime recently, she'd been eating cinnamon, leaving her mouth as spicy and sweet as a Christmas candy. He had to stop. He was going to stop. Stopping was the right thing to do.

She moaned into his mouth, and he pulled her even closer, sliding his hands down her arms to hold her waist. He wanted to grab her delectable ass, but he was a gentleman through and through, and he'd be damned if he was the sort of man who ass-grabbed after only a day's acquaintance.

When they finally stopped, she pulled away from him and they both took a steadying breath. After a minute, she said, "Thank you," quietly leaving him feeling bereft and frustrated and with a raging erection that was going to make walking extremely uncomfortable.

He looked down at her face, slightly sunburned from her time at the windmills, the scattering of freckles across her nose and chin making a warm glow deep in his belly. "For what?"

"The pity kiss. Normally, I'm against them, because nothing is worse than knowing someone is driven by pity into kissing you. I mean, how embarrassing is it to admit that people kiss you not because they want to, but because they feel like that's probably the only kiss you're going to get? But that was a nice pity kiss. It was a pity kiss that says that you aren't the type of person who would have kicked me out of our condo and found a new woman without at least suffering a bit. It was a pity kiss that says I'm in the right, and Patrick is an ass, and while you empathize with my sad situation, you don't feel sorry for me. It was a pity kiss that said you want me to feel better about myself, and to not let Patrick's idiocy ruin a really good trip. Right?"

He wanted quite badly to tell her that he kissed her

because he wanted to, and not out of respect for her feelings, but long association with his mother and sisters kept his tongue behind his teeth. He nodded.

She gave him a dewy smile, sniffed twice, and thankfully blinked back the last of the tears. "You're really a nice guy, your royal lordship. Tell you what, I'll take you to dinner tonight, OK? So long as you don't order any wine. It's really expensive here, and my daily spending budget isn't huge. Deal?"

"If I desire wine, I will be happy to pay for it," he told her gravely, and allowed her to tug him along toward their destination.

"I hope you're hungry," she said again as they wound their way through the sometimes confusing maze of streets, guided by a map she had on her mobile phone. "Did you get your book written today?"

"I reached my goal for the day, yes, but the book is far from being done."

"Ah. How long does it take you to write a whole book?"

"It depends on the book in question. Where exactly is this restaurant?"

"Just around the corner ahead. Do you not like talking about writing?"

The neighborhood they had entered had a decided seedy tinge to it, one that raised a few mental warning flags. He wasn't opposed to people indulging in minor recreational drugs, so long as they didn't harm others, but he didn't care to participate, himself. The question was, how did Alice feel about coffeehouses and the drug patronage they offered?

Different strokes, he reminded himself, and decided that he would not attempt to kiss her again. Not until he knew whether she was likely to be getting stoned at every opportunity while they were in Holland. Emotional distance—that was what he needed, at least until he knew her a little better. Not only did he not need a romantic complication in his life, he certainly did not need one that used drugs.

"Elliott?"

"Hmm? Oh, no, not in particular. What's the name of the place we're having dinner?"

"The Ladybug. I hope that isn't too cute for you, but Ricardo said it was the best place to go in all of Holland, and that I shouldn't miss the experience of visiting it."

The warning flags fluttered a bit more in his head. "This wouldn't happen to be a coffeehouse, would it? One that happens to also serve Ethiopian food?"

"Like a Starbucks, you mean? No, they have meals. I'm so looking forward to a big bowl of wat."

He slid a glance at her. Did she think that he was not aware of the fact that coffeehouses in Holland were infamous for the consumption of cannabis, or was she simply naive? He sincerely hoped it was the latter. They turned the corner and ahead indeed was a sign that hung directly over a purple door.

"There it is. What a cute ladybug sign. You ready for an exciting Ethiopian experience?" She fairly skipped to the door she was so excited, and Elliott couldn't tell whether it was because she was anticipating a drug-filled evening or a spicy stew.

"Ugh, they let people smoke in here. I thought that was illegal. Boy, they are seriously busy. That's a good sign—it means their food is good. Oh, those people in the corner are just leaving. Let's grab their table quick like a bunny."

Before he could come right out and ask her if she was

aware of what a coffeehouse was in the Netherlands, Alice had commandeered a small table tucked away under a couple of hanging ferns. Two cushioned armchairs sat at a white rattan table, the center of which held a paisley-painted hookah. He took the seat opposite her, batting away a fern tendril that caressed the back of his head.

"This is so exciting. I can't believe I'm really sitting in Holland having dinner. With a lord, yet! My friends back home are going to die when I tell them. Sec, picture so they know I'm not lying. Smile!" Obligingly, he smiled when she snapped first a picture of him, then took a few shots of the coffeehouse. "I just hope there's going to be enough room for all the food I want to order," she finished, moving aside one of the hookah mouthpieces. "This centerpiece is a bit big."

"That *centerpiece* is a water pipe," he said, giving her a long look. She didn't look at all like someone who was waiting impatiently to fill it up and begin smoking. She looked, as she had told him, hungry. "Alice, are you aware of why there is smoke here?"

"Because people are smoking. Drat, that waitress didn't see us. You're in a better position than me. Can you flag her down?"

"You are aware of what they're smoking, yes?"

She looked puzzled. "Cigarettes?" She sniffed a couple of times. "Sorry, my sense of smell is a little weird. I had allergies a lot as a kid and I think it killed off some of my smell receptors. It's not a cigar bar, is it? I really hate cigar smoke, but I don't see a blue haze that normally goes with a cigar bar."

"I see that I'm going to have to explain a few things about the drug culture in Holland."

"I know all about drugs." Her back stiffened, and she

gave him a little frown. "Just because I don't like booze doesn't mean I'm clueless about other things. Oh, wait! You mean the fact that you can get pot in Amsterdam really easily, right? I saw on a travel Web site that it was legal here, but I didn't read much past a warning that it wasn't smart to try to smuggle drugs out of the country because pot just makes my tongue go numb."

It took Elliott a moment to work through that last sentence. "I am relieved to know that you won't be smuggling drugs, which I should point out are actually illegal in Holland. Partaking is not a crime punishable by the law, though, so the effect is a form of legality. However, the practice is not confined to Amsterdam."

Her eyes widened. She pointed at the hookah. "You said the centerpiece was a water pipe! So it's a working bong, not just a funky decoration? Oh my god, we're in a drug shop?"

"Coffee shop." He caught the eye of a passing waitress, who nodded at him. "I'm happy to find another restaurant for us to eat at, if you wish to find one that has less . . . ambiance."

A slightly stubborn look passed over her face. "Do you have any problems with people smoking pot?"

"Not unless they become violent, no."

"Good. Neither do I. It's not my thing, but I don't think it's any worse than booze, and lord knows that's much more readily available, and kills a whole lot more people each year." She took a deep breath, coughed a couple of times, then said with a lift of her chin, "We'll eat here. I'm looking forward to you trying the wat."

He hesitated. He didn't want to have to point out the obvious, but on the other hand, he felt obligated to at least mention it. "Will it bother you? Will being in an environment where people are leaving the air rife with cannabis smoke cause an issue for you?"

"No, I'm fine around a little pot smoke. Patrick used to indulge now and again, and although it probably wouldn't be smart to smoke a bowl, or whatever the latest pot slang is these days, the buzz you get off of second-hand smoke is really minor. At least, that's what Patrick always said, and I have never had reason to argue with that opinion."

"Very well, but I hope you don't have any drug tests scheduled in the next twenty-four hours."

The waitress appeared at their table.

"What do you mean? Oh, hello. Do you speak English?"

When the woman shook her head, Elliott offered to help. "I don't speak Dutch per se, but I could probably find enough words common to German that I could make myself understood."

"No, no, I said you weren't going to have to tax your brain tonight, and I meant it. I have a Dutch/English translator app on my phone. Let me just look up the dining-out section, and we'll be set." Alice bit her lower lip as she tapped on her phone's screen for half a minute. Elliott watched the little pink lip, and felt a familiar drawing sensation in his groin.

Dammit, he was becoming aroused just by watching those white teeth take possession of the deliciously soft lip, a lip that he himself wanted to gently bite, then suck into his mouth, and caress with his tongue. He shifted in the chair, telling himself that thoughts like that were going to ensure the evening was a painful one.

"Do you mind if I order for us both?" Alice asked.

"If you feel up to doing so, then by all means go ahead. I look forward to trying the stew you mentioned."

"Awesome. You won't be sorry. OK, here we go." Consulting her phone, Alice stumbled over a collection of words that didn't sound to him as if they were correct, but perhaps the app she was using was having her speak more formally than colloquially. The waitress nodded, collected the used dishes and cups that had been scattered around the table, and left them.

"I think you're really going to like the wat. At least I hope you will—it depends on how good this place makes it, but Ricardo swore it was worth the visit. Although . . ." She frowned and idly played with the mouthpiece of one of the hookah hoses. "Maybe he recommended it because he could smoke pot here rather than because it had great wat. I'll be really annoyed if that's true, because my mouth is all set for spicy goodness."

"If we are to eat with our right hand and not utensils, then I suggest you wash your hands before the meal arrives."

"Oh, they should bring us a bowl of water to wash with. If they don't, I'll hit up their bathroom." She looked curious. "Was that just a general warning, or are you hypersensitive to germs?"

"Neither." He nodded toward the mouthpiece. "They generally change those for new customers, but the waitress didn't bring a clean one. Judging by the contents of the pipe, the people who were here before us were using it."

She looked in horror at the mouthpiece, and flung it away from her, exclaiming she would be right back. He reached into his jacket pocket for a small travel bottle of hand sanitizer that he carried for just such situations—

although he had to admit, he'd never used it before for a water pipe—when his phone began buzzing.

He held the phone a bit away from his ear, well aware of his mother's habit of speaking loudly into all telephones. "Hello, Mum. Is anything the matter?"

"Elliott, dear, how nice to hear from you."

"You called me," he pointed out. Usually, his mother only called him when trouble was brewing. "What has happened? Is anyone bleeding? Have parts of the castle collapsed?"

"No one is bleeding, and of course the castle hasn't collapsed. That's why those very annoying men are here pounding away and making all sorts of messes outside with their scaffolding, and buckets of water, and loud, obnoxious power tools buzzing away just when one wishes to take a nap."

Alice was visible through the haze of smoke that hung off the ceiling, carefully picking her way through the tightly packed tables back to her seat.

"What's the trouble, then?" he asked. "And more to the point, how much is it going to cost me?"

"Nothing is wrong, dear heart. That is, nothing in the sense you mean. Josiah, my love, would you please tell your brother to stop wailing. Elliott is not going to string him up by his balls."

"Oh, lord," he muttered to himself, half rising from his chair when Alice returned. "Which brother, and what has he done?"

"Well, that bathroom was a trip in itself. Oh! You're on the phone. Sorry."

Silence met his questions. He was about to repeat them when his mother asked, "Who was that?"

"Are you talking to me or someone at home?"

"You, dear. That's why we are speaking on the phone. Who is that woman who apologized for interrupting you?"

Elliott flashed Alice a smile, but she was too busy looking around the room, and taking covert snaps with her camera.

"A fellow traveler on the cruise. What has this unnamed brother done?"

"I don't have to ask if she's pretty, since you have exquisite taste in women, except, of course, for that interlude with the Page Three girl who insisted on baring her breasts to all and sundry."

Alice had obviously been attempting to give him privacy while apparently interesting herself with people-watching, but she slid a quick, startled look at him before busying herself with her camera. No doubt his mother's voice was audible to everyone near them. He just hoped no one else spoke English.

"Mother," he said in a firm, no-nonsense tone of voice. "What is wrong at home that forced you to call me?"

"It's Rupert. He and Josiah thought it would be nice if they painted your office, since the mold has crept in around the window, and stained the north wall, and of course, you aren't here, so it really is the perfect time to paint without disturbing you. Wasn't that thoughtful of them? The boys were most energetic with their work, and had everything but that ugly old desk covered—"

He closed his eyes for a moment. He had a horrible premonition as to what was coming. "You mean the desk that has been in the Ainslie family for the last three hundred years?"

"—and Rupert evidently jostled Josiah—you know how boys can't help but roughhouse at their age—and unfortunately, a small amount of paint was spilt. Very small, almost so small you can't notice it, especially if you put a large blotter on the desktop, or perhaps, drape it with one of those oversized shawls that my grandmother used to say tarts put on pianos in their boudoirs. Although really, when you think about it, what good is a piano in a boudoir? If you use it to play seductive music, you can't either be seducing or be seduced, because you would be concentrating on playing it. And if you had someone playing it for you, then you would need to be a voyeur, and I just don't see the greater population of Victorian tarts being voyeurs. You would know more about that than I do, since you studied that sort of thing in university. Did the tarts enjoy being watched while going about their sexual congress?"

He took a deep, deep breath, and opened his eyes to find Alice giving him a commiserating look, one tinged with deep amusement. He spoke before his mother could get started again. "First of all, I studied languages, not the history of Victorian prostitutes, and second, those *boys* are twenty-six and twenty-nine, respectively, so no, I don't see how you can claim that roughhousing is part of their day-to-day routine. That desk was a valuable antique, one laden with family history, and if the paint is not removed from it and the desk restored to its former state by the time I return home, I will have many and varied things to say to both Josiah and Rupert, much of which will feature assorted tortures until such time as the desk is restored."

The corner of Alice's mouth curled up in a smile. He had the worst urge to kiss that corner.

"I think that most unreasonable of you, Elliott. Just because your brothers did you a favor does not give you the right to threaten them."

"Actually, it does."

"It was just high spirits that caused the unfortunate accident, high spirits and a driving desire to please you, their much loved eldest brother."

"I appreciate the thought."

"So you don't know about the Victorian tarts?" His mother sounded disappointed.

"I'm afraid not. If that is all—"

"I don't see why your father and I sent you to Cambridge if you weren't going to learn something useful. What is her name, this fellow traveler of yours?"

He felt profoundly uncomfortable. He didn't want to discuss Alice with his mother, especially not with the former sitting right there in front of him, trying to look like she wasn't listening to the conversation, but he knew full well the tenacity of his mother's mind, and rather than field phone calls from her all night, he attempted to feed her just enough information to leave him in peace. "Her name is Alice."

"Alice. What a nice old-fashioned name. Where is she from?"

"The States." He gave Alice a feeble smile. She flashed a grin that expressed her understanding.

"And her surname?"

He stopped smiling back at Alice, a suspicion suddenly entering his mind. "Why do you wish to know that?"

Her response was given in a vague tone of voice. "Oh, you know, darling, it's always nicer to think of someone by their full name rather than just one name."

"Are you at this moment sitting in front of a computer Googling Alice?"

"No, of course not. You know I don't like computers."

He thought for a moment. "Which of your sons is in front of you at the computer?"

Righteous indignation dripped from every word. "Really, Elliott! You have the most suspicious mind of any man I've ever met."

"Josiah? Teddy?"

"It's Emanuel, if you must know, and I think you're being quite, quite odious to call me up and harass me in this manner."

"Good night, Mum."

"Good night, dear. Don't forget to use protection."

He hung up with an apologetic twist of his lips. "I'm sure you heard every word of that."

"I'm afraid I did. Your mom is one of those people who feels like she has to yell into the phone, huh?"

"Sadly, yes. I apologize for any untoward interest she has expressed in you. She's been after me to get out more and meet women, and tends to be a little extreme in her interests in my social life."

"I hear you on that. My mom gave me up when I was really young, but I had a lot of foster moms, and a couple of them were real drama llamas. Sorry to hear about the desk. I love old furniture, so I can see why you're upset, although I have to say, it's still kind of a shock to hear you talk about things like your house being a castle, an actual castle, not a metaphorical one, but a real, honest-to-bullfrogs castle type of castle, and of having a desk that's hundreds of years old, and going to Cambridge and all. I just knew you went to somewhere like Cambridge. I mean, it all fits, doesn't it? How many brothers do you have? Supposedly I have two half brothers, but I've never met them, and given the foster brothers that I had to endure, I'm not really angsting over the unknown birth sibs. I am so hungry! You'd think they'd bring us some injera to nibble on until the wat is ready. My stomach is growling to beat the band. I'm so hungry I could eat a hookah. Hahahah. Wow, I seem to be talking a lot. Do you think I'm talking a lot? I don't usually talk a lot. Not that I'm an introvert or anything like that. I bet you're an introvert, because you're a writer, and someone told me once that writers were classic introverts because they liked to be around themselves and tell stories. I'm also willing to bet your mom isn't an introvert. I mean, no one who goes on and on about Victorian tarts and their boudoirs is going to be an introverted person. Although, who knows, I could be totally blowing it out my piehole, huh?" She giggled in a very endearing fashion.

"I think," he said with grave portent, feeling that one of them had to keep a cool, dispassionate head, "that the secondhand smoke has gotten to you. Unless you normally chatter like that, and I don't recall you doing so in the past, although it is true that we met only yesterday, so perhaps I don't have a solid basis of data upon which to make that judgment. Are you normally a person who indulges in stream-of-consciousness soliloquies, or is this abnormal behavior? I'm afraid that I'm not terribly cognizant of just how extroverts behave when afflicted by secondhand cannabis smoke, since I have, as you rightly surmised, introvert qualities that dominate my personality." He paused, watching her as she continued to giggle. "Since I now am possessed with an almost overwhelming desire for pie, I'm inclined to believe that I am being affected by the smoke, as well. And ham, for some bizarre reason. A nice ham sandwich and a piece of berry pie would be very welcome right now."

"Oooh, pie," she said, her eyes growing large. "Lemon meringue. Oh, I know—key lime!"

"That does sound good," he agreed, and gestured at the waitress. "I shall ascertain whether or not this establishment carries such a thing."

"You're just talking like that to make me laugh," Alice said in between giggles.

He waggled his eyebrows at her in a manner that both shocked and amused him. He'd never waggled his eyebrows in his life, and here he was waggling at a woman he just met, one with tantalizing lips, and nicely rounded breasts, and an even rounder ass. He liked Alice's ass. He liked everything about her, but her ass was especially wonderful. He had a sudden mental vision of sitting with one hand on her naked ass, while the other held a piece of berry pie, and he knew he had to get them out of there before he explained the vision to her. "I believe we should leave. This smoke is getting to be a bit too much."

"Not until we eat," Alice begged. "I'm so hungry. Oh, look, the waitress is coming back. That looks like dinner. You're going to love this, I promise."

"Very well. We shall leave directly after we've eaten."

The waitress set down a platter that contained twelve fried eggs and immediately left. They looked at the eggs.

Alice frowned at them. "I don't understand. Where's the wat?"

"What's on first? No, that's second base," Elliott said, laughing silently so hard that his shoulders shook.

Alice prodded aside one of the eggs. "Is it under the eggs? I don't see it at all. Did they forget it?"

"'Did they forget it?' is on third." This time, he laughed out loud, unable to keep his amusement in any longer. Dear lord, who knew he could be so intensely funny? Perhaps he ought to consider writing a humorous novel next.

Alice stabbed one of the eggs with a fork and gestured at him with it. "You, sir, are punch-drunk."

"I have had no punch. Are you intending to accost me with that egg? Because if you are, I will be obliged to inform you that I do not care for fried eggs." He looked closer at the plate of them. "Although I will admit, those appear to be particularly fine examples of eggdom. Perhaps a taste or two is in order. For politeness' sake, you know."

"Politeness?" Alice asked, looking with growing interest at the egg on the end of her fork.

"Yes, since you went to all the trouble of ordering us many eggs, it would be rude of me not to eat at least some of them." He scooped several eggs onto a small bread plate and passed it to her, then repeated the process for himself. *"Bon appétit."*

"I wonder if this is the Dutch idea of an appetizer," Alice said around a mouthful of egg. "Not that I'm complaining, because you're right, these are really good fried eggs, and I'm not normally a big fan of them, either. But still, it's odd that I ordered us delicious wat, and we got fried eggs instead. I like the crispy bits at the edges the best. Yum."

They consumed their eggs in silence for a few minutes. Elliott had to admit to feeling much more relaxed than when he began the evening, a pleasant sense of well-being making his limbs tingle. And his lips. For some reason, his mouth was highly sensitized. He looked at Alice. He wondered what kissing her with tingly lips would feel like.

"I'll just save these last couple of ones in case we get

hungry in the middle of the night," Alice said, sliding three fried eggs into her small handbag. "Unless you wanted them?"

"No, I believe ten eggs is my limit," he said, wiping his mouth carefully, extremely aware of the sensation of the roughened cloth across his lips. "If your hunger has abated sufficiently, we should probably leave before we become even more affected by the environment."

"I suppose it wouldn't be good to show up at the ship stoned out of our gourds, especially since we didn't hoo-kah. I have to say, though, that I've become fond of this one." She gave one of its brass appendages a pat. "It just kind of represents Holland, doesn't it? I know every time I see a hookah, I'll think about having dinner with you here."

He stood up, and made a bow to her that got a little involved when he straightened up and knocked his head into the hanging fern. "Allow me to present it to you as a souvenir, madam. Ow. Waitress! How much for the hookah?"

She giggled and giggled and giggled, and was still gig-gling when, some twenty minutes later, they arrived at their ship. Luckily, most of the others were off having dinner, although they did encounter Tiffany as they were attempting to make the key work at their cabin door. She eyed the hookah with pursed lips.

"It's a souvenir of a most delightful evening," Elliott told her.

"Like an egg?" Alice asked, opening her bag and of-fering it to Tiffany.

Tiffany peered into the bag's depths. "Erm . . . no thank you."

"She's one of those non-egg people, clearly. She

doesn't know what she's missing," Alice said once he had the door opened. "Damned good fried eggs they do here. Boy, it's ten already? I didn't think we were at the restaurant that long."

"Time flies when you are having eggs," he said, laughing inwardly at the sudden emergence of his humor. Definitely, he needed to write a funny novel.

"Elliott."

"Hmm?" Perhaps a whole series of funny novels. Ones with eggs, and hookahs, and women with wondrous asses. He could be the new P. G. Wodehouse!

"I want to thank you for the pity kiss earlier, and the only way I know how to do that is to give you a nonpity kiss." She stopped for a moment, her face screwed up in thought. "Or do you think all that secondhand smoke has made me horny?"

Hell, he could even make a character named Egg. Wodehouse always had oddly named characters. He stopped that train of thought, suddenly diverted by what she was saying. "You wish to kiss me?"

"Yes, I do. Would you mind terribly? I mean, I won't if you'd be offended, or repulsed, or if you're gay and just aren't into women, but I don't think you are gay, because gay men don't usually go around kissing women, not even pity kisses."

"It wasn't a pity kiss. It was an 'I fancy you' kiss," he explained, wondering even as the words left his mouth why he was saying them. He certainly had no intention of doing so earlier. He even had a vague memory of patting himself on the back for his deft handling of the situation. "I wouldn't mind if you kissed me, although to be honest, I'd rather kiss you."

Her face screwed up again in obvious thought. On

any other woman, he would find such an act off-putting, but on Alice, it was nothing short of adorable. She pulled an egg from her bag and absently nibbled on it. "Is there a difference?"

"There must be. Shall we see? You may kiss me first, and then I will kiss you, and we will compare the experiences."

"Sounds good to me." She kissed him.

"That was nice," he said, trying to form subjective thoughts about the experience. "I believe it would be nicer without the egg, however."

"It did kind of get between our mouths, didn't it?"

"Yes. I shall conduct my kiss without it. Do you mind?" He plucked a bit of fried egg from where it dangled from her mouth, and placed it carefully back into her bag, then took her in his arms, and tilted his head slightly to the left so he wouldn't smash his nose into hers. "Ready?"

She giggled. He took that as an assent, and kissed her. She tasted decidedly less sweet, and more eggy, than earlier in the evening, but still, it was a highly pleasurable experience, one that his tingly lips greatly enjoyed. Even his tongue gave a thumbs-up when it got into the action, playing with hers in a way that reminded him of dolphins leaping about the bow of a ship in the Aegean.

"That *was* better without the egg," she said when he had to come up for air, since he evidently had forgotten how to breathe while kissing. "What did you think?"

"Dolphins," he told her. "Riding the bow wave."

She blinked at him. "OK."

"I think we should go to bed."

"Yeah, I'm tired. Wait, did you mean together, or separately?"

He glanced down at his trouser front. Alice glanced

with him. There was a pronounced bulge behind his fly, and a distinct ache in his groin. He looked back up and met her gaze. "I'll leave that to you."

"Well, I see you're willing and able and all, but I'm heartbroken and devastated by Patrick's betrayal, so I'm going to say separately."

He made another bow, smacked his forehead on hers, and said while rubbing his head, "As you wish. I shall bid you good night."

She giggled some more while rubbing her own forehead. "I love it when you talk like a lord. Night, Elliott."

He retired to bed, not finding it necessary to remove his clothing or his shoes, so relaxed and peaceful was his mental state. Clearly she felt the same way, and they were both soon asleep.

Chapter 5

Diary of Alice Wood

Day One (for real this time—the other two Day Ones were practice)

It was a new day, a new dawn, and a new life. Unfortunately, awareness returned to me with all the stealth of a manatee clad in anvil shoes. "Urgh. Pleb. Flrng. Stupid drug hangover effect thing."

"I second that 'flrng,' and raise you a 'What the hell was I doing last night?' Which prompts me to ask: What the hell *was* I doing last night?"

One eyelid peeled back with an almost audible fwapping sound, kind of like a wet blind being pulled up. I rolled my eyeball over to see what was wrong with Elliott, but his bed was empty. Had I lost my mind? Were his spy ninja–like skills so great that he could speak to me without being in the room? Was he talking to me via a hidden intercom?

A slight movement caught my peripheral vision. I leaned down over the edge of my bed and considered the man lying on the floor on his back, fully clothed, hair adorably tousled, and eyes scrunched closed.

"Hello, Elliott. I'd ask if you were checking under the beds for assassins, but since there's drawers under the bed, and no space for a person, that can't be."

His eyes opened. I winced when I saw just how bloodshot they were. "Assassins?"

"Yeah." I thought for a minute. My brain seemed to be working very slowly this morning, kind of like a fog bank had rolled into my head and was smothering all those hardworking synapses. "You know, like double agents and their ilk. People sent to kill you in order to keep you from talking about what you know."

"That's a strangely specific thing to believe might be under your bed."

I remembered at that moment that I was supposed to be covertly digging into his past, and that mentioning the assassins and double agents that no doubt were once part of his daily life didn't quite qualify as covert. "Um. Yeah. Ha ha. Just a joke."

"How you can make a joke at a time like this is beyond me."

"A time like what?" I squinted at the small clock on the dresser. "Seven after eight? Are you not a morning person?"

"Not at a time when my head feels like it's full of cotton. Usually, I *am* a morning person. At least, I am when I don't feel as if my entire body has been run through one of those damned historic windmills. What did I do last night?"

"We went to a coffeehouse. I guess that secondhand

smoke was more potent than Patrick let on. I've definitely got a drug hangover thing going on, and since you said you get the same way, I assume that's why your head is full of cotton." I touched my forehead. "Mine feels more like my brains have turned to molasses."

"Coffeehouse. That's right. You dragged me to a coffeehouse and insisted I kiss you."

"I did no such thing. That was a pity kiss, and it was bestowed upon me of your own volition, not that I didn't appreciate it at the time. I'm a little less happy with it now, although I seem to recall kissing you later on, too." I rubbed my temples. "I'm having a hard time braining, to be honest."

"I empathize completely." He sat up, moaned a little, and, with an unseemly grunt that I thought it best not to point out, got to his feet. "My mouth tastes like the inside of a tart's piano. Do you have immediate need of the facilities, or may I use them?"

"Knock yourself out. I took a shower in the middle of the night. Don't you remember?"

"At this point in time, I remember nothing other than there is a reason I dislike this country." With great dignity, he staggered into the bathroom and closed the door.

By the time he emerged, I was dressed, had collected my gear for the day, and was flipping through a guidebook to review what sites were to be visited. "Evidently, we're in Cologne, Germany, already. Cool. And we're going to see the cathedral this morning. It sounds really interesting." I looked up, making a sympathetic face when Elliott walked stiffly by me. "You really look like you've been through a war or two. You going to be OK?"

"Possibly." He sat down heavily at the small table, pushing his laptop away as if it was suddenly repugnant.

"Possibly not. If I do not survive, would you see to it that my mother receives my personal effects? Also, tell her I forgive her."

"For what?" I asked, curiosity getting the better of me once again.

He waved a hand about vaguely. "Everything. Anything. Nothing in particular. What are you doing?"

I had opened up my bag to tuck the guidebook into it, but stopped. "I'm wondering why I thought it was a good idea to fill my purse with eggs."

He blinked at me.

I pulled a cold, flabby fried egg from my bag, followed by its twin, holding them up so he could see. "Eggs."

"You couldn't carry a packet of peanuts like a normal person?" he asked.

I smiled. "I've never done normal particularly well. I won't ask you to go up to breakfast with me, since the way you're looking at the eggs indicates extreme revulsion, so I'll just say happy writing, and get out of your hair."

"Actually . . ." He waited until I reached the door before stopping me. He rose and stood in the middle of the room, with a chagrined expression on his face that I found oddly endearing. He cleared his throat and tried again. "Actually, I thought I might give myself a day off. I did quite a bit of writing yesterday, and it's no use trying to write anything coherent when my brain feels the consistency of one of the eggs in your bag. And I've always liked Cologne."

"And you speak German, right? You can translate stuff! That'll be awesome, because we're on our own after the tour of the cathedral, and I have to admit I was planning on glomming onto one of the other people because I'm intimidated by German. But now we can go off by ourselves, because you won't let me get lost and end up at some kinky sex club full of dominatrixes."

"You are wise to avoid that eventuality. Why come all the way to Germany for bondage experiences, when I assume you could have the same at home at a greatly reduced cost?" He slipped his wallet into his pants, and pulled a lightweight sport coat from the tiny little closet.

He had that same deadpan look on his face as when he joked he'd have to kill me if he told me the truth about himself, so I couldn't tell for a minute if he thought I was seriously into kinky sexual acts, or not.

He stopped in front of me, gently placing a finger beneath my chin and pushing upward to close my mouth. "I was joking."

"Oh, good, because I'm really not looking for sex, kinky or otherwise."

"You are devastated and traumatized by Patrick's betrayal, yes, I remember."

I narrowed my eyes at him. "Are you mocking my devastated trauma?"

"I would never do such a thing."

His eyes revealed nothing but a hint of amusement.

"All right, because I have been really upset. I mean, I was supposed to be getting married."

He tipped his head to the side, grimaced at the obvious pain that followed such a careless act, and carefully straightened back up. "Would you be offended if I made a comment regarding that?"

"That depends," I said warily, wondering if he was mocking me. "You tell me the comment, and I'll tell you if I'm offended."

He was silent for a moment, then brushed a bit of hair

off my cheek in a gesture that suddenly made it seem like there wasn't enough air in the cabin. "In all your ranting about Patrick, you seem to be more focused on the fact that you aren't going to be married than regretting the loss of a man you assumedly loved beyond all others."

I opened my mouth to dispute that fact, but the words wouldn't come out. Instead, I took a step forward and poked him in the chest while pointing out, "He kicked me out of our condo."

"Yes, and that was not at all well-done of him."

The smell of him—the slightly piney aftershave tinged by something that I decided was pure pheromones—seemed to spiral around me in little tendrils of sexual interest. I reminded myself that I wasn't attracted to him, but the more I argued that, the more the tendrils of pure chemical lust wrapped around me.

"He dumped me for another woman!" It took a major effort to get the words out—I wanted nothing more than to nestle against his neck and breathe in the heady scent of him—but I managed by telling my body that nothing was going to come of the nonattraction.

"Which tells you that he didn't truly care for you, not in the way you deserve."

I was standing so close to him, I could see the little flecks of black in his eyes. I stared at them, wondering how a man could have such dense, thick black eyelashes, all other thoughts but those of a purely carnal nature leaving my mind. "I am not attracted to you," I said savagely.

He cocked one eyebrow. "No? Your pupils are dilating. Your breath is ragged. Your breasts"—his gaze dropped down to the front of my gauze shirt—"appear to be of another mind."

"I'm hurt and devastated and traumatized," I reminded him, biting back a moan when he swept his thumb across the pulse point in my neck.

"Your pulse is rapid. All classic signs of physical attraction."

"Yeah? Well, so are you," I said, sliding my hand slowly down his chest. It was as if there were no cloth between us, the heat of him almost singeing my hand. "I can feel your heart beating like crazy, and your eyes are all spotty, and if you had boobs, I bet they'd be demanding that they place themselves in my hands just like mine are insisting that they're going to be very, very pissed if I don't walk them straight into your hands. And possibly mouth." I thought for a moment. "Definitely mouth. So if I'm attracted to you—wholly against my will, I'd like to point out, being the injured party in a monumental breakup—then you are, as well. Worse, you're all dilated pupils, heavy breathing, hard little nipple nubs for me, a person who is on the rebound, and we all know how easy rebound pickups are."

He looked a little puzzled. "Did you just call yourself easy?"

"Perhaps, but if I did, it's because your cologne is befuddling my mind, and I can't think straight with my boobs clamoring at me, and your mouth right there in front of me, and dear god, man, do you have a fever? Your chest is so hot."

He clamped a hand over where I was now simply stroking the deliciously hard bulges and valleys of his chest terrain. "If you don't stop referring to your breasts and the smell of a warm, freckled woman, not to mention driving me insane with your fingers on my nipples, then I will be forced to take defensive action."

"Really?" I tipped my head, smiling smugly because I could do it without incurring a headache. "What defensive act did you have in mind?"

"I will kiss you," he said, his voice seeming to thrum inside me. It was a deep voice, and the way he enunciated each letter made me want to leap on him. "I will kiss you until you are giddy, and your breasts are sated."

"My breasts are notoriously hard to please," I said haughtily, attempting to look down my nose at him. It's not easy when the person receiving such a look is many inches taller than you. "It's going to take more than a few smooches to put them into overdrive."

"Are you saying I couldn't please you sexually?" His eyes widened, and I smirked to myself that his pupils were huge in them. The man was clearly just as aroused as I was. I didn't even have to glance down at his zipper to see that.

Of course, on that thought, I had to look. And Elliott caught me at it.

"I am not responsible for my penis's reaction," he said quickly, in the same haughty tone I used on him, only his was much more effective.

"Was that an insult?" I asked, outraged.

"No more so than your statement regarding your breast satisfaction."

"You are so toast, buster," I said, and boldly placed my hand on his crotch. He sucked in an inordinate amount of air, and twitched behind his zipper.

"So, it's going to be like that, is it?" His beautiful voice seemed to have lost some of its polish, but that fact went right out of my head when he placed both hands on my breasts.

I moaned slightly, the warmth of his palms seeping

into my flesh, and heading straight for my lady parts, where it settled deep within. Before I could react to his move, he rubbed both thumbs over my respective nipples, making my knees want to buckle.

"That is not fair," I said in a husky voice that I was a bit shocked to find belonged to me. "I'm not using my thumbs. I'm just holding you. Well, part of you. You appear to be quite . . . long."

"Not unnecessarily so. I will grant you the right to use your thumb if you so desire. In the interests of fairness."

I started laughing then, mostly because of his deadpan delivery, but also because I had a sudden image of what we looked like standing there arguing while holding each other's erogenous zones. "Are you going to kiss me or not?"

"Do you want me to?"

"Very much so."

"I will be happy to oblige upon one condition."

I rubbed my thumb along the part of him that was beneath my hand. "That I use my thumb."

His eyes crossed for a few seconds, and he seemed to be having difficulty breathing. "No. I want no recriminations that I am taking advantage of your rebound status. If I kiss you, it's because you want me to do so, and not because you are seeking to assuage your feelings of hurt and betrayal."

I thought about that for a moment. Was I guilty of seeking attention to soothe my bruised ego? Or was it Elliott that stirred me so? And if it was the latter, what did it say about my relationship with Patrick?

"You were right," I said slowly, not wanting to admit the truth even to myself. "I think I have been more upset about the result of the breakup than the breakup itself."

He took his hands off my breasts (which instantly demanded they return), and slid them around my waist, pulling me forward against him. I had to release his crotch to do so, but my hands were happy enough to slide around to his back where they found more muscles to caress.

"I'm sorry if I was poking my nose into something you wish to keep private."

I said nothing, just looked into his eyes for a few seconds, then brushed my mouth against his. "I hope this doesn't make me a tramp, but there's just something about you that makes me want to do all sorts of extremely illicit things to you."

"Thank the lord," he said with a sigh, and kissed me, really kissed me, not just a little peck, or even an open-mouthed snog, but a full-bodied kiss, the kind where every inch of him worked along with the kiss until it overwhelmed me and left me feeling boneless, and very, very aroused.

"Elliott," I said, my lady parts tingling for all they were worth.

"Yes," he said, pulling my shirt off me, stopping to add, "There's no rebound in this?"

"None whatsoever. This has nothing to do with Patrick, and everything to do with needing your flesh applied directly to my flesh this very instant," I answered, quickly unbuttoning the buttons on his shirt. He shucked his shoes. I peeled off my retro plaid Capri pants, shoes, socks, and, after a moment's hesitation and regret that I hadn't stuck with the Zumba class, underwear and bra. By that time, he was naked, as well, and without any amount of awkward standing around assessing the other person's body, we toppled into the nearest bed (mine).

"I suppose we should be adult about this," I said, writhing when his mouth closed around one needy nipple. "Oh dear god, yes, do that thing with your tongue again."

His tongue swirled. My body hummed.

"What was I saying? Oh yes, adult. Responsible. All that crap. Do the other one, Elliott, it's getting jealous." He obliged by swirling his tongue over my other nipple, making my fingers dig deep into his shoulder muscles.

"You taste like honey," he said, looking up from my breasts.

"Is that good? Do you like honey? What kind of honey? The kind that's put on wounds that won't heal, or honey from happy and contented bees? Please god, tell me it's the happy bee honey!"

"It is. Very happy bees. Bees that are so happy they're about to burst into show tunes. You smell like flowers, and you taste like honey, and your skin is so soft I want to lick it."

"Far be it from me to stop you—wait!" I remembered what it was that I had been about to say when my breasts distracted me. "I've had my shot last month, so I'm fine so far as birth control goes, but we don't really know that much about each other, and—"

"I have no diseases, social or otherwise," he interrupted, leaning down to rub his cheeks between my boobs.

My toes curled into the sheets. "Neither do I. Great. So we're good to go?"

"Roger, as you Yanks say, wilco and out."

"Well, I'd rather in, because, frankly, if my lady parts tingle any harder, they might just go up in flames, and I can't tell you how painful that's going to be."

He squinted up at me. "You are making jokes during sex?"

"We're not having sex. We're having foreplay."

His hand slid down my belly, one finger curling into me. I almost came off the bed at the sensation of it. "My finger is inside of you. I think this qualifies as sex."

"No, it's just very, very good foreplay. Oh, dear god, two fingers? Really? Holy crapballs, that's good. To the left, please. Nnrng!"

"Your *nnrng* pleases me," he said with a wholly male, extremely smug smile as his fingers danced a seductive dance. My hips bucked, my hands clutched at the sheets of my bed (unmade, because I am basically a slob), and I swear my eyes all but rolled back in my head. "But I think we can do better than that. Shall we try for a *foowah*?"

"What's a foowah?" I panted, trying desperately to keep from falling over the edge into Orgasmland.

"It's the sound I make when someone pleasures me to the limit of my tolerance. Can you foowah for me, Alice?"

"I will if you let me get my hands on you," I said, desperately trying to reach that part of him that caused the foowahing.

He moved just enough that he was out of my reach. "No, I believe we will focus on you this time."

"That doesn't seem fair, although I'm hardly in a position to complain."

"Indeed you are not. Later, perhaps, if you are very good, I will allow you to pleasure me in ways that have me nnrnging, but until then, we are striving for a fullfledged foowah."

His thumb brushed sensitive flesh, and that was all she wrote. So to speak. "Foowah!" I shouted, my intimate muscles spasming around him. "Oh, holy hell, foowah and then some! Foowah squared! My god, Elliott, where did you learn to do that? You haven't been to those kinky German sex dungeons, have you?"

"Actually, I have, just once, and no, I did not particularly enjoy myself. I prefer my women willing and not tied down."

It took a few minutes for me to come down off the orgasmic high, but when I did, I couldn't help but ask, "Wow, you really went to one of those places? I've always wondered what they were like. I mean, you see shots of them in porn—not that I've watched porn, although Patrick loved some weird studio out of Lithuania, and was always trying to get me to watch it with him—I wonder if that's why he dumped me?—but I've always wondered if they were as wicked as they looked. Was your place as wicked as it looked?"

"Do you always talk this much during sex?" Elliott asked, licking a path up my belly to the valley between my breasts.

"I'm afraid I do. Is that a turnoff for you? If it is, I can try to be quieter, but honestly, I've found that people who don't like me for who I am really aren't my problem."

"It's not a turnoff; I simply didn't know if you are nervous, and chatting because of that, or if you are normally this vocal. As a matter of fact, I agree with you about other people's perceptions. They usually don't concern me. Do you like it when I do this?"

He gently took my nipple between his teeth. It wasn't a hard bite, and I had to admit, the sensation fired up my already steaming-hot blood. "Oh, yes! You're very gentle, aren't you? Do they do this sort of thing in the German sex clubs?"

He stopped molesting my breast to look up at me. "Do

you happen to wish to visit one of those establishments, but don't want to suggest it?"

"I can't help it. I was raised Lutheran. Lutherans never go to German sexy-time clubs." I waved a hand in the air. "Was I that obvious?"

"No. I am simply that perceptive." He looked down at my breast for a moment, then slid his gaze lower to my hips and belly. "I will make a deal with you. If you allow me to choose the restaurant in which we shall dine, I will accompany you to one of the clubs your Lutheran heart so desires to see."

"Deal," I said, stroking my hand down his chest, pausing just long enough to gently tweak one of his nipples. "So long as you don't leave me in the hands of some leather-clad dominatrix who has a whip and one of those benches they bend you over and do wicked things to you."

The look he gave me could have steamed clams. "Oh, we will have the bench, have no doubt about that. The whip is optional, but the bench? Yes, my sweet little Alice. That is one Wonderland you will most definitely remember visiting."

"Oooh," I said, my legs moving restlessly next to his. "I like that glint in your eye. Elliott?"

"Hmm?"

"Are we done with foreplay? Because my engine is more than warmed up, and I think I may go out of my mind if you don't continue."

"I couldn't agree more," he mumbled as he nuzzled my neck. "Do you prefer to be on the top or bottom?"

"I don't care," I said on a gasp, pulling him down on top of me. Just the feel of all that warm, solid flesh made me feel as if my skin were alight.

"Bottom, then." He slid into me, making my intimate muscles give a cheer of happiness and embrace the welcome intruder.

"Wow, you are . . . Oh, yes, that is a really nice move. . . . You are a lot more robust than I thought you were. Not that I'm saying you were inadequate in any way."

"It's all in the technique, or so I've been told," he panted against my shoulder. "Would you mind doing that again?"

"What, this?" I tightened all my inner muscles around him.

"Oh, Christ. Don't do that again or it will be all over for me."

"This, then?" I dragged my fingernails softly down his back. I had been careful to be gentle the first time, since some men didn't care for the sensation, but evidently Elliott really did, because his back arched, and his hips thrust forward, and I saw stars for a second time.

"Nnrng!" I gasped, wrapping my legs around his hips and giving myself up to the unprecedented second orgasm.

"Foowah," he corrected, and gave in to his own climax.

"I can't believe," I said some minutes later when I had the brain function and coordination to use my mouth again, "that I had two orgasms. I've never been multi-orgasmic. Usually, it's just bang! One, and I'm done for the night." I squinted at the hair resting against my cheek, Elliott still being clasped in my arms. "You must have learned things at your previous visit to the German sexland. Secret things."

"Am I too heavy for you?" he panted into my shoulder.

I stroked my hand down his damp back, to the lovely muscles of his butt. He had a very nice butt, with those little swoopy indentations on either side that bespoke a man who had a regular exercise regime. That or fabulous butt genes. "Not in the least. You might be a big man who eats like a horse, but I'm no frail, delicate flower."

He reared back to give me an outraged look. "You said you were not going to make any further references to the quantity of food needed to give me energy to perform secret German sexual techniques."

I giggled, and kissed the tip of his nose, swatting his butt when he rolled off me. "Sorry. Since there's not enough room in the shower for two, and we're both too messy to go out without one, do you want to go first, or shall I?"

He collapsed onto his own bed, waving an airy hand. "You go first. I must recover from your voracious sexual demands. I hope there's time for me to consume a side of beef or the like before we must tour the Dom."

I giggled again, and took a fast shower, focusing my attention on just how wonderful a lover Elliott was, and shying away from the fact that I had just jumped into bed with a man I'd known for two days.

I did not once think about Patrick.

Chapter 6

Diary of Alice Wood

More of Day One (version three)

Elliott's voice echoed in a suitably dramatic manner. "I believe the cathedral is best tackled in the following manner: first we will explore its history, then view the important artworks and discuss the various points of architecture, and following that, we can descend to the lower levels to explore the history of the crypt, after which those people who do not mind heights can ascend the viewing platform, which has an excellent view of the Rhine. The platform has five hundred and nine steps, so be warned. And now, a few dimensions to get us started. The external length is one hundred forty-five meters—that's about four hundred seventy-five feet for you, Alice—and it's eighty-six meters wide, or two hundred eighty-three feet. The cathedral was begun in 1248 in order to house the relics of Three Kings, which had been pillaged from the Basilica of Saint Eustorgio, in Milan, and was still undergoing work two hundred years later. In fact, one could say that it wasn't really completed until the Victorians got their hands on it."

"Fascinating," Deidre said, clinging to Elliott's arm and simpering in a manner that made my hand itch to yank her hair. Or smack the smug look off her face; either option appealed to me at that moment.

"Sod that. I'm not going to have all the joy stripped from the experience by a recitation of facts and figures. Besides, this is one of the most visited tourist sites in Germany—Dahl and I shall be conducting some research, if you want us," Anthony said, and, with Dahl, wandered off down the nave, no doubt intending to snag unwary visitors and question them about their experiences.

The Japanese schoolgirls giggled. Even the teachers snickered.

"Mr. Ainslie, much as I appreciate your comments on the history of the cathedral, I should point out that I have given this tour many times, and I am fully qualified to do so again today." Tiffany held up a pamphlet that had been heavily highlighted and annotated.

"Then I'm sure you're ready for a break," Deidre said smoothly, actually batting her eyelashes at Elliott. Thankfully, he was looking at Tiffany, and didn't see such a shameless act of hussitude.

"I'm so sorry about this," Laura said softly next to me. "I tried to talk to her, but for some reason, she has set her sights on him, and refuses to admit that her actions are not at all reasonable."

"Not to mention the fact that Elliott here has a much bigger guidebook," Deidre cooed, putting her hand over his to hold up the (admittedly quite thick) guidebook that Elliott had picked up in the gift shop. "It's even in German. That has to be more authentic than an English abridged version, don't you think?"

"Oh, dear," Laura said, glancing worriedly over at me.

I smiled, fully committed to hanging on to my temper. Just because Elliott and I had become a bit more than mere roomies didn't mean I had to act like Jealous McJealouson. Deidre could maul poor Elliott all she wanted—within reason, of course—and I wasn't going to so much as bat an eyelash. "It's fine, don't worry about it. Elliott and I are both aware that she's got the hots for him, so it's not like she's going to have any effect. Or at least, not the one she desires."

"I can assure you that there is nothing the least lacking in the tours that we provide," Tiffany meanwhile said huffily, and went into an explanation of all the research she'd done on the cathedral to make her qualified to talk about it.

"I have to admit," I said sotto voce to Laura, who was standing with me at the back of our little group, "I'm kind of with Anthony on this. I'd rather just wander around and see the cathedral without all the facts and lengths and widths and discussion of architectural types used."

"To be honest, I'm with you," Laura said with a little smile. "I'd much rather just soak in places like this. I mean, does knowing how and when the cathedral was built make you appreciate it any more?" She waved a hand at the high vaulted ceiling, which was indescribably gorgeous. "Not that I mean any insult to Elliott, of course. He's obviously one of those people who values structured learning."

"You should see how he folds his socks and under-

wear," I told her as Deidre and Tiffany squared off. Elliott, I noticed, was reading a text message. "The man's
downright anal when it comes to those things. I suppose
it's that attention to detail that makes him a very good
writer."

"I suppose so." Laura gave me a conspiratorial nudge
of the elbow. "I bet that's an excellent cover for a spy."

Elliott suddenly announced, "My apologies, ladies. I
have a call I must take. Tiffany, I'm sure you will do very
well guiding everyone. If you will excuse me . . ." He hurried past us with an abstracted look on his face that had
me wondering what was up.

"I wonder if that was his mother?" I asked absently.

"Is she ill?"

"No, just . . . kind of funny, actually." I shook away the
need to rush after Elliott and make sure everything was
OK in his world. I wasn't really his girlfriend, and didn't
have the right—or desire—to push myself into his life.

"You know," Laura said, the group moving off to look
at a famous painting. We trailed behind, our steps lag-
ging. I half hoped Tiffany would forget about us and just
let us wander around. "You know, if I was a spy, I'd use a
busy place like the cathedral here to meet up with my
contacts."

"Yeah, I suppose it would be a good cover." I looked
around. There were hundreds of tourists all over the
place, some in guided tours, others viewing various
nooks and crannies, and still others sitting with blissful
looks of relief on their faces. Guess we weren't the only
tourists who got tired feet. "With all these people, who'd
notice if two of them came together for a few minutes?"
Laura was silent for a few seconds. I caught her eye, and
asked, "You're not thinking what I'm thinking, are you?"

"I wager I am." An impish look came into her eye. "Are you game?"

I thought for a moment or two. "I shouldn't. I mean, it's kind of . . . underhanded."

"Covert," she corrected. "But of course, if it would make you uncomfortable, then I wouldn't dream of going through with it."

I bit my lower lip. The truth was, I was fairly itching to know what was so important that it stopped Elliott in midstatistics. "Well . . . oh, what the hell. So long as he doesn't see us, it won't be an issue, right?"

"Oh, this is so exciting!" Laura said as we both turned and hurried back toward the entrance. "I've always wanted to be a private detective, you know. I positively consume mystery books! I've watched ever so many American shows about that sort of thing, and I'm quite sure that we won't be seen. Which way, do you think?"

By that time we'd emerged into the sunshine. As we were coming from the dark into the brilliant light and buffeted by folks who were entering the cathedral, it took a moment to get oriented, but as soon as I had my bearings, I grabbed Laura's arm and dragged her away to the left. "There!" I pointed to where I caught a glimpse of Elliott's head bobbing above the crowds. "He's going toward the river."

We looked at each other. "I thought he said he needed to take a call?" Laura asked.

"So did I." The mood changed from one of silly companionability to something much more adult . . . and serious. It was one thing for us to joke around that Elliott was involved in something secretive, and pretend to spy on him, and another thing when the man made an excuse to leave the group, only to go off on an unexplained journey.

My curiosity ratcheted up several notches as we hurried after him, dodging people on the busy sidewalks, once losing sight of him entirely, but luckily, Laura found him again after a panicked search in which we split up to cover different streets. *Outside the Ludwig Museum. Have him under observation,* she texted me. I turned and retraced my steps until I came to the oddly shaped building that my map said held a noted collection of modern art.

Am on west side. He's in front, on steps. Meet me by coffee shop.

"That must be one heck of a phone call," I said, a little out of breath, when I found Laura. She was lurking behind a bus stop sign, periodically peering around it to check on Elliott.

"I know! That's exactly what I was thinking. He's moved to the little garden area. You see it? There are some benches. He's on the third one."

I peered with her. Sure enough, Elliott sat by himself on a bench, looking down at his lap, not around as if he was enjoying some private time away from everyone (the only reason I could think of why he ran off and left the group). "He's looking at his phone. Probably texting someone."

"That's what I thought." She gave me a long look. "Alice . . . look, I know this sounds idiotic, but maybe we should go back to the cathedral. It's obvious that Elliott is here for a reason, and . . . well, it seemed like a fun idea a few minutes ago, but now . . ."

"Not so fun," I finished for her, nodding. "I agree, but I also would like to know what he's doing. Oh, not in a nosy sort of control-freak way. If something is wrong with his mom, or another member of his family, then maybe I could help in some way."

She didn't say anything to that, taking it for granted that Elliott and I were so well established that I'd have a say in his life, but the truth was much more unforgiving. I did feel a bit like a stalker, but one who quite honestly wanted to help if he needed it. And if he didn't need help, if he was behaving in this mysterious manner because something covert was going on . . . well, I couldn't help but wonder what it was. "Maybe I am being a nosey parker, but I'd dearly like to find out what he's doing—"

Laura grabbed my arm at that moment, her nails digging into my flesh when she yanked me back behind the bus shelter. "Did you see that?"

"The guy who sat down on Elliott's bench? Yeah. I wonder if we can get closer?"

"I think so. Over there is a big cement planter. That screens the area behind the benches. You could probably slink around there without being seen, since Elliott's back would be to you."

I looked at her.

She made an apologetic face. "I just don't feel right spying that much on him, if you know what I mean. It's fine for you—you're his girlfriend. But he might be upset if he found out I was eavesdropping."

Well, that made me feel like a great big boil on the buttock of honor and dignity, but not enough so that I didn't make my way over to the screened area behind Elliott and his mysterious visitor. Unfortunately—or, rather, fortunately for my smarting conscience—I wasn't close enough that I could overhear them. But I could get a good look at the man who was chatting so intently with Elliott—he had straight, shoulder-length black hair, skin the color of milky coffee, a short-cropped beard, and hands that seemed to dance in the air when he spoke.

One of those hands held a camera with an impressively large lens on it.

The two men seemed almost to be arguing, although I couldn't detect the sound of raised voices. After about three minutes of this, Elliott reached into his pocket and pulled out something. It looked like one of the leaflets from the cathedral, but I couldn't see it well enough to be sure. He passed it on to the other man, who tucked it away in his coat. He rose, and playfully pretended to take Elliott's picture. Elliott made a sharp gesture, and got to his feet. I didn't wait around to see more—I high-tailed it back to where Laura was waiting, her eyes big.

"Did you see? He gave that man something. A secret message sort of something."

"We have to run if we want to beat Elliott back," I said, shoving her forward. She didn't argue. We dashed madly down the street back toward the cathedral, careening into both people and various other obstacles, scattering apologies indiscriminately to all.

"You were in a better position than me; could you see what Elliott gave the other guy?" I asked when we raced up the steps of the cathedral. We didn't stop to see how close Elliott was behind us—we ran through the doors and immediately took a sharp left, tucking ourselves away in front of an obscure plaque depicting some patron or other.

"Not really." Her brows were pulled together in a frown. We both were out of breath, panting from the jolt of adrenaline brought on by our flight, and the heat of the day. "All I could see is that he gave Tall, Dark, and Handsome something white and thin, like an envelope, but not one, if you know what I mean. You don't know what it was?"

"Tall, Dark, and . . . ?" For a moment, I was startled, thinking she was talking about Elliott. "Oh, you mean the other dude. No, I don't know what Elliott gave him." We both stiffened into attitudes of studied (and awkward) indifference when Elliott reentered the cathedral. Luckily, a small group of elderly women were right on his heels, and screened us from his view.

"That really was strange. Alice . . ." She frowned at the floor for a few minutes. "I wasn't quite serious before, when I said he was a spy and that we should follow him to see what he was doing. It was . . . kind of a fun little game, you know? But now . . . now I don't know. You don't think he really *is* a spy, do you?"

"I don't know," I answered after a few seconds' silence. Elliott's head bobbed above the crowds as he strolled down the main aisle. "But I have to admit that I really, really want to find out the truth."

"That's your right," she said, giving my arm a pat before leading me down the left side to where our group was visible. "You have to live with the man, after all. Er . . . assuming you do live together, not that it's any of my business. Oh, heavens, I really am putting my foot in my mouth today, aren't I? I'm leaving now, before I say anything more embarrassing." And with that, she wandered over to the other side of our group.

My gaze remained on Elliott even though my conscience pricked me mightily. *You don't have the right to pry into his life,* it reminded me. *You may have gotten sweaty with him, but that doesn't mean he has to tell you his private business.*

That's all well and fine in theory, my brain argued, *but real life is different. What if he is in some sort of trouble?*

If he was, you'd just make it worse, my conscience said with a self-righteous sniff.

Haters gonna hate, I told it, then realized I was bickering with myself, and decided that sanity demanded I stop right that instant.

"I'll just keep my eye on him," I said softly to myself, feeling that compromise was the best way to proceed. "If he's in trouble somehow, I'll offer my help. And if he's not, then . . . well, we'll see. After all, it means I have a good excuse to spend lots of time admiring those curls. And his chest. And dear lord above, his ass."

"It is a very nice ass," a voice cooed beside me.

Deidre! The hairs on the back of my neck stood on end.

"Not that I've seen it in its natural state," she said with a feline smile. "Yet."

"Really?" I asked. "That's the best you've got? Oh, don't give me that faux look of surprise. We both know what you're doing. If you think a slinky walk and inappropriate touching of Elliott's chest—yes, I saw you earlier pretending to be brushing a crumb off his shirt—if you think that's going to cause any trouble, you had better think again." I spoke with a bravado that I wasn't quite feeling, but I felt it was important to make it absolutely clear to Deidre that I was on to her nefarious plans.

"Dear, sweet Alice," she said, patting my cheek. "You really think you stand a chance against me, don't you? The truth is that I haven't yet decided whether or not I should take Elliott away from you. I'm mulling it over." Her eyes were hooded as she gazed at the subject of our discussion. "He's certainly not hard to look at, and I'm sure he's divine in bed, but I'm just not sure if he's sufficiently interesting to make him worth the effort."

"He's very interesting," I said, outraged on Elliott's behalf before I realized what I was doing. I crossed my arms over my chest. "He's also mind-numbingly fabulous in bed, so you can just suck on that."

She pursed her lips.

"Yes, all right, that was a poor choice of phrase, but you can just take the gist of the comment, because I don't really give a damn what you decide to do about Elliott. If you want to make a fool of yourself fawning over a man who isn't interested in you, then by all means knock yourself out. Literally or metaphorically—the choice is yours."

She tossed her head, her mane of black hair flicking back dramatically. "Thank you, dear heart. You just helped me make up my mind. You've annoyed me enough that I think I will have Elliott." Her smile was filled with acid. "Enjoy the rest of your trip."

"Oh, it's on now," I said under my breath when she sauntered off. So she wanted Elliott? Well, I might not be sure I wanted him in my life on a permanent basis, or even one lasting longer than the cruise, but I certainly didn't intend on handing him over to her on a plate.

He was a nice man, and deserved better than that sort of predatory she-devil. He deserved someone who was nice, too. Someone who appreciated his dry, rather quirky sense of humor. Someone who didn't care that he lived in a castle, or might be a spy, or even that he gave the best pity kisses in the world.

He deserved me.

You don't want him, my annoying inner self pointed out. *You are devastated, and betrayed, and all that other crap that you keep going on and on about. You're not looking for a man, any man, especially not one like Elliott, who, despite what his mother said about that woman on Page Three, probably takes relationships seriously.*

I sighed, and slowly moved toward the group. The problem was, I was beginning to think that maybe I had a lucky escape with Patrick, especially if it meant I got to meet the delightfully mysterious Elliott.

A little smile curled my lips as I came up behind him. Oh, yes, I was going to enjoy unraveling the puzzle that was Elliott. I was going to enjoy it more than I'd enjoyed anything in a very long while.

Chapter 7

Expense Account
  Item one: forty-two euros
  Remarks: entrance to club
  Item two: eighty euros
  Remarks: room rental, plus one nipple-abusing parrot

Elliott was aware of Alice the second her delightful scent tickled his nose. He didn't have to turn around to know she was behind him—he could detect her nearness even over the sounds and scents of thousands of visitors to the great Dom. It was almost a prickling sensation along his skin, one that made him very aware that he was a man, and she was a woman, and they had fit together extremely well earlier that morning.

There was the fact that he probably shouldn't have given in to those urges that seemed to overwhelm him whenever she was near, but she seemed quite honest in her statement that she wasn't using him to make herself feel better about the breakup with Patrick.

"Did Tiffany run you off?" he asked without turning his head, knowing by the tightening of the skin on his back that she was very close.

"Uh . . . not so much. Laura and I were talking about how we'd rather look around on our own than be guided through." She moved up to stand beside him, giving him a look he had a hard time putting a name to.

"Ah. I'm sorry I had to run out for a few minutes. There was a slight family issue I had to take care of."

"Nothing wrong with your mother, I hope?" she asked.

"Not in the sense you mean, no. She is quite hale and hearty. A little too hearty for my comfort, but there is little I can do about that short of moving her to the dower house, and that's unfit for habitation at the moment. Once the work is completed on the castle, however, that is next on my list for repair."

And he'd certainly be having a word or two with his mother about her ploy of sending Gunner out to check up on him. Just the idea that she would be investigating Alice was annoying enough, but when she coerced his own brother into meeting with him to find out what was going on, well, that was outside of enough. He'd sent Gunner on his way with a proverbial flea in his ear, and he wouldn't hesitate to do the same to his mother.

Alice took his hand, her fingers warm against his, reminding him of just how aroused those fingers had made him feel a few short hours before. "Most of the time, I'm just coasting along thinking my thinky thoughts about stuff, and then you say things like *castle* and *dower house*, and it makes me feel like I'm in a Georgette Heyer book."

"Not Jane Austen?" he asked, smiling down at her. Lord, she was pretty. How could he ever think she was just a normal woman, one with requisite bits and pieces, but not the amazing package of femininity that he now knew her to be? "I always fancied being the dark, brooding Mr. Darcy."

"Oh, he was definitely hunky, but while you're dark enough, and handsome enough, to be him, you don't brood." She gave his fingers a squeeze. "Although I bet you could do the haughty lord of the manor thing pretty damn well."

"It goes with the title," he said in his plummiest voice. "We are required by law to cut the hoi polloi at least once a year, or the title passes to the snobbiest relation."

"I just bet," she said with laughter rich in her voice. "What would the people in your castle do if you started talking like that?"

"Probably drag me out to the pond and throw me in it. Or call a mental health official," he admitted, returning to his normal voice.

"I would totally support a pond scene like the one in *Pride and Prejudice*, but only if you were stripped first."

He slid her a glance out of the corner of his eye. She was giving him a lascivious grin that made him feel like singing at the top of his lungs. "You have a smutty mind, Alice. It's one of the many things I admire in you. Unfortunately, we are in a holy place, and although I don't particularly hold strong religious feelings, I feel it would be insulting to the caretakers of this cathedral to give in to your lustful desires and engage in sex right here and now." He thought for a moment. "Although I have to admit it is a tempting thought...."

"Good lord, you really *did* know what I was thinking.

I agree, however—we shouldn't get it on here. Maybe later, in our cabin. Or if we can find a dark alley. Or even a moderately dim one. Oh lord, there's the she-hussy. She told me she's going to steal you from me, not that you're mine to steal, but I just thought I should warn you that you're in her sights."

He glanced to the side. Deidre was indeed moving their way, a sultry look of invitation in her eyes. "How unfortunate. Come. Let us make our escape while we can." He took Alice's arm and steered her to a pack of tourists, weaving skillfully through the people until he found a secluded niche featuring the stone depiction of a saint. "I don't think she'll find us here, not unless she comes looking for us."

"I wouldn't put it past her. That woman seriously wants into your pants." A mischievous glint lit up her eyes. "Which, I have to admit, is on the top of my to-do list, as well."

"This insatiability in you is somewhat shocking. I don't know whether to be pleased that our lovemaking was of such a high quality that you immediately want more, or if it's an indication you are one of those sex-addicted people who are never satisfied."

Her expression went from teasing to serious in a flash. She blinked. "Oh. I'm sorry. Did I come on too strong? I'm not really one of those sex fiends—"

He wanted badly to kiss her at that moment but, mindful of their surroundings, contented himself with taking her arms in his hands and giving them a little squeeze. "I was teasing you, Alice. I know you're not a sex addict."

"Oh, good." She slumped in relief. "Because I was enjoying conducting highly charged sexual banter with you."

"As was I, although if we continue along that line,

you're going to make it extremely painful for me to walk. Shall we cool down our libidos with a spot of crypt viewing?"

She glanced at her watch and scrunched up her nose in a way that reminded him of a rabbit. An adorable rabbit. "Actually, as interesting as the cathedral is, it's kind of crowded, what with Deidre likely to appear at any moment. Would you mind giving the rest of the tour a pass? I'd much rather just walk around and kind of soak in the atmosphere of Cologne. Maybe have lunch at a cute little place. That sort of thing. Does that sound too boring?"

"It sounds," he said, turning her and giving her a gentle push toward the door, "like a much more pleasant way to spend the day than here. The ship doesn't sail until nine tonight, so we can have dinner in town, too, if you like. And yes, I will order for you."

Elliott felt a slight twinge of guilt over the next few hours. He really should be working, not enjoying a delightful day sightseeing with Alice, but he told himself he wanted to make sure that she wasn't secretly feeling guilt about their recent intimate activities. The truth was much less altruistic; he simply enjoyed time spent with her too much to give in to the demands of his tight writing schedule.

As it was, the hours passed quickly by with his regard for Alice growing even more. She wasn't just easy on the eyes—there was a sharp, fast wit behind that pretty face, one that made him feel pleasantly off-balance. She was impulsive, to be true, and made giant leaps in logic that he didn't always follow, but even those traits, which he would consider flaws in anyone else, were oddly attractive in her.

"My feet are about ready to drop off," she said in the late afternoon, after they had left the Jewish Museum and its attached archaeological dig. "I could really use a break, and something cool to drink. That looks like a bar. Let's go in there and rest a bit before we decide where to go for dinner, OK?"

They had turned off the main avenue onto one of the lesser side streets. Alice made a beeline for a brightly lit window through which a neon bar gently glowed. His eyes widened at the sign, and he hurried after her, trying to stop her before she entered. "That's not a bar, Alice."

"It's not?" With one hand on the door, she peered through the window. "Sure it is. See the people sitting there? They have drinks."

"I can guarantee you that what they are drinking contains no alcohol." He tried to tug her away from the door, but a mulish look flitted across her face.

"How on earth can you guarantee that?"

"Because they don't allow alcohol in sex clubs."

Her mouth dropped to form an O of astonishment. She turned to look through the window again. "Wow. It's one of the sex clubs? How come people are sitting at a bar drinking and not having wild orgies?"

"The orgies are conducted in the private rooms. They have a social area out front where you can mingle and meet someone with whom you can partner up. They make it look like a bar, but it's really not. Let's go a few streets over. I believe I spied a more suitable establishment there."

She looked thoughtful. "Can couples go into the sex places, or do you have to pick up a partner there?"

"You can't seriously be saying you wish to go in there," he asked, nodding toward the entrance.

"Well . . ." She made a face, then gave him a half smile. "Actually, I am. I mean, how many opportunities do you have of going to an authentic kinky German sex club? I wouldn't go by myself, but if I'm with you, then I wouldn't worry about someone trying to pull a fast move on me."

A little devil made him say, "I assure you, my sweet little squab, if we go into that club, I will most definitely be pulling moves on you, although I can't guarantee as to the speed or lack thereof."

Her eyes appeared to darken. He knew it was just a sexual flush, and the reaction of her pupils growing, but it had the result of making his penis stir, which in turn had him thinking that perhaps a visit to the sex club wasn't as outrageous as he first thought.

"Not many men can get away with leering at a woman while saying formal phrases like 'lack thereof,' but boy, did you manage it. And speaking of that, you're on. So long as you don't get too wild on me. Should we have a safe word? I think we should have a safe word. What should it be?"

"Sauerkraut?" he suggested.

"Ew. Don't like. I know, Wiener schnitzel! That makes a great safe word. Can we sit at the bar first and pretend we're looking for other people?" she asked as they entered the club.

"We can, although I assumed you would wish to avoid bars."

"Because I don't like to drink? Naw. It's never bothered me when people around me are drinking, although I will warn you that if you're going to indulge, I'm not going to enjoy kissing you a whole lot."

He was about to ask why when the answer occurred to him. "The taste of the alcohol?"

"Yeah. You try kissing someone whose mouth tastes to you like rubbing alcohol, and see if you can keep from making a face. It's very off-putting."

"I understand completely, and promise that if I feel the need for a drink, I'll do it when you aren't around. Not that it will be an issue at this establishment."

He stopped at the desk and paid the (substantial) fee for a couple to use the facilities, and received in turn a sheet explaining the rules, and the prices of various theme-oriented rooms. He had to admit that he was a bit disconcerted by her desire to sit at the bar, reminding himself that although he was attracted to her, *highly* attracted to her, that didn't mean she didn't have some odd kinks that he hadn't discovered yet. Perhaps she enjoyed the idea of picking up a stranger?

She seemed to sense his concern, because she leaned into him and whispered into his ear, "Don't look so shocked, silly. I don't want a threesome or to hook up with someone; I simply want to sit because my feet hurt, and I really am thirsty. I won't be able to say 'Wiener schnitzel' if I don't rehydrate, let alone have the strength and stamina to do anything else. Wait—are these places clean enough to do anything else? Because if it's going to be all scummy motel inside, then I'll give it a pass."

"I've only been to one club such as this before, but it was quite clean, and judging by this lobby and the price of admission, I assume it won't give offense. Although . . ." He gave her a long look. "Forgive me, but I'm not sufficiently acquainted with you to know if you just are curious about the club, and want to see what goes on here, or whether you're so horny you are looking for a reasonable place to have what is usually called a quickie."

She sank onto a free chair with a sigh of obvious relief. "Can you get me a tonic and lime? No booze, just tonic water and lime. A really big one, preferably with ice, if they have it."

He cocked an eyebrow at her until she giggled and poked him in the stomach. "Perhaps it's a little of both? Or maybe I'm just keeping my options open."

"Hmm." He said nothing more, just got them both drinks, his suitably nonalcoholic, and returned to the table, which was now being shared with two men.

" — and that's flattering as hell, but really, I don't think my boyfriend would be at all into that. He's not the sharing kind, and he's big, and actually, he's a lord, so he might have some sort of a pull with whatever royalty you guys have here. Or even be related to them! So thanks for asking me to be your . . . what did you call it? Pony leader? Man, I don't even know what that is, but I'm pretty sure I don't want to be it. . . . Anyway, thanks, but no thanks. Oh, hello, Elliott. This is Elliott, boys. Note his size. Note the fine definition of his bicep. Note the scowl that says he doesn't want to have a foursome. Elliott, this is Jurgen and Fritz."

"Charmed," he said drily, giving the two men a look that let them know they'd best take themselves off.

They took themselves off.

"You were right, this bar is kind of hookup central," Alice said, taking a long pull on her drink before holding the glass to her cheeks. "That feels sooo good. I didn't realize how hot it was out until I started getting parched. So, I found this." She slid a piece of paper over to him. "I can't read what it says. My German tourist app is evidently quite lacking. Is it a menu for food, or sex?"

"Sex," he said, glancing at it. He did a double take at a couple of the items available.

"That good, huh?" She scooted her chair over until her breast was pressed against his arm. "Translate for me."

"Mostly these are just rates for standard rooms, use of the pool and sauna, and additionals like a video camera and something that I assume is equivalent to aromatherapy."

"I sense a however in there," she said, nudging him with her elbow.

"Yes, well." He tapped the lower half of the menu. "Evidently this establishment caters to some different tastes. There are standard sex club rooms—flogging, voyeurism, standard BDSM setups—and then specialty rooms. There is a historical room containing stocks and a mock thatched cottage, a medieval dungeon, complete with torture implements, an upside-down room where clients can hang upside down suspended from the ceiling, a faux doctor's office, complete with instruments of a gynecological nature, a pirate ship, and a children's room."

"Ew," she said, wrinkling her nose again. He had to fight back an urge to kiss her. "They cater to pedophiles? We're leaving."

"Not pedophiles, no." He consulted the sheet. "It sounds more like fairy tales and the like."

"Oh. That might be fun. But I have to admit, I really want to see the pirate ship. I love pirate stuff." She squinted at him. "Do they hire out costumes? Because if we put a Johnny Depp wig on you, I'd totally hoist your mainsail."

"Are you saying my mainsail won't receive any attention unless I don the garb of a pirate?"

"I like it when you do that," she said with a big smile.

"Do what?" he asked, somewhat startled when she pointed at his face.

"Cock your eyebrow. It's just so . . . you. No, of course

I don't need you in a pirate outfit to ogle you and want to lick you all over, and basically jump your bones from here to next week, but come on! We're in a sex club, we have four hours before the ship sails, and there is a piratin' to be done! Is the pirate room expensive?"

He glanced at the sheet again, calculated how much money he had budgeted for the trip, adjusting it to include the price of the specialty room. He'd simply cut back on the redecoration fund for the dower house. "No," he lied, the tingly feeling back as Alice gave him a sloe-eyed smile before sipping her drink.

"If you asked me a few days ago if I ever had piratical fantasies, I would have answered no," he said some twenty minutes later, closing the door to the pirate room behind them. They surveyed their new domain—theirs for the next hour—with interest. Alice held a stack of fresh bed linens in her arms, an indigo and lavender captain's hat upon her head. "And yet, here we are."

"Yeah, it wasn't high on my bucket list, either, but hey, you have to take life by the horns. Do you want to wear the hat first?"

He eyed it before setting down the plastic-wrapped set of faux-leather cuffs, plastic rum bottle (containing their beverage of choice, which in this case was a cola), nylon lightweight version of a cat-o'-nine-tails, and stuffed parrot with alligator clips on its feet. "No, thank you."

"It's new." She held up the plastic bag that had contained the hat. "No cooties from a former user."

"Indigo and lavender make me look sallow," he said, holding out the parrot. "Do you think the clips on this are intended to be used to attach him to your shoulder, or for nipples?"

She pursed her lips. "I think they probably leave that

up to you. I have to say, I'm a bit sad we didn't go for the full costumes, because that Elizabeth Swann dress was just gorgeous. But I felt a bit weird wearing something that someone probably had sex in. I mean, I know they clean them and all, but still."

"It's not something I wish to use, either. So. What do you think?"

Alice set down the sheets and looked around the room, her hands on her hips. "I like the pirate ship. Can we climb on it, do you think?"

"The sign says so." They strolled across the room to where the forepart of a ship, and part of a cabin, projected from the wall, as if the ship had docked right there. To the right of that, a mural depicted a town set in the Caribbean. A small cannon sat next to the wall, as did small wooden stocks, a few barrels and crates, and, opposite that, a wooden shack about six feet deep that held a utilitarian bed.

"I guess I should make the bed," Alice said, taking the linens into the shack. Elliott wondered whether she expected him to role-play—he'd never been one to get into make-believe like that. He didn't think his imagination worked that way. Would she expect him to be a swashbuckling pirate, and sweep her up in his arms whilst scattering *yarr*s and *ahoy*s hither and yon? He eyed the stock. Perhaps she wanted him to use that on her. Now, that was a much more interesting idea. He could definitely see himself standing behind her, admiring that wonderful ass of hers while she pleaded with him to satisfy each and every one of her many needs.

Yes, the stock was good. The nipple-clamping parrot another matter. He had no real use for it, but since it was included in the price of the room, he felt obligated to take the beastly thing. Perhaps Alice might like to keep it as a memento? He examined the parrot again, wondering idly what nipple clamps felt like.

"What on earth are you thinking about? You look like someone just asked you to circumcise yourself with a dull table knife."

"I was wondering what nipple clamps felt like. These look painful."

She came over to look with him. "They do."

"Have you ever tried them?"

"Once."

"And you didn't enjoy the experience?"

"Are you kidding?" She covered both breasts protectively with her hands. "There is no way on god's green earth anyone is ever again using anything on my boobs that contains the word 'clamp' in the name."

"I would tend to agree with you on that. I just wondered if there was something I was missing, since the establishment seemed to feel that they would be used enough to justify the expense of making up these parrots."

Her face screwed up in thought as she absently patted the parrot's head. "Plus there's the silly factor."

"Pardon?"

"The silly factor." She waved her hand toward his chest. "Let's say you are turned on by nipple clamps. That's fine and well, and I could even deal with it, although I'd take you down if you ever came close to using one on me, but there's a bit of a difference between a guy lying back being all sexy and come-hither and mmrowr-worthy, and a man who has a toy stuffed parrot hanging from his nips."

He got a mental image of just that, and had to agree. "No nipple clamps, then."

"Well, I don't know. You haven't tried it. I did. Mind you, I almost decked my boyfriend at the time, and swore never to let anyone abuse my poor little nipples again." She cupped her hand around her right breast. "But you haven't tried it. Maybe we should give that a go. You know, just so you can see if it's something that turns your crank."

"My crank," he said, tossing the parrot onto the bed behind her, "has no need to be clamped in order to be turned. In fact . . . I hope you're not going to take this the wrong way, because I'm happy to indulge you, but I don't know that we really need this room. I find you exciting enough as you are, without pirate trappings to stir my interest."

He was relieved to see her nod her understanding. "Because we're not an old couple who needs to spice things up, you mean? I'm with you on that. Just thinking about you today has made my tongue swell a good two or three sizes, but YOLO."

There was a moment when he was convinced that his brain had stopped working, because he hadn't the slightest idea what she said. "Yolo? Is that another safe word? I haven't even put you in the stocks and started admiring your ass, and you're safe wording me already?"

"YOLO is a popular acronym these days," she said, looking with interest at the stocks. "It means you only live once. I figured that since we were here, and there was a pirate room, we might as well take advantage of it. You really want to lock me into the stocks? I thought you said that you don't like your women tied down."

"I don't," he said, then realized he just contradicted himself. He swallowed hard. "Erm . . . perhaps just the stocks. It holds much promise, don't you think?"

"Maybe," she said, giving him an odd look. "Well. I

suppose we should get down to business, since we just have the room for a little bit. Um. I guess we should take off our clothes."

"That would probably be best. Less staining that way," he agreed, feeling more than a little uncomfortable. He didn't want to disappoint Alice, however. Not when she was so clearly looking forward to having sex in a risqué club. He unbuttoned his shirt, trying to keep his attention on her, and not on their surroundings.

Alice pulled off her shirt and hesitated a moment, then removed her walking shorts. She stood in front of him in nothing but her pirate hat, sandals, and underwear, her skin pricked with goose bumps, her arms wrapped around her middle.

He slid off his shoes, removed his pants, and folded them, placing them with his shirt on the nearest barrel. "Well," he said, not knowing how to begin. Was she expecting him to be a pirate?

"Yeah," she said, sounding as uncomfortable as he felt. "Here we are."

He eyed her. "Are you in any way aroused by this situation?"

"Not in the least. You?"

"Sex is about the furthest thing from my mind at this moment," he said.

They stared at each other; then without a word they both hurried back into their clothing. "We can at least play on the pirate ship," Alice said a minute later, now fully dressed. She clambered up the wooden ladder, the parrot in her hand. "Yarr 'n' stuff!"

"Play?" He frowned at her when she took hold of the ship's wheel and gave it a spin.

"Yeah, you know, play. Don't tell me you don't play?"

"I am an adult," he said sternly.

"So am I, but all work and no play makes Elliott a dull baron."

"Regardless, it's not something I do. At least, not in the sense you mean. I'm quite fond of playing several video games. They can be quite relaxing."

"So can regular playing. Don't make that face—I'll be happy to show you how to let down your hair and have a little fun. Come up here, Cap'n Sexy Pantaloons, and if you're good, I'll let you bend me over the capstan."

Elliott didn't quite know how to take that. He wasn't used to a playful sexual partner—all his girlfriends had been businesswomen or relatives of neighbors, and although they were pleasing in bed, they didn't play. "I thought you weren't turned on by this situation," he said, slowly climbing the ladder to the faux ship. "I should warn you that I do not know how to role-play, let alone how to pretend I am a pirate captain."

"You don't have to be a pirate if you don't want to. I can be the captain, and you can be my sexy captured prisoner." He frowned, but before he could protest, she continued with a little laugh, "Elliott, just because I agree that this room isn't conducive to wild jungle sex doesn't mean I don't want to kiss you, and touch your chest, and maybe bite that line of muscles at the top of your shoulders that drives me wild." She held up the parrot. "And I really want to try a nipple clamp on you."

"No nipple clamps."

"You big poop," she said with an exaggerated sigh. "Fine, we'll leave the parrot for another time. We'll just play a little. You liked the stocks, right? Well, let's try this.... I'll put you in the stocks and molest you a little bit, and then we can switch and you can do the same to me. Sound good?"

"I agree with the stocks, but I insist that you take the first turn in them."

"Nuh-uh," she said, taking his hand and jumping off the side of the ship. He leaped after her, allowing her to lead him over to the stocks. "You had your way this morning. It's my turn to touch you. How does this work? Oh, there's a latch on the side. OK, in you go."

He hesitated, but in the end did as she directed, not wishing to ruin her entire experience. He was fully clothed, after all, and since she obviously intended for him to stay that way, it wouldn't hurt to indulge her a bit. He placed his hands and head in the appropriate spots, reminding himself that he would have his turn, a turn that he planned to enjoy for a good deal of time.

Alice closed the stocks over his head with a metallic snap of the latch. "There we go. Now you're my prisoner, Lord Hunkybuns."

"I refuse to be a Hunkybuns, lord or otherwise," he said firmly.

"Boy, you really are new to playing, aren't you?" She stood in front of him in an attitude of deep thought. "Prince Punkypants?"

"No."

"Lord Largeloins?"

He rolled his eyes. "Does playing always involve a name change? I don't see why you can't just call me Elliott."

"I know!" She leaned forward and kissed the tip of his nose. "You can be Dirk Dashing, the Earl of Erogenous, and I'll be Jasmine, Queen of the Midnight Sea. All right,

Dirk, now that I have you in my grasp, prepare to be molested like you've never been molested before."

He shifted his weight. "It goes without saying that I look forward to any and all molesting you care to enact upon me, but if you could speed it along, I would appreciate it."

"Oooh, anxious for it, are you?" She smiled and held up the parrot. "Shall we start with the nipple clamps?"

He glared at the parrot. "I distinctly remember telling you no just a few minutes ago. I haven't changed my mind since then."

"I know, but it seems like too good of an opportunity to waste." She giggled; then, before he could protest, she spread the parrot's legs and clipped each foot to his shirt. "OK, that's just funny as hell."

He looked down, sighing to himself at the sight of the parrot dangling spread-eagle and upside down from his shirt. "It's so hilarious I'm surprised I haven't ruptured a spleen or two in reaction."

She laughed, a sound he relished, even in his present ignominious circumstances. "I'm so going to get a picture of us before I let you out. Consider it my blackmail picture of you."

"I'm sure it will be worth millions. Would you consider me churlish if I asked you to continue with whatever you have planned for me? These stocks are a bit low for someone of my height, and I suspect being bent over like this won't be good for my back."

"Got a bad back, huh?" she asked, placing the pirate hat on his head before running her fingers down his sides.

"Unfortunately, yes."

She moved around behind him. He rolled his eyes to the side in an effort to see what she was doing.

"Poor Dirk, with all those sore muscles. Maybe I should massage them."

Her fingers grasped his ass, making him jerk upward against the top rail of the stocks. He swore at the pain of the wood against his neck. At the same time, a muscle in his back, protesting the unusual attitude, gave a twinge of protest.

"Oh, sorry! I didn't mean to startle you like that. I just couldn't resist because your butt was right there, and to be honest, I've been wanting to do that for what seems like forever." Alice's voice was contrite. "Did you hit your head?"

"No, my neck, but if you could unhook this thing, I believe I need to straighten up before my back begins to spasm."

"You're a baron," she pointed out, coming around to the front of the stocks. "Barons aren't supposed to have bad backs."

"I'm also six foot four, and hover around the fifteen-stone mark, both of which mean I'm pretty much guaranteed to have back problems, so if you could release me, I'll do a few stretches that the physiotherapist recommends, and then we can switch positions."

"Not so fast there, Lord—damn, this is a stiff latch—Erogenous. I barely had any chance to molest you, and ... dammit! That broke my nail. ... And you can ogle my butt without me being in the stocks, not that I think you should be ogling it anyway, because it's not particularly ..."

Her voice trailed away to nothing. Elliott's back gave another warning spasm. He turned his head as far as he could. The hat slipped down over one eye, giving him an unintentionally rakish appearance. "Alice, I realize you enjoy playacting and such, and I hate to appear to be such a feeble creature that I can't stand doubled over for more than a few minutes at a time before my back fails me, but I assure you that it will soon become uncomfortable for me—"

"I'm not playing with you, silly. I know backs are nothing to mess with when they go hurty," she interrupted, her head bent over the metal latch that closed the stocks. "This stupid thing is stuck or something. I can't pry the bit up that needs to move so it'll unhook."

His back gave a massive twinge. A sense of panic filled him when he tried to pull his hands free, but apparently, the people at this club ordered their stocks from a source that believed in truly confining the participants. "Use something to pry it up, Alice," he demanded, wincing against the pain jabbing upward along his back.

"Like what?" she asked, spinning in a circle as she looked around the room.

"I don't care what you use. Anything! Break the damned thing if you have to."

She took one look at his face and ran for the door. "I'll get someone to help."

That was all he needed, he thought as he tried to flex his back in an attempt to forestall more spasms. There he was, doubled over and confined in a German sex club, a lavender and indigo captain's hat on his head, parrot hanging from what appeared to be his nipples, and a grimace of pain on his face. The way his day was going, Alice would have a blackmail photo to keep her in wealth the rest of her life.

Ten minutes later, three of the club personnel, two maintenance men, and a cluster of bystanders applauded when the hinge was unscrewed and removed, allowing

Elliott to be released from his bondage. He straightened up with an audible groan, his hands on his back in an attempt to stretch the cramping muscles.

"I'm so sorry," Alice said for the fifth time, hovering around him in obvious desire to help him, but not knowing how. "I'd never have locked you in that damned thing if I thought it would hurt you. Oh thank you, Herr Keller. I much appreciate you getting that off Elliott. *Danke, danke*, everyone."

It took another fifteen minutes of stretching, and having Alice walk on his back, before he could stagger out of the club, Alice clutching his arm in case he needed her. He wanted to laugh at the idea that she could prop up someone of his size, but to be honest, her fussing around him was the only thing that made the experience worthwhile.

They left the club, the parrot, hat, and cat-o'-nine-tails in a carrier bag that swung between them as Alice assisted him down the street. He couldn't quite straighten his back entirely, but it wasn't as bad as it could be, so on the whole, Elliott was hopeful that he'd be right as rain after a night's rest.

"Are you angry?" she asked after a few minutes of silence.

"Me? No," he said, honestly surprised at her question. He had tried hard not to give her the impression that he was angry about the accident with the stocks; he knew full well it was due to faulty equipment, and nothing she had done. "I don't blame you at all, and I'm sorry if you took my silence for condemnation. I was just trying to remember if I brought any muscle relaxers with me."

"Oh." She bit her lower lip. "Regardless, I feel terrible that our playtime ended so badly. But at least the sex club gave your room rental back, so it wasn't as bad as it could be."

"It could have been quite worse," he agreed magnanimously.

"And those two guys who felt up your butt while the maintenance dude was working on that hinge were kicked out because they violated the 'must have fondlee's consent' rule, or so that pink-haired woman who spoke English said, so at least they won't do that to the next guy trapped in the stocks."

"I will sleep easier knowing that."

"As for the photos, I have Herr Keller's assurance that they won't post any of the pictures of you on their Web site. I'm afraid I couldn't confiscate the phones of the people who stood around taking videos, but no one but the manager knows who you are, and I made him promise he wouldn't tell anyone, so at worst, at very worst, all that would happen would be a few videos are put up on You-Tube of some unknown British tourist who got stuck. There should be no mention of your name, so none of your friends will ever find out this happened."

He sighed. He didn't want to think about all those people with their damned phones.

Alice glanced worriedly at him. "I will be happy to walk on your back again once we get you back to the ship. That seemed to make it feel a bit better, didn't it?"

"A bit, although I'd prefer that you sat on my front rather than walked on my back."

She blinked a couple of times. "Did you just proposition me?"

"Yes, yes I did, Jasmine of the Midnight Sea."

Her eyes lit with amusement. "Oooh, someone wants

to play despite a hurty back, and the guys with cameras, and the unwarranted butt-gropage."

It wasn't easy, but he trotted out a smile. Truly, none of the horrible events were her fault, so it wasn't fair to blame her for what had turned out to be a nightmarish visit. "I thought it only right since I ruined your pirate experience."

She stopped, and despite the fact that they were on the middle of the pavement, with people streaming to and fro around them, she kissed him, her breath warm on his lips as she said, "You really are one in a million, Elliott. I don't know of another man who would have withstood all that indignation, not to mention real pain, and not bitten my head off at least once during the evening."

He gave a one-shouldered shrug, and put his arm around her waist, pulling her in close to his body, her scent working its usual aphrodisiac magic. "You weren't to blame. Besides, it was an enjoyable day up to that point."

"It was, wasn't it?" She looked pleased for a few seconds; then a shadow seemed to come over her mood. "What . . . uh . . . you never did tell me what the family problem was. If that's not being too nosy, and assuming that it was a problem you were dealing with."

Elliott frowned at the reminder. He didn't know if the budding relationship with Alice was going to go anywhere, but he knew that because of her situation, he'd have to leave the pace up to her lest he push her too far too fast. And interference from a brother sent to investigate would be bound to put her back up—it certainly made Elliott feel itchy just knowing his mother was sending in siblings to spy on him. "Not a real problem, no. More a situation that had to be dealt with."

"Oh? Nothing serious, I hope."

Alice looked as if she'd like to know more, but if there was anything he'd rather talk about than his family, he couldn't think of it. "No, just the usual distractions of being the oldest of twelve."

"Twelve! Man, your parents . . . oh, jeez, that was rude." Alice's eyes had widened, but she gave his arm an apologetic squeeze. By that time, they had approached the ship. Luckily, no one else was present to watch him lumber in.

"There are only three of us related by blood. The other nine are adopted," he told her, waving her forward to go up the gangway to the ship. "My mother was a firm believer in adoption, and my father wouldn't dare contradict her desire to adopt every needy child she came across. No, thank you, I'm fine. Just a little incident, nothing serious." This last was spoken in response to Tiffany, who emerged from the bar to ask if he was injured.

"You're back early," Tiffany said, frowning. "The schedule was quite clear in stating that you are responsible for your own dinner tonight."

"I'll grab something takeaway for us," Alice told her, tugging him toward the stairs. "Don't worry about us. Oh, would you happen to have some ice for Elliott's . . . sprain?"

"I will bring you some shortly, although room service is discouraged," Tiffany replied with obvious disapproval.

"Thanks. I think between the ice and the muscle-rub stuff I have, Elliott should be just peachy." They managed to escape any more of Tiffany's disapproval, but only because Alice took control of the situation, sending him to the shower to loosen up the aggravated muscles.

"It always does my legs good when they cramp up after a long run," she told him, pushing a large clean towel into his arms. "No one else is on the ship, so go ahead and take a nice long shower, and when you're done, I'll rub some of the muscle stuff into your back. We can ice it later, if it's still bothering you. You eat cow, right?"

"I beg your pardon?" He paused in the act of folding his shirt after removing it.

"Beef. You eat it, right? I ask because I've only seen you eat ham and chicken, and I didn't know if you were anti-cow-consumption or not. There's a burger place at the end of the dock, and I thought I'd run down there and grab some dinner for us."

"Oh, yes, I eat beef. No onions, though, please."

"Gotcha." She made a shooing gesture. "Go shower. Hopefully it'll stop you from walking like Quasimodo."

He tried to stretch his back. It protested the action. "I sincerely hope so. I don't relish the idea of spending the rest of the trip looking like my grandfather at his most frail."

When he emerged from the tiny bathroom, the room had been transformed.

"You've been busy," he said, toweling his hair as he looked around. The two twin beds had been shoved together, his laptop had been moved over to where their luggage had been stacked into a makeshift desk, and the table was covered with a scarf that had been around Alice's waist the day before. On it lay a collection of fast-food items that had Elliott's mouth watering.

"Yup, I thought since I wasn't going to insist on you keeping your distance anymore, we might as well be more comfy at night. Not that I expect to . . . you know . . . tonight, what with your ouchie back and all." She clipped the parrot to the curtains and gave him a once-over. "Although I have to say, you look much better. You're standing straight."

"I found that I did have a couple of muscle relaxers with me, and took two. That and the shower have returned me to human again." He sniffed. "Is that strudel?"

"Yeah. The Germans sure know how to stock their fast-food joints—fresh pastry for dessert. You said you had a sweet tooth, so I got a couple different kinds."

"Sadly, I do. This looks excellent." By the time they finished eating, the muscle relaxers were really beginning to kick in, but there was one thing he very much wanted to do before he gave in to the pull of the drugs.

He helped Alice clear up the trash, then proceeded to remove his shirt and trousers, placing both out of the way in one of the drawers. Alice was watching him with interest when he said matter-of-factly, "I believe I owe you a bend over the capstan."

"You do?" Her brow furrowed for a moment before she understood. "Oh, you mean you want to . . . but your back is sore."

"That is why I shall allow you to be on top," he said, lying down on one of the beds. "Not that I'm opposed to this position in normal circumstances, you understand, but it seems advisable to take it easy, so if you have no objections, you may mount me at will."

There was a devilish twinkle in her eye, and a suspicious twitch of her lips, both of which were reflected in her voice. "Is that so? Well, far be it from me to miss such a splendid opportunity. I'll just freshen up, and then we can see about playing Cowgirl and Baron, hmm?"

"Cowgirl?" he asked the room after she went into the

bathroom. Was he now expected to be a cowboy? He shook his head. He barely had a grasp of the pirate role play—he knew even less about cowboys than he did pirates.

Alice's captain's hat sat on the bed next to him. "If she wants to play," he told the hat, "she can just stay with pirates. My brain is too befuddled from the drugs to cope with anything else. The very fact that I'm speaking aloud to you confirms that fact, since I seldom talk out loud. It's a sign of an untidy mind, and mine is very tidy. It has to be, given my family." He thought for a moment, then removed his underwear, folding them and placing them in the zip bag he had for soiled laundry. "There," he said to his penis. It struck him that he should, by rights, feel awkward speaking to it, but oddly enough, it seemed perfectly natural. "If a man can't speak to his own genitals, then who can?"

He wouldn't mind Alice speaking to it, especially if she used her hands while doing so. He wondered how she felt about oral sex, and hoped she was in favor of it. He certainly was. Just the thought of her speaking to his penis (using both hands and mouth) had him erect and more than ready for her attentions.

"Hell," he said, looking down his body. "I shouldn't have thought about that just yet. Now Alice is going to come out of the bathroom and see you standing there being demanding. That's not very gentlemanly. Ladies like time to be wooed, not presented with a fait accompli."

Deflation didn't seem to be likely, especially not since he was now remembering the events of the morning, and how hot she had been, hot with amazingly strong muscles that seemed to squeeze him like a hundred little fingers.

That just made him even harder.

With a sigh, he snatched up her pirate hat and slapped it over his crotch. "There. Now we can at least present the semblance of a man who doesn't have a single-track mind."

He put his hands behind his head, his toes bobbing gently as he thought about Alice, and was still thinking about her two minutes later when he drifted to sleep.

Chapter 8

Diary of Alice Wood

Day Two (at last!)

"*God morgen.*"

"Morning, Dahl. Like the lederhosen."

"*Takk.*"

I jogged past where Dahl was doing some sort of calisthenics involving various stretches, made my way around the bow of the ship, and started back along the port side to make another circuit.

"Morning, Izumi. How are your chicks?"

The teacher looked confused. I jogged in place for a few seconds. "Sorry, that was too colloquial. Chicks as in little ones, i.e., your students. Did you guys have a good time in Cologne?"

"Oh, yes, very good," she said, her face clearing. "The cathedral was very beautiful, was it not?"

"Very." I nodded over her shoulder. "And you can't beat this scenery, can you?"

She turned to admire the crumbled remains of a castle set high on a verdant hill, its broken tower seeming to scratch the morning sky. "Oh!" she squeaked. "I must take a picture! My camera!"

"I got some great shots earlier this morning," I called after her as she ran off to scurry belowdecks. "And already uploaded them to my Facebook page, along with some from yesterday. My friends love them. Well. Now I'm talking to myself. Onward, Alice."

Confined as I was to the top deck of the ship—not to mention being fairly unenthusiastic about jogging in the first place—my morning exercise was done at a slow pace. Mostly I was jogging to work off some of the sexual tension that held me in its grip even after a (restless) night's sleep.

I made another lap, swerving around Anthony when he lurched up the stairs looking like he had a hell of a headache. He flinched when the sunlight reached him, snarling to Dahl, "Where the hell did you put the bag with the medications? My head is going to split if I don't get something. . . . Oh, hello, comrade Alice. You are energetic this morning."

"Not overly so," I said, jogging in a circle around him. "Hangover?"

"No, thank you," he answered, rubbing his head. "The one I have is sufficient."

"And yet you can make old jokes like that." I gave him a gentle buffet on the arm, which sent him reeling backward three steps. "Woops. Sorry. I'll just go on my way."

He muttered something under his breath, and headed

downstairs with Dahl. I had the deck to myself. I jogged around it twice more, greeting two of the schoolgirls when they emerged with cameras, and finally, tired out enough that I felt I could sit still, went back to the cabin.

"With luck," I said aloud, digging in my pocket for the room key, "Elliott will be awake and wanting to play."

"What a lovely thought," came the dulcet tones of the resident man-eater. Before I could so much as slam the door in her face, she pushed past me into the cabin, calling out, "Elliott, dear, Alice says you wish to have a threesome."

"I did not!"

Dahl walked past, his face carefully devoid of expression.

I snarled to myself and closed the cabin door. "I never said anything even remotely like that, because even if I did want a threesome, and I certainly don't, then I wouldn't want one with a she-hussy."

"'She-hussy' is redundant," Deidre said with sickening sweetness. She was sitting on the side of the bed, leaning across Elliott to brush a strand of hair off his forehead. He looked sleepily confused. A delicious sleepily confused, and I realized with a start that although I wasn't looking for a relationship so soon after Patrick's betrayal, I definitely viewed Elliott as something more than just a bed buddy.

"Hey!" I crawled across my bed and sat on the other side of him, pushing his hair back to where it was. "If he needs his hair arranged, I'll do it for him."

She gave a delicate shrug. "If you are unable to perform even the simplest of attentions for dear Elliott, I feel obligated to rectify the situation."

I wanted to growl something about rectifying her situation, but I've always felt that one should be prepared to back up one's threats with actions, and I wasn't really the sort of person to get into a physical fight without a really good reason. Elliott's unruly lock of hair didn't seem to qualify.

"I don't believe I've ever had two women fight over my hair while I was still half-asleep," Elliott commented, looking from me to Deidre and back again. "I am unsure of the protocol. Should I thank you for the compliment, or point out that I am not in a state conducive to the reception of visitors?"

"Definitely the latter," I said, getting up and taking Deidre by the arm. I hustled her toward the door. She didn't like it, but short of getting into the aforementioned physical fight, she didn't have much of a choice. "I'll give an A for effort, but man, did you fail this exercise. You're going to have to try harder than that if you want to win the Queen Hussy crown."

I was still smiling when I shut the door on her angry face.

"You do realize that the implication is that you yourself hold that crown, yes?" Elliott asked.

I considered his naked form as he made his way to the bathroom. Parts of him looked happy to see me, but that could just be the fact that he'd been asleep for a long time, and had to use the facilities. "I realize that, but it seemed like a really good line, and I hate to miss the chance to use a good line. How do you feel?"

He waited until he'd finished washing his hands before he answered. "A bit groggy, since I was dreaming when Deidre barged in, but if you are referring to my back, quite well." His face screwed up for a moment. "Am I misremembering, or did I fall asleep waiting for you? I have vague memories of not wishing to startle you with my erection, but there are no follow-up memories of you reassuring me that you weren't in the least bit startled, and were, in fact, quite approving of the manner in which you cause me to be almost instantly hard."

I looked at his penis. It was decidedly less happy now that he had visited the bathroom, but even as I watched, it started to look more interested in me.

"That's got to be just about the nicest thing a man has said to me. Yes, you were asleep when I came out of the bathroom last night." I dragged my gaze up from his nether regions. "Is there a reason you had my pirate hat on your crotch? Were you expecting me to play hide-and-seek with your naughty bits? Or did you just want a hat for him?"

"I have a hat for it, actually." Elliott made a vague gesture with one hand. "Well, it's more of a full-body suit, really."

"Is that a euphemism for a condom?"

"No." He marched past me and lay down on the bed. "My mother knitted me a willy-warmer a few years back when we were having a cold stretch. She felt I wasn't likely to produce the grandchildren she desires if I had, as she put it, frost-shriveled parts."

"What a thoughtful mom." I crawled onto the bed and sat on my heels, leaning down to kiss him. His mouth was warm and intriguing. "Do I take it that you want to have rompy time now? Because I'm game for it if you are."

One of his hands slid up my thigh to my hip. "You have too many clothes on, if we are. And yes, I'd like that, assuming you're not angry with me."

My breath hitched when his fingers splayed across my bare thigh. "Friends don't let friends have angry sex?"

"Something like that." He pulled me down so he could nuzzle my breasts through my T-shirt.

"Is that what we are? Friends?" My voice had a decidedly rough edge to it that I blamed on his morning whiskers as they brushed across my breasts. Even through my T-shirt and bra, I could feel the abrasion. It made my nipples cheer with happiness.

"I'd like to think so," he murmured against one breast before tipping his head back. His reddish brown whiskers glinted in the sunlight that streamed in through the window. Through it, I had a glimpse of another castle ruins, but at that moment, the only sight I wanted to see was sprawled out before me. "If you are asking if we are anything more, I would have to say that I don't know. Do you?"

I bit his nose, then kissed it, then kissed him properly, little shivers of delight rippling down to my toes at the rasp of his tongue next to mine. "I don't know what we are, either," I managed finally to say. "Other than—"

His cell phone, which was on the nightstand next to his side of the bed, buzzed and started playing a tune indicative of a call.

"Really?" I said as he reached for it. "'Moves Like Jagger'?"

"That would be one of my brothers' fault. Rupert got to my phone one day and reprogrammed my manly, uncomplicated ringtone with various embarrassing songs. I still haven't cleaned out all of them." He frowned at the phone. "Er . . . I should probably take this."

I patted his leg as I got off the bed and headed for the bathroom. "That's fine, I need to take a shower after jogging around the deck a bazillion times. Tell your penis to think happy thoughts until I'm back."

It was tempting to stick my ear to the bathroom door in an attempt to overhear what call Elliott had to take, but I told myself that there was nothing unusually mysterious about getting a phone call. If the cost hadn't been so prohibitive, I would have been calling back home and gloating to various girlfriends about the fact that I was snuggle-bunny to a real-life baron. As it was, I managed to post online for their delectation not only pictures of the various sights I'd visited but several shots covertly taken of Elliott. My Facebook page never had so many likes. I was still smiling smugly to myself over that when I emerged from the bathroom. "All righty, here I am, all clean and ready to get dirty again."

Wrapped in nothing but a large towel, I sashayed my way over to him, but stopped when I got a good look at his face. It was as unhappy as his penis. "What's wrong, Elliott?"

He set down the phone that he was still holding. "I'm not sure if I should tell you."

For ten horrible seconds, every disasterous scenario I'd ever imagined ran through my brain. "Oh my god, has a war broken out? Another terrorist attack? Is one of my friends dead?"

He got up quickly, and took my hands in his, saying, "No, nothing like that. I'm sorry to have frightened you."

"Oh, thank god." I took a couple of deep breaths and willed my pulse to return to normal. "I hope it's not something with your family."

"It's not." He stood holding my hands, an odd look on his face. "Alice, you haven't been in communication with Patrick, have you?"

"No. Why?"

He let go of my hands, rubbing his face while looking

extremely thoughtful. "Then how the hell did he know we had . . . erm . . . become lovers?"

Confusion quickly gave way to overwhelming guilt. "Um . . . he might have seen it online."

"Seen *what* online?"

I sat on the edge of the bed and felt about three inches high. "I . . . er . . . posted some pictures of you on my Facebook page. I didn't put your name or anything, so no one can identify you, but I wanted to show you off to my friends. So I put up a couple of pictures of you, and said we were having a great time, and . . . and . . . well, it's possible he saw them there, and drew obvious conclusions. Why, did he call you?"

"Yes." His lips twisted, and he, too, sat on the edge of the bed. "He tore a strip off me, as a matter of fact. I pointed out that he had broken up with you, and you had accepted that fact and moved on, but evidently Patrick feels that I had no right to, as he put it, put my move on you."

"Now it's my turn be annoyed and flattered at the same time," I said, wanting to lean into him, but feeling too unsure of myself to do so. "It's nice to think that he was having regrets, but . . ."

"But you've moved on," Elliott said, nodding his head. He said it so matter-of-factly that it didn't occur to me that it might have been more a question than not. I was too busy wondering why Elliott was so bent out of shape over the pictures I'd posted.

"I defriended him after we broke up, but I guess he's using a mutual friend to spy on my posts and pictures." I gnawed my lower lip. It wasn't as if I'd posted anything risqué, I told the judgmental side of my mind. There was one shirtless picture that had all my girlfriends swooning, but the rest of them were perfectly decent. Well, perhaps the one where he was naked on the bed, sound asleep, with the pirate hat over his naughty bits might have pushed the limits of the word "decent," but that picture was grainy and slightly out of focus, so I didn't feel it provided too much of an invasion of Elliott's privacy.

Guilt hit me even harder. I was in the wrong, and I knew it. While an ordinary man might not mind his lover posting pictures of him online, someone who was involved with a covert activity certainly wouldn't want his image plastered all over the Internet.

If I needed more proof that Elliott was involved in something secretive, I just had it. And what had I done? Only blown his cover, that's all. "I'm so sorry. I didn't think about ... er ..." Should I mention that I knew he had a secret life? His expression was grim—maybe now wasn't the best time to let him know I was on to the truth about his covert activities. "I just didn't think. That's my biggest failing if you hadn't figured it out by now. My friends are always telling me that I don't think before I do stuff, and boy, are they right this time."

I grabbed my phone and stabbed at the screen, deleting all of the pictures of Elliott that I'd so happily posted. I wanted badly to tell him that I'd do whatever I needed to do to fix his cover, but I had a feeling he'd had enough of my interference.

"It's not your fault," he said slowly, looking as if a boa constrictor had a hold of his testicles. "I thought you understood ... I thought we were clear about it all, but I gather I was mistaken."

Clear about what, the fact that he was a spy, or at least involved in something very covert? Did he know that I knew? Was I supposed to acknowledge that, or were we pretending that I didn't know? I was so confused, I just sat there in a big, unhappy lump. "I'm sorry," I said again, at a loss. I didn't know what I should say out loud, and what he wanted to remain unsaid.

He patted me on the leg, and I flinched when his freezing fingers touched my bare skin. We both looked down at his hand, me to chastise myself for having ruined the moment (his sad, deflated penis made it quite clear that happy fun time wasn't going to be happening any time soon), and him to think whatever thoughts he had about women who didn't respect a man's covert activities.

He snatched his hand back and rose, gathering up some clothing with a muttered explanation that he would take his shower. I continued damning myself while I got dressed, and later, when I sat in one of the deck chairs, my gaze turned too far inward to watch the small towns and villages of the Rhine as they flowed past.

An hour later, a shadow fell over me.

"Where's lover boy?"

I squinted up at Deidre before making an annoyed *tch* and returned to contemplating my misery. "He's busy. And by that, I mean he doesn't want to be disturbed. If you ignore me, which I fully expect you will, and go ahead and interrupt him, then you will find out for yourself that he takes his privacy very seriously." My conscience twinged at that, but I continued on in a tired tone, "Do what you want. I'm not your mother, or his."

"I wouldn't dream of disturbing him if he desires some time away from annoyances," she said with particular emphasis on the last word. I knew that she classed me as such, but at that moment, I didn't really care what she thought.

Another two hours went by. Castles, cute towns, the

occasional famous statue, and lots of greenery melted past as we spent the day on the Rhine sailing to the next stop, which we'd reach about midnight.

I didn't enjoy any of it.

"Would you mind if I sat here?"

I stopped staring at my toes long enough to smile at Laura. "Not at all."

She settled next to me with a bottle of suntan lotion, a big floppy hat, and a paperback. "I didn't want to disturb you earlier. You looked like you were thinking deep thoughts, and I know how annoying it is to be bothered when you're doing that." She slid me a sidelong look, hesitated, and went on slowly, "It's absolutely none of my business, to be sure, but I can't help but ask you if something is wrong? You're normally so full of joie de vivre, and now . . ."

"I'm a big fat wart on an equally big fat toad, yes," I said glumly. It struck me that I was enjoying my wallow in self-pity a bit too much.

"Not in the least. I ask because if Deidre has been causing problems between you and Elliott—"

"No, it's not her." I looked out blindly at the scenery passing, wanting badly to unburden myself, but not knowing if that would make my earlier breach of Elliott security worse. I didn't see how it could—Laura already knew that there was more to him than appeared. "Not that she hasn't tried, mind you, but I can't honestly blame this on her. I did something stupid, Laura."

She donned an attentive expression. "I'm sure it wasn't intentional, if you did."

"Kind of. I mean, I didn't intend on putting Elliott in danger, but I did think it would be fun to put up some pictures of him so my friends could see. Online, you know."

She looked confused for a moment; then her eyes widened. "Oh! You mean he wouldn't want people knowing he was in Germany?"

I nodded. "That or he just doesn't want people to know where he is at all. For all I know, he could be pretending he's back home, and there I go blasting pictures everywhere of him standing outside the cathedral in Cologne. I took the pictures down as soon as I realized what I'd done, but ... well, he's not very happy with me. And due to the nature of this problem, I can't ask him how bad it is."

"How do you mean?"

"Elliott's never actually come right out and admitted that he's doing something ... covert," I explained. "He kind of referred to it circularly, but he's not actually ever said anything out loud about it."

"And that makes it hard for you to do the same," she said, nodding. "I see the problem. Alice ..." Laura fidgeted with her book for a minute. "I don't want you thinking I'm casting aspersions on Elliott, but are you sure that what he's doing isn't ... illegal?"

I stared at her.

"That came out so bald," she said with a distressed gesture. "I don't quite know how to say it without being offensive, but I was thinking about the situation yesterday, and while he could have been passing along some sort of a message, or microdot, or any number of things that spies pass on to other spies, I wondered if maybe it wasn't possible that he was doing something a little less dashing."

"Drugs, you mean?"

She shrugged. "Or money laundering. Or something of that ilk."

I shook my head. "With anyone else, I'd stop to consider that, but not Elliott. He's a nice guy. I mean, really decent, the sort of man you'd happily take home to meet your family. He takes care of his own family, and he thinks of others, and he's got honor and stuff like that. I was going to marry one of his friends, but we broke up, and when Elliott and I got together, he was all, 'Are you sure you're over Patrick, and this isn't rebound sex?' and things like that, and a lot of guys wouldn't even be concerned about that. So no, I don't think Elliott's doing anything nefarious."

"You know him best," she said, clearly relieved. I didn't tell her that I knew him about as long as she did. "As for your problem . . . well, I've always believed that the best way to avoid misunderstandings is to talk about the situation. Is there any way you can do that without mentioning his . . . occupation?"

"I don't know." I was back to feeling miserable again. "The truth is, I feel like I've ruined the relationship. I don't know if he wants it fixed."

"That is certainly difficult." She flipped through her book until she found a spot she liked. "I won't pry any more, I promise."

"You weren't prying at all. I offered to talk about it, and to be honest, I'm glad I did. I've been wallowing in a big ole vat of self-pity for the whole day, trying to decide if I messed things up beyond repair, or not, and whether I should try to fix it. But talking to you has helped." I didn't tell her that despite my bold statements to Elliott, I was trying to figure out if he really was someone I wanted to know a whole lot better, or if he was just a fun vacation fling, one that massaged my hurting ego while entertaining my mind and body.

Shallow, shallow, shallow, my inner critic said disgust-edly.

Hey, I'm being honest here, I pointed out. *I need to know this stuff, because if I lie to myself and go forward with a relationship, then it'll all end badly, and likely will hurt Elliott in the process. Not to mention bash you, my fair little ego, around, as well.*

And what did you decide? it asked.

I watched a line of colorful houses perched high above the river, looking like they were superglued onto a sheer rock face, as they drifted past. Could I imagine spending the rest of my life in one of those houses with Elliott? Day after day, putting up with his fussy ways, and general crankiness when he wanted to work, and the fact that he had a secret life that he obviously didn't want to share with me?

I just don't know, I finally acknowledged. But one thing I did know for sure—I wasn't interested in him simply to make myself feel better about Patrick. I liked Elliott *because* he was fussy, and cranky, and mysterious. And that had to be a good start, right?

My inner self shook her head, but stopped nagging me, which was a relief because I'd spent almost the whole day in introspection, and that was just too much self-knowledge for my tastes.

"Right," I said a short time later when I entered our cabin. Elliott looked up from the computer. "Time for sex."

He blinked at me. "Pardon?"

"You heard me." I pulled off my tank top and lacy shrug, and kicked off my espadrilles. "If you want me to apologize again, I will, because I'm truly sorry that I messed up and put your pictures online without first asking you. But after that, it's sexy fun time."

He just stared at me for a moment before pinching the top of his nose, like he had a headache coming on. "I . . . I'm not . . . Alice, I'm working right now."

"Yeah, I can see that." I shucked my shorts and tried to strike a pose that made a woman clad only in her undergarments attractive. "But surely you can take a break?"

"A sex break?"

"Call it what you like. You've been in here for five hours, Elliott. You didn't come out for lunch, and judging by the way you're stretching your back, I bet you haven't gotten out of that chair except to use the bathroom. So you're due a break, and what's more fun than a nooner held a few hours late?" I gave him my most winsome smile, hiding the uncertainty and worry that I had, truly, ruined our budding relationship.

He gestured to the laptop. "I can't just stop writing to have sex, Alice."

"Why not? Your boy parts stop working?"

"No, of course not, but there's such a thing as keeping to a schedule. I've told you how important it is that I keep to that, and I've already lost yesterday's time, so I can't just run off and make love to you the way I'd certainly like to." He was frowning now, not a good sign. "Besides, there's the other issue."

Fear clutched at my stomach. He *was* still angry at me. I *had* screwed things up beyond repair.

"I don't know what else I can do about that other than apologize yet again. I've contacted all my friends, and asked them to delete any copies they have, but beyond that . . ." I suddenly felt very naked despite my underwear and bra.

"What are you talking about?" He shook his head. "I think we're talking at cross-purposes. I don't care about you sending pictures of me to your friends, assuming they don't include me naked with a pirate hat."

Guilt dug into me with sharp, stabby edges. I tried to smile, but it came out pretty horrid. "Uh . . ."

"What I was referring to was Patrick."

It was my turn to stare at him in utter confusion. "What does he have to do with the price of tea in China?"

"I told you he called me earlier today. He was upset that you and I had been intimate, and told me in no uncertain terms that I was to cease continuing. He didn't say it in as many words, but I suspect he means to fly out from Paris to confront you."

I sat down on the edge of the bed, and clutched the parrot to my chest. "Why on earth would he do that?"

"I have no idea." Elliott's gaze seemed to crawl over my exposed flesh, making me feel very warm. Hot, even. Downright feverish. "I can only gather that he wants you back."

"Well, he can't have me. I don't want him."

"Are you sure? Earlier this morning, you seemed to think otherwise."

"Me? You're nuts. I've washed that man right out of my hair. The only thing I want from Patrick is an apology for how he treated me, and destroyed my dreams, and stole my home from me. But since I doubt I'll ever get that from him, I'm not going to hold my breath."

Elliott looked adorably doubtful. "You don't want to be with him? You aren't sorry that we engaged in lovemaking?"

"Of course I'm not sorry. Sex with you is awesome." I searched his face. He really had thought I would leap when Patrick snapped his fingers for me! What a silly man. What a sexy, endearingly, wonderfully silly man. "I don't know how else to say this, so I'll just spell it out. I don't want Patrick. I want you."

"Alice . . ." Elliott hit the save button, and stood up to face me. "We've fallen rather headlong into a relationship of sorts."

Of sorts? What the hell?

His hands were on his hips, as if he was lecturing me. Or speaking to an unusually obtuse person. "I am not normally so heedless about women, and I assume you are likewise with men, although you do seem to live your life rather . . ."

"Enthusiastically?" I asked, getting annoyed at his high-handed manner.

"I'm trying to think of a nice term for 'without due consideration of consequences,' but am having little luck. I realize that you embrace spontaneity, and even allow that in certain circumstances it can be beneficial and enjoyable, but this demand to engage in sexy fun time, as you insist on calling it, is a good example of how disruptive it can be."

"You are such a stick-in-the-mud sometimes, you know that?" My annoyance faded. Elliott, poor man, truly believed what he was saying. He thought life was better when it was organized and structured until all the fun had been squeezed out of it. "Look, one of the things I've learned from life is that you have to grab what you can take, because you never know if it'll be there later. I'm here right now. So are you. And I just bet you if I stick my hands down your pants, you'll be ready for a little fun in no time."

His nostrils flared, and his voice took on that haughty lord-of-the-manor tone that made me want to giggle. "I assure you, madam, that I am in full control of my libido. If I did not wish to become aroused by you, I wouldn't."

I put my hand on his fly. Just that, no caressing, no stroking, just my palm on his zipper. I could feel him getting hard within seconds. I cocked an eyebrow at him.

"As it happens, I want to be aroused," he said with an attempt at dignity. "I have decided that I will, just this once, bend my inviolable rule about not stopping until I am done with my daily quota of writing."

"If you bend it, it's not inviolable." I let my fingers do a little walking, which had him moaning at the same time he reached behind me to unhook my bra.

"Now you're being pedantic," he murmured against my neck, pausing when I tugged his shirt off over his head.

"Gloriosky, man, that's going to melt my knees." I clutched at him when he nibbled a spot behind my ear that seemed to be seriously erogenous.

"We wouldn't want that. I like your knees." He started to bend down, no doubt to pick me up in true he-man style, but mindful of his back, I scooted backward onto the bed, patting it.

"We don't need to stress your back. Come and lie down, and I will work my womanly wiles upon you as I intended to do last night."

"Did I apologize about that?" he asked, doing as I requested.

I looked at the seemingly vast smorgasbord of Elliott before me, and tried to decide where to start. "Yes, you did. Hey! No hands. This was my turn to have my way with you, remember? You got to be all 'I'm giving and you're receiving' yesterday. Now it's my turn."

"You had your turn while I was in the stocks." He slid his hands around my breasts, rubbing his thumb across nipples that were suddenly extremely demanding.

"That was not a full turn. I was just barely getting started—oh dear god, yes, I love your manly stubble! It's so soft and yet seriously makes my boobs tingle—and didn't have a full turn, so I'm still in charge. All right, one little nibble, but that's it. I'm taking over after that."

He took each nipple by turn into his mouth, making me want to rub all of myself on every last inch of him, but when his fingers slid down my belly and headed south to my party zone, I came to my senses.

"Hold it right there, buster," I said, grabbing his wrists. "You're going beyond the terms of our agreement. Stop that! Hands to the side."

"Are you always this bossy? I don't recall you being this assertive yesterday. Except for in the club, and I assumed you were simply trying to guide me into the proper frame of mind for piratical acts."

"It's my turn to run things, so yes, I'm being bossy." I peeled off my undies and slid over until I sat on his thighs, making sure he kept his hands to himself. His penis was waving away at me, but I ignored that for the moment, enjoying just looking at Elliott's chest, and arms, and those wicked gray eyes that now seemed to be smoky with passion. It sent a little shiver of pure pleasure down my back. "You look positively edible, Elliott. All those tasty bulges, and nibbleworthy spots, and not so much body hair that I think 'Get that man a razor!' No, you're a feast for both the eyes and the mouth."

"And hands. Don't forget hands. Your hands are good," he said, his eyes hopeful.

I gave the part in question a long, hard look. "Hmm. I

was going to save this for dessert, but you look a bit . . . anticipatory. Are you going to last if I start nibbling at your ankles and work my way up?"

"No. You might make it to my knee, but only if I think about starving children and venereal warts."

"We can't have that," I said, rising up on my knees, and taking him firmly in hand to position him appropriately.

"No foreplay?" he asked, looking astounded.

I nestled the head of his penis right where I wanted it, and paused. "You said you wouldn't be able to last, and mindful of the time, I thought we'd get right down to business."

"But . . . women need foreplay. They need time to get ready. They need kissing and touches, and much rubbing of the breasts, none of which I object to, far from it. But you haven't allowed me to do but the bare minimum of that. You can't be ready for me."

"Sweetness, I've been ready since last night, and no, that's not a criticism."

"But—," he started to protest.

I stopped him by the simple act of sitting on him. Oh, I did it slowly, because he was no lightweight in the penis department, but I was telling the truth in that I was more than ready to go to the main course.

The groan of sheer, unadulterated pleasure that he gave was matched by one of my own.

"Oh, my, you're so much . . . more . . . this way. And I do like that this position lets me tweak your nipples if I want. Do you like nipple tweaking?"

He moaned something unintelligible, his eyes closed tight, his hands convulsively clutching the sheets covering the bed.

"That's OK, we can leave it for later. Wow, you really are there, aren't you? Woof! Let me try a Kegel. Can you feel this?"

He began panting.

"Oh, good, so those are paying off. They're not my favorite thing to do, but I'll keep up on them if you like them. Hey, are we going to do pirates or not? I can go either way, to be honest."

Elliott opened his eyes to shoot a glare at me. "How is it you can do this and talk at the same time?"

"Women are creatures of delight and mystery. Worship us."

"No pirates, and yes I like the squeezing thing. You may do it again."

I did it. He bucked beneath me. "I have changed my mind. If you do that again, I risk disappointing you."

"Got a hair-trigger dick, huh?" I asked, bending down to nibble on his nipple.

His fingers spasmed. "Not normally, but you seem to bring that out in me. I shall commence thinking of scabies and syphilis and gonorrhea."

"You have the best lovemaking banter," I said, giving him another squeeze.

His eyelids, which had drifted closed again, snapped open. He released one handful of sheet in order to slide his hand up my thigh, gently rubbing his thumb over sensitive flesh. I swear that my eyes just about crossed when a familiar spiral of pleasure tipped me over the edge. It didn't take him long to follow, his shout of pleasure still ringing in my ears as I collapsed onto him.

"Can I just say," I said in between pants, "that I love the fact that you're not quiet? Not to compare you to He Who Doesn't Deserve to Be Named, but I like to know that the man I'm with is enjoying himself, and that's quite clear with you."

Elliott's big chest rose and fell with rapidity beneath me. Once he had enough oxygen in his lungs, he swatted my butt with a languid hand, and managed to gasp, "Vixen. You go too far. Also, I have never met a woman who talks during lovemaking as much as you."

I pried myself off his damp chest to look in his eyes, suddenly worried. "But you like it, right?"

"Yes," he said, pulling me back down until we lay in a tangled mass of arms and legs and sticky flesh, and two hearts that might not be beating as one, but were sure starting to match their rhythms. "I like it."

Chapter 9

Expense Account
  Item one: twenty-two pounds fifty
  Remarks: That was one of my favorite shirts!

The phone chirruped. Elliott snatched it up quickly with a glance over to the bed. Alice rolled over mumbling something, but didn't appear to wake up. "Yes?" he said softly, sliding open the door to the minuscule balcony, and stepping out into the soft night air.

"Sorry to disturb you so late. And by disturb, I mean I hope I didn't catch you in the middle of any form of congress, sexual or otherwise."

"What do you want, Gun?" he asked with an annoyed glance at his watch. It was almost midnight, and he'd been working for the last two hours, ever since Alice had gone to sleep.

"Is that yea or nay on the congress interrupting?"

"Nay, not that it's any of your business. If it will ease your mind, I was writing. Nothing more."

"Pity. Did you say your next port of call was Miltenberg? My trip to Portugal was canceled, and I can't get into the Bulgarian factory for a couple of days—evidently some government team is crawling all over the site right now—and as I have a few days to kill, I thought I'd spend them with my favorite brother and his mysterious American bit of fluff."

"She's not a bit of fluff," Elliott said, annoyed with himself the second the words emerged from his mouth. Dammit, now Gunner would get all sorts of ideas about Alice, ideas that he himself hadn't yet fully considered, let alone approved for general announcement.

"No? Glad to hear that." Gunner's voice was neutral, but Elliott knew better. He had a strange reticence to introducing Alice to his brother that he analyzed, with some surprise, as jealousy.

"As a matter of fact, I'm working late so I can take the time to accompany Alice tomorrow. She wishes to go to some of the tourist sites, and I told her that assuming I got tomorrow's work done tonight, I would go with her."

"I'll let you get back to it, then. I'll be at the Miltenberg dock around ten. That is, if you want me to meet your bird."

"She's not a bird any more than she is a bit of fluff. She's a woman, an intelligent, attractive, amusing woman, and if you want to meet her, you'll have to promise not to be a bigger fool than you already are."

"Now, when have I ever misbehaved in front of one of your women?" Gunner asked on a laugh.

"When haven't you? is more the question. Ten it is.

See that you're not late," Elliott warned before ending the call.

He returned to his chair, intending on finishing the chapter at hand, but his eyes kept drifting over to the sheet drawn over the delicious curves that made up Alice. She was so warm, so full of life, and a joy that seemed almost childlike, and yet he sensed in her a deep sadness. He'd never felt overly protective around anyone that wasn't family, but there was something about Alice that made him want to shield her from the trials of the world.

And then there was the siren lure of her person. Even a few yards away, he felt the pull of her, like she was a lodestone, drawing him ever closer until he could stroke that soft, satiny skin, and breathe in the wonderful warm Alice scent, not to mention the taste of her. . . .

He was on his feet and headed toward the bed before he realized what he was doing.

It took more effort than he would have liked, but he managed to sit back at the computer, and shut Alice out of his mind while he wrote for three more hours.

Seven and a half hours later he entered the dining room seeking several cups of extra-strong coffee, and wondered if it was such a good idea to spend the day out seeing sights when he'd rather be back in the cabin with Alice.

"Are you going on the group tour to Rothenburg?" he heard Laura ask Alice as the latter rose from the break-fast table. Their backs were to him as he approached, but he heard them clearly.

"No, Elliott said he didn't care what we saw today, so I figured it would be more fun to visit that sword factory here in town. They have sword-fighting classes there, and they'll teach you the basics in an hour. I've always wanted to learn how to fence."

"It's very James Bondian," Laura said in a low voice, followed by a little laugh.

"I know, right? It's a good skill to have in case you're ever stuck in a castle and forced to fight for your life," Alice responded with her own light laugh.

"Evidently Elliott told Deidre that you were going to Rothenburg, so she has us going there."

"That was my fault, I'm afraid. I figured she'd pump him for details of our plans, so I told him to tell her we were going to Rothenburg. I apologize if you wanted to spend the day poking around the town instead."

"Oh, I don't really mind. I enjoy going on the Manny van Bris tours. Tiffany is actually quite good, although she doesn't let one linger long." Laura leaned into Alice. "You'll have to let me know if there's any further *activity* going on, though, since I won't be there to help watch for it."

Elliott wondered what the hell she was talking about. What sort of activity? Something Alice was doing? A cold chill gripped him. Was she meeting with Patrick? Had she lied to him about that? It wasn't out of the question that she could be using him to make Patrick jealous . . . something his old friend evidently was, judging by the texts he'd received.

He moved closer, but Alice must have sensed him, because she stopped in the middle of her sentence.

"You know I'll definitely tell you if he—oh, there you are, Elliott. Get enough coffee in you to wake up?"

Both women turned bright, dazzling smiles on him. He was instantly suspicious. They were up to something. The question was whether it was something that was any of his business.

"There isn't enough coffee in the world for that, but I

have consumed enough to remain awake for the day. Are you ready to go?"

"Yeah, let's get out of here before Deidre the Leech suckers onto you. Have fun, Laura!"

"Enjoy your fencing lesson," she said with a wave.

"You didn't tell me you wanted to learn how to fence," Elliott said a few minutes later, when they had escaped the ship without seeing anyone else. Most of the other passengers were going on the tour provided by Tiffany and company, but he noticed Anthony and Dahl lounging at an outdoor café, chatting with a couple who were obviously tourists, and making copious notes. He lifted his hand in acknowledgment when Anthony gave them a nod. "If you had told me that before, I would have been happy to show you a few basic moves."

Alice gawked at him. "Don't tell me you know how to fence, too!"

"Too?"

Her lips compressed for a moment as if she was holding something back. "Er . . . you speak a lot of languages. That's kind of different, just like knowing how to use a sword is different."

"I learned from my father, as a matter of fact. He was something of an amateur expert at many forms of swordplay, and I took a bit of it at university, as well." He gave her a long look from the corner of his eye. "It's not all that extraordinary."

"Well, I think it's cool." Her expression was placid, showing excitement and pleasure, but no shadow of secrets, no sense of hiding something. Certainly nothing as heinous as playing him along in order to attract another man.

He had to be wrong. He misheard the conversation, or he put the wrong interpretation to what he did hear. Alice wasn't devious, and she wasn't using him for her own purposes. She was exactly what he had told his brother—an intelligent, attractive, amusing woman, and nothing more.

As if on cue, Gunner loomed up before them. Alice paused to take a picture of an ironbound door just as Gunner, his eyes on her, said, "Right on time, I see. Hello."

"Of course we're on time. Punctuality is a courtesy that is far too often overlooked. Alice, I'd like you to meet my brother Gunner, who finds himself in Germany for a few days."

Alice's eyes were huge as she looked at his brother. "But that's ... you're ... he's the one ... *brother*?"

"Yes." He gave her grave consideration. She looked flustered as hell, and he didn't understand why that was. It couldn't be because Gunner was of an obviously mixed ethnicity—Alice didn't hold with prejudices of that sort, that much he knew. What was it then that so startled her? "He's the first child that my parents adopted. We are, as a matter of fact, both thirty-seven."

"We've been brothers since we were wee babies," Gunner said with a dazzling smile. He took Alice's hand and bowed over it, something he did with great effect.

At least it annoyed Elliott greatly. He took Alice's hand back, and kept it safely in his.

"Gunner ... I ..." Alice seemed to get a grip on her emotions, because she rallied quickly. "How nice to meet you. That's an unusual name. Is it German?"

"No, it's spelled with an *er* on the end. The orphanage said I was named for one of the founders, who had been a gunner on a warship. I'm delighted to meet you. Elliott has told me nothing at all about you, so I look forward to finding out everything there is to know."

"You'll have to forgive his atrocious manners and blunt personality," Elliott said with a glare. "He was raised by monkeys before the orphanage found him."

He thought Alice's eyes might pop out of her head. "He was?"

Gunner laughed, and fell into step on the other side of her as they walked up the hill toward the upper part of the town. "Elliott likes to embellish the truth. That's why he's such a good writer. There were no monkeys involved in my early life, I assure you, although Elliott did have a pet hedgehog named Rory that he grudgingly shared with me. But enough about us. Tell me about yourself."

"I . . . I . . ." Alice didn't seem to know what to say.

Elliott took pity on her. "Gunner, she's on holiday. She doesn't want to undergo the third degree."

"I'm just trying to be friendly," his brother said with a faux expression of innocence.

"I'm really not that interesting," Alice said, giving Elliott's hand a little squeeze.

He smiled down at her. "I think you are."

"I'm sure I'd think you are, as well, if I knew more about you," Gunner piped up. "It's hard to say otherwise, because I was taught not to judge someone by their appearance, not that your appearance says anything but that you look like a fascinating woman, but the fact remains that if I knew more, I'd be able to second Elliott's character call with firm approval."

"I like how you talk, too," Alice told Gunner. "It's more stream-of-consciousness than Elliott, but you both have that quirkiness that isn't apparent on the surface."

"She's perceptive," Gunner told him. "That's always nice in a woman."

"What I'd like to know is how you ended up here at the same time we are," Alice said, her thumb rubbing against Elliott's hand. He liked the feeling of her fingers twined so naturally in his. She felt right next to him, and he could see by the admiring glances that Gunner was sending her way that his brother liked her, too. Alice flinched a little before adding, "That sounds accusatory, and I don't intend for it to be, but you being here is rather curious, you have to admit."

"Not at all curious," Gunner said cheerfully, giving her a wink. "Elliott mentioned you would be in this area, and since I was waiting for some government officials to vacate a place I have to do some work, it made sense to spend my heel-kicking time here rather than by myself in a strange Bulgarian town where my presence wasn't particularly welcomed."

"My brother, the industrial spy," Elliott joked.

Alice's hand jerked in his. "You're a . . . spy?" she finally managed to ask. "Does it . . . uh . . . run in the family?"

Elliott was about to explain that he was joking, when a shadow fell across them as a man stepped out from a doorway. "I thought I'd find you here."

"Patrick!" Alice said in a voice that was (reassuringly) filled with surprise. "What the hell?"

Elliott eyed his old friend. Patrick looked as dashingly handsome as ever, but his eyes were filled with ire, an ire that Elliott could almost feel. Elliott held firmly to Alice's hand when she would have jerked his fingers from hers. "That's a very good question. Mind answering it, Patrick?"

"I came t'see if it was true that you were doing everything you could t'undermine me with my woman."

"Whoa, now," Alice said, jerking her hand from his in order to put both hers on her hips. "One, I am not your woman. And two, I'm not your woman."

Gunner frowned. "I believe those are actually—"

"And three," Alice said loudly, loud enough that people passing by them sent curious glances their way. "I can't believe I ever was your woman, because that had to be the stupidest thing I've ever done in my life. So you can just stick that in your pipe and smoke it."

"What pipe?" Gunner asked Elliott. "I feel like I'm missing something."

"I believe it's an American colloquialism," Elliott told his brother. "I seem to recall reading it somewhere."

"So you admit that you've shacked up with him!" Patrick pointed dramatically at Elliott.

"I had no choice since you gave your ticket to him!" Alice snapped. "How dare you come here and act all butt-hurt."

Gunner pursed his lips. "Erm . . ."

"Yes, that's another colloquialism," Elliott said.

"I really must spend more time in the States. Evidently I'm missing quite a lot."

"I am simply pointing out that you took no time at all before you started sleeping with my friend," Patrick argued. "So much for being brokenhearted, as you insisted you were t'anyone who bothered t'read your Facebook page."

"I don't see that the matter is anything to do with you, Patrick," Elliott interjected in what he deemed his argument-soothing tone. "You broke up with Alice. That act in and by itself negates any further say in her romantic choices."

"Yeah," Alice said, taking Elliott's arm. She shook her head, then said, "I can't believe you flew all the way around the world to be jealous."

"I didn't, as it happened. There was a trade show I had t'attend in Paris." His gaze shifted from Alice to Elliott. "I left your sister there. She was shopping. I'm sure you will enjoy the bill that follows."

Elliott swore under his breath.

"So what are you doing here, then?" Gunner asked.

"Gunner. It's been a few years, hasn't it?" Patrick looked him up and down. "I could ask you the same."

"No, no, we're talking about you, not him," Alice said, then suddenly shook her head. "What am I saying? No, we're not talking about you. You know why? Because I'm through with the conversation, just like I'm through with you, Patrick. You dumped me, and I've moved on. I'm not going to spend my life pining for you, and if you say one word about Elliott and me being together, then I'll punch you in the nose."

"I think it's important also to point out that Patrick has done exactly what he has accused you of," Elliott said with aplomb. "Since he just admitted that he went to Paris with my sister Jane."

Alice looked even more incensed. Elliott enjoyed that greatly.

"You bastard!" she said, smacking Patrick on the arm. "You dumped me for Elliott's sister?"

"Jane? Really?" Gunner eyed Patrick. "Interesting."

"So why are you here, then?" Alice asked, then immediately took Elliott's arm again. "Never mind. I said I was through with the conversation, and I am. Come on,

Elliott. Let's go to the sword place, and you can show me how to sword fight."

Elliott was unable to keep from throwing a slightly triumphant glance at the sputtering Patrick as Alice sailed past him, but that moment faded quickly when Patrick said, "Sword fighting?"

"OK, why did Patrick say the word 'sword fighting' like that?" Alice asked him as they hurried up the hill, Gunner right on their heels. "Like it meant something to him?"

Elliott sighed. "Patrick attended the same fencing classes I did."

"Crap. I should have known he would do something like that. He always did admire old film actors who could do all the Errol Flynn stuff. Is he following us?"

"Yes," Patrick answered, and, shoving Gunner aside, took up a position on Alice's far side. "This isn't over, Ainslie."

Alice snorted and said something derisive under her breath that Patrick obviously pretended not to hear.

"You're wasting your time, but so long as you don't bother Alice, then I can't stop you from doing that," Elliott told him. Alice gave him a look of approval that had warmth spreading inside him. He loved it when she looked at him like that, just as if he'd done something heroic. She made him feel like he really could do anything.

He regretted that feeling some three hours later when, after a tour of the sword-making factory, a visit to the attached fencing school, and Alice's hour-long lesson (during which a form of peace had been achieved by Patrick sitting in the spectators' area texting and making phone calls, while Gunner and Elliott watched Alice and the other pupils in the center floor), Patrick put Elliott's newfound heroism to the test.

"You need t'put your money where your mouth is," Patrick said loudly when Elliott was adjusting Alice's grip on her training foil.

They both looked up. Patrick strode across the floor, a pair of sabers in his hands.

Elliott sighed. "You can't possibly be about to do what I think you're about to do."

"I can't?" Patrick tossed one of the sabers toward Elliott, hilt-first.

Elliott deftly caught it and spun it in a manner that used to make his fencing master smack him on the head. "Just watch me."

"Whereas I don't have anything to prove." Elliott placed the saber on a nearby table. The practice room was empty of students now, it being the designated lunch period, which meant that Elliott could speak his mind without outside witnesses. "What the hell is the matter with you, Patrick? This jealousy doesn't make any sense. You told me yourself not ten days ago that you were through with Alice, and were assumedly defiling my sister at will. Alice has stated numerous times, both to you and to me, that she has no further interest in you. And yet, here you are, apparently playing the role of the jealous scorned lover. Why? Why are you here, and why are you doing this?"

To his astonishment, Patrick seemed to deflate in front of them. His antagonistic expression quickly faded to one that was more embarrassed than anything else. "I . . . ah, t'hell with it. I don't know why I'm here, t'be perfectly honest. I was quite happy with Jane in Paris. She's got one hell of a sex drive on her—and then a friend of mine sent me a screenshot of Alice's post with you lying naked in bed with naught but a fancy hat covering your cock, and a red wave seemed t'wash over me right then and there. Next thing I knew, I was on the plane t'Germany with murder in me heart." He waggled the saber. "I'd be the first t'admit that it makes no sense at all."

Elliott turned his eyes to Alice. She looked horrified. "Oh man, I thought I took that down fast enough. Sorry, Elliott."

He took a deep breath, reminded himself that getting angry would serve no purpose, and simply said to Patrick, "At least you've admitted that you have no business being here."

"I didn't say that," Patrick said with his trademark roguish wink to Alice. "There is a fair lady t'be won back, after all."

"What part of *I don't want you anymore* are you having trouble understanding?" Alice asked, looking delightfully put out. "Because as I see it, you're just making an ass of yourself, and ruining what was going to be a very nice time with Elliott and Gunner, although admittedly Gunner was an unexpected addition to today's activities."

"That is my fault," Elliott told her. "It simply slipped my mind to mention to you that my brother would be joining us."

"I'm waiting for the Bulgarian government to clear out of a factory," Gunner told Patrick.

"If he can be here, then so can I," Patrick said, and picked up his saber. "Besides, you fell for me once, you can do it again. I intend on giving Elliott a run for his money."

"We're on a cruise," Alice pointed out. "Even if I did want your attentions—and I don't—there's no room on the ship for you, and you can't very well follow us from town to town."

"Sure I can." He waved the saber at Elliott again. "And I'd like t'start winning Alice back with a round of fencing. You up t'it, Elliott? Or are you afraid that Alice's affections will waver once she sees how badly you're beaten?"

"As if I care," Alice said, turning to Elliott. "We can go have some lunch if you like. I'm done here."

He looked at her for a moment, weighing the need to spend the rest of the day in enjoyable pursuits with the need to show off for Alice. He made a mental *tsk* at the fact that even he, the most logical of men, felt the desire to impress his woman, but honesty forced him to admit that at the moment it was the strongest desire.

"Very well," he said, picking up the saber. "But we don't have any masks."

"We don't need them; we'll exclude the head from the target area. Acknowledged touches only, since we lack the proper gear. Winner at three, all right?"

"As you like."

"This is stupid. You could get hurt," Alice protested when Gunner, at a glance from Elliott, pulled her back to the sidelines.

"These are practice sabers," Elliott said, holding up the weapon. "The blades are dulled and there are plastic tips on the point of the sword. Ideally, we'd be hooked up to the usual fencing electronics if we were having a proper match, but since this is just to satisfy Patrick's ego—"

"You accepted the challenge. Your ego is just as involved as mine."

"—then we'll just use gentlemen's agreement rules, such as they are." He saluted Patrick with the saber, and took an opening stance. "You need not worry that either of us will be—bloody hell!"

Before he could finish reassuring Alice, Patrick lunged

forward and slashed across his chest. Elliott just barely parried the thrust in time, and even then, the tip of Patrick's blade snagged on his sleeve, and ripped a long gash in the material.

Patrick bared his teeth in a feral smile. "Will you look at that? My sword seems t'have lost the cap."

"Oh my god, I knew it! Are you all right?" Alice ran forward to examine his arm.

"I am unharmed, if that's what you mean. You did that on purpose," Elliott said to Patrick, examining his torn sleeve. Dammit, this was one of his favorite shirts. "My mother gave me this shirt two Christmases ago!"

"My apologies." Patrick took up his position again. "Shall we continue, or are you going to whinge some more?"

"Look, I realize you guys are now in a pissing match, but since it involves swords, I think you need to take it down a few notches," Alice said, trying to piece together his torn sleeve. She added to Elliott, "I don't want you getting hurt, and no, that's not a reflection on your skill."

"I could get hurt, too, you know," Patrick said.

She tossed, "I don't give a damn about you," over her shoulder to him before continuing on to Elliott, "Some women may think it's fun to have men fighting over them, but I'm not one."

"We aren't fighting over you. At least I am not. And for your information, Patrick, I am not whinging. I am simply pointing out that you have willfully destroyed the sleeve of a very nice shirt that was a gift. That is not very sporting, a fact that I have no doubt Alice noticed."

She sighed in a dramatic manner, shook her head, and turned on her heel. "You two want to do this, go right ahead. But you'll do it without me watching."

"She left," Patrick said, all astonishment.

"She said she didn't care for us fighting." Elliott raised his saber. "Evidently you never learned that about Alice, and yet I instinctively knew it. *En garde.*"

"Yes, but women love it when men—you bastard!"

Patrick had automatically returned Elliott's salute, which meant he was free to attack. With two swift strokes, he slashed both shoulders of Patrick's polo shirt. Patrick stared in astonishment first at his shirt, then moved his gaze to Elliott's sword. The tip had mysteriously disappeared from it, as well.

Elliott smiled.

"Oh, it's on now, lad," Patrick said, raising his sword.

"Lighting isn't great in here, but I think I can get a few good shots," Gunner said from the sidelines, his camera in hand. "No one splash any blood my way, please. I don't want to get my Nikon dirty."

"There will be no blood," Elliott promised, narrowing his eyes. "Patrick will be lucky if I leave him with a shirt, however."

Patrick tossed his head in his usual dramatic fashion, and snarled, "You'll be lucky if you walk out of here with your trousers intact."

Ten minutes later Elliott exited the building (trousers fully intact), immediately going over to where Alice sat in the lotus position on a small swath of grass, her eyes closed and her palms upraised. She cracked one eye open when his shadow fell across her, the other eye popping open in surprise. "What the hell?"

He made a wry face, gesturing toward his chest with the hand that held both detached sleeves. "Patrick was better than I remembered."

"Evidently. I only hope you returned the favor...."

Oh." Patrick and Gunner stopped next to them. Patrick was shirtless, holding the remains of his shredded shirt. "I see that you did."

"Put your shirt back on, man," Elliott told Patrick when he noticed the latter was flexing his muscles in Alice's direction.

"What shirt? All I have left is a rag, thanks to your damned insistence on ruining a perfectly good garment."

"Pot, kettle, black," Elliott told him, offering his hand to Alice. She took it and rose, frowning when two women walked by, giggling at Patrick.

"You look like a male prostitute," she told him, then turned to Elliott.

He wanted to kiss her at that moment. And although he wasn't a man to give free rein to his emotions when it came to public displays, he felt that since *he* could still wear his shirt, he was the victor, and thus, he was due a boon. He caught Alice up and laid his lips on her in a way that gave no uncertain message to Patrick.

"Bah. I don't need t'see that sort of abuse," Patrick spat out, then stomped away. "I'm going t'fetch another shirt. I'll catch you up later."

"Would you like to try that again, this time without having Patrick in mind?" Alice asked when he shot a triumphant smirk at Patrick's back.

He looked back down at her. One eyebrow was cocked in a very jaded expression. "My apologies. Yes, I would like to try again, but only if Gunner puts down that damned camera. I think he has enough shots of us snogging."

"That," Alice said, grabbing him by the tattered stubs that were all that remained of his collar points, "was not snogging. This is."

Her mouth was warm and wonderful, and he wanted badly to be back in their little cabin, so he could do more than just be the recipient of a kiss that all but steamed, but after allowing her to suck his tongue for a few seconds, he remembered that Gunner was likely even at that moment e-mailing pictures of them to his mother.

"That was exceptionally good," he told Alice softly, relishing the feel of her in his arms. "Remind me to thank you later. When we're alone. And naked."

"Deal." She smiled at him, making him feel as if he were standing in a spotlight of heat.

It was her eyes, he decided, gazing into them. They were particularly mossy-colored today, standing out in the bright sunlight. The little flecks of gold and brown were particularly pronounced, but it was the warmth in them that had him thinking seriously about escorting her straight back to the ship. Surely they'd done enough sightseeing for the day?

The clicking of Gunner's camera brought him to his senses. With reluctance, he let go of Alice, offering her his arm. She took it, and they started down the hill toward the town proper. "Shall we have some lunch?"

"Sounds good to me. Although do you think they'll serve you without sleeves?"

"If I explain that I lost them in a dueling accident, perhaps they will."

She slid him a sidelong glance. "What are we going to do about Patrick?"

"What can we do? Short of bodily putting him on a plane back to Paris, I am at a loss as to how to keep him from following us. Unfortunately, he knows the cruise schedule."

"Mum says thanks for the photos, and she'll be in contact with you shortly, El," said Gunner, who had been busily sending pictures out via his phone, as he caught up with them wearing a delighted grin. "She really liked the one where Alice grabbed your head with both hands."

Elliott sighed. He knew any protest about the invasion of his (and Alice's, for that matter) privacy would be futile. Even before he could say anything, his phone buzzed, indicating a text received.

Alice laughed at the look on his face. "It could be worse, you know."

"I don't see how."

Her smile was pure cheek. "She could have seen the picture of you with my captain's hat."

"Oh, yes, about this picture that Patrick has seen but evidently was removed," Gunner started to say, but Alice just laughed and released Elliott's arm to dash ahead, cooing over an outdoor café on the next block.

"I like her," Gunner said as the two men strolled down the cobblestoned street. "She doesn't seem like the sort to play games."

"Patrick, you mean?"

Gunner nodded.

"I agree." Elliott watched as Alice, with her phone in hand, attempted to decipher a menu posted on the café's wall. "Patrick being here is none of her doing, nor is it her desire."

"What are you going to do about him?"

He shrugged. "What can I do?"

"Not a lot, although I have to admit you're a better man than me if you're willing to put up with her ex trying to woo her out from under you." They walked in silence for a few seconds before Gunner asked, "You going to keep her?"

"I don't know," Elliott answered, his gaze still on Alice. Her hair glistened with hidden golden highlights in the sunshine, the wind causing her light dress to caress her lush form in a way that had the blood pooling in his groin. "I suspect that's going to depend on if Alice can be persuaded to put up with a stodgy, hidebound man who couldn't be a pirate if his life depended on it."

Gunner jostled his arm. "You'd better get on it, brother, before someone comes along who's better at persuasion than you are."

Elliott couldn't agree more. The question was, did he have what it took to make Alice agree, as well?

Chapter 10

Diary of Alice Wood

Day Three (really Day Six, but eh.
We'll go with Day Three)

"Well," I said, moving over to the deck rail next to Laura. The glittering lights of the towns glowed like fireflies in the darkness, making me wonder for a moment what it was like to live in one of those adorable little towns that dotted the Main River, upon which we were now cruising. "It's been quite the day, huh?"

"Has it?" Laura gave me a curious glance. "We had a very interesting time at the glassblowing demonstration—I'm sure you would have enjoyed seeing it—but I don't know that it has been anything I would classify as *quite a day*. Did something happen to you? Something ... mysterious?"

A quick look around determined that the others who were enjoying the soft evening air were not close enough to overhear us. Elliott, I knew, was dealing with some emergency his editor had dealt him, and was closeted with his laptop.

"You could say that." I tried to look urbane, as if it were a normal thing for me to be hanging out with two spies. "I got confirmation of what we were thinking."

She grabbed my arm. "You didn't!"

"I did. And what's more, I found out that his brother is in the same line of business."

"Oh!" she said, her eyes huge. "How exciting!"

"I know, right? Makes you wonder about the rest of the family."

"Have you met them? Do they have that air about them that says the whole family is in it, or do you think it's an isolated circumstance?"

"I've only met one of his brothers, so I can't really say about the others." I thought about the snippet of the phone call I'd overheard in the Dutch coffee shop. "Although his mother is a character, so I wouldn't put it past her to be involved somehow, too."

"Well, that's just . . . imagine knowing a real—" She glanced around quickly and bit off the word. "Imagine knowing a real one. It must be hell for you, though."

"Uh . . . must it?" I was at a loss as to what she was driving at.

"Yes, of course." She leaned in a little closer. "You must worry about him when he goes off on missions and such. I know I would be a bundle of nerves if my boyfriend— not that I have one right now—if I knew he was placing himself in dangerous situations."

What a horrible thought that was. Worse was the fact that it never occurred to me that Elliott might be doing just that—putting himself in situations of danger. My blood seemed to freeze solid in my veins when I thought about Elliott facing down some desperate opposing agent. Or the local authorities. Or a foreign government, determined to rid the world of him. "Eep," I said, choking on my sudden fear. "I have to talk to him."

"To make him stop?" She gave a little hesitating head bob. "That's tricky, isn't it? It follows that he must love what he's doing, or he wouldn't be doing it. So to beg him to stop doing that . . . well, it has to be hard to know your partner doesn't approve of your employment, and wants you to stop."

"But he could be hurt. You know how volatile some countries are these days—there're coups and violence and wholesale murders popping up all over the world."

"And that's why it's tricky. You just want him safe, but really," she said in a philosophical sort of manner, "should one live one's life in fear of what might be? I've always thought that was the coward's way, and your Elliott doesn't seem at all cowardly."

"He's not," I said miserably. "He's very honorable. He had the opportunity to beat the crap out of my ex when the jerk was taunting Elliott, but he didn't. He maintained his cool because that's the sort of man he is. Holy crapballs, what am I going to do?"

She patted my hand. "I have no idea, but I'm sure that if you discuss the subject with him in a calm and reasonable manner, you'll work out a solution agreeable to you both."

I had no such confidence, but I wasn't going to dwell on that with Laura. We chatted for a few more minutes before I wandered belowdecks, the magical quality of the evening having paled to nothing. Elliott found me a few hours later, huddled in one of the chairs in the dark and empty lounge, watching the darkness drift past us in a heavy silence that seemed to permeate the ship itself.

"Alice?"

I turned from the window at the sound of the voice whispered in the shadows. "Elliott?"

"What are you doing in the dark by yourself?"

"Just sitting here."

His silhouetted form moved over to stand next to me. He wasn't so close that he touched me, but I was very aware of him just a few inches away. He knelt, one hand on my knee. "Are you ill?"

"No." That lovely spicy, smoky scent that was uniquely Elliott wafted around me, embracing me in a cocoon of want and desire, and something I had only just admitted to myself. "I've just been thinking."

"Would I be prying if I asked about what?"

His hand was warm on my knee. It was warmer still when it slid up my thigh.

"I was thinking about you, mostly." I hesitated for a moment. "You're a very nice man, you know."

"Oh lord." His hand dropped from my leg. I missed it. "You're breaking up with me, aren't you? Patrick hypnotized you into thinking you want him, didn't he? Alice, you have to fight the compulsion. He's not right for you."

I wanted to laugh, but realized that he was being serious. Instead, I slid off the chair to my knees so I faced him. "And you are?"

"Yes." I couldn't see him well in the darkness, with just occasional lights from passing ships flickering across his face, but his voice was filled with emotion. "I am exactly the right person for you. There has never been, and never will be, another person more perfectly suited to you. We complement each other in a way that should eliminate any doubts you might have."

I bit my lip to keep from giggling, but oh, how my heart sang. I had an idea that Elliott would return my feelings, but here he was declaring himself in a way that I'd never imagined. "In what way?"

"You are . . ." He cleared his throat and took my hands in his. "You are a bit impetuous. I don't think you'd deny that."

"No, I won't deny it. Spontaneity has always been my byword. It keeps life from getting dull."

"Whereas I tend to think things through before acting. Thus, a little of your spontaneity and a dash of my caution blends to a nice state of adventure without undue risk."

"Undue risk is very bad," I agreed. "It's something I want to talk to you about, but it can wait until you're done. What other way do we complement each other?"

"You like my accent."

I smiled even though he couldn't see it. "It's very sexy."

"I don't see that, myself, but I'm delighted to have you believe it to be true. In other regards, we fit together well in bed, pirate gear aside."

"Oh, come on now, the pirate stuff was fun. Except for the part where you hurt your back."

"I am not averse to having you teach me to play a bit more. I may not be any good at it, but I trust that you will not give up on me."

"No," I said, leaning forward to brush his hair back off his forehead. It didn't need brushing, but I just wanted to touch him, and if I did anything else, I'd end up pouncing on the man and having my way with him right there in the lounge. "I will never give up on you."

"Also, there is your living situation."

"What about it?"

He cleared his throat again. "You mentioned that you had just moved into a small little flat with a shared bathroom, and that you hadn't even unpacked before you arrived for the cruise."

"Yes, but a good part of that is because I'm lazy," I admitted. "Also, it's just easier to leave things boxed up. That way you don't have so much to do when you move."

"You need roots," he said, his voice as warm and intoxicating as brandy. "I own a castle that is approximately four hundred years old. Parts of it go further back, but those are unsafe. Also, there is a lot of room, and you wouldn't have to have all your belongings crammed into one room. You would have to share a bathroom, though."

"Not a lot of plumbing going on at Castle Ainslie?" I asked, breathing deeply of the Elliott Scent.

"I meant that you'd have to share a bathroom with me."

"Elliott."

"Alice?"

"Are you by chance proposing to me?"

The silence was broken by the distant sound of a car alarm going off. "I believe I am."

"OK. I just wanted to make sure, because it sounded to me like you were presenting me with a list of all the reasons why I should be with you, which I have to say is a really Elliott thing to say. Other men might tell me they love me, and want to be with me forever, and that my eyes are like the purest jade, and that sort of thing, but you make a list of your qualifications."

He sighed. "I apologize. I have to be the most unromantic man in the history of the world. Naturally, I think your eyes are like the purest jade, and I do want to be with you forever, and at some point in time that I can't exactly pinpoint, I have fallen intensely, intoxicatingly in love with you."

"I like the alliteration of that," I told him, rubbing the back of one of his hands on my cheek.

He made a choked sound.

"Sorry," I said, dropping his hands. "You're waiting for me to tell you that I am intensely, intoxicatingly in love with you, too, aren't you?"

"It might make things go easier, yes," he said in that dry British humor way he had that delighted me down to my toenails.

"Well, I have to be honest, Elliott—I'm not. Because intense intoxication implies a sensibility, giddy to be true, but still a sensibility, and the fact that I'm ass over ears in love with you makes no sense at all. No, you don't have to list the reasons for me to be in love with you—my statement has nothing to do with your adorableness, and the fact that you make my breath hitch every time I see you, and how I want to tell you everything I think and see and feel, and has everything to do with the fact that when I first met you, I was devastated and betrayed and figured I'd never, ever fall for another man so long as I lived. And yet here it is, a few miraculous days later, and I can't imagine existing without you."

"Thank god," he said in a rush, and I realized to my amazement that he'd been holding his breath. "I've never proposed before, and when you said you weren't in love with me . . . good god. I hope I never have to go through that again. Wait a moment—you did accept me, didn't you?"

"Well, you didn't actually ask me to marry you, but assuming you did, then yes, I accepted."

"Good. Can we please get up? My knees are beginning to hurt, and I want very badly to kiss you, then strip you naked and frolic upon your body in ways that will make you see stars, and I can't very well do that out here in the open."

We made it back to the cabin without molesting each other, but just barely. By the time we worked out whose turn it was to be in charge (his), and whether to include the parrot in the aforementioned frolicking (Elliott vetoed that), we were both wound up to the point where it didn't take much to set off our mutual bonfire.

"Have I mentioned how much I love your legs?" Elliott said from where he knelt between them. He rubbed his stubbly cheek along the tender inside of my thigh, and leaned forward to press a kiss to the center of all my desire.

"No! Don't touch me there!"

He looked up, a question evident in his eyes.

"I'll go over the edge," I said, panting and trying to keep my body from spiraling out of control. "Just don't touch me there!"

He looked down at my lady parts. "Where? Here?"

I shuddered at the feel of his breath, moist and hot. "Aieee!"

"Or here?"

Inner muscles started to cramp with the strain of holding back the orgasm. "Nnrng. For the love of god, nnrng!"

"I believe, my love, that the term you are seeking is foowah." He moved upward, wrapping my legs around his hips and entering me with one, smooth, foowah-making move.

"Oh, lordy, yes, do that some more!" I damn near sang the words, so good did he feel. He warbled his own song of happiness a moment later, making me extremely grateful that he wasn't the sort of man who dallied at his business. "I like ..." Pant, heave. "... the fact that you ..." Deep breath for much-needed oxygen. "... don't insist on wasting time." My body shivered convulsively with wonderful little aftershocks. "Some men feel like they are too quick, and drag things out forever, when what you really want is to just finish. Holy hellbeans, Elliott. You are really, really good at sex."

"I thank you," Elliott said just as breathlessly, rolling off me, but taking me with him so that I was draped across his chest. "My penis also thanks you, as does every other part of my being. Also, I'm pleased that you didn't think I was rushing things. I wouldn't have been able to last much longer."

I snuggled into him, relaxed, sated, and oh, so very happy ... if amazed that I had found him. What were the odds of it? I wondered. "People are going to think we're insane, you know. We've only known each other for a couple of days, and yet whammo! It kind of hit us like a sledgehammer. And that in itself is curious, don't you think? I mean, we are very different people. We don't have a lot in common."

"The very fact that you've made me love you is in itself an explanation," he murmured sleepily.

I tried to figure out what he meant, and was about to ask him when his gentle snore ruffled the top of my head. Poor guy was exhausted. My lady parts gave languid applause, and pointed out that he certainly had earned his rest.

His comment stayed with me through the next morn-

ing, however. "What did you mean?" I asked him over the
roar of the tiny hair dryer that Tiffany had provided. "Is it
because we're in love, so it doesn't matter if we have a lot
in common?"

"Hmm?"

I repeated his statement from the night before.

"Oh, that. No, I meant the fact that I've fallen in love
with you after having known you for less than a week is
in itself a remark on how much you've changed me. I've
never been a fall-in-love-at-first-sight sort of person. The
fact that I have done so despite my nature and what
most people would consider common sense is proof that
we are meant to be together."

"Common sense?" I glared at him. "Did you just do a
Mr. Darcy insult?"

"What the hell is a Mr. Darcy insult?"

"You know, asking Elizabeth Bennet to marry him
despite his own better judgment and the wishes of his
friends and family. Because if you did, you had better
practice your groveling apology."

He looked so confused that I turned off the hair dryer.
"What most people would consider common sense?" I
reminded him.

"Ah. No, that wasn't an insult, Mr. Darcy or otherwise.
You yourself acknowledge that we fell into this relationship quickly—common sense would dictate that to do so
would be a recipe for disaster."

"And you think we'll avoid that?"

"Yes, I do." He put away his shaving things, splashed
some of the woodsy aftershave on his cheeks, and then
realized I was staring. "You've changed me in a fundamen-
tal manner, Alice. That, to me, says that our emotions are
not of the transitory nature, and although I'm aware we

are both going into this with only limited knowledge of each other's foibles and habits, I am confident that we will be able to work out any issues, and have a long and happy life together. I wouldn't have asked you to spend your life with me if I thought otherwise."

I leaned across the sink to kiss him. "That has to be the nicest thing anyone has ever said to me."

He leered. "I have quite a few other things I could say, but they would result in us returning to the bed that we just left, and since you are insisting on visiting Würzburg and the Bishops' Residenz, I shall forgo further commentary until a more appropriate time."

"Hey, it's an honest-to-Pete baroque palace. Of course I want to see it. I mean, how often do you have a chance to do that? Is Gunner going to be joining us?"

"He asked to, but if you'd prefer that he not, I can tell him to take himself elsewhere."

"No, I don't mind having him with us. He's nice, and he's going to be family, and since he's waiting for the all clear to do his covert activities . . ." I let the sentence go, hoping Elliott would fill me in on just what exactly Gunner was doing, but damn his circumspect self, he simply said something noncommittal and sat down at the laptop to check his e-mail.

Gunner was waiting for us when we left the ship. Unfortunately, so was Patrick . . . and Deidre.

Laura hurried across the gangplank as we greeted Elliott's brother.

"I'm so sorry," she said in a rush to me, gesturing toward Deidre. "That's your ex, isn't it? He tried to get on board the ship last night, but Tiffany ran him off, unfortunately *after* he had time to chat with Deidre. We were supposed to be taking the optional Romantic Road tour, but once Deidre chatted up your ex, she changed her mind, so here we are." She made an apologetic gesture.

"I should have known that my two most favorite people would manage to band together in their attempt to be annoying," I told her in soft sarcasm before introducing her to Gunner. "This is Elliott's brother. You know, the one I told you about."

She blinked, holding out a hand, which he took. "I hope Alice had only nice things to say about me. I'm a wonderful person, really. Charming, some might also say charismatic, intelligent—"

"Modest," Elliott said, taking my hand, and leading me down yet another cobblestone street to where the bus to the palace waited.

"I hope you don't mind that your boyfriend and I tag along, dear," Deidre said, falling into step next to me. "We met last night, and dear Patrick's plight plucked at my heartstrings. How you can resist such a handsome, erudite man is beyond me."

"Just wait till you get to know him," I said, shooting Patrick a look filled with ire. He blew me a kiss. "Then you'll understand."

Tiffany was waiting for us at the bus. The Japanese group was already on board, but I noticed that Anthony and Dahl were not.

"They went on to Rothenburg," Tiffany answered when I asked about them. "Something about there being more tourists to chat with." She then turned to Patrick and said, "Sir, I believe you are on the wrong bus. This vehicle is for the Manny van Bris tours only. You'll find public transportation across the square."

"Oh, he's all right," Deidre said, pulling Patrick past

Tiffany, who had blocked the aisle. "He's Alice's boy-friend."

"No, he's not," I said, and took a seat toward the back. Elliott sat next to me.

"I used t'be," Patrick objected.

"Used to isn't worth squat. Feel free to kick him off, Tiffany. He has nothing to do with me."

"I like that! If it wasn't for me, you'd never have met Elliott!"

"And just who are *you*?" Tiffany had turned when Gunner entered the bus.

He smiled and offered her a couple of twenty-euro notes. "I believe my brother asked if I could accompany you? He said this should cover the costs of my inclusion in the tour."

"Oh, yes, that's all right," Tiffany said with a sniff. She took the money and stuffed it into a pocket before turning back to Patrick. "I'm sorry, sir, but you will have to leave."

"He gets to go," Patrick said, pointing to Gunner, who had taken a seat across from us. "Why can't I?"

"Mr. Ainslie made arrangements for the inclusion of his brother last night. No such arrangements were made for you, sir."

Patrick whipped out his wallet and dangled a few notes in front of her. "I'm sure that was just an oversight on Alice's part."

"It's nothing to do with me," I said loudly, making shooing gestures. "Boot him off the bus!"

"Deidre, then," Patrick said, pulling out another wad of money.

Tiffany looked annoyed, but she jerked the money

from his fingers with a terse, "Very well, just this once I will make an allowance, but you must not bother any of the rightful passengers. Take your seats, please. We will commence our tour to the famed ornate Bishops' Residenz, which you must know is one of Germany's biggest palaces, and is in fact a UNESCO World Heritage site."

"You think we can break away from the others and see the palace on our own?" I asked Elliott while Tiffany droned on tossing out dry facts and figures.

"We can certainly try. I'd like to get Gunner alone so we can tell him our news."

"Really?"

Elliott looked surprised at my question. "Did you think I wasn't going to mention it to him?"

"Well . . ." I made a noncommittal gesture. "Kind of. I thought maybe you would give it a bit of time before you mentioned it to your family, since we haven't known each other for long."

"As I told you earlier, the very fact that I feel so strongly about you should alert my family that something extraordinary has happened." He took my hand, giving it a little squeeze that warmed me through and through. "Are you worried that you won't receive a welcome reception from them?"

"Honestly?" I thought about it for a moment. "No. But I think we may both be in for a little ribbing."

"Ribbing I can take," he said, nodding when Tiffany pointed at something out the window. "But you should have no fear that our marriage will meet with any objection. My mother will be thrilled beyond words."

That I would wait to see, but I didn't voice that opinion to Elliott.

The rest of the trip out to the palace was spent listening to Tiffany. We did manage to lose her once we had toured the (huge and incredibly ornate) palace, and were released to wander around on our own. Elliott, Gunner, and I made a beeline for the gardens, handily ditching the others so that we could have a little privacy.

"This place is so incredible," I said, snapping a picture of a particularly lovely fountain. "It's like a dream, it's so perfect. I can almost picture a carriage rolling up the drive, and a woman in a long, flowing dress running out to greet her returning lord."

"You have quite the imagination, don't you?" Gunner asked with a smile.

"Yes, but even you have to admit that this place is the epitome of romance." I gestured toward the massive structure behind us. "I'm surprised they haven't made a bunch of period movies here."

"Speaking of romance," Elliott said, taking my hand. "We have something to tell you."

"Oh?" Gunner looked up from where he was fiddling with his camera. His eyes widened. "You don't mean—"

"Yes. Actually, yes and more. I've asked Alice to marry me. She said yes."

"Marry you?" Now Gunner looked dumbfounded. Thankfully, that changed almost immediately to delight. "You're not joking, are you? What am I saying? You never joke around like that. You're really engaged?"

"Yes," I said, then laughed when he whooped and crushed me in a bear hug. "I'm glad that you, at least, aren't going to flip us any crap about getting together so quickly."

"Oh, I'm going to rag Elliott for years about that, but it doesn't mean I'm not delighted." He hugged Elliott, who socked him on the shoulder. "Fancy you two finding each other like this. It's definitely like something out of one of El's books."

"Hardly," Elliott said with a wry twist to his mouth. "Not unless Alice turns out to be a secret agent, and shoots us both to escape with a bag full of priceless jewels. Or cocaine. Or, for that matter, illegal arms."

"I promise I won't do any of that." I kissed Elliott on his nose, so happy I felt as if I could burst.

"You have to let me marry you," Gunner said suddenly, an expression of joy on his face. "Please, El, you know I've always wanted to marry someone ever since I was ordained."

I gawked at him. "You're a minister?"

"No, he's not," Elliott said with a long-suffering look.

"Don't listen to him, he's a nonbeliever. I'm duly ordained by the Church of Jante."

"The who now?"

"It's an Internet religion," Elliott said, tugging me away, his fingers laced through mine as we strolled through the impressive gardens. "It's not real, and he can't marry people."

"Of course I can, although you are recommended to follow up with a civil ceremony, just in case the government refuses to recognize my authority. I could officiate at your wedding ceremony, and then you can slip out to the registrar's office afterward and take care of any remaining legalities."

"That's actually a very cool idea," I said, thinking that there was no better way to be welcomed into Elliott's family than to have his brother marry us. "We could have the ceremony at your castle!"

"That is not at all a good idea," Elliott said over the top of Gunner's enthusiastic agreement.

"Why not?"

"Because the Ainslie Castle is in the middle of being restored. One entire wing is off-limits since parts of it have crumbled, and the rest of it is receiving much-needed structural work to keep it from falling down. We could hardly host the sort of ceremony you're thinking of. A visit to the registrar's office sounds appropriate, though. We'll have to review the laws regarding an American-English marriage once we get home."

My joy dimmed somewhat. "But your castle would be so romantic. I can't imagine a woman alive who wouldn't want to be married there."

"It's just not viable, Alice. I'm sorry. If you like, we can look for some other stately home venue in which to hold the wedding, although I hesitate to point out that such places tend to be rather expensive. . . ."

"I have it!" Gunner said with a snap of his fingers. "We'll marry you here."

"Here in Germany? Wouldn't it be harder, legally speaking, for an American and an Englishman to marry here than it would in England, where at least one of us is a citizen?"

"Nonsense. I've seen the marriage application form that churchofjante.com states must be filled out in order to have a marriage officiated, and there is no occupancy requirement. Citizenship, yes, but you don't need to live in the location where I marry you." He waved an arm encompassing all of the grounds. "You wanted a castle for your wedding backdrop—how about one of the grandest examples in all of Europe?"

"Your Internet ordination is hardly going to be viewed by the Germans as legal—," Elliott started to protest.

"No more so than in England, I agree, and more fools

they are." He whomped his brother on the arm. "That's why you follow up with a civil ceremony when you get home. And bonus for your thrifty ways: you could take the rest of the tour as your honeymoon. There's, what, a week left?"

"Oooh," I said, starting to like this idea more and more. "That would be awesome. Some people might think it's a bit odd having the honeymoon before the legal ceremony, but I've never been overly concerned about things like that. How about it, Elliott? Do you want to marry me in one of the most romantic spots on earth?"

Elliott was at a loss for words, and I realized that he was truly flabbergasted by the idea.

"OK, time-out," I told Gunner, taking Elliott by the hand and heading for a small group of topiaries. "I think I need to speak to the groom alone."

"You do that," Gunner said, nodding. "I'll run up to the castle office and see if I can print out a copy of the marriage application. I'll need you to fill that out before I can marry you. This is going to be excellent, most excellent!"

I waited until we were out of earshot of the other tourists before I turned to Elliott and said, "The whole idea of a marriage here has you freaked out, hasn't it?"

"It's not that I don't want to marry you," he said quickly, pulling me up for a quick kiss. "I don't want you thinking that at all. But this . . . it's no more than playacting, really. Gunner isn't really a minister. Any marriage he officiates would just be an agreement between us, and nothing more."

"If you come right down to it," I pointed out, "that's all that marriage really is, isn't it? All the legal stuff is a way for governments to recognize a joining of two people, and if we plan on doing that later anyway, I don't see that there's a difference between Gunner marrying us here and Gunner marrying us a day before we go sign a marriage license in England."

His eyes were shaded, but I could clearly read doubt in them. "But this would be your wedding. Don't you wish to have your family and friends attending?"

"Believe it or not, when Patrick and I were going to get married in Budapest—man, I can't believe I even wanted to do something so stupid—all we were going to do was to say our own vows, toss some flowers into the river, and then go to the registrar's office. So if you're asking if I'll miss the white dress, and bridesmaids, and flowers, and a huge expensive wedding that would make everyone insane, the answer is no. I'd far rather stand here in this dress and marry you right here and now. But it's not all about me, Elliott. This would be your wedding, too, and if you'd rather have your mom and all your brothers and sisters and friends, then I will have no problem whatsoever telling Gunner that we're going to wait."

He hesitated, and I knew that I'd have to give up my dream of being married at a castle.

"It's all right," I told him, giving his lower lip a swift lick. "We'll find somewhere cheap and romantic in England to get married."

"No, Alice, I—" He stopped, his brow furrowed. "I don't know how to say what I want to say. It's most infuriating. I'm a writer, for god's sake. I should be able to put words together in a manner that is understandable."

The poor guy really looked like I had pulled the rug out from under him. I took pity on his obvious need to reassure me. "Maybe I can help. Is it marrying me that you object to?"

"Christ, no. I want to marry you. You know that."

"OK, is it being married without your family? Does that bother you?"

"Not particularly, no. Like you, I've never been a fan of large ceremonies." He gave a little shudder. "Especially ones where I was expected to be the focus of attention. And as for my family—they would be just as happy with a party thrown after the fact. Probably more so, since less decorum will be expected."

"I love that you're such an introvert," I said. "All right, then, is it getting married in Germany?"

"No, it's not that—"

"Is it the spur-of-the-moment aspect?"

"You have to admit it is very spontaneous." He rubbed the bridge of his nose. "But I am trying, for your sake, to go with the flow. I would be quite happy to marry you today if it could be arranged."

"Is it Gunner? You don't want your brother being the officiant? Did you want him for your best man, instead?"

"I would have him for a best man, naturally, but I also like the idea of him officiating, if only—" He stopped again.

"Gotcha. It's the fact that it's not a legal ceremony."

"It just seems . . ." He made a vague gesture. "It's so . . . unstructured."

"If we made our wedding vows in bulleted lists, would that help?" I asked.

He laughed, and hugged me despite the fact that a family was strolling past. "It might. Don't listen to me, Alice, I'm a fool, and we both know it. If you wish to be married right here, right now, in what clothes we have on, and with what friends we have around us, then I would be honored and grateful and blessed to the ends of my days."

"You're sure?" I asked, nibbling his chin just a little before letting go of him. "No regrets? Patrick and Deidre are bound to show up for it."

A look of satisfaction spread across his face. "I have to admit that is a bonus I hadn't considered. Very well, we'll do it. But I will want us to be married again in England as soon as we can arrange it."

"Deal," I said, and shook his hand.

Which is why, diary mine, approximately an hour and twenty minutes later, Elliott and I stood in a semicircle comprised of Izumi, Megumi, the Japanese schoolgirls, Tiffany, Laura, Deidre, and a resigned Patrick.

The last actually surprised me—I thought he'd be a bit more surly, or even hurt that I was marrying his friend after such a short period of acquaintance—but I suspect that he had finally realized that we really weren't meant to be together.

"Do you have vows you would like to speak to each other?" Gunner asked.

"Yes, we have prepared some," Elliott said, all businesslike, just like he was testifying in court.

I buried my face in the clump of silk flowers that Laura had plucked from a garish tourist hat, and tried not to giggle out loud.

"Would you care to speak your vows?" Gunner asked me.

"Certainly." I could do the dignified mien as well as Elliott. I handed my bouquet to Laura, and pulled out two slips of paper, giving one to Elliott. "Here is a copy for your records."

Elliott smiled, looking down at the paper I had handed to him. My vows were, indeed, bulleted.

I took a deep breath, and took his hands in mine. His eyes were warm, like liquid silver, and filled with so much love that I almost broke down. "I, Alice Little Wood, do solemnly swear in the presence of these, our friends and fellow travelers, to cherish you, and trust you, and think about your needs, and love you to the end of our days. I promise not to bother you when you're working, unless it's a matter of life or death, and I promise not to make you wear silly hats unless you are willing to do so, and I promise to be there when you need me. I promise that even when I don't agree with what you say, I'll always listen."

"Oh, that is lovely," Laura said, applauding lightly.

Deidre rolled her eyes and looked pointedly at her watch. "Is this about over? There are several other things I'd rather be doing."

"And Elliott?" Gunner nudged his brother.

"My vows are not written down," Elliott said, kissing each of my hands. "Except on my heart."

"Aww," Laura said.

I sniffled happily.

"They are simply I love you, and I want to be with you for all the days that remain to me." He paused. "And that I honestly cannot think of my life without you in it. For those reasons, I take you as my wife."

My lip quivered. "That is so romantic," I told him, fighting to keep from flinging myself upon him right then and there. "No one has ever said anything like that to me."

"I did," Patrick said, raising his hand. "Well, something similar. Somewhat. Without all the frills."

We ignored him.

"Since you have both decided to forgo rings—"

"Only for the present," Elliott interrupted, rubbing his thumbs over the backs of my fingers. "We'll have them for the civil ceremony."

Tears pricked hard and hot behind my eyes. I was marrying him! It was the single most romantic moment in my life!

"Then by the authority granted to me via the Church of Jante (churchofjante.com), I pronounce you brother and wife." Gunner beamed at us. "You may snog the wits right out of the bride."

The group (minus Deidre and Patrick) cheered as Elliott proceeded to do just that. "We're married," I said as soon as I got my lips back from him, laughing with the sheer joy of the moment. "We're really married!"

"Well . . . ," Elliott started to say.

"Don't be so pedantic. It'll ruin everyone's fun." I turned my back to our group, saying as I did so, "Time to throw the hat flower bouquet!"

I flung the clump of silk flowers. Deidre almost dislocated Laura's shoulder when she thrust her out of the way to grab the bouquet.

"So," the former said, sauntering over to Elliott, and giving him her Cheshire cat smile. "You've had a make-believe wedding. . . . Would you like to try a pretend divorce?"

I laughed. I couldn't help it—life was just too good to let people like Deidre rain on our parade.

Chapter 11

Expense Account
   Item one: two hundred eighty-nine pounds
   Remarks: plane ticket
   Item two: six thousand, four hundred, twenty-two pounds
   Remarks: Why wasn't Jane born first, and male, so the expenses of the estate fall to her?

"So, you're a married man now." Gunner sipped appreciatively at the champagne for which Elliott had splurged. Music from the ship's lounge stereo system blasted out tunes that Tiffany had assured him would be danceable, yet dignified. Thus far, all Elliott had heard were swing tunes and a few fifties oldies, but that didn't stop the members of the ship from dancing as if they were at an elite club. The schoolgirls were dancing in a group with Anthony and Dahl, while Deidre was grinding against the bartender, who had abandoned his duties with fervor.

"Mum will be thrilled. She'll expect your first child in exactly nine months."

"She can expect all she wants; I'm not going to rush Alice into anything. Lord knows the courtship has been conducted in fast-forward speed. And with all due respect to your so-called religion, I won't consider us truly married until we have a proper marriage certificate."

"You have one from me, duly signed and sealed with a bit of the wax that man from the palace business office lent me. I thought that gave the document a nice touch. You can't go wrong with a royal seal on wax."

"We aren't royal, it wasn't the Ainslie seal, and your marriage certificate isn't recognized by the British government," Elliott couldn't help but point out. Around them, the denizens of the ship danced, ate the appetizers that were part of the midnight buffet, and drank champagne, all in celebration of his earlier nuptials. His gaze went immediately to where Alice was chatting with Laura, the former's laughter floating above the thumping of the music.

He had married her—in a manner of speaking—and she stood there glowing with happiness. He had done that. He had given her that glow. It was a heady feeling, one that was mingled with intense sexual desire, and the satisfying knowledge that he loved, and was loved in return. Yes, it may have been a heedless act to propose—and marry—a woman without knowing her for a more reasonable length of time, but all that paled in view of Alice and her glow. She was like a beacon, calling him to her, drawing him in until he could warm himself in her light.

"Yes, but look at it this way—" Gunner interrupted his thoughts by thumping him on the chest. "Now you can have honeymoon sex."

"There is that," Elliott admitted, his trousers growing tight as he contemplated the joys of marriage. "Not that we've had any issue in that arena, but I will admit that there is something about the thought of being on a honeymoon that appeals."

"Frankly, I'm surprised you didn't drag her back to the ship immediately after the ceremony and get down to it," Gunner said with blithe insouciance. "I know I would have."

"I had to arrange for you to travel with us to Nuremberg. That took some time, not to mention money. Speaking of which, you owe me thirty quid for your passage."

"Ouch. That's a bit stiff, isn't it? I could have gotten a train for less than half of that."

"You wanted to travel with us for the six hours it takes to sail to Nuremberg—that's what it cost. You didn't hear Patrick complaining about it, did you?"

Gunner looked over to where Patrick was slouched on a barstool, chatting up one of the schoolteachers. "What the hell is he doing here? I reckoned he'd have left after you married Alice."

"He says that Jane made a scene when he called her this evening, and that she'd thrown his things out of their rented flat, so he was at a loose end."

"Good for Jane, although if that means you have Patrick hanging around your neck like a human-sized albatross, then perhaps we should talk her into taking him back."

"That's not likely. You know what Jane's like."

"True." Gunner drained his glass and set it down on the bar. "Well," he said, smoothing back his hair. "If you're not going to dance with the bride, then I surely am."

Elliott shoved his glass of cranberry juice at his brother. "Don't even think about it."

Gunner laughed. "Why you aren't in your cabin right now enjoying the benefits of marriage is beyond my understanding."

"The boat will dock in two more hours. Alice thought it would be rude if we disappeared before then, since you had come along for the celebration."

Gunner gave him a long look.

"You're right. We can see you any time. It's time to reap what I have sown." Elliott skirted the dancers, putting his arm around Alice in a way that was both satisfying and tantalizing. She was his now, truly his, every odd little quirk of her mind, every delicious curve of her body, every inch of that silken skin. His wife, his lover, his charming, wonderful woman.

"So, we've been married for four hours now. What do you think?" Alice whispered in his ear. She smelled of flowers and lime (from her beverage of choice), a heady mix that went straight to his loins.

"You're mine," his mouth said before his brain could regulate such acts.

Alice stared at him. Laura laughed, and murmured something about leaving them alone. She moved off to chat with Gunner, who promptly dragged her onto the dance floor.

"You didn't just say that?" Alice finally said.

"I did. I don't know why I did, but I did. I apologize for it, nonetheless. It was an aberration. Some deep, primitive part of my mind was rejoicing in you, and that's how it was vocalized."

"Hmm." She sniffed the air. "Did you have some of that champagne?"

"No, of course not. I wouldn't be able to kiss you if I had, and you, madam wife, are going to be in for some quality kissing tonight. Now, would you like to dance, visit the buffet table for a light snack which will allow you to keep up the strength you are going to need later for all of the aforementioned kissing, or stroll on deck and enjoy the romantic moonlit evening?"

"Shouldn't we stay here? The party is for us, after all, and Gunner and Patrick paid to be here."

"We were just pretend married, so—"

She pinched his side.

"Er . . . we were just married, so no, I don't think anyone will think anything if we escape early."

"Good point. In that case . . ." She bit her lip. He wanted very much to do the same to that adorable lip. "I think if we're not going to be sociable, then I'd rather jump your bones."

"I like how you think, Lady Ainslie."

She stared at him just as if he'd turned into a turnip. "What did you call me?"

"Lady Ainslie. I would say that you won't be able to use the title until we are legally married, but I'm afraid you'd just tell me I was ruining the illusion, so I have gone with the flow. You may express your appreciation of such thoughtfulness by tormenting my poor man's body in ways that will ensure neither of us sleeps until dawn has stretched her rosy fingers across the sky."

"Oh my god," she said, still staring at him. "I'm a lady! Just like Lady Cora on *Downton Abbey*! She was American, too, and she married this English lord and became Lady Cora. And I'm the same thing. Holy Moses, I'm a real lady. Lady Alice! My friends are going to *crap their pants*!"

"I'm very happy to tell you that your friends need not go to any such lengths to prove their amazement," he said, delighted with her even more than he had been a few seconds before. He never knew from one moment to the next what was going to come out of her mouth. "The correct title will be Lady Ainslie. I'm afraid you won't be able to be Lady Alice unless your father was an earl or duke."

"Still," she said, giving him another pinch. "You're a baron, and that's going to floor them."

He took her arm, and escorted her from the lounge, asking, "Did you really forget that fact?"

"Would you be offended if I said that I kind of keep doing that? It's not that I'm making light of your heritage or anything, but barons are so ... I don't know. British upper-crust sort of thing, like a story by P. G. Wodehouse."

"Or *Downton Abbey*?"

"Exactly!" She took his hand, rubbing her thumb over his palm in a way that had him suddenly breaking out in a sweat. He didn't ever remember wanting a woman as much as he wanted her, and she was quasi-legally his to enjoy. "I mean, I know you're a baron and you have a castle, but it's kind of like ... I don't know, it's kind of like you being Lord Largeloins."

"I thought I was the Earl of Erogenous?"

"That, too. It's a fun thing to think about, but you are more than that, if you know what I mean. You're ... Elliott. Just Elliott, without all those trappings." She gave him a crooked smile, one that was endearingly shy and uncertain. "I like plain old Elliott. The rest is fun, but I'm glad that underneath it all, you're you. I hope that doesn't offend you, because I mean it in a nice way."

He took her into his arms right there in front of their

cabin door. "My darling wife, I can assure you that as someone who's been seen and sought for his title alone, your words are quite simply the greatest compliment I have ever received."

Her lips were warm and welcoming, and the fact that it took him several tries to open their door gave testament to the fact of just how distracting she was. At last he got it opened, though, and escorted her into their little sanctum.

"You say that like you've never been complimented before," she said, sitting on the bed and kicking off her sandals. "And yet, you've won an award for your books. It's on the cover of the one you have next to your laptop."

"That," he said, picking up her foot, and kissing her anklebone, an act that gave him a delightful view along the length of her leg, "was the merest trifle compared to your words."

"Jealous!" she said, offering her other leg. Obligingly, he kissed that ankle, as well, stroking his hand up her bare calf. "And I'm glad you're not offended, because I meant every word, although I think you're letting the mood of the day exaggerate your feelings a wee bit. You must have received accolades in other areas."

He stopped kissing his way up her calf to look up at her. "Such as?"

She wiggled her toes. "Well . . . like your . . . you know. Abilities."

"Sexual?" Dear lord, would he ever come to know what she was going to say next? He fervently hoped not. "I've never had any complaints, but to my best knowledge, I've never received an award for my sexual prowess."

"No, not that, although god knows you deserve it." She gave him a steamy look that faded into one that he could only classify as coy. "I meant your other abilities. Your . . . covert abilities."

Now what was she talking about? "Covert in what way?"

She slapped her hands on the bed. "You're going to make me say it right out loud, aren't you? OK, we're married—almost completely married—so I'll just say it. Your espionage abilities, Elliott. You must be highly thought of in that area or else you wouldn't be so successful."

Ah, she was talking of his books. No doubt she had a touch of the same awe that some of his fans had. He never understood it himself, but he was flattered that she viewed his ability to write a detailed and intricate thriller plot with such admiration. "That's very sweet of you, but that doesn't have anything to do with us, right here and now, and that, my fair little squab, is what I'd like to concentrate on. Is your other calf jealous, too? Ought I pay it my respects before proceeding forward, or do your thighs yearn for me the same way I want them?"

"Oh, they yearn, man do they yearn!"

"Good. I like them yearning." He slid his hands up both legs, and was about to spread kisses everywhere he could reach when she sat up.

"I think this is officially my turn, Elliott."

He looked at her thighs, her delicious, tempting thighs. "But, your thighs," he protested. "You just said they yearn for me."

"And they do." She scooted off the bed, giving his ass a pat in the process. "But a turn is a turn, and it's mine, which means I get to tell you what I want to do, and right now, I want you naked and on your back. I'm just going to brush my teeth, because that smoked salmon appetizer has left my breath a bit fishy, and there's nothing that kills romance faster than salmon breath." She winked at him and disappeared into the bathroom.

"Which makes me all the more thankful that I don't care for salmon," he said, about to remove his clothing. He thought for a moment, then dug through his shaving kit until he found a small tin of cinnamon mints, popping one in his mouth. He was just unbuttoning his shirt when his phone buzzed against his hip.

"You are going off for the night," he said, fishing it out of his pocket, fully intending to suit action to word, but once he caught a look at the text that had just come in, his whole body froze for about five seconds.

West tower collapsed, read the text from his brother Dixon—who acted as steward to the estate. *Workman injured. No deaths so far, but not out of woods yet. Liability will be huge. Talking to lawyer in morning. Will update you when I know more.*

He had the phone up to his ear before he even realized that he had punched Dixon's number. "How bad is it?" he said when Dix answered the phone.

"Well . . ." Dixon hesitated, obviously not wanting to ruin his vacation.

"Out with it. Do I need to come home?"

"I don't want to tell you to do that." Dixon's voice told the whole story, however.

"But it would be better if I was there?" Elliott was almost sick to his stomach. "What exactly happened?"

"A couple of the workmen were storing lumber near the tower. Three of them were shifting some of it when the lower section of the tower just gave way. It brought the entire thing down on them."

"Oh, Christ," Elliott swore, his stomach turning over at the thought of it. "No one was killed?"

"No, but two of them are having surgery right now. The doctors aren't saying much about their odds one way or the other. The third managed to get away with just a broken leg, and some superficial injuries."

"I should have torn that entire wing down," Elliott said, regret filling him like bitter poison. "Why the hell did I leave it up?"

"You weren't to know it was going to come down like that. Richardson said that he could repair it just as he's doing the rest of the castle. Elliott, this isn't your fault."

"Perhaps not, but I could have prevented it." He thought for a moment. "Why was anyone near the tower? We blocked off access to the entire wing just in case something like this happened."

Dixon didn't say anything for a few seconds. "Mum complained about having all of the material where it could be seen by the tourists, and asked them to move it where it was out of the way. You know how Richardson is around her."

Elliott knew. One of the reasons he had chosen Richardson for the restoration for the castle was that he was willing to give them a reasonable price—and that was due to the man's interest in Elliott's mother. "Christ, Dix."

"I know." His brother's voice sounded as devastated as he felt. "I'll be talking to the insurance people tomorrow, but if the worst happens . . ."

Elliott closed his eyes for a few seconds. He wasn't a praying man, but he sent fervent good wishes to the poor men who'd been injured. "I'll get a flight out of here."

"I really hate to throw this on your lap when you're trying to get some work done—"

"That's not what's important right now," Elliott said,

clamping the phone between his ear and shoulder while pulling clothing from the dresser and placing it into his open bag. "I'll text you my arrival time. Keep me updated on how the workmen are doing."

"Will do. Sorry, El."

"It's not your fault."

"No more than it is yours, but if I had known what Mum was doing—well, we'll deal with that later."

Elliott hung up, his mind shoving aside the emotions of the situation to deal with the facts. He had to get a flight out of Nuremberg. He had to inform his publisher that there would likely be a delay in the book, which would throw their schedule out of whack, but he couldn't help that.

A lilting voice bursting into song in the bathroom had him shaking himself. Alice! He had Alice to think about, as well. What was she going to say when she found out that his negligence had injured innocent people? He wanted to hide that fact from her, like it was a shameful secret, but he knew that he'd have to tell her in the end. If she damned him for it . . . He shook his head. He couldn't cope with that right now. Later, once he had a chance to assess just how bad the situation was, once he had seen the injured men himself, and talked to Richardson, then he would explain to Alice what had happened. Until then, he'd have to trust that she was so madly in love with him that she'd forgive him running off on their wedding night.

He had just finished booking a flight that left in three hours, summoned Gunner to his cabin, and quickly explained the situation by the time Alice emerged from the bathroom.

"Now, about my thighs and their desperate need for

your thighs—," Alice started to say, coming to an abrupt halt when she caught sight of not only Gunner standing in the middle of the cabin but Elliott packing his laptop into its bag. "Um?"

Elliott exchanged glances with Gunner, who murmured something about checking with the captain about when they'd be docking at Nuremberg.

"What's going on?" Alice asked, watching Gunner leave. She was clad in a towel and little else, but even the sight of all that smooth, enticing flesh couldn't distract him from his purpose.

"Alice, something's come up, a situation that requires my attention immediately. I can't give you any details about it just yet—I will, as soon as I can—but I'm going to have to leave as soon as we get to Nuremberg." He took her arms in his hands, caressing the soft flesh with a need that was almost painful. "I don't want to go, but I must. I know you're thinking the very worst things possible about me, but I assure you that I will make it up to you just as soon as I can."

To his surprise, she was silent, her eyes searching his for the count of seven before she finally said, "I don't think anything bad about you, Elliott. This whole business—" She waved her hand. "It's part of you. It's part of who you are, and I know that. I accept that about you. I just don't— I just don't want you to get hurt."

"I don't deserve you," he said, pulling her close until he could kiss her face, her cheeks, her eyelids, and her adorable little nose. "I truly don't, but I'll be thankful to the day I die that I found you."

"Just so long as that day isn't any time in the near future," she said into his collar. She hugged him with a ferocity that surprised him. They stood there for a few minutes, just holding each other, him breathing in her scent, wishing like hell he didn't have to be the responsible one, and that he could shirk it all just to remain in her arms.

"Promise me you won't do anything dangerous," she said once she released him.

He smiled down at her, every bit of him warmed in the knowledge that she loved him, she truly loved him. "I won't do anything stupid, I assure you. I have a wedding night to look forward to."

"Damn straight. How long is this . . . mission . . . going to take?"

He stuffed the few remaining notes on his book into the laptop case, and glanced around the cabin, looking for anything he'd left behind. If they arrived in Nuremberg in the next hour, he could get a cab to the airport, and be in London by dawn. Two hours by train and he'd be in Ainston. . . . "Hmm? Oh, there won't be time to come back to the ship, I'm afraid. Can you come to England once the tour is over, or do you have to return to the States first?"

"You expect me to stay on the tour?" she said, toying with the edge of her towel. Her worried expression made it clear she wasn't doing so to entice him.

"There's no reason for you to leave it now. There's still six days left. . . . If you can come to me after that, I'll have the situation in hand. At least, I hope I will. I'll call or text you if I don't, but I can't imagine that I wouldn't be able to receive you by then."

"All right." She sat down on the edge of the bed and watched him shake out his jacket. "It won't be much fun without you, but . . . well, as I said, I know you have a job to do."

There was a tap on the door. He opened it to find Gunner.

"We're coming in to Nuremberg early," Gunner said, his expression grim. "We should dock in the next few minutes. I told them that you have to leave. Did you get a flight?"

"Yes." Elliott shoved his suitcase at his brother, slinging the strap of his laptop case across his chest before returning to Alice. He knelt, his hands on her bare knees. "You are one in a million, Alice Wood."

"Ainslie," she said sadly, trying to give him a smile, but failing.

He felt bad about the way he was running out on her, but didn't feel it was fair to drag her into the mess before he knew just how bad it was. Once he had evaluated the situation, and dealt with the worst of it, he'd be ready to bring her home, to introduce her to the family, and to her new life.

"Lady Ainslie." He kissed her hands, wanting to do more, but knowing if he did, he wouldn't be able to stop. "*My* lady. I do love you, Alice. More than I can express at this moment, and not nearly as much as you deserve, but I want you around every day of my life."

"Except for situations like this," she said with a forlorn smile, brushing a strand of hair back off his forehead. "Stop looking like you've just been asked to do something heinous to a baby seal, and go do it so that we can get back to the Earl of Erogenous, and his wife's needy thighs."

He kissed her hands again and, without another word, left the cabin. Already his mind was racing ahead to what needed to be done. He'd pick up his passport from

Tiffany, then head straight to the airport. En route to England, he'd place calls to the Ainston Hospital, his solicitor, the insurance man, and Richardson. By the time he landed, he hoped to at least understand exactly what he had to deal with. . . .

Chapter 12

Diary of Alice Wood

Day Five or something. Six? No, Five.

"Where's comrade Elliott?" Anthony asked the following morning, when we both stood at the breakfast buffet waiting our turn at the fruit compote. He leaned close to speak, catching a good look down my sleeveless tunic in the process. "Dare one make a comment about wedding-night activities, and grooms too exhausted to get out of bed the following morning?"

"Why do you pretend you're gay?" I asked him in an equally hushed tone.

His jaw sagged for a minute before the edges of his mouth curled. "What do you mean? Dahl is quite clearly my partner. We live together in London. We share a bed here on this ship. We have excellent fashion sense."

"Stereotype much?"

"It seemed called for." He gave a little shrug. "Perhaps what you are interpreting as heterosexuality is merely curiosity. Perhaps in you I've found a woman who makes me question my life choices. Perhaps I wish to see what it is I'm missing and simply want to know if in you I might find someone who shares a desire to learn all there is to learn, to try all that is available, to experience all that—"

"Bullshit," I interrupted rudely. "You and Dahl may live together, you may even share a bed. For all I know, you even have sex. But if so, you're not exclusively gay, because I've seen you look down four different women's shirts, one of which was an underage schoolgirl. So you can just stop the 'why don't you have sex with me so I can see if I'm not gay anymore' strategy, because it's not going to fly with me."

"Comrade," he said, drawing away from me with a wounded look. "You misunderstand my motives. Grossly misunderstand them. I am an equal opportunity lover. So if you are, in fact, less than fulfilled by comrade Elliott, I will be happy to entertain you. I take it he's recovering from the nuptials?"

"As a matter of fact, he's not. He had an emergency at home, and he had to return there immediately." I had decided on that explanation as being suitably vague, which would cover all bases with the fellow passengers without blowing Elliott's cover.

Anthony's eyebrows rose. "I hope it is nothing serious."

"Not at all. Elliott's very responsible, though, and he felt he had to be home to help his family." I eyed Anthony for a few seconds. He seemed oddly disconcerted by the news that Elliott was gone, almost distracted. "You're not going to tell me that you have the hots for him, too?"

Anthony looked amused, and for a tiny fraction of a second, I felt like I was seeing a different Anthony. That sensation was gone almost instantly when he leered at me and said, "Your husband? Would that turn you off if I was? I know some ladies enjoy a little man-on-man action." He gave me a roguish wink. "Don't tell me you're interested in a threesome so soon in married life?"

"We're back to that, huh? No, I'm not interested in having sex with anyone but Elliott, and while we're on the subject, I'd advise you to keep away from those schoolgirls. No one likes a lecher, but especially when they ogle kids."

"Indeed." He gave me a little bow. "Such advice is worth its weight in gold. If you will excuse me, I believe Dahl wishes to speak with me about interviewing some tourists in Nuremberg."

He moved off, leaving me to scoop up some fruit, toss a fresh croissant onto my plate, and take a seat at Deidre and Laura's table, which was pleasantly Deidre-free at the moment.

"I'm going to make absolutely no comment about how happy you look this morning, lest it turn ribald," Laura told me around a mouthful of toast. There was a wicked glint in her eye, nonetheless. "I will simply say that you look well, and assume that means that married life agrees with you."

I sighed, and stuffed one of the croissant's arms into my mouth. Around it, I said, "Any ribald comment would be welcome if it was grounded in fact, but alas, married life at this moment is rather lonely."

"Lonely?" A spoon of yogurt wavered in front of her face. "Why lonely?"

"Elliott left as soon as we docked in Nuremberg last

night." I took a quick look around, but no one was paying us any attention. "He had business to attend to."

"What sort of business ... oh!" She raised her eyebrows in mute question.

I nodded. "Some sort of an emergency, I gather. And he took Gunner with him. I think. I know they both left at the same time. I told you about Gunner, right?"

"About his being in the same business? Yes. I wonder what took them so urgently? I listened to BBC radio this morning, and didn't hear anything about a foreign crisis. You don't have any idea where he went?"

"I didn't think it was right to ask him. You know, he probably swore to keep that sort of thing secret."

"No doubt that's so. You're going to stay on the cruise until he returns? We only have six days left."

"I know, hence the sigh a minute ago." I tore off the second croissant arm, considered whether to slather it with orange marmalade, and, deciding that would be a minor travesty of food-dom, popped it into my mouth. "I'm not going to be one of those needy women who have to have a man at her side in order to have fun, however. There are lots of fun cities coming up, and of course Vienna, which I'm really looking forward to."

"We will see the sights together," she said, patting my arm. "So long as you don't mind Deidre, that is."

"Where is the she-wolf of the Danube?"

"Ah, that is a very good question. She said last night that she was going to have a drink with Patrick—this is after we docked, mind you—and she didn't come back to our cabin."

"Really," I drawled, wanting to say so much more, but being (for perhaps the first time in my life) circumspect. "Well, now. That's interesting."

"Mmhmm. I thought you'd like that. So, what would you like to do today? According to the schedule, we can take the tour to see the Zeppelin Field."

I wrinkled my nose. "Too Nazi for me."

"Yeah, I think I could miss that. How about the Palace of Justice? That's where they held the Nuremberg Trials, so it won't be a happy fun site, but still interesting."

"Eh." I tried to jolly myself out of the self-pity that was threatening to swamp me. I meant what I had said— I didn't need Elliott to have fun. He just made things that much more enjoyable.

"There's the Documentation Center Museum." She looked at me, and shook her head. "How about a ramble through the Old Town area?"

"Don't let me dampen your fun, Laura. I'm just being a big ole pouty-pants today. Why don't you go do whatever you want to do, and I'll wander around a bit, and then maybe curl up with a book."

"If that's what you want." She gave me a searching look. "Just let me know if you suddenly get too down with the loss of Elliott. And do tell me if you hear from him. I can't help but wonder where he's gone to in such a hurry, and if we'll hear about an international incident."

"One would suppose that if he was doing his job right, we wouldn't hear anything," I said absently. A thought had struck me at her words, and I wanted to think about it. I finished breakfast in a hurry and ran back to the cabin, pulling out the journal that did duty as my diary. I flipped back through the pages, rereading select passages. Should I be writing things down about Elliott being a spy? What if someone found my diary? It took an hour (I may have gotten sidetracked with the descriptions of our sexual activities), but at last I reassured myself that I hadn't given anything away about what he was doing, other than the bit about meeting Gunner in Cologne. I ripped out those pages, then walked around the cabin with them in my hand, looking for a safe way to dispose of them.

"Great, I don't smoke, so I don't have a lighter. I can't tear them to shreds and throw them into the river, because someone could tape them back together. Likewise with the toilet. I could eat it, I suppose." I looked at the pages, covered with my loping handwriting. They didn't look in the least bit appetizing. In the end, I folded them up very small, and stuffed them into a tampon package. "That ought to keep anyone from finding them," I said, satisfied.

The remainder of the day passed. It wasn't quick, not that I blamed the town of Nuremberg. I took a solitary walk, and found the Old Town section was sufficiently cute and interesting. I took lots of pictures, but every single one was taken with the view of sharing it with Elliott.

"Damn the man, I'm always thinking about him," I told Laura later that night, as we sailed toward Regensburg.

She laughed. "You've been married a day—obsessing about your new husband is *de rigueur*, I believe."

"Yes, well, I've worked hard to quell my compulsive tendencies, and I don't need to stir them all up by being so focused on him."

"Maybe you just need to talk to him. Why don't you call him?"

"Holy Moses, I never thought of that. Should I? I

mean, what if he's out . . . you know . . . spying." The last word was spoken in a whisper, since others were enjoying the nighttime spectacle of floating down the river in the dark. "I wouldn't want to interrupt him at a vital time."

"He's a professional. I'm sure he knows enough to turn off his phone if he's going to be . . . I don't know, creeping around a warehouse, or interrogating a captured baddie, or sneaking into an embassy, or whatever it is that he's doing. Surely they must teach them things like that."

"You'd think," I agreed, pulling out my phone.

That's when the horrible truth hit me. "Oh no! I don't have his number."

"You don't?"

"No. I never got it. There . . . er . . . wasn't time. Hell's bells."

"Is there someone you can call who has it?"

"Yes, Patrick probably does, but he changed his number after we broke up. Something about too many annoying calls." Briefly, I smiled at the memory. "I don't have his new number, but I bet I know who does."

I looked pointedly at where Deidre sat on the other side of the deck, chatting with Anthony.

"Most likely. I should warn you that you'll likely have to grovel for it. I'd ask her for it, but she's sure to know it's for you, and quite frankly, she's a bit sore about what she calls you spiriting Elliott away."

"Deidre can just bite me," I said under my breath, and slapped a friendly smile onto my face, preparing to do what it took to get Patrick's number out of her.

It took fifteen minutes of pleading (and forty euros), but at last I had Patrick's cell number. I waved the slip of paper upon which I'd written it at Laura, and dashed down to my cabin to make my calls.

"I need Elliott's cell number," I told Patrick a few minutes later.

"You what, now?"

"Don't play games, Patrick, please don't. I'm tired, cranky, and possibly hormonal, so if you could keep the arch comments to yourself and just give me the phone number, I'd be very grateful."

"Why can't you just ask him for it?"

"He had to leave suddenly." I waited for it. It came right as I expected. I waited until he was done laughing and said, with no little amount of acid in my voice, "Got that worked out of your system? Good. Now, can I have the number, please."

"You may, but on one condition."

"I am not going to sleep with you—"

"Such a mind you have! It shows quite clearly that you're not over me as you insist you are, but far be it from me t'point that out. I wasn't going t'demand sex, love. I simply reserve the right t'call Elliott myself and find out what happened."

"I don't care what you do, so long as you give me the number."

He rattled off a number so quickly, I had to have him repeat it. I wrote it down on a page in my diary, then thanked him.

"I can't say that I'll be available long, but if you come t'your senses before Jane realizes what a mistake she made, then feel free t'call me. I'd be very happy t'console you about the breakup of your one-day-old marriage."

I hung up, quickly saving the phone number into my contacts. I stared at it for a moment, then took a deep breath and dialed the number, my fingers crossed that I wasn't disturbing Elliott at a dangerous time.

It rang and rang and rang, and just when I was expecting Elliott's voice mail to kick in, someone said hello.

Someone female.

Visions of suave, sexy female spies danced in my head when I said, "Um. Hello. Could I speak with Elliott, please?"

"I'm afraid Lord Ainslie is being prepped for surgery. You may leave a message, although I cannot say when he will be able to receive it."

My entire body froze in fear. Dear god, some horrible fiend was doing terrible surgical experiments on Elliott! "What . . . holy shit, lady! If you hurt him, so help me god, I will hunt you down and make you the sorriest person on the face of the earth!"

"Madam, I assure you that harming Lord Ainslie is the furthest thing from our minds," the voice said, clearly offended.

"Who are you?" I demanded.

"Nurse Malweather. I am the duty nurse at Ainston Hospital."

Ainston? That was the name of the town where Elliott lived. What was he doing in England? More to the point, why was he in a hospital having surgery?

"I apologize for what I just said. I'm very upset, naturally. Has Elliott been hurt somehow?"

"I'm afraid that I am unable to discuss Lord Ainslie's status with you. If you wish to contact the press department of the hospital, all updates will be released through them."

"Updates? Is he that bad?"

"I'm sorry, I must hang up now."

"Wait, you don't understand, I'm his wife—"

The connection went dead. I stared at nothing in particular, my skin crawling as the conversation replayed itself over and over in my head. After the twelfth time, I dialed Patrick's number again, and quickly explained what I'd heard.

"Are you sure he's not having one of his sisters play a prank on you?" Patrick's voice was sleepy and irritated. "He might be trying t'get rid of you, and feels this is the best way of doing it."

"Don't be ridiculous. Elliott loves me. The real kind of love, not your pale imitation thereof. What am I going to do, Patrick? I don't know the number of his house to call so I can talk to his mom. Or even Gunner. Do you have Gunner's number?"

"No. Jane would, but she's blocking my calls. I can give you her number, but she's very touchy about her privacy, and I don't know that she'd give his number t'you without Elliott or Gunner first introducing you." He was silent for a moment. I clutched my hands together and thought seriously of breaking down. "I can get the number for Ainslie Castle easily enough—it's bound t'be online—but if he's truly been hurt, then you will want t'be there."

"Yes, yes I do. I should be there. Oh my god, Patrick." My voice broke as the tears burned in my eyes.

"Steady," he said warningly. "Crying won't do Elliott any good. Can you get on a plane to London?"

I mentally totted up the balance on my credit card. "Probably."

"Then I tell you what you should do. Do you have something t'write with?"

I scrambled for a pen and grabbed my journal. He proceeded to give me details on how to take the train from

Heathrow to Ainston. "Once you get there, call the castle and tell them who you are. Someone will no doubt be sent t'take you t'the hospital."

"Thanks, Patrick. I appreciate the fact that you're not being a dick about this."

"My dear, Elliott is one of my oldest friends." I waited, knowing there was more to come. "Besides, I've decided Jane is, in fact, the one that I want, not you, so it behooves me t'keep on his good side. And speaking of that good lady, I believe I shall go find her in order t'tell her of this terrible event. Let us hope she won't have me thrown out of the hotel again."

I promised to keep him up-to-date, and then hurried out of the cabin, intent on finding Tiffany, horrible images of death and dismemberment lurking in the back of my head.

What happened to Elliott? And why hadn't he told me he was going to England?

Chapter 13

Diary of Alice Wood

Day Six, aka Day of Sheer and Utter Hell

I've never felt as alone in the world as I did during the twenty-two hours that followed. Tiffany was sympathetic when I woke her up and begged her to help me, but short of handing over my passport, she was of no use to me.

"Unfortunately, my ability to help is governed by the terms of our insurance, and they do not allow me to assist passengers to book flights to countries that are not their own. That does not, alas, fall under the term 'medical emergency,'" she told me, standing at her cabin door.

"It's for Elliott!"

"Yes, but the insurance company would not recognize you as married. Thus you would not be able to take advantage of our accident assistance, not to mention the fact that he was not injured on a Manny van Bris tour, but was apparently out of the country when he suffered this mysterious calamity that you cannot describe."

"I can't describe it because I don't know what happened to him. At least can you refund the rest of the tour price to me? I checked with the airlines, and I'm short the price of a ticket."

"Tickets are nonrefundable," she said firmly. "I'm sorry, but there is nothing I can do."

I slumped away, falling into a chair in the dark lounge. A few tears did sneak down my cheeks then. I felt as if the world had been stripped of the sun—everything was darkness and gloom. Solitary gloom. Mentally, I ran over my list of friends, wondering if I could hit up any of them for the money needed for a plane ticket. Unfortunately, no one came to mind. Maybe the U.S. embassy? I shook my head. Even if I knew where one was, I doubted if they'd help send me to England.

Patrick was the only person I knew who had any money to spare. Reluctantly, I tried his number, mentally rehearsing a plea. It was wasted, however. . . . His voice mail answered. I left a message and told him to call me back, but after another hellish hour passed with no word from him—and he still wasn't answering his phone—I decided that enough was enough.

I'd been on my own for what seemed like my entire life—as usual, I'd have to rely on my own self.

I decided that traveling light was going to be easier than hauling along my big suitcase, and the second bag that had started to fill with souvenirs, including one giant hookah. Accordingly, I left the bulk of my luggage on the ship, with a note taped to the top explaining that I'd pick it up after the tour, and giving the address of Ainslie Castle in case they wanted to forward it to me.

I stepped off the ship in the cool light of dawn, silvery gray fingers of fog drifting along the river, and wrapping the normally bustling Nuremberg in silence. I glanced back at the ship, giving it a sad, but fond, smile. It still looked like a bucket of rusted bolts, but our cabin had been a little haven of happiness.

Would I ever have that happiness again? What if Elliott . . . I choked aloud, a hard lump of tears making my throat ache.

"Stop it," I told myself, hoisting my day bag and marching resolutely toward the train station. "He's going to be fine. He has to be fine. I don't want to be a widow before I'm even legally a wife."

I was more than a little surprised when a familiar face was waiting for me at the train station platform. Anthony sat on one of the benches, luggage at his feet, his nose buried in a magazine.

He looked up, startled, when I stopped next to him. "Comrade Alice! You've left the cruise? Going to meet up with comrade Elliott, are you?"

"No, he—" I stopped, not wanting to speak of Elliott in case I lost it, emotionally speaking. "I have somewhere else I have to be. What are you doing here?"

"Ah." If he was disconcerted by the question, he didn't show it. "I'm afraid that Dahl and I have had a slight parting of the ways, and I thought it best to continue my research on my own."

"That's . . . sudden," I said, not wanting to point out that his excuse sounded lame, lest he point out that mine was just as bad. "I'm sorry that you and Dahl broke up."

He shrugged. "It wasn't a breakup per se, but I thought now would be a good time for a little period of solitary reflection. You are returning to America?"

"No, actually, I'm going to England." I held his gaze, willing him to make a snarky comment about following Elliott.

"Indeed. I'm headed to London, myself. Are you flying, or taking the train the entire way?"

"Train. It's cheaper."

"It is that. I am, as well." He made a little grimace. "I dislike flying, and avoid it whenever possible. Well, it looks as if we shall be traveling companions. How exciting for us both."

"Uh-huh." I was anything but excited by the prospect of spending so much time with Anthony, but there wasn't much I could do about it.

In the end, he turned out to be a pleasant travel companion. He chatted politely with me about my life back home, and then Elliott, and how I would cope with living in a different country. By the time we exhausted that subject, several hours had passed, and we had traveled through Germany and France, up to Belgium, where we had a two-hour delay before we could catch a ferry from Ostend to Dover.

Every now and again I'd sneak away from Anthony and call the hospital, but they continued to refuse information. Nor did I have any luck with Patrick. Either he had connected with Elliott's sister Jane, or he had turned off his phone for another reason. By the time I reached England, my phone battery was dead, and I was down to just a few dollars.

"Well, here is where we part," Anthony said with a smile only slightly touched with salaciousness. We emerged from the ferry with the hundreds of other passengers, buffeted and jostled as everyone headed for the taxis and train station. "I can honestly say that you've made the journey quite pleasant, comrade, and I wish you and comrade Elliott only the best in your future life together."

"Thank you, I'll pass that along to him." In a moment of sentiment, I patted his arm. "And thank you for not hitting on me. That was really getting old. It's been nice knowing you."

"The pleasure is all mine. Who knows?" he said, donning a cap and pulling out the handle on his wheelie suitcase. "We may see each other again someday."

"That would have been such a good parting line if you could have managed it without ogling my breasts," I told him.

He laughed aloud. "I didn't want you to think I wasn't open to a little life experience if you were. Au revoir, comrade Alice."

"See ya." I watched him leave, a sense of sadness gripping me as he melted into the crowd heading for the trains. I stumbled forward feeling as if the weight of the world had settled unceremoniously smack-dab on top of my shoulders.

It was afternoon by the time I got off the train in the town of Ainston, and it took nearly another hour for me to find my way to the hospital. Ainston wasn't a large town, but the hospital evidently served several nearby communities, which meant I had to take a couple of buses before I finally staggered in the door, by now exhausted from lack of sleep and food, and an overabundance of worry.

"Hello," I said to the woman at the reception desk. "My name is Alice Wood Ainslie. My husband was admitted a day or so ago. I've been in Germany, and just got here. Can you please point me to his room?"

"Ainslie?" A little frown appeared on her forehead as

she tapped at a keyboard. After a few moments, she gave me a critical look over the top of the monitor. "Lord Ainslie's family is with him. I have a note here that some-one has been calling repeatedly inquiring for informa-tion, claiming to be his wife. You wouldn't happen to know anything about that?"

"That was me," I said with as much dignity as I could muster. It wasn't a lot, considering how tired and travel-worn I was.

"I thought it might be." She tapped at the computer again. "Unfortunately, Lady Ainslie has no knowledge of you, so I'm afraid that we can't let you bother his lord-ship."

"She doesn't know about me because Elliott—Lord Ainslie—and I were just married yesterday. No, day be-fore that. In Germany. At the Bishops' Palace, to be ex-act."

"Indeed." She looked bored.

I rubbed my forehead. I was so tired and worn down I just wanted to crawl in a hole. "Look, ask Elliott. He'll tell you who I am."

"Unfortunately, Lord Ainslie has only just been taken to his room from recovery and is not available."

Fear clutched my heart. "Oh my god, I didn't know. He was in surgery that long? What happened to him? Is he OK? Please, you have to let me see him. I need to know he's all right."

"I'm sorry, but that's just not possible." There was a note of finality in her voice that I ignored.

"This is so stupid! I've traveled all the way from Nuremberg to see my husband, and despite what El-liott's mom thinks, we really are married. If you just tell me where he is, I will explain it all to her."

"I'm afraid not. Now, if you would please move away from the desk, there are others who wish assistance."

"Gunner, then. Gunner knows me. Hell, he married us. He can tell everyone who I am."

"Mr. Gunner Ainslie is not here. Next person, please."

"No," I said, clutching the counter with both hands. Stubbornness gave me strength. "I'm not moving until you tell me where my husband is."

"Madam, you will please move, or I will be forced to take action," the woman warned.

"Like what? You going to have me thrown out?" I held firm to the desk. "You're British. You guys don't do that sort of thing."

As it turns out, they did. Two security men pried my hands off the counter, and hustled me out the door despite my pleading to be taken up to see Elliott. They were dispassionate and immovable as they frog-marched me off the property.

"If you return, we will be forced to call the police," one of them warned before they went back inside.

"That's fine with me! Maybe the police will take me to see my lawfully wedded—in an Internet way—husband!" I yelled after them.

Neither responded. I slumped against a bus shelter, wondering how I was going to find Elliott. At the very least, I needed to find out how he was, and what happened to him.

"How am I going to do that if they think I'm some sort of baron stalker?"

I didn't realize I'd asked that aloud until the female who was slouched in the shelter, hiding in her hoodie, her nose almost touching the screen of her phone, turned to look at me and spoke.

"Wot?" she asked, lowering the phone.

"Sorry." I tried to give her a reassuring smile, but the way her eyes widened in alarm told me much about my state. "I'm overtired, and when I get that way, all my inhibitions melt away to nothing."

"Oh." She glanced back at her phone. "You're American?"

"Yup."

"You here for the castle?"

"No, I'm here for the castle's lord and mast—" As her words sank into my sleep-deprived brain, a lightbulb went off. "The castle!" I said loudly, spinning around to look at the bus schedule printed on the wall. "They would know what happened to him, right? I can explain who I am there, and they'll clear me with the hospital, and then I can see Elliott. Hell's bells, I don't know where these places are. Do you know how to get to Ainslie Castle?"

"Yais," the girl said, burying her nose in the phone again. "Oi works there sometimes on weekends, cleaning up after you lot."

"My lot? Americans, you mean?"

"Tourists." She looked up long enough to nod across the street to another bus shelter. "Take the number four. It'll drop you at the grounds if you tell 'em where you want to go."

I hurried across the road, taking up my place at a second bus shelter with renewed hope. Surely someone at the castle would help me. Elliott had spoken warmly of his family, and although they would have no idea who I was, I was confident I could make them understand.

The bus was another hour in coming, but at last it delivered me to the entrance to the castle grounds. I was surprised to see so many cars filling a parking area that had been carved out of velvety lawns.

"Today's Tuesday," the bus driver said as I asked him about the number of visitors. "Castle is open every Tuesday and Friday."

"Gotcha. Thanks much." I descended the bus steps, and started walking up the long drive that curved through an arch of willow trees. There were a few people walking with me, but most of the families were straggling back down the shaded drive toward the car park, their faces red with sun and exertion, many of them clutching little flags bearing the words "Ainslie Castle" that hung limp in the heat of the day. A few of the folks heading home bore shiny plastic bags, indicating the castle had a gift shop, as well. A little thrill of anticipation wormed its way through the heavy weight of worry when the treelined drive that obscured the house gave tantalizing little glimpses of it through the foliage.

"At last," I said to myself. I was about to see Elliott's castle, his home, the home that would embrace me and welcome me and immediately become part of my very being.

I was home . . . if only someone but me would recognize that fact.

The warm yellow stone of the castle was the first thing I noticed. . . . The second was the extensive scaffolding that covered the front and right side of the building. Elliott had said there was restoration work going on, and he wasn't kidding. The builders weren't present at the moment—they probably didn't work when the castle was open to the public—but there was a vast amount of machinery and materials stacked neatly next to what appeared to be the stables. The castle itself was three stories, and looked more like something out of *Downton Abbey* than what I thought of as a castle. There were no round crenellated towers with arrow slits, and murder holes out of which one could pour boiling oil, no moat, no draw-bridge, not even a proper portcullis with spiky bits that one could drop on attackers. It looked like a glorious grand house. At least, most of it did. The left side looked like it had been bombed, with raw, jagged edges jutting out into space above a pile of rubble. That end of the house was roped off with bright pink tape, evidently to keep the tourists from getting into trouble—or taking souvenirs.

At the entrance of the house stood a little kiosk bearing the sign TICKETS. I waited while a large family bought their tickets, then greeted the woman manning the booth with a smile.

"Just one? Entrance to the castle itself is six pounds. The grounds are three," she told me, looking more than a little bored. "Both, including the dower house, are eight pounds."

"Oh, um . . . Actually, I don't think you can sell me what I want. I'm looking for information, not a tour."

She pursed her lips.

"This is going to be a bit of an odd story. My name is Alice Wood. Er . . . Ainslie. I married Elliott a couple of days ago in Germany. I realize you don't know a thing about me, because Elliott was evidently injured before he could tell his family about us getting married, but I've come all the way from Germany, and I really need to see him. Can you please get me whoever's in charge so they can tell the hospital who I am?"

The woman just looked at me unblinking.

"OK, that came out kind of crazy, but I don't want you

thinking I'm a nutball who stalks barons or anything, because I'm not. I told Elliott that I don't care about him being a baron, and that's the truth. I like him for who he is, not what he is, if you know what I mean. Anyway, I'm not crazy or a stalker, but I am really, really tired, and I think my blood sugar is, like, nonexistent at this point because I haven't eaten in a couple of days, so I really, really just need someone to tell the hospital that I'm OK. Can you do that for me"—I consulted her name tag—"Beryl?"

"I'm only authorized to sell tickets," she said after a moment's consideration.

"Right. You can't take the responsibility." I nodded. "I understand, I really do. You're trying to protect Elliott. I'd likely do the same thing in your shoes. I applaud your willingness to keep the crazies away from him, and will mention your devotion to his well-being when I can talk to him. I'm sure you'll be in line for a raise. Tell you what—you point me to someone who can help me, and I'll leave you alone."

"Someone in charge?" she asked.

I nodded some more, then had to stop myself because I was enjoying it too much. "Yes, please. Someone in the castle."

"Entrance to the castle is six pounds," she repeated.

"Yeah, I got that, but see, I'm Elliott's wife—"

"Lord Ainslie is unmarried," she said stiffly. She looked like she'd been sucking on a lemon.

"Right, he was before he went on the cruise, but we got married while we were on it. Is Gunner back from Germany? He'd verify everything I'm saying."

"Mr. Gunner Ainslie is out of the country and thus cannot confirm your story." If her mouth puckered any more, her face might implode.

"Crap, that means he's probably in Bulgaria doing . . . er . . . things. Um. Isn't there someone in charge while Elliott is gone? Someone I can speak with? Someone inside?"

"Entrance to the castle—"

"—is six pounds, I know." I sighed, dug out my wallet, and counted out my change. I had enough to get into the castle, and possibly buy myself a cup of tea at their tea shop, but not much beyond that. I doled out the money. "Fine, but I'm going to tell Elliott that you're not at all flexible."

I took the ticket and stomped my way up the shallow stone steps to the grand entrance, part of my mind oohing and aahing over the graceful arches over the windows, the little stone decorations of flourishes and some sort of flowery leaf, and the fact that it was a real, authentic castle, even if it didn't have a moat and murder holes.

The entry hall was everything I hoped it would be—a black-and-white checkered tile floor, dark oak paneling, gigantic fireplace at the far end, lots of uncomfortable-looking wooden benches, a few bits of tapestry hung out of the reach of the tourists, and a no-nonsense woman with poufy red hair, and a businesslike blue blazer with white piping, who was rounding up the available visitors into a contained herd.

"The tour is about to begin," she said, looking meaningfully over at me. "It is the last one of the day, madam, so if you will join us, we can get started."

"I'd kind of rather just look around on my own," I told her.

She looked horrified. "Ainslie Castle is available via guided tour only. You must join us."

"See, I'm really just here to talk to someone in charge. Is there like a manager or someone? I need to find out about Elliott."

"Lord Ainslie is indisposed," she said stiffly.

"I know, that's why I am trying to find someone in charge!" I was about ready to pull out my hair. It was an emotion that continued when she insisted that I either join the party or leave the castle. With no other choice, reluctantly I tagged along, keeping my eyes peeled in case I saw someone who looked like they worked there.

I had to admit, as Cecily (the fluffy-haired, iron-willed tour guide) steered us through a number of staterooms, there were definite "Elizabeth Bennet touring Pemberley" moments. I kept thinking that all the paintings, the objets d'art, the gorgeous furniture ... all of it was Elliott's, and just as soon as I got someone, anyone, to tell me what was going on with him, I would be able to walk around and enjoy the fact that I had married a man who had such a tangible link to the past.

Failure was, unfortunately, my lot to bear. No one appeared in the distant hallways. Cecily ignored my repeated pleas for assistance. And by the time the tour was finished, she had evidently had enough of my attempts to bribe her into helping me.

"The castle is now closed," she told me firmly. We stood at the entrance of the great hall, the other tourists making their tired way down the drive to the parking lot. "You must leave."

"But I've explained to you a dozen times—"

"And I have told you almost as many that I will have no part of your shenanigans. I know Lord Ainslie. He is not married. That is the end of it."

"Is there no one else—his mom? She knows about me—"

"Lady Ainslie is occupied elsewhere. If you do not leave now, I will be forced to have you bodily removed."

I gave up. There was no hope for it. I took the three steps needed to leave the hall, wincing when the door slammed shut behind me. Ahead of me stretched the treelined drive, with a few figures straggling down it. The ticket kiosk had been removed. A few birds sang, but even their songs were tinged with despair and depression.

"Alone in a strange country, with no money, no way to get to Elliott, and absolutely no friends," I said. My voice sounded as dull as the stone steps before me. "Now what the hell am I going to do? It's going to be night, soon, and I don't have enough money for a hotel room. Hell, I don't even have enough for a meal, and I'm going to pass out if I don't get something to eat soon."

No one answered me. No one was around to hear me. No one cared.

It was with those melancholy thoughts that I trudged back to the bus stop, waiting almost two hours to catch a bus back into Ainston, and from there—with nowhere else to go, and a vague idea that I could prowl the halls of the hospital at night in order to find Elliott—out to the hospital.

The bus let me off on the other side of the hospital from where I had entered before. My hopes, pretty non-existent by that point, rallied momentarily. There was a slight chance that the woman at the reception desk who had denied me entrance earlier wouldn't notice me if I went in via that entrance . . . or perhaps she'd gone home for the day?

I walked through the large parking lot, and into the front entrance of the hospital. A large, well-lit waiting area greeted me, one with scattered televisions for those people waiting for news of loved ones. There was also a small shop, but it was now closed. There was a different woman at this desk, so I marched up and asked for Elliott.

"I'm afraid Lord Ainslie is only seeing family members."

"If I told you that I was married to him, would you believe me?"

She looked a bit taken aback, but recovered quickly enough. "No, I wouldn't."

"I didn't think so. Is there a problem with me waiting to see him?" I asked, gesturing toward the mostly empty waiting area.

"No, although I can't say when Lord Ainslie will be receiving friends."

I nodded. I was so exhausted, it was about all I could do. "Gotcha. I'll be over there if anyone cares, not that anyone does, because . . . well, because no one does but Elliott, and he doesn't know I'm here."

The chairs were surprisingly comfortable. I chose a bank of them that was located next to a vending machine. I plugged the last of my sparse money into the machine and was rewarded with two candy bars and a cup of tepid coffee. I claimed three of the seats as my own, ate and drank my meager dinner, and curled up on the chairs, too tired and too hopeless to care if the reception woman noticed me camped out for the night.

Wicked dreams chased my sleep, dreams in which strangers circled around me taunting and jeering at me, calling me a liar. I tried pleading with them just as I'd begged others to listen to me, but the dream people were just as obstinate, and dragged me off to a high cliff where they threatened to throw me over the edge.

One of them, the fluffy-haired Cecily, shoved her way forward and taunted me by name. "Alice, Alice, no one loves Alice," she said in a singsong voice.

Tears leaked out my eyes, hot and burning on my face. I touched my cheek and saw blood.

"Alice," she said again.

I wanted to shriek with the unfairness of it all. I *was* loved. Elliott loved me . . . didn't he? Or had I dreamed him up, as well?

"Alice!"

"Hrn?"

The realization that it wasn't Dream Cecily calling me dragged me out of the deep well of sleep. I blinked up at the person who was bending over me, trying to get my eyes to focus.

"Are you awake now? Were you dreaming? You were making squeaking noises like my dog makes when he chases rabbits in his sleep."

"Nightmare," I mumbled. I stared at the man for a moment, then shrieked, "Gunner!" and flung myself off the chairs onto him.

"Steady, now, or you'll have us both on our arses," he said, wobbling slightly, but managing to keep on his feet. "What are you doing out here? Why aren't you with Elliott?"

"They won't let me see him," I said on a sob, and then, to my eternal embarrassment, burst into tears. I told him my tale in between blubberings, clutching his sleeve like it was a life preserver. I had a horrible fear that if I let go, he might disappear into a puff of smoke.

"It's all right," he said, patting my shoulder, and shoving me back onto one of the seats. "Let's have a cup of tea—that's how I found you, by the way, so smart thinking parking yourself here—and we'll work it out."

"Elliott!" I said, leaping back to my feet.

"Is all right. He's sleeping now, which is why I came down to fetch some tea."

"What happened to him?" I asked, mollified enough to take the milky cup of tea that he offered. "How badly was he hurt? Was he shot? Knifed? Poisoned? No one would tell me what was wrong!"

"Shot? Poisoned?" Gunner shook his head. "I have no idea where you came up with that. There was an accident at the castle in the old wing—the tower collapsed, injuring some workmen. Elliott flew out to examine the damage, and part of the remaining wall came down while he was doing so. His collarbone is broken, that's all. They had to put in a couple of pins to piece it back together—that's why he had surgery. But he should be fine, so stop worrying."

"Can I see him?" I clutched my cup of tea hopefully. "I want to see him. I want to make sure he's all right. I want to make sure he still loves me."

"You really *were* having a nightmare, weren't you? Of course he still loves you. Why wouldn't he? You're perfect for him. And if he won't have you"—he winked at me—"I will."

"I thought you were in Bulgaria. They said you were out of the country."

"They who?"

"The people at the castle."

"Ah." He rubbed his nose. He looked almost as tired as I felt. "As it happens, I was at the airport, just about to board a flight to Sofia, when my brother Dixon texted me that El had been hurt. I changed tickets and got here a couple of hours ago. Since Elliott was sleeping comfortably, I said I'd stay so the family could go home and get some rest."

"I'm just glad you came out to get tea. I think I would have gone mad if anyone else refused to tell me what was wrong with Elliott."

"Sounds like you had a rough time of it."

I willed him to drink his tea as fast as possible, telling him again about my hellish day. I was still telling him when he escorted me up a couple of floors, and introduced me to the nurses at the nursing station as Elliott's wife, asking them to make a note on the official records as to who I was, and that henceforth I was to be given all possible courtesies.

I was ready to kiss Gunner when we entered the darkened room containing the man who had consumed all my thoughts. Instead, I said, "Elliott!" in a tiny voice, and rushed to the bed.

He had been asleep, but groggily turned his head and blinked at me. "Alice?"

"Yes, my darling, it's me. Oh my god, you look so horrible."

One side of his mouth curled up. "You certainly know how to make me feel good. What are you doing here? You should be on the tour."

"Don't be an idiot. Of course I'm going to be here. It took me longer than I would have liked because no one would believe that someone as handsomely wonderful as you would marry a lowly American, but I'm here now, and I'm going to take care of you."

"Good," he said, his eyes drifting closed. "Tired."

"Go back to sleep, then." I leaned down to kiss him. "I won't leave you."

The hand that wasn't strapped to the front of his chest fumbled around until it found mine. His fingers were warm and strong, and brought tears of gratitude, relief, and love to my eyes.

"Love you," he said slowly as he drifted off to sleep.

I didn't answer. I couldn't talk around the massive lump in my throat.

Chapter 14

Expense Account
  Item one: five thousand pounds, quarterly
  Remarks: Increased insurance premiums. The bastards.

"What do you mean, you're married?"
        Elliott held the phone away from his ear, grateful that Alice had just gone off to have a quick breakfast in the hospital canteen. His eyes rested on the clock. It was three minutes after six. What other mother would call and wake up her son just to demand information that could wait until a more civilized hour? "It means exactly what you think it means—I have taken unto my bosom a wife."

"Gunner says that he married you to the American who was staying in your cabin. That can't possibly be true. He is well-known for pulling my leg; thus, he was jesting. Which of your former women did you marry?

The one with the birthmark on her neck? The actress? The one with the short legs?"

"Gunner isn't joking. He did, in fact, marry Alice and me while we were in Würzburg, and yes, I'm aware that the government won't consider it a legal marriage. That is why we plan on having a civil ceremony just as soon as it can be arranged, when I'm able to get around, I assume. Speaking of which, I'm fine, not that you asked."

"Of course you're fine. You have a broken collarbone. Your father broke his collarbone at the drop of a hat, and you never saw him making a big fuss about it."

"I'll wager he didn't have half the damn castle come down on him," Elliott said darkly. The memory of standing out with Richardson, assessing the damage, only to have half the remaining wall come down would haunt him for a very long time. Although Richardson escaped without injury, and a broken collarbone was the worst he himself had to suffer, he was well aware of just how close to death he had been. It wasn't at all a comfortable feeling.

"But who *is* this woman?" his mother asked, returning to the reason for her call.

"You should know—you had her Googled. By now I expect you know more about her than I do." That wasn't exactly true, but Elliott was more than a little surprised—not to mention annoyed—that his mother had not greeted news of Alice with more enthusiasm. "She's a wonderful woman who you will love as soon as you get to know her."

"But that's just it, my darling son—you don't know her. You only just met her. You can't possibly form any sort of a reasonable judgment on her character in such a short amount of time. You'll simply have to annul the marriage. I will devote myself body and soul to finding you a proper woman, one who doesn't show up expecting you to give up part of your cabin."

"She had a ticket. It was as much her cabin as it was mine."

"Don't be ridiculous. You're Baron Ainslie."

Elliott rolled his eyes and shifted slightly, in order to reach the drip that held his pain medications. He bumped it up a notch. "That doesn't give me any rights beyond the castle grounds. You will love Alice as much as I do when you meet her."

"I highly doubt that. Tell this woman that I will be down to take charge of you immediately after breakfast. Don't do anything rash until I get there."

"There is no need for you to come rushing to my side. Alice is here, and Gunner said he'd be back after he had a little rest."

"A fine sort of mother I'd be if I left my eldest son to the wiles of some title-hungry American!"

"I thought you wanted me to get married? Isn't that why you were grilling me on the phone about Alice? Isn't that why you sent Gunner to find out what he could? And yet now when I tell you that your fondest wish has come true, you act like a stereotypical mother who doesn't wish to give up her son."

"Elliott! I forbid you to call me stereotypical. The very word is an insult. I simply wish to ensure that you marry the right sort of woman."

He couldn't help himself. He had to ask, "And just what is the right sort of woman?"

"Certainly not one who would marry a man after knowing him for only two days!"

"Alice and I knew each other for longer than that, and we cohabited the entire time, which I think you'll agree speeds up the getting-to-know-you phase. No, no more, Mum. My shoulder hurts, and Alice will be back any minute. You may come to see me if you insist, but you will treat Alice with the respect due her as my wife."

"Thank the lord that you have not yet married her!" was his mother's final cry before hanging up the phone.

He got himself and his IV to the bathroom, and was being put back into bed by a thickset male nurse when Alice hurried into the room. "Oh, you're up? How are you feeling?"

"Sore, and I'm not up. The doctor won't be by to see me until around lunch. Did you eat?"

"Oodles and oodles. More than enough to make up for missing a few meals." Alice waited until the nurse checked the IV and went off to deal with other patients.

"He seems nice," she said, nodding after the nurse.

"Everyone has been very kind," he said, eyeing her. He didn't like to see the deep purple smudges beneath her eyes, a sign that she had not gotten any sleep. At least he'd seen to it that she had some food. "I should warn you that my mother will be here shortly."

"Warn me?" She curled up on the visitor's chair, hugging her knees to her chest. "That sounds ominous. I kind of got the impression that your mom would be super happy that you finally got married."

"I assumed she would be, as well, but evidently she is determined to bring drama to our lives." He reached out with his good arm and took her hand. "I want you to promise me that you won't let anything she says or does upset you."

"Uh-oh." Her fingers tightened on his. "That sounds worse than ominous. Is she mad that we got married without her? Did you tell her we're going to have a big party to celebrate after we have the civil ceremony?"

"She's . . ." He thought for a moment, trying to explain the complexities that were his mother. "Mum can frequently be a contradiction. She has very strong beliefs in equality and justice, and the idea of every person making his or her own way through the world, and yet, she can be single-minded in her attempts to force things the way she wants them. Right now she's clinging to the belief that all Americans are bad, and thus, she must rid me of you."

Alice's shoulders slumped. "Oh, great, I'm going to have a mom-in-law who hates me."

"Hate is too strong of a word."

"Dislike?"

He shook his head, grimacing when his shoulder pulled. Alice immediately got up to readjust his pillows. He settled back on them with a sigh of relief. "Dislike implies knowledge of whatever is being disliked. This is more an unreasonable prejudice, if that is not too repetitive a description. She thinks all Americans want a title; therefore, you must be after me for my title, and nothing more."

"Then I'll just have to show her I don't give a damn about your title. Or rather," she said quickly, obviously seeing the little frown that formed between his brows, "that it doesn't matter to me whether or not you have a title. Is that better?"

He let the frown go. "Much better. I may not make a fuss about it, but the barony is an ancient one, and not all of my ancestors were oddballs like my parents."

"Just so . . ." She stopped and did that lip-biting thing that never failed to make him want to kiss her. And frequently more. "Just so you don't end up being brainwashed, and want to dump me. Because honestly, Elliott, I don't think I could go through that again. It was bad enough with Patrick, and he was a jerkwad. You're every woman's dream."

"Hardly that," he said with a gentle laugh. Anything else hurt too much. "You shouldn't need the reassurance that I am not so fickle with my affections, but since you do, let me just say right now that there is nothing my mother can say that will change my mind. You're stuck with me."

"Good," she said with a happy sigh. "Now, would you like to tell me what happened? Gunner told me briefly, but I'm confused how that part of the building fell down twice."

"It didn't fall twice—the bulk of the tower collapsed two days ago, injuring a couple of workmen, who are luckily recovering nicely. That's why it was so urgent that I leave you and return home. When I went to see the damage, part of the existing wall that supported the now-destroyed tower fell. Richardson and I weren't standing under it, if that's what your frown means—we weren't that stupid. The part of the wall that fell landed on the rubble of the tower, and knocked some of the larger stones aside. One of them caught me on the shoulder."

"You're lucky you weren't killed," Alice said with a gratifyingly frightened face. "Oh, boy, do I want to climb on that bed and hug you like you've never been hugged before."

To hell with the pain. He held up his good arm, trying hard not to show how his broken bone hurt when she carefully curled into his good side. He breathed in the smell of her—now a somewhat antiseptic version of her usual flowery scent, since she had taken a fast shower in the attached bathroom—and put aside the pain for the pleasure of holding her.

That was how his mother found them—Alice sound asleep, drooling slightly on his shoulder, while he made mental lists of all the things he needed to do once he was released.

"What on earth is that woman doing up there! Elliott! Release her at once!"

"Shh," he warned, glancing down at Alice, but the damage was done. She slid off the bed with a guilty, sleepy look, shoving her hair back from her face, and trying to straighten her clothing at the same time.

"Oh, sorry. I must have fallen asleep. Why didn't you wake me up?"

"Because you needed your sleep, and there was no reason to move you. Mum, may I introduce you to Alice Wood."

"Ainslie," Alice prompted.

"Ainslie," he agreed, knowing that where it concerned his mother, it would be best to start out as he meant to go. "My wife. Alice, this is my mother, Rosalyn, Lady Ainslie."

"I'm so happy to meet you at last," Alice said, her hand outstretched as she came around the bed to where his mother stood. "And I know that I must come as a huge surprise to you, what with Elliott and I deciding that we were meant for each other, and all that sappy stuff that must seem really weird to you, but we really did decide that. I mean, how could one not? Elliott is so wonderful, and I thank my lucky stars that Patrick dumped me when he did, because if he didn't, then I would never have met Elliott, and I wouldn't be standing here right now. I'm babbling, aren't I? I'm so sorry about that. I babble when I'm nervous, and Elliott told me that you weren't best pleased about the fact that we got married without him even telling you about me, and that you have a thing about Americans, but I assure you that I don't give a hoot about the fact that he has a title. I mean, I think it's neat and all, but I didn't want him because of it. In fact, it still strikes me as being weird." She stopped for a breath, looking so endearingly miserable and unsure that Elliott was ready to leap to her defense.

His mother had listened in silence to Alice's monologue, then turned to Elliott. "Why?" was all she asked.

He took a deep breath. "Mum, I told you that I love Alice, and nothing you can say is going to change that."

"Why would I want to change anything of the kind?" she asked.

Elliott felt out of his depths, an emotion that he frequently experienced around his mother. "You said you didn't want me marrying her—"

"Nonsense!" She gave him a little buffet on the top of his head, then turned to examine Alice. "This girl is perfectly charming, not at all like what you told me she was. She's quite clearly head over heels in love with you, and if you feel the same way, then I would be the last person on earth to interfere. My dear, you look peaked. Have you been ill?"

"Oh my god," Alice said, suddenly releasing a breath she'd obviously been holding. She shot a look of mingled confusion and relief at Elliott before suddenly embracing his mother. "I can't tell you how happy you've just made me! I thought you were going to be a horrible mother-in-law, and were going to try to break us up whenever you could, and would make snide comments and digs when Elliott wasn't around."

"You poor child," his mother said. "What horrors has Elliott made you imagine? How like a man to scare you like that. Now, you must come back to the castle with me. It's clear that you have been suffering, and need care and attention, and you shall have it in abundance. I will move immediately from the baroness's bedroom, and make it available to you. I hope you like peach. Elliott, you must move into your father's room—it's long past time you did that."

Alice protested, but his mother was having none of it until Elliott said loudly (frequently the only way to get through to his mother), "I'm quite happy in my own rooms, and there's ample space for Alice there, so you do need not move anyone, Mum. Although I do agree that Alice needs care and attention—she will tell you what she had to go through to get here, so I'd be grateful if you would tell everyone to give her all due consideration."

"Of course I will. You don't imagine I'd let the mother of my grandchildren be abused and neglected, do you?" Mum asked with a disgusted look cast his way. She steered Alice by the shoulders to the door. "I shall take you up to the castle now, Alice dear, so that you might meet Elliott's brothers and sisters. They will be delighted to know you. And then I will show you around the grounds, and you will appreciate just how old and vaunted the barony is. After that, lunch, and perhaps a visit to Ainston so that you might get to know the town, too. It is important to us, the town. So many of the tenants live there, you see."

"But—but Elliott—," Alice said, gesturing as she was shoved out the door.

"Oh, he'll be fine. It's just a broken collarbone. Did he tell you how many times that Edmond, my beloved hus-band, broke his collarbone? It seemed as if he was forever doing it. No doubt Elliott gets his weak collarbones from his father's side of the family—"

His mother's voice drifted back as the ladies left, Alice with one last startled glance. He smiled to himself, pleased that his mother saw what he saw in Alice, and content that all would be well in that regard.

The following day, Alice, Gunner, and his mother were on hand to take him home. Elliott gritted his teeth against the pain of the ride to the castle, regretting the loss of his IV drip filled with painkillers. Bertie was waiting for them on the front steps, dancing around excitedly while inquiring if there was anything he could do.

It seemed to take forever, but at last Elliott was settled in bed, Alice at his side, and his mother dashing in and out of his bedroom scattering random facts she felt were pertinent to the situation. Elliott couldn't help but be amused by how quickly his mother had taken to Alice—it must be something in their genes, he mused to himself as Alice arranged pillows and adjusted the drapes so that the sun didn't shine in his eyes. His mother never said the word "Alice" without appending "dear" to it.

"Walston has some new sheep in the south meadow. Walston is one of our tenants, Alice dear. You will like him. Bertie, don't fuss with Elliott's laptop. You know how he dislikes that. Alice dear, close the drape just a bit more. The sun will soon move and it will make Elliott uncomfortable. Did Richardson—he's the builder, Alice dear—did he tell you that the insurance man called at the castle this morning? He said he would be back later today, so that he might speak to you, but that you were not to worry about the payouts to those men who were injured, so all is well there."

"Other than the increases in insurance premiums,

yes," Elliott said, and immediately felt like a heel in being concerned by monetary issues when three men had been injured working on his home.

"Should he see the insurance man, do you think, Alice dear?" His mother frowned, and tweaked the duvet covering him. "He looks pale."

Alice's lips twitched as her eyes met his. He let a little of the exasperation show, which she answered with another twitch of her lips. She got control of herself, though, and turned a placid face to his mother. "I think he'll be fine so long as he doesn't try to cartwheel his way out to meet the guy."

"Yes, but he looks so horrible."

"Thank you," Elliott said, shooting his young brother a look when the latter cackled, and slumped into an easy chair that sat next to the fireplace.

"Elliott's a big boy," Alice said, taking a page from his mother's book, and gently escorting her to the door. "If he didn't feel well enough to meet with someone, I'm sure he'd tell us."

"Men can be so stupid about things like that," Mum answered, but allowed herself to be persuaded. "Is that the time? I must be off. There is a meeting of the dramatics society that I said I would attend, even though that sort of thing isn't really me. I'm the least dramatic person I know, aren't I, Bertie dear?"

"Yes, Mum," Bertie answered without bothering to look up from Elliott's laptop.

"Leave it, Bertie," Elliott growled. He disliked others touching his computer. They had a way of messing up things that made him tetchy just thinking about it. "Don't you have something to do?"

"Summer hols," Bertie said, poking at the keyboard.

Alice came back into the room, and took in Elliott's growing frustration with one swift look.

"Beat it, kiddo," she told Bertie, holding the door open.

He looked up in surprise.

Alice jerked her head toward the door. "Now."

Bertie grinned, slammed closed the laptop in a way that had Elliott saying something quite rude, and got to his feet, slouching his way to the door in his usual manner. "So it's going to be like that, is it?" he asked Alice, pausing in front of her.

"You got a problem with me?" she asked in a voice that was surprisingly tough.

His grin grew, and he shook his head. "No, but I bet old El doesn't have a clue as to what he's let himself in for."

She gave him a little push out of the door, closing it and leaning against it with a tired sigh. "OK, let me preface this by saying that I love your family—"

"But a little of them goes a long way? I am in complete agreement with you."

"So what now?" She moved around his room, clearly at a loss as to what she should be doing.

"The doctor said I should stay in bed for another day or two in order to minimize jarring the bones, and then I will be released from this room. If you hand me my laptop, I can do a little one-handed work."

"I meant now what do I do? I'm happy to take care of you, but other than shooing people out of your hair, I'm not sure what you need done." She set the laptop on the bed, plopping down next to him.

His shoulder screamed with the movement of the bed.

He waited until the sharp burn of pain dulled into a bearable level, and answered, "You're free to do whatever you like. Gunner said he'd be here for a few more days, and he'd be happy to show you around, or you can wait for me to do the same."

"Do you have any work I could be doing?"

"Work? Such as?"

She shrugged. "I don't know, something secretarial? You're a writer—you must have tons of paperwork and the like. Do you need something typed?"

"I have a voice program that will take my dictation."

"There's got to be something I can do. I hate feeling like I'm being a burden."

He gave her hand a squeeze. He wished he could do more, but even that movement had him braced against the resulting pain that not even his medication would alleviate. "Now you're being silly. You aren't a burden. I'm quite serious when I say you can do what you like. My home is now your home. I want you to feel comfortable here."

"Oh, Elliott!" She snuggled up to his side, careful to avoid the injured area, but still making him wince. "You really are the most amazing man. I'm sorry to be such a pill when you're feeling crappy, and I don't mean to whine. I'm just feeling a bit . . . lost. I love your family, and of course, the castle is fantastic, but it's all so . . . strange. I can't shake the feeling that Cecily is going to pounce on me from a dark corner and make me leave the house."

"You've been introduced to the staff as my wife, so that won't happen."

She bit her lip.

He had to look away so as to keep from kissing her.

He tried to think of something for her to do that would give her a feeling of involvement without working her too hard. "Why don't you plan our wedding party?"

"You're kidding, right?" She pulled back to look up at him. "Your mother would kill me, Elliott, kill me if I dared to disrupt the plans she's already making for that. It's going to be on a Sunday, so she can thumb her nose at some local preacher dude by having your lesbian sister and her partner present, not that I understand all of that, but with your mom, it's really just easier to let her roll ahead with her plans. Besides, she's planning a kick-ass party, much better than I could have done. I don't suppose I could help you with your book?"

"No, I've never been one who could work with a collaborator."

She hesitated, then said, without looking at him, "What about your *other* work?"

He thought about that. Dixon acted as steward, but there were still some tasks that he as baron had to do. "I don't know what there really is that you could do. It's mostly things I have to attend to myself."

"I kind of figured that must be so."

"There is something," he said slowly, desperately searching his mind for an occupying task and finally coming up with two ideas. "Two somethings, in fact."

"What?"

"First, the castle, as you know, is open to the public twice a week. Dixon has been pressing me to open up all week in order to make the estate pay for itself, rather than having me pump money from book sales into it, and I have to admit it is an enticing thought. The estate being profitable, not having the house opened to tourists all week long."

"And?" she asked, clearly eager to help.

"If you could put that clever brain to work on ways for the estate to turn a profit without filling the house with tours all day long, I'd be eternally grateful."

"Hmm." She looked thoughtful. "Brainstorm fundraising, you mean? I did that in my last job, and if I say so myself, I was pretty good at it. What's the second something?"

"This one is a bit trickier, at least so far as my mother is concerned. All of the family—other than Jane and Gunner—are what is euphemistically referred to as employed by the estate."

"Euphemistically?" Her nose scrunched up in an adorable manner. "How so?"

"Other than Dixon and Gabrielle—she's a sister you haven't yet met—there is little to no work done for the salaries they draw. Those were set in place by my father, of course, encouraged by my mother, who firmly believes that as head of the family, I should have no problem supporting all my siblings."

"That's hardly fair!" she said, indignation clearly visible in her face. "You work hard writing all those books just to pay for things!"

"And Dixon works hard to keep the estate as profitable as he can, yes. Unfortunately, we can't continue this way. I told my siblings who aren't working for their wages that they would have to find new jobs, but my mother tells me that they didn't take me seriously. That's where you come in."

"You want me to find them jobs? I'm not sure I know how to do that."

"Jobs, internships, a sabbatical somewhere far away—hell, you can even find them spouses, so far as I'm concerned. Just get them off the estate accounts and onto their respective own two feet."

She giggled. "I may not be any great shakes as an employment agency, but I'm a wonderful matchmaker. At least, I always figured I would be, and it will be great fun finding significant others for your brothers and sisters."

"Or jobs," he cautioned. "Employment is going to be much easier than finding them all their soul mates."

"Aye, aye, Lord Erogenous," she said, saluting. "Consider it done!"

"Let's . . . erm . . . let's keep that second job quiet, shall we? My mother is giving me enough grief about it; if she finds out that I've asked you to help shoo her chicks out from under her wings, we'll both feel her wrath."

"No problem. I like your mom, and wouldn't want her to think we were plotting against her, even if it is for everyone's good. Oh, about the fund-raising . . . did you have any suggestions?"

"No. If I did, I'd have Dix looking at them, but my attention has been focused of late on getting this book done, and the first of the renovations finished."

She patted him on the hand and rose, sending another sharp jolt of pain through his shoulder. "Don't worry, Elliott, I'll take care of everything so all you have to do is heal up, and finish writing that book."

He was about to tell her that he didn't expect her to have much success at either task, but she looked so damned happy and pleased with herself that he didn't have the heart to do so. "I would be greatly relieved if you'd do so."

"I'll go take a quick look around the castle and grounds, and start working on things. You should be resting now anyway. I'll be back with your lunch, OK?"

"Tell Gunner to show you around," he told her as she left.

He settled back with his computer, relaxing at last. Alice had an occupation, his mother was happily planning a party, and he would be able to finish writing the book. All in all, life was looking pretty damned rosy.

Chapter 15

Diary of Alice Wood

Day Fourteen. Holy Moses, has life been crazy busy.

I can't believe it's been a week since I last wrote in my diary! My only excuse is that I've been so busy, all my creativity has been sucked dry. Since today is the first day of Phase One, I've decided that I need to document it, so that we can look back later and tweak anything that went weird. Assuming, that is, that we're still together.

Great. Now I'm foreshadowing. I hate it when I read a mystery that does that! I guess since this is just a diary, it's OK, but maybe I'd better start over.

Let's see, it was a week ago, the day after we got Elliott home from the hospital, that I sat down and thought about the jobs he'd given me. The matchmaking (since I discounted finding jobs for people when I could get them married off so they were as happy as Elliott and I were) sounded like the most fun, but realistically, I figured I'd have a better shot of bringing some money into the coffers if I focused on ways to make the castle profitable, and that's where I put all my brainpower.

"I have a list of things," I had told Elliott that morning. He was sitting up in bed, his laptop on his legs, and had been speaking into a headset so that his words would be transcribed into text. "Oh, sorry, didn't know you were writing. Er . . . talking. Writing via talking."

He looked just as adorably irritated as he had back on the ship, making a little curl of nostalgia pinch my stomach. "It's called dictating. What does your list concern?"

I held out the tablet of paper. "It's my moneymaking ideas."

"Ah." He looked back at the computer. "Have you shown them to Dixon?"

"I started to, but he was just hauling his suitcase out to his car, so he told me to discuss them with you."

"He's leaving?" Elliott's frown cleared a little as he answered himself. "Oh, the agricultural course he's taking in Scotland. I forgot that was starting this week."

"He's going to be gone for eight weeks, and I'd like to get some of these things started." I held out the tablet again. "I can explain them, if you like."

He started to say something, but checked himself. He gave me a long look. "Do any of the plans include vast herds of tourists stomping through the castle at all hours of the day?"

"No, of course not. I know you don't want that."

"Are any items being created with my face, or yours, on an undergarment?"

I laughed. "No Lord Ainslie undies, I swear. Just simple stuff meant to appeal to people with sizable money at their disposal. For instance," I said, tapping on the tablet. "The dower house isn't being used as anything but a site for tourists to see. I thought we could use it as a wedding venue. Castle wedding spots, as you mentioned, make oodles of money, and although I know you don't want anyone up near the castle itself until it's repaired, the dower house is gorgeous by itself, and there's that cute little pond, and if we fixed up the rooms, we could rent it out as a reception area and B&B for wedding guests."

"That is an excellent idea," he said, looking back at his laptop. "I wholly approve of it, and assuming your other ideas are along those lines, then you have my full approval to enact them."

"Well, admittedly, there's only a couple of other ideas that I had, one of which involves corporations using the gardens, but there's one big one that I think is really fabulous—"

"I'm sure it will be a splendid success," he said, tapping one-handed on the laptop.

"Yeah, but you should probably hear about exactly what I want to do," I said, feeling a bit shoved to the side.

"That's not necessary. I trust you."

It's hard to bitch when someone says that, but I felt that this was a big deal, and Elliott needed to give it his full attention. "It's your house that's at stake, Elliott. I don't want to plow ahead doing something that you wouldn't like."

"If you are concerned, speak with my mother," he said, his eyes fixed firmly on the laptop. "I really must get this book done if I am to have time for the wedding and party next week."

"All right, I'll do that. Elliott . . . you're sure you're going to be well enough for the wedding?" I asked, sidetracked by the thought of our upcoming nuptials. We'd decided to have our wedding itself at the local registry office, with just a few of Elliott's family in attendance, and then on the following weekend, we'd have the big party for his extended network of family and friends.

"I'm sure I'll be feeling fine by then."

I will admit to feeling a bit bereft at that point. Elliott hadn't even kissed me since he had come home from the hospital, let alone initiated anything else. Not that I expected sexual activity with a broken bone, but I'd noticed a sort of reluctance to have me near him that worried me.

"You're just being weird because you're the stranger here," I told myself when I went in search of his mom. "He's not going to suddenly unlove you just because you're in his home and now everyone knows that we hooked up so fast. Stop being a drama queen, and count your blessings."

"I count my blessings every night when I retire for the evening," Elliott's mom said, strolling past me from the entrance hall to the wing that contained the family's private (as in, not on the public tour) sitting room. "It's better than sheep for putting you to sleep."

"Is it? Oh! Hi. Um, Elliott told me to talk to you . . . Lady Ainslie." That last bit came out all shades of uncomfortable. I hadn't yet settled on what to call her, and Elliott was absolutely no help, saying that her name was Rosalyn, and that she wouldn't at all mind being called that.

"About what?" she asked, stopping before the door to the sitting room. She held a sheaf of papers in her hand, and looked with mild interest at me.

"Elliott asked me to come up with some moneymaking plans for the castle. I did a lot of fund-raising in my old job, and for a local animal shelter, so I know my way around that sort of thing," I said by way of an explanation. "And he really likes one of my ideas—turning the dower house into a wedding venue—but he's too busy to hear the rest of my ideas. He just said to make them happen, but I thought it might be good to bounce the ideas off of someone first."

"A wedding venue," she said thoughtfully, her eyes on me but obviously her thoughts elsewhere. "Yes, I believe I can see that. The house is in excellent shape, although it desperately needs painting."

"I'm sure we could freshen it up a bit," I said hastily, feeling very much like a puppy seeking praise. "That cost would pay for itself in no time." I spent a few minutes explaining my vision for the dower house, which she appeared to like.

"That seems like a most excellent plan," she said, giving me a little pat on the cheek, something she was prone to doing. "By rights, I should move out there, especially with Elliott marrying, but I've never admired the house, and there is ample space here at the castle, so there's no need for such an extreme action. Besides, this is a much better use of the space, and I'm sure we can leave all of the planning in your capable hands."

"You sure can," I said, beaming with pleasure.

"Now, if you will excuse me—"

"There's another idea I had. Elliott really doesn't seem to like tourists visiting the house much."

"No, he never has." She sighed. "He was resistant to the idea to begin with, claiming that it disturbs his muse, which is just ridiculous, but we must humor him."

"Dixon wants to open the house up every day, and I

thought if there was a way that we could make about the same amount of money as would be brought in by daily admittance, but with fewer people, then it would be win-win all around. So I thought of Medieval Times."

Lady Ainslie's forehead furrowed. "The Dark Ages?"

"No, it's a place in the U.S. that has jousting and knights and things, and people dress up and eat food like they did in ye olde days, and it's a hoot and a half. We're talking really popular, and it isn't at all cheap. Since this place is a castle, a real castle, then we could do something similar. You know, playing up to all the history that the house has seen."

"You wish to open a restaurant?"

"No, that would be a lot of people tromping through, which is what Elliott wants to avoid. I thought, why not have just a couple of people who have to pay through the nose to stay in an actual historic castle with the actual historic castle's owners!"

She just looked at me.

"For example, let's say we picked an Elizabethan theme. Elliott says the castle was originally built then, right? So we put out an ad saying that for beaucoup bucks, people can stay here for ... oh, I don't know. A week? Four days? We'll have to work out rates and such, but let's say four days. So if people have to pay two thousand pounds to stay here for four days, they'd get to have dinner with the baron and his family, hang out in parts of the castle that aren't open to the public, and would participate in an authentic Elizabethan banquet. We could all dress up in costumes from that period, and maybe hire a minstrel or something, and it would be a blast, don't you think? And the best part is that we'd make money hand over fist, and yet we'd limit it to just a couple of people at a time, so Elliott wouldn't feel like the place was overrun."

I stopped talking, waiting to hear what she thought. I hadn't missed the way her eyes lit up when I mentioned dressing up in Elizabethan clothing.

"It seems very promising," she agreed. "Where would these people stay?"

"Well, that's one of the things that I wanted to talk to you about. Are there a couple of spare rooms that we could have done up for the VIP visitors? I was thinking maybe two rooms, and we could limit it to two people maximum per room. That way there wouldn't be tons of people hanging around with the family."

She waved that thought away. "There are always extraneous people here. Is that the word I want? Perhaps not, but regardless, the children always have friends visiting, and it's a rare day when we sit down to just family. A few extra people would likely not even be noticed."

"Especially if those people were paying a lot for that honor," I said, cannily playing up to a facet that I knew would please her.

"Two thousand pounds for four days?"

"Per person."

Her eyes brightened even more. "Yes, that would be most acceptable."

"I'm so glad you like the idea. And I had a thought while taking a bath this morning—two of the ladies we met on the cruise work for some upscale travel place. I know that one of them would definitely spread the word among her clients." A thought struck me as I spoke. "And I bet I could get Patrick to talk it up to his rich buddies, too. Now that he's done being weird about Elliott and me, there's no reason for him not to. Especially if he's dating Elliott's sister."

"Hmm?" Lady Ainslie asked, clearly thinking of something else.

"Nothing, just talking to myself."

"I do that, as well. It's very satisfying. Now, Alice dear, I'll leave it all up to you. I really must go write this article about the sale of ivory. So tragic, and really, people should know better, but still they do it. . . ." She toddled off to her sitting room, leaving me with all sorts of plans tumbling around in my head.

I dug through the entries on my phone until I found the number I wanted, and put in a call to Laura. After catching her up with the latest news about Elliott and me, I explained my idea to her, and waited to hear what she thought. "I was thinking we'd call it the Ainslie Elizabethan Experience. Do you think your clients might be interested in something like that?"

"Absolutely! That entire program sounds incredible," she said when I was finished. "Truly magical. Alice—oh, this is going to sound insane, I know, because I just got back from the trip—but would you mind if I booked the first Ainslie Experience for myself? It's a bank holiday in two weeks, and if I tack on an extra day off of work, that would give me four days to stay at Ainslie Castle."

"Done!" I said, then suddenly worried about the cost. "Um. It's pricey, though, Laura. I'm sure we can give you a little discount, but—"

"Pfft," she interrupted. "Don't worry about that. The agency pays for a certain number of research trips per year. I'll just make sure that this is one of them."

"Awesome! I'm so pleased. I've been wishing that I

could see you again, since I couldn't even say good-bye when I had to dash last week."

"I'm dying to see you and Elliott again, too," she said, her voice dropping to add, "You never did tell me the nature of Elliott's injury. Was it something related to his . . . job?"

"Um . . . in a way, yes." I hated hedging like that, but I didn't think it was the best advertising plan to announce that part of the castle was prone to falling on innocent bystanders. I made a mental note to discuss a more permanent structure to keep people away from the danger spots, and focused on the happier idea of raising enough money to have that wing repaired. "But he doesn't like to talk about it, Laura."

"I totally understand. Can you e-mail me a brochure, so I can run it by my boss? I don't anticipate any trouble, but I will need it and an invoice for the accounting people."

"I'll have both to you by this afternoon."

I waited until it was time for lunch (and Elliott's pain medications) before taking both to him along with the news that not only had his mother approved of my plans, but money was already rolling in.

"Should you be out of bed?" I asked, setting down the tray of food and medication, and glancing around the small, dark room that served as Elliott's workplace. "The doctor said you need to rest."

"I can't write in bed. I just fall asleep there, so I came down here. Sitting in a chair and speaking to the computer is well within my abilities, so you can stop making that mother-hen clucking noise."

"Yes, well, I reserve the right to mother you if you do something to hurt yourself. Now, about the plans I came up with. I've already knocked up a brochure, and printed out enough copies to get us by until I can have some professionally made, and have put ads in at several spots, and have started collecting bids for a wee bit of renovation to the dower house. Not a lot, because I know you don't want to spend big bucks just to get going, but a bit of paint will do wonders for it, and shouldn't cost an arm and a leg."

"That's good to know," he said, reaching for the bottle of pain medication that I'd brought in with a bowl of pasta salad and a roast beef sandwich.

"Now," I said, waiting until he'd washed down the pills to sit on his lap, being very careful not to lean on the owie side of his chest. "You may duly reward all my hard work with many breath-stealing kisses."

He gave me a swift, almost impersonal peck. The look on his face was anything but romantic. "There's nothing I'd like to do more, love, but I really have to keep working. I'm just over the halfway point of the book, and I can't slow down until I'm closer to the end. I lost too much time to the accident to be able to spend my day stealing your breath as I'd like."

I studied him, trying to decide if he really was simply so stressed about the book deadline that it was consuming him, or if something else was going on.

Something more ominous.

Something familiar.

He's getting ready to dump you, my inner self warned. *It's Patrick all over again.*

It is not, I argued. *Elliott isn't like Patrick. Elliott is sweet and warm and loving, and he'd never boot me out of my own home.*

Which is why he's so uncomfortable now. Just look at

him. My inner self pointed to Elliott. *Look at that expression. That is not a man who is so head over heels in love with you that he wanted to marry you after knowing you just a couple of days.*

She had a point. Even when he was Mr. I-Must-Write-or-Else on the ship, he still made time to be with me. And go places with me. And kiss me.

Tentatively, I nibbled on his earlobe. Maybe the problem was that he was waiting for a signal from me that I was comfy enough in his home to do those things that people in love did.

"Alice, I'm sorry, but I really must get back to this chapter."

I released his earlobe, my stomach wadding up into a tiny little dense ball of misery. "I thought we could have lunch together."

"I wish we could, but I need to get this chapter finished." He kissed me on my forehead—my forehead!—and urged me off his lap.

I got up with a sense of doom that suddenly made the world dark. "I wanted to tell you about the plans that your Mom and I made."

"And I want to hear about them," he said, his eyes back on the laptop. He held up a small microphone with one hand, obviously wanting to continue dictating. "After dinner, all right?"

I nodded, too choked up to speak, not that he noticed. He leaned back in his chair and closed his eyes, his voice rolling around the small room. "Chapter Eleven. New paragraph. With the blood of the assassin washed off in the cloakroom at the airport comma Damon Reeves fast-talked his way onto a flight from Geneva to Amsterdam."

Sadly, I closed the door behind me, confused and unhappy and unsure of what I should do. Why was Elliott acting so indifferent to me? Was he tired of me already? Embarrassed by me? Out of love with me so quickly?

The hallway in this part of the castle was dark, since the public tours didn't go through the area. I stood for a moment, hearing in the distance the voice of Cecily's partner (and coworker) Clive as he brought yet another batch of tourists through the castle.

There was no safe place for me to go, nowhere I could curl up in a ball and cry, no room that was mine. I've never felt more out of place than I did at that moment, desperate for something comforting, something familiar. With a sob, I ran up the stairs to Elliott's bedroom, throwing myself on the bed and indulging in a good cry.

But even that was ruined when I realized that I was sobbing into his pillow, and that the Elliott smell of it was breaking my heart.

My stupid inner voice was right. He didn't want me anymore. I don't know what happened, but it was plain as day that he no longer loved me, but was too nice to simply come out and say that. He knew how devastated I had been with Patrick, and was trying to be nicer about his breakup.

"Devastated," I said, blowing my nose. My voice was thick and wobbly. "I didn't know the meaning of the word. Now I do. Now I really am devastated." The last word was a wail, and brought on a fresh volley of tears that utterly drenched Elliott's pillow.

"Good," I said when the tear storm faded. I glared at his pillow. "Maybe he'll get a cold in the head from it." The instant I spoke the words, I regretted them. I didn't want Elliott to be sick. I wanted him well and happy and warm and sexy and all the things that he was.

Except mine. He wasn't mine any longer. He was going to dump me, and I'd be alone again. Homeless, loveless, and hopeless.

"Well, not this time, Lord Ainslie," I said, leaping to my feet. I hurried over to a massive wardrobe and yanked out my suitcase, ripping clothing out of drawers and off hangers to fling into it. "This time, I'm the one doing the dumping. I'm going to walk away from you with my head held high. I don't need you, Elliott Ainslie!"

Liar, my inner voice said.

"I don't love you anymore, either!" I zipped the suitcase closed, and jerked it off the bed, hauling it after me as I stalked toward the door, snatching up my purse en route.

And again, a lie. Of course you love him.

I ignored the voice in my head.

"This is over," I said loudly, marching down the hallway, my suitcase in tow. "I will seek a divorce from the Church of Jante!"

Now you're just being stupid. And overly dramatic. No one loves an idiot drama queen. Get over yourself already.

"And I'm breaking up with you, too, voice in my head!" I shouted, starting down the grand staircase to the main floor. "We're done, do you hear me? No more advice, no more snide comments from the peanut gallery, no more so-called insights! I hereby divorce you, too!"

The group of eight people waiting for the next tour watched with interest as I stomped across the black-and-white stone floor, jerking my suitcase viciously. Cecily was in the middle of pointing out something in the brochure. The look on her face was indescribable.

"Don't say it," I said, leveling a finger at her as I stormed past. "Or I'll divorce you, too! Just see if I don't!"

Halfway down the long drive, the growl of a motorbike came up behind me. I moved over a bit so that whichever one of Elliott's brothers it was could get around me. I was distracted, desperately trying to feed my anger so I wouldn't throw myself on the ground and dissolve into a giant puddle of heartbroken goo.

The motorcycle stopped next to me, and the rider flipped up the visor on his helmet. It was Bertie, Elliott's youngest brother, a nice kid whom I liked, despite the fact that he regularly hit me up for money I didn't have. "You going into town, Alice?"

"Yes." I marched on.

"Want a ride?"

It was on the tip of my tongue to refuse, but the sane part of my mind—which I was mostly no longer listening to—managed to point out that I didn't need to cut off my nose to spite myself. So I accepted.

"Hop on."

"What about my suitcase?" I gestured toward it.

He held out his hand. "You'll just have to hump it."

"I beg your pardon!"

"Carry it. Here, get on behind me, and put it between us."

It wasn't very comfortable, but at least I wouldn't have the indignity of standing at the bus shelter with my suitcase, looking every inch the woman who had been rejected by the local baron.

By the time Bertie dropped me off at the train station, my face was lashed with tears. He cocked his head as I climbed off the bike and pulled the handle out of the suitcase. "You going up to London?"

"I'm going home."

"Oh." He gave me a friendly smile. "Gotta get your things, eh? I thought Elliott said he was going to go with you to help you pack up, but I guess with his shoulder such a mess, he's not able to. See you later."

He zoomed off without giving me a chance to correct his false impression, not that I would have. I was in enough pain without telling him that his brother didn't love me anymore.

I sat on a hard, uncomfortable plastic bench at the small station, facing the track and a scraggly line of vegetation that marked the border of some field. The grasses were brown and lifeless, sagging limply downward toward the steel of the train tracks. Two trains arrived, spat out a handful of people, and took off without me. I sat with my hand on my suitcase, watching the trains arrive, eject small groups of people, and take off again. The faces of the passengers in the train had a sickly hue to them, their eyes expressionless, their faces masks of indifference.

Is that what I'd look like one day, the day that this pain stopped tearing me apart inside? I tried to see into my future, to imagine myself riding on a commuter train, or bus, heading to some boring job, the same look of indifferent numbness on my face.

I didn't want to be that way. Even if I had to live without Elliott, I didn't want to have to be numb just to exist.

People came and went around me, but only a few cast curious glances at me. Most of them ignored me, no doubt figuring the crazy lady who sat clutching a suitcase, tears running down her face, was best left alone. In time, the tears stopped, but still I sat, watching trains come and go, and wondering if I'd be able to survive this. And that was when I realized that running away wasn't the answer. I had to go back and face Elliott. I couldn't just leap before I looked anymore, not where he was concerned. He mattered too much.

I was rehearsing the things I was going to say to Elliott, how I would explain that I understood that his feelings had changed, but that I wasn't ready to give up on us, when a man sat down next to me.

I was irritated by his presence. How could I formulate a good argument for why Elliott needed to see reason when there were distractions all around me? This was important, the most important thing I'd ever done. I needed to get it right.

"Where are you off to?"

"I don't know," I answered without turning my head to look at my seatmate. My gaze was firmly affixed to a clump of dead grass that swayed gently in a tiny breeze sweeping along the track. "I'd like to say home, but I don't have a home. Not really."

"Everyone has a home."

I shook my head. "Sometimes, you just live in a place. But it's not a home. A home has heart. It has meaning. It welcomes you and wants you, and you want it. Not every place you live is a home."

"I have a home. It has heart and meaning and welcomed you, Alice."

"Did it?" I turned my head to look at Elliott. "It's not enough, though, is it? Not without the master of the house wanting me, as well."

His gray eyes were solemn as they considered me. "Why do you think I don't want you? Is it because I couldn't have lunch with you?"

"No, it's not just today. It's every day since you got out of the hospital. You're a nice man, Elliott. You're not a

Patrick. I know that you don't want to destroy me when you tell me that you made a mistake, and you don't really want to marry me after all. So you're letting me stay at the castle and maintain the fiction that all is right until ... well, I don't know until what. Or when. Maybe you figured I'd get tired of you and want to leave. The problem is, I don't want to leave you, and I never will get tired of you. I don't know what I've done to change things between us, but I can't stand trying to kiss you and not having you want to kiss me back." My voice caught when my throat tightened. Tears were rolling down my face again, but I didn't care who saw us. My heart was breaking, and I truly didn't know if I could live with the pain for the rest of my days.

"When have I not wanted to kiss you?"

I laughed, more than a bit hysterically, and dripping with bitterness. "When have you? I've tried for days to cuddle with you, and you spurn me at every opportunity. Just today you kissed me on my forehead. My forehead, Elliott! The least erogenous part of anyone's body. You only kiss someone like that when you don't want them. And since you've made it clear you don't desire me physically anymore, not even to kiss, what am I to think but that you're sick and tired of me?"

"Oh, god, it's that, is it?"

His words jolted me out of my black well of pity. I finally looked at him. The pain in his eyes had me blinking back the rest of my tears.

"I'm sorry, Alice. I hoped you wouldn't notice. I hoped you'd be so busy with doing things around the castle that you just ... wouldn't care."

"Wouldn't care about the fact that you don't want me anymore?" I wanted to hit him. "What the hell sort of person do you think I am? I love you, Elliott. I fell in love with you, and I married you, and I went through hell to get to you even though you couldn't be bothered to tell me where you were, or that you were hurt, or even to let your family know about me so someone could call me."

"I didn't have your mobile number," he protested. "I was going to have Dixon hunt you down via the tour line, but I was so out of it with the surgery and drugs that I hadn't had time yet."

That mollified a bit of the pain and outrage, but I still had a veritable sea of grief to get through. "You admit then that we made a mistake."

"No, I admit that I made a mistake."

My heart shattered into a billion jagged pieces. I stared dully at him, wondering how anyone could live with a shattered heart.

"Sweetheart, don't look at me like that." With a pained look, he put his arm around me, pulling my limp body against his. "I didn't mean that I made a mistake in marrying you, not that the marriage—never mind. I meant that I made a mistake in not telling you the truth."

Wildly, my thoughts shot to his secret spy career. Dear god, was he working for the other side? "What truth?" I asked in a squeaky voice.

"You're right that I didn't want to kiss you."

I stared at him some more. My brain didn't want to process those words.

"But not because I don't desire you, or want you in my life, or, hell, even want you sitting on my lap when I should be working." His face twisted, and he dropped his arm from around me. "I didn't want to tell you the truth because ... well, because of pride."

"It's because you're a baron and I'm a nobody—"

"Hell, no. You should know me better than that. It was my pride that was threatening to be hurt if you knew the truth about me."

Oh my god, he *was* an enemy spy!

He took a deep breath, and said quickly, "I'm a weakling, Alice. I have a low pain threshold, and this collarbone has been the very devil to live with since I left the hospital."

I stared in utter surprise at him. That was the last thing I expected him to say.

"I've been going through the pain medications like they were candy, but I know that can't continue, and they aren't very strong to begin with. I thought if I could keep you busy and at arm's length, then I wouldn't be tempted by you."

"I don't understand. What does your broken collarbone have to do with kissing me?"

He looked intensely embarrassed. "It hurts to kiss you. Just putting my good arm around you makes the bone ache, and there's no way in hell I can kiss you without wanting to touch you. Without wanting more. I decided that if I focused on writing this damned book, and you were busy organizing things with the castle, then my collarbone would have time to heal."

"You hurt?" I asked, mentally shaking out the cobwebs of confusion that clogged my brain. "But I was so careful. I made sure I wasn't touching your owie side."

"The break is such that when you sit next to me on the bed, it jars my collarbone."

I clapped a hand over my mouth for a moment before saying, "Oh, Elliott. I'm so sorry."

"I know it wasn't intentional; that's why I didn't want to say anything."

"Even when you were standing up? That hurt, too?"

"You try moving any part of your body without the movement also moving your torso," he said with a wry twist to his lips. "Yes, even when we were both standing, it hurt. And when you sat on me, or leaned into me, or hugged me—"

"I am the worse fiancée and wife ever," I said, wanting to bang my head on the wall. "You were so cold and uninterested. . . . It never occurred to me to ask why. Well, other than the obvious—that you'd decided you made a mistake in marrying me."

"I would like to be outraged that you had such a lack of confidence in me, but the truth is, my darling, you married a coward," he admitted with a watery smile. "I didn't want you to know the truth that I was so . . . weak."

"You're not weak; you're an idiot!" I said, and was about to throw myself against him when I realized what I was doing. Instead, I leaned forward, careful not to touch any part of his body but his lips, and kissed him very, very gently. "Elliott, why didn't you tell me? No, I know you believed I would think the worst of you, but seriously, you idiotic man, why would you not tell me that sitting with you and on you and near you was making your broken bones hurt? I love you, you foolish man. I thought you didn't care about me anymore."

His eyes were suddenly grave again. "Were you really leaving me?"

I sat back against the wall of the station, placing my hand on his where it rested on his leg. "What time is it?"

"Half four."

"I've been here for almost four hours. At least three trains going to London have stopped." I looked at my friend the clump of dead grass. "I couldn't bring myself to get on any of them. I wanted to. I wanted to leave in a huff, to show you that I didn't give a damn. But every time a train stopped, I couldn't do it. I couldn't take those steps to walk away from you. My inner self kept shouting that I was being a world-class idiot, and that I needed to go right back to you and demand an explanation, and I was just agreeing with it when you sat down."

"Thank god for your inner voice." He lifted my hand to his mouth and kissed my fingers. "And thank god for Bertie calling to tell me he'd need seventy-five pounds for a new front tire, or I wouldn't have known you'd left. Alice." He leaned back, as well, his good shoulder brushing against mine. "I want to kiss you very badly right now. I want to hold you, and breathe in the scent of you, and stroke that lovely freckled skin that covers you. I want to make love to you. Several times. And in many varied ways, some involving your captain's hat. But most of all, I want to know you forgive me for being so selfish."

"I forgive you for being human, and for feeling pain, and for having a perfectly normal amount of vanity," I said, smiling at him. "You're going to have to work on my forgiveness for the idiot part of not telling me I was hurting you, but since I'm going to have to do the same for the fact that I didn't talk to you about my feelings, we're pretty even. Well, no, we're not, because I was so self-absorbed that I didn't notice you were in pain."

"I tried my best to hide it. You're not to blame for not seeing that."

He rose. It was quick, but even so, I noticed a flash of pain in his eyes at the movement. He held out a hand for me. I took it, holding on when he was going to let go in order to grab my suitcase. "We really are a pair, aren't we?"

"We are. But I think we're suited, despite that."

We walked out of the train station. Elliott's car was sitting outside. I tossed my suitcase into the back and, with a long look at him, slid into place behind the steering wheel.

"Do you know how to drive?" he asked, slowly getting into the passenger seat.

"Of course." There was a clash of gears, a low, ugly grind as I put my feet on the wrong pedals, and an explosive backfire when the car lurched backward. I grinned at him as I got the car into the proper gear. "Driving on the left will be an experience, but I expect I'll soon get the hang of it."

He said nothing, but hurriedly put on his seat belt.

"You really want to use the captain's hat?" I asked after a few minutes.

"Yes," he said, surprising me. "You've convinced me that role play might be a fun element to introduce into our intimate moments. Not that I wish to indulge in it all the time, but now and again it might be welcome."

"Admit it—you really dug the German sex club."

"I enjoyed the experience before my back seized up, yes."

"I knew it. We're going to make a fly-by-the-seat-of-your-pants-er out of you yet. You'll come to see that spontaneity is the spice of life, and that flinging yourself into adventures without worrying about pesky details brings a zest that makes you feel alive."

"Adventures like leaving your husband without bothering to tell him?"

I shot him a look. "I didn't say that all adventures turn

out well. Some of them might have benefited from a little more . . . er . . ."

"Forethought?" he offered.

"I was going to say communication, but that does as well, I suppose. You know, when you think about it, we really do complement each other nicely. You'll keep me from doing crazy things like running away because you didn't love me, and I'll keep you from becoming a stodgy man who wouldn't recognize a spontaneous act if it bit him on his extremely biteworthy ass."

"No doubt it will all work out admirably."

"I notice you didn't include the parrot in your plans for pirate hat sex—"

"No nipple clamps. I draw the line there."

"Fair enough." I laughed.

We drove along in silence for a few minutes before Elliott said, "I have to admit that I'm relieved you didn't leave me because of my family or the castle."

"What do you mean?"

He made a little gesture without taking his hand off where it rested on his leg. "My family can be a little over-whelming in both number and character. You've only met a couple of my brothers—the full contingent will be sure to arrive for the wedding party."

"I don't think you have anything to worry about," I said in a reassuring tone. "I like Bertie and Dixon and of course Gunner, and your mom is really sweet now that she's over that weird little Americans-are-bad shtick, and is no longer the Red Queen. You know, off with her head? Your castle is Wonderland, I'm Alice, and your mom is the Red Queen, although as I said, she's not anymore."

"If my mother is the Red Queen, then what am I? The Caterpillar?"

"Of course not, hookah aside. You're the White Knight."

"As I recall, he was quite elderly. And also in *Through the Looking-Glass*, not *Alice in Wonderland*."

"Pfft," I said, waving away those objections. "Pedantics. The White Knight was young once, and so you're simply a younger, sexier version."

He gave me a look that just made me giggle.

"Your ideas of Wonderland aside, you must be aware that there will be certain demands that go along with being Baroness Ainslie. No doubt the local groups will ask you to join committees, and open fetes and participate in various rural schemes. My mother will be delighted to hand those duties over to you—she'd far rather devote her energies to needy causes abroad."

"Yeah, she said something about being happy that she wouldn't have to go to one more Women's Institute meeting."

"You don't mind?" he asked, a little worried line between his brows.

"Are you kidding? I'm a baroness—at least I am according to an Internet religion, and I'm going to be a real one in a couple of weeks. I can't wait to swan around and be all Lady Grantham. Can we have some sort of a shindig on the lawn that all the locals come to? With tea tents and pig races and that sort of thing? I will walk around with a big ole hat on, and a pitcher of lemonade, dispensing cooling refreshments and polite chitchat to everyone. It'll be so much fun!"

"You have a strange concept of fun, but you may have a fete at the castle if you like, although I'd prefer you wait until I have the west wing taken care of. I am concerned about the safety of it with the tourists as is." He gave me an approving smile.

"I know you are. That's why I ordered up some of this plastic barrier stuff that comes on a roll. They use it back home for chickens. It'll make sure that no one gets near the bad section." I explained the technical details of the barrier product I'd found online and promptly ordered. "It should be here in a couple of days."

"That is an excellent thought. Thank you." He leaned his head back against the seat rest, saying tiredly, "I can't tell you how delighted I am that you have made the castle your priority. It has long needed a mistress who held its interest uppermost in her thoughts. My mother has done her duty, of course, but her interests have always been elsewhere."

I was silent for a few minutes, not sure if it was wise to taint our newly restored happiness.

Elliott must have sensed the dark turn of my thoughts, because he looked over at me and asked, "You do like the castle, don't you?"

"It's amazing," I said honestly, but picking my words carefully nonetheless.

He sat up in his seat. "I sense an unspoken 'but' in that sentence."

I made a little waffling gesture. "The house is gorgeous, except the bit that's crumbling away and hurting people. But the rest of it—it's very historic. I mean, you can just feel the centuries of history rolling off it."

"I know it's not in the best of shape, but once the restoration is finished, it will be quite impressive. The facade—"

"Elliott, it's not the facade," I interrupted. "Or anything to do with the work you're having done. I think the castle is gorgeous just because it's a castle. I mean, you live in a friggin' castle! Not many people can say that."

"But . . . ?" he prodded.

I bit my lip, then just blurted it out. "But it's not my home."

"Of course it is. I own it, and you are married to me; thus it is your home."

"It's not that." I was miserable again, wishing I'd never brought the subject up.

"Is it because the estate is in my name? It was entailed upon me, although the entail will be broken with my death, so we will be able to leave it to whichever of our heirs we decide."

"No, that's fine, I don't care about that. It's just . . ." I bit my lip again, sorting through the feelings I wanted to express. "You know I was a foster kid growing up, right?"

"Yes. You said you did not have a pleasant childhood."

"It wasn't horrible. I mean, none of my foster parents abused me or anything, but there was never one family who really wanted me. It was like—there's the family . . . and then me, standing to the side. I used to pretend that one day my real mom and dad would swoop down and scoop me up, and tell me how they'd been off in the wilds of South America finding cures for cancer and stuff, but now they were back and I'd have a family again, a real family with a real home."

Elliott digested this for a few seconds, then, ever the practical man, asked, "What can I do to make Ainslie Castle into a real home for you?"

"I don't know," I said miserably. "I don't even know

why I brought this up. Really, anywhere you are is going to be my home."

"No," he said, looking out of the window, his jaw tight. I wondered if I had angered him. "No, it's not the same thing."

"I'm sorry. I know you don't need my wimpy feelings dumped on you right now. I shouldn't have said anything—"

"What sort of parent leaves their child to be raised by strangers?" he suddenly exploded. "If they could not keep you, why did they not give you up for adoption, so that a family might have taken you into their home as their own?"

I had to pull over to the side of the road because I was so surprised by his anger. "I . . . I don't really know what to say. I was told my parents had drug problems, and couldn't take care of me, and put me into the system because of that. Given that lifestyle, it was much better for me to be floating around the foster system, even if I didn't have a permanent home. I appreciate your indignation on my behalf, but it's nothing you need to get irate about now. I got through it. I had counseling all through my teen years, and I'm OK now."

"You shouldn't have to have been so alone." He turned back to me, his eyes alight with little silver glints. "And by god, I will see to it that you do not feel the same way at Ainslie. The public rooms must be left as they are for the tourists, but you shall have charge of redecorating the private rooms. All the private rooms, from the sitting room on up to the bedrooms. You will put your own stamp on them, and they will be your home."

"You know, if I didn't love you to the very tippy top of my tippy top-dom, then I'd love you even more right now. I really appreciate that offer—"

"It's not an offer," he said with grim finality that had me biting back a laugh. "It's an order. You will redecorate, and make the castle a home."

"—but it's not necessary. For one thing, it'll cost an arm and a leg. For another . . . I like the castle the way it is. Well, OK, your bedroom is a bit dark, but it's a guy's room, so that's understandable."

"You will redecorate that, as well," he said, pinning me back with a look that did not allow for discussion.

I did laugh then. "You really are a hoot, you know that? Any woman would leap at the chance of a carte blanche for redecoration, but no, Elliott, we have to be sensible about this. We need that money to freshen up the dower house, and also to buy the things we need for the Ainslie Experience."

"You will redecorate my room—our bedroom—and the attached sitting room," he said after a moment's grumpy silence. "I am willing to let the other rooms go since you are right—it would be ill-advised to spend that much money without need. But I will have a haven for just the two of us."

"All right," I said, patting his hand and pulling back onto the road. "That I will accept. It would be nice to have a private little retreat where we can go and play with the captain's hat."

He gave a sharp nod, and puffed softly to himself in diminishing indignation. I thought it best to drag his mind off my checkered past, and on to something more pleasing. "What exactly did you have planned with the hat?"

"Pardon?"

"You heard me. Come on, out with it. We might not be able to get it on until you heal up, but at the very least you can tell me what you'd like to do."

"No, I can't." His face was obstinate.

"Why not?"

"Do you have any idea how uncomfortable it is to walk around with an erection?" He shot me an annoyed look that made me giggle under my breath. "You may have thought I was uninterested, but I assure you the opposite has been the case. In fact, I've been ready to swear that you've been doing your damnedest to give me permanent blue balls, what with the way you prance around in those tiny negligees, and flounce about the bedroom in just your knickers, not to mention wearing those bras that make everyone with eyeballs in their head stare at your breasts. It's damned frustrating to think about all the things I want to do with you . . . tasting you . . . touching you . . . and not be able to do any of them. Hell. Now look what you've done."

He gestured at his crotch. The fly did look unusually bulgy.

"I'd say I'm sorry, but I had no idea that you were all hot and bothered. You definitely hid that well."

"It was self-defense," he said grimly. "Please don't hit that cottage. It is an old one, and our former gardener has retired to it. I enjoy visiting him."

I swerved just in time, mentally reminding myself to stay on the left side of the road. "All right, I won't make you discuss what you'd like to do with the hat, although I have a couple of suggestions involving some silk scarves, and . . . oops. Sorry. That made you more bulgy. I'll stop now."

"Too late." Out of the corner of my eye, I caught a glimpse of him glaring at his crotch.

"Change of subject time. I'm glad to hear you say you're interested in role play."

"Really? Why is that?"

I grinned at him, and put my foot down on the accelerator. We were close now to the borders of Elliott's land, surrounded by gently rolling pastureland. "Let me tell you about what's in store for the castle."

Chapter 16

Diary of Alice Wood

Day Twenty-nine

The day of our wedding just happened to coincide with the first official Ainslie Experience (as I decided to call it). We didn't plan it that way—in fact, the whole Ainslie Experience almost went down the toilet once Elliott understood that people would be paying to stay for a couple of days with him, and not even the high price tag on it mollified him.

"Since you've already collected the money from these people," he stormed the day I had tried to leave him (very careful not to move his body much as he strode up and down in his tiny office), "I will allow it to go forward, but only because the visitors are people we know, although why you felt it vital to have your ex-lover as one of the participants is beyond my understanding. There will be no other such events, however."

"But, Elliott—we'll make money hand over fist! And it'll just be a couple of people at a shot. You'll only have to see them at meals, and maybe watch a little TV with them, or shoot some pool. Nothing horrible."

The look he settled on me told me just what he thought of that plan. I sighed, and decided to wait until after Laura and Patrick left before broaching the subject again. He'd see just how noninvasive it would really be.

Confident that he would eventually see the wisdom of my ways, for the next two weeks I threw my energy into two main projects: the refurbishing of the dower house, and redecorating our private rooms. The suite consisted of three rooms: a small, dark bathroom that had been converted from a servant's room, the bedroom, and a large-sized sitting room. I had the bathroom painted a cheery yellow, redid the bedroom in pleasing greens and robin's-egg blue (as well as installed a much-needed new bed with ultra-bouncy mattress), and completely gutted the sitting room of its old, heavy Victorian furniture. I had found some furniture stored in one of the attics that probably hadn't seen the light of day for at least a hundred years. The pieces had the long, graceful lines of neoclassical Regency England, and the colors of the upholstery had faded into soft moss greens, rose, and gold. I arranged them around the room, added in a chair that Elliott had said was his favorite, and placed a small lady's writing desk for myself. I also had Elliott's beloved desk carried in by his two youngest brothers.

"What's this?" the man himself asked about a week before our wedding, when he returned from a visit to the doctor. Bertie, Gunner, and I had pulled him into the redecorated room to see the end result. "What's my desk doing here? Why isn't it in my office?"

"Your mother says your so-called office used to be a storage room. A boxroom? Is that the right term? Anyway, it was small and dark and cramped, and I can't for the world imagine how you could write there."

"I could write there because no one bothered me in it," he said, giving his brothers a look that neither of them acknowledged. He strolled around the room, noticing the bookcases filled with his favorite books, and one that I had arranged for myself, and only just started to load. "This is very nice, Alice. I like the furniture. I like the colors. And I like that I have an actual window I can look out of while writing. Yes, this is very nice indeed. I will be able to work here."

"And play," I said with a little waggle of my eyebrows. Instantly, he looked interested, but since we had decreed a hands-off period until after the wedding, so as to give his bones time to heal, I didn't investigate that look.

That didn't stop the tension surrounding us, though. It hummed with electricity, enough that after Bertie hit me up for payment for his part in moving the furniture, and departed to spend it on who-knew-what girl (I swear, the kid was a babe magnet), Gunner looked from me to Elliott and shook his head. "I don't know how you two do it."

"It's not easy," I said with a sigh.

"You're a stronger man than I am, Gunga Din," Gunner misquoted to Elliott. "I couldn't hold out against someone as lovely as Alice. You're sure there's no way you can lie back and let her proceed without you hurting your collarbone?"

Elliott, who had sat at his desk, and was adjusting the placement of his desk pad, and a metal penholder, didn't bother to look at his brother when he answered, "No, there isn't, not that it's any of your business."

"What about a reverse cowboy?" Gunner said after a few seconds' thought. "That's when the girl—in this case Alice—sits on your—"

"Yeah, we know what a reverse cowboy is," I interrupted quickly, seeing the flash of outrage in Elliott's eyes. He might have unbent quite a bit since I had met him, but I could tell that discussing our sex life with his brother was going too far. "You can take it as read that since I'm sleeping in the guest room until after the wedding that we tried and decided it was best to let him heal."

"Well, your loss," Gunner said.

Elliott was now looking at me, a familiar, steamy glint to his eyes that had my breasts and girl parts suddenly clamoring to be placed immediately in his hands.

"Oh," I said, feeling my nipples harden under that potent look.

His eyes narrowed until they were thin slits of bright silver, glowing with passion.

My back arched just a little of its own accord. I blamed it on my breasts. They were shameless hussies who desperately wanted Elliott's notice.

"I feel dirty just standing here," Gunner said, still looking from Elliott to me and back again.

"You could leave," Elliott suggested, his voice low and rough and with a quality that seemed to rub along my skin like velvet.

"I almost feel as if I should stay and chaperone you. Who knows what damage you might do to your broken bone if I were to leave and you fulfill that look you're steaming all over Alice's body?"

"My body likes his steam," I cooed, and took a step toward Elliott.

He stood up, his body lines taut and filled with coiled power, his face a mask of desire.

"Oh, Elliott," I breathed, and prepared to run across the room, unable to resist him any longer.

Gunner caught me on the second step, wrapping an arm around my waist, and hauling me backward toward the door. "See? This is exactly what I'm talking about. You two clearly can't be left on your own together."

Elliott made an annoyed sound of deprivation.

"Bad brother! Stay!" Gunner told him, pulling me out of the door. He shoved me through it, then blocked it with his body, saying to me, "Don't give me that look — you both said he needed time to heal, and it's only been a week. He needs longer than that. Go do something somewhere else, Alice."

"But Elliott needs me — "

I could hear Elliott's footsteps across the wooden floor.

Gunner looked over his shoulder, and flung out a hand, pointing down the hallway. "Flee, sweet maiden! I'll hold back the beast as long as I can, but there's no telling how long I can last."

I waited until Elliott loomed up over his shoulder, then blew a kiss, and dashed off down the hall to the ground floor, chuckling to myself. Gunner was quite right — it had been a near thing, and I made a mental note not to be alone with Elliott again until after the wedding.

That day couldn't come too soon, and despite the feeling that time was crawling by, the morning of our wedding finally did arrive.

I traipsed into our sitting room wearing the new gauzy, flowery tea dress that I planned on wearing at many a garden party. Rosalyn—as I'd finally decided to call her—had taken me to buy it the day before, and I was very pleased with how girly it made me feel.

Elliott stood with Gunner, who was giving him a once-over. We'd decided to go very informal for the wedding itself, with just the few members of his family who were currently in residence as witnesses, saving the big celebration for a month hence. "Mmrowr," I told Elliott, taking in just how handsome he looked in his dark suit.

"Thank you, although I should point out that it's unseemly for the bride to be ogling the best man," Gunner said, giving Elliott's tie a tweak.

"That was Elliott's mmrowr, as you well know," I told him.

Elliott's eyes were mercurial with simmering sexual tension. "Turn," he said.

I made a little pirouette. The layered chiffon of the skirt spun out as I did so.

"Yes," he said slowly, a catlike smile on his face. "Yes, I will enjoy greatly taking that dress off your nubile and wholly desirable body."

"Yes, please," I said, my body instantly one giant erogenous zone.

"Oh, for the love of—thank god this is the last time I have to keep you two chaste," Gunner said, rolling his eyes as he shooed me toward the door. "Stop teasing my brother, you jezebel. You can't slake your lusty thirst upon him until he's been wedded by the government official duly authorized to validate the wedding that I performed over two weeks ago. Now, be off or I'll tell Mum that you came in to molest him."

"Tattletale," I said, mouthing *I love you* to Elliott.

He growled a low, sexy growl in response.

Gunner slammed the door in my face. I sang a happy little song to myself as I ran downstairs, and waited impatiently for Rosalyn. She made me wait for an hour, confining me to a room that used to be a conservatory, but was now a greenhouse for vegetables and dwarf fruit trees. By the time we arrived at the registry office in Ainston, Elliott and three of his brothers (Gunner, Bertie, and Rupert, whom I had just met the night before) were waiting.

The ceremony itself was quick and anticlimactic. It was over in a matter of just a few minutes, following which we signed the register, and then found ourselves outside in the sunshine, the sense of something lacking lying profoundly over us all.

"Your version of the wedding was much more memorable," I told Gunner.

"It's what we in the Church of Jante strive for," he said complacently, then buffeted the air next to Elliott's shoulder. "All right, old man, you're truly tied down now. Happy?"

Elliott took my hand and kissed my fingers, then gave a what-the-hell look, and pulled me into his arms. "Very much so," he said, his eyes all but stripping me naked. He added in a tone just for me, "And very ready for a second wedding night."

I touched the hollow at the bottom of his throat. "You're not hurting?"

"I didn't say that." He waggled his eyebrows at me. "But my collarbone is healed, yes. It's been a long two weeks, my love."

"Has it ever," I said on a sigh, and squealed softly to myself when he kissed me with the passion of a man long deprived of such actions.

We had a celebratory lunch in town (enlivened by risqué comments from Elliott's brothers, and reminiscences by Rosalyn of her own wedding), following which the family went their separate ways, with Elliott and I returning home.

"Race you to the bedroom," I said as we got out of his car. "We've got three hours before the first Ainslie Experience—"

"And last!"

"—kicks off, and the guests arrive, which is just enough time for me to jump your newly healed bones on our brand-new bed."

"There you are," a voice called from the house. Patrick strolled out, a tall, elegant woman on his arm. "We wondered where everyone was. Elliott, you're going t'have t'do better than this if you want people t'shell out four grand for a few nights, not that I object t'doing so, since Jane tells me that you're in desperate need what with more of the castle falling t'pieces, but really, old man. At least have the paying guests met at the door with a little champagne, and perhaps a few nibblies."

I looked at Elliott. He looked at me. We both wanted to cry.

"Alice," Elliott said, pulling himself together faster than me. I really had my heart set on some sexual tension relief. "May I introduce my sister Jane. Other than being cursed with a dubious taste in men, she is normally a very intelligent woman, and I'm sure you'll like her."

"Of course I will." With an effort, I beat down my libido and put out my hand for her to shake. She looked at my hand, looked at Elliott, and then embraced me in a bear hug that was surprisingly strong.

"How nice to meet you at last, Alice. I've heard so

much about you from Mummy and Gunner. And of course, Patrick, although I don't for a moment believe half the things he says about you. Elliott would never fall in love with a woman who was no better than she should be."

Patrick coughed and said quickly, "That's enough of the polite chitchat, my love of loves. Shall we not see the rooms that you inventively convinced me t'pay for? My man, show us the accommodations."

"I hope the day comes when I won't want to punch you in the face for leering at my sister," Elliott told him, taking my arm to stroll inside. "But until then, you're welcome to Ainslie Castle."

"Nice going not rising to the 'my man' bait," I told Elliott in a low tone. "He's clearly feeling inferior and trying to make you feel like a loser because of it."

"I'm well used to him throwing around the fact that he's made a fortune while I have to spend every pound I have on the castle. He won't get a rise out of me that way. You, however . . ." He pinched my behind, making me squeal loud enough that Jane and Patrick, who were in front of us, turned to see what was going on.

Jane was nice enough, although she spent a good deal of time chatting with Elliott and Patrick, and later the rest of the family as they returned home, about people and things that I had no knowledge of. I did my best to hold up my end while not making it overly clear that I really, really wanted time alone with Elliott, but it wasn't until Laura arrived that I relaxed.

Until I saw her companion.

"Well, this is a pleasure, isn't it? It's quite like we were back on board that dreadful ship," Deidre said, sashaying in a line straight to Elliott, who had risen to greet the new-comers. She paused to cast a glance around the family's sitting room, taking in not only Patrick but Gunner and Rupert. She ignored the women present. "Who would have guessed that dear, charming Elliott was a peer? A baron, no less." She turned back to him and simpered. "I suppose by rights I should curtsy, and say 'my lord,' but as we're old friends—"

She planted her lips right on his, pressing herself against him.

Secure in the knowledge that Elliott loved me, I ignored Deidre and went to Laura, giving her a little hug and telling her how nice it was to see her. "Although I'm surprised at your choice of companion," I told her, nodding toward Deidre.

She made an exasperated face. "You wouldn't believe the fuss she made when she found out who Elliott really was. Lord Ainslie, I should say. I suppose I should call you Lady Ainslie, too."

"Pfft. He's Elliott, I'm Alice, and you really are a friend, although not an old one." I took her around the room and introduced her to Elliott's brothers, sister, and mother before sitting down with her on a small sofa. "So, tell me, how are things in Windsor?"

"Oh, you know, much the same as ever." She waited a moment until Deidre, with her usual style, dominated the conversation in the room, and then said, "Elliott looks well. Has he recovered from his accident?"

"He has, thankfully."

"You must be dreading the thought of him going out on more . . . assignments."

I shifted uncomfortably. The truth was, I'd been meaning to bring that subject up to Elliott, but the time never seemed to be right. "I will admit that I'm hoping he's going to hang up that particular hat now that we're married. I mean, most spies don't like to have families, do they? They're always used against them in movies."

"Very definite pressure points." Laura nodded. "He must have an especially effective security system here in order to protect himself and his family."

"I think so," I said slowly. "The windows and doors are all wired up to a system, and you have to punch in a code to turn it on and off, so there's that. But I don't think he's overly worried that he'll be attacked here. I mean, there's lots of people around. He has oodles of brothers and sisters, some of whom live and work here, while others drop by for periods when they need a break, or just want to visit."

"And there are servants," Laura said, her gaze going around the room. "Their presence must reassure you."

I looked over at Marie, one of two daughters of Franklin the groundskeeper. Marie served as daily help—doing some cooking and a little light cleaning of the family's rooms, while her sister, Anne, kept the public rooms tidy. For the Ainslie Experience, I'd promised Marie a bonus in her salary if she helped serve the drinks and meals. She agreed, although she demanded a sexy serving wench outfit for the costumed evenings.

Elliott had told me that although the castle had, in times past, engaged more than a hundred servants, now they mostly did for themselves. It helped that many of the rooms where closed up, the furniture covered, and only aired once a year in summer, when any signs of decay were noted.

"Yes," I said slowly, wondering how Marie in a wench costume was supposed to make me feel better. I decided that it wouldn't enhance Laura's experience to know just how broke the estate was, and how few employees there really were. "They're a great help."

"You said you did some redecorating? I imagine that was great fun."

"It was a blast. So much fun, and I found some wonderful pieces in the attic that just fit perfectly into my vision of the sitting room. Would you like to see it?" I was relieved to be off the subject of servants and, when Laura agreed, took her (and Deidre, who insisted on tagging along) to see the renovated suite. Everyone was duly impressed, even Jane, who had made a disparaging comment about the odds and bobs that had been tossed into the attic.

"This is a lovely room," Laura said, standing at the window and looking out at the drive. "What a glorious view you must have of the park when the scaffolding isn't ruining it."

I made a face at the metal structure that spread across the front of the castle. To be honest, I'd gotten used to seeing it there. "It's just temporary, and it's easy enough to see through it."

"I would find it highly disconcerting to be making love knowing there could be workmen standing on the other side of the window watching everything," Deidre drawled, running a finger down Elliott's arm.

"On the contrary, we've found that spectators heighten the sense of forbidden fruit," he replied, giving her a bland smile.

I thought her eyes were going to pop out of her head, and had to smother a sharp bark of laughter at Elliott's teasing. His eyes were filled with amusement when they met mine.

"Naughty," Deidre said at last, and followed the others when they exited.

"I think it's time for dinner. Tonight is just a normal,

nonhistorical dinner, and there's no need to dress up for it," I told them all, herding them toward the door. "But if you wish to wash up beforehand, we'll gather in the sitting room in twenty minutes, all right? Do you all know where your rooms are? Awesome."

I closed the door on the last of them and turned to face Elliott. "Quickie?" I asked.

He pursed his lips in thought, looked like he was about to agree, and reluctantly shook his head. "I think after waiting these endless months, we should take our time."

"It's only been two weeks, silly," I said, and went over to give him a kiss. "You're right, of course, but all that talk of voyeuristic sex . . . well, enough said."

He pinched my butt again, and we parted, me to go to my temporary room and take off my wedding clothes, and Elliott to do likewise.

We both tried our best to be witty and entertaining hosts, but the truth was that we so badly wanted to be together, we spent a good amount of the time just sending looks fraught with desire and need down the length of the dining room table. Rosalyn had yielded her spot at one end to me, with a grace that made me feel truly part of a family for the first time in my life. I beamed first at her, then at Elliott, looking with contentment at my new family and friends as they laid into the roast beef that Marie had worked on all day.

The hours passed, neither especially slow nor too quickly. We ate; we strolled around the grounds showing off the garden to the visitors (although Patrick had been to the castle before); we held an informal tour of the house with Elliott and Jane describing all the historic points, finishing the evening with a couple of rounds of billiards, the ladies against the gentlemen (they won, but only because Gunner turned out to be nigh on par with a pool shark).

At long last Elliott and I managed to leave the party without too many undue comments.

"Happy sex," Gunner called after us as we made our good-nights. "Don't break anything else, El, or Alice may just spontaneously combust with sexual frustration."

Elliott closed the door to the billiards room and looked at me. "Shall we have that race now?"

"Just stay out of my way," I said before bolting. I beat him to the bedroom, but only because he let me. I snatched up the sexy nightie I'd left off earlier in the day, and with a look that had him pausing while standing on one foot, in the act of pulling off his shoes, headed to the bathroom while saying, "I expect you to be naked and ready to rumble when I return."

He was.

"Is this ready enough?" he asked. He was lying naked on the bed, the captain's hat on his head, and the parrot clipped to the headboard, where it hung down drunkenly.

I laughed aloud. "OK, that is sweet, you bringing the pirate hat back for wedding night number two. I came prepared, too." I held up a bottle of massage oil. "Or rather, your mother did. She thought a little oil would make things easier."

He looked concerned as I moved over to the bed, and popped the top off the oil. "Won't that make a mess?"

"We will make a mess, but this?" I shook the bottle at him. "This is nonsticky, superslick stuff that is supposed to help you give the most amazing massages. And before you demand that I hand it over so you can use it on me, I'll point out that it's my turn."

"It most definitely is not."

"Well, either way, it's the bride's prerogative to pick who uses the slicky oil first, and I choose me." I dribbled a line of it up both his legs, and knelt between his ankles. "Since I know you like organization, I'll let you in on the schedule for this evening. First, there will be an erotic massage, mostly meant to relax some of your muscles which appear to be so tense, they're about ready to snap."

"It's been a very long two weeks," he admitted.

"I agree. Hence the massage. Following that, the oral sex."

He smiled. "Was that a Monty Python reference, or do you mean it?"

"Both. *Holy Grail* is one of my favorite movies, but we'll discuss that another time. And finally, the big finish in which you and I get down to business and see if we can beat our previous record."

I put my hands on his calves, and rubbed the oil in, not able to do much in the line of a deep muscle massage since he was lying on his back, but if the state of his penis was anything go by, the erotic part was most definitely working.

"What record? Oh, lord, yes, right there." He moaned softly when I used the heel of my hand on his thighs, his toes bobbing happily with each stroke. I had to say, the oil was very good, leaving no sticky residue, but providing a seemingly frictionless surface. I did the same to his other leg, then slathered a little oil on his penis and testicles before moving past them to his chest and arms.

"Hmm? The record in which we had the orgasm to end all orgasms last time. I don't remember how long it took us, but it was quick. I think we can be quicker."

"Most women," he commented, his hands clutching

the sheets when I oiled up his nipples and gave them a gentle tweak, "most women don't like a man who's quick. They prefer longer experiences. You're the only woman I've ever met who wants me to be faster than I was before."

"That's because there's such a nice payoff, and if you don't spend all night doing it, then you have time to recover and do it all over again. OK, let me know if anything hurts. No holding back and being brave, all right?" I dribbled a little oil on his shoulders, and very, very gently rubbed it into the muscles.

"I promise I will tell you if my collarbone hurts, but right now, there are other parts of me that are aching, and yet you cruelly ignore them."

"I'll get back to them. This is supposed to relax you, first." I looked down at him. He didn't look relaxed. In fact, the way his eyes were focused on my breasts, he looked about ready to spring. "You are feeling the benefits of this, aren't you?"

"Yes. Now take off that thing and let me oil you up. I know you said I couldn't, but it's my wedding night, too, and I have the right to oil you and make you relax."

"How about a compromise?" I asked, setting aside the bottle. His body glistened in the soft light, every bit of his front from the neck down slick and inviting.

"What would that be?"

I peeled off the nightie and straddled his hips, pressing his penis between us as I lay out on top of him. The oil allowed me to slide in a very sensual way, one that not only stirred him to new heights of arousal, but made my body alight with need and want and all those things that only Elliott seemed to stir. "This. Look, I can slide around on you."

He groaned and grabbed my hips to keep me from doing just that. "You're about to have an answer to just how quickly I can break our previous record."

"Well," I said, thinking about all the things I had planned for that evening. "I'd hate to waste that, and since my motor has been running nonstop the last two weeks, I'd be more than happy to skip right to the main course, but that does mean you owe me the chance to lick you up one side, and down the other."

He just stared at me for a second, then tipped his head back and laughed loudly. "You are the most amazing woman, Alice. I don't know what I did to deserve you, but I thank god that you decided to put up with me. You may lick me another time. But for now . . ."

I was on my back before I realized what he was doing. He loomed over me, now wantonly rubbing himself on me, transferring some of the oil so that we were both wonderfully slippery.

"And now, as you said, the oral sex." He gave me a roguish look before sliding downward, his breath hot and moist on my thighs as he spread my personal paradise, and went to town. So to speak. Between the heat of his mouth, the feeling of his stubble on my thighs, and his dancing fingers that seemed to know exactly where to touch, I was soon at the point of no return.

"Now!" I yelled, tugging at his hair. Luckily, he gave in to my demands, and slid upward along my oil-slicked flesh, taking my legs over his arms as he did so, and sliding into me with one long move. That was all it took for me— my muscles clamped down around him as I went soaring. I did something I never do—I yelled with the glory of it all: my love, the feeling of the orgasm, and, most of all, the knowledge that we were bound together in ways that went beyond a mere legal event. He was mine, my Elliott, my love, my family. He was the part of me that I'd been waiting for since I had become an adult.

It took him a little longer, all of another four seconds, before he, too, gave in to his own orgasm. He sprawled on top of me, his hips twitching a little with the lingering sensations of the moment, his breath hot on my neck.

I slid my hands down his back before wrapping my arms around him, holding him tight, tears burning the backs of my eyes.

"Alice?"

There was concern in his voice. I opened my eyes to smile at him. He kissed the edge of my eye. "Why are you crying, love?"

"I'm just so happy." I couldn't help giving a watery chuckle. "It's stupid, I know, but I never thought I'd be this happy. I love you, Elliott Edmond Richard Ainslie, eighth Baron Ainslie, lord and master of all you survey, except me because I don't go in for that business about men mastering women. Did we beat our record?"

He blinked at me, glanced at the clock, and then looked back down at me. "No."

"Damn."

He smiled then, a smile that lit up his eyes, and filled me with warmth that I knew was permanent. "We will have to try again. And keep trying, until we get there."

"Absolutely. I'm so glad you see the benefit of not spending hours at this."

"You really are the most amazing woman," he said, laughing a little as he rolled off me, pulling me until I was draped partially over him. "I will do my utmost to fulfill your every desire."

"You already have," I said, pulling up the blankets,

and snuggling into him. "Except for the nipple clamps, and we'll get there in time."

Life, I decided as we drifted off to sated, happy sleep, could not be any better.

But three hours later, I had a chance to bitterly regret those words. I stood shivering naked, awkwardly clutching a blanket to myself, while I watched my husband get dressed at gunpoint.

"I don't understand," I said for what must have been the fifth time in as many minutes. "Why are you doing this?"

"You explain it to her," Deidre said. She was dressed in a black pullover and black pants, and had her hair pulled back into a no-nonsense ponytail.

I looked from her to Laura, who was holding the gun on Elliott while he pulled on his clothing. "Is this some sort of a weird joke that Gunner set up? Because I have to say, I don't think it's very funny."

"It's no joke, Alice. And I'm sorry that you had to be here to see this—I was hoping that we might be able to accomplish this without you witnessing it, but there's no help for it. We can't have you talking, you see. It wouldn't go down well at all."

I shook my head. "I really do not think this is funny—"

"It's not a joke," Elliott said, slipping on his shoes before standing up. He seemed to be much less fuzzy-minded than me. I was still having issues processing the fact that one moment we had been sound asleep, and the next Laura and Deidre had prodded us awake with identical guns, and a demand that Elliott get dressed. He turned to face the two women. "I don't know what you think you're doing, but I assume you're kidnapping me, no doubt in hopes for a big ransom."

"We're not kidnapping you for ransom, darling," Deidre drawled, her eyes eating him up. For some reason, that really irritated me. Not only had she seen Elliott naked, but now here she was ogling him right after dragging him out of our bed. "Our handler wishes to talk to you. To find out just who you are, and who you work for."

"Handler?" Elliott's eyes narrowed. "You're joking."

Deidre waved her gun carelessly. "I never joke about work, darling. Now if you'd be so kind as to disable the alarm, I believe we'll be on our way."

"Elliott?" I asked, a sudden cold chill coming over me that had nothing to do with the fact that I was naked, and everything to do with the suddenly frightened look in his eyes.

"Your lover boy and I are going to take a walk," Deidre told me, her teeth flashing in a cruel smile. "Since I'm a romantic at heart, I'll allow you one last farewell."

"What is going on?" I asked Elliott, my eyes on the two women.

"They're . . ." He stopped, then made an abbreviated gesture. "For lack of a better term, spies."

"*They* are?" My mouth dropped a good inch as I stared at Laura. "But . . . how can that be? Laura?"

"Sorry, Alice." She gave a shrug. "I didn't want you to find out, I really didn't. But this was too good of an opportunity to miss. Once we told our handler about Elliott, he very much wanted us to bring him in for interrogation."

"Is everyone in the whole world a spy but me?" I demanded to know, a headache suddenly blossoming at my temples.

"Who do you know who is a spy?" Elliott asked me. He had moved ever so slightly, I couldn't help but notice, shifting a bit to the side in a way that blocked me from

Laura. I suddenly realized a number of things, none of them good. Laura's oblique references to me meant she was going to shoot me. They couldn't have a witness running around, so she planned to shoot me right then and there.

"I thought you were my friend," I told Laura, moving to the side so I could level a real quality glare at her. "I would never have told you about Elliott being a spy if I thought you were going to turn out to be one yourself. Oh! You're a bad spy! You're working for bad people, aren't you? Oh my god, how could you do that? You seemed so nice!"

"I *am* nice," Laura said, giving me an annoyed look. "I'm very nice, and I did apologize. But business is business, and capturing a British agent is just too good of an opportunity to let slip through our fingers."

"What the hell is this about me being an agent? I'm not an agent. I'm a writer," Elliott said loudly. "I write books about spies; I'm not one myself."

"You're not?" Was he lying to protect his cover? Or was he telling the truth? I thought back over the time Laura and I had followed him. "But you met with Gunner in Cologne. You gave him a mysterious paper, and you told me he was a spy."

The look Elliott gave me was filled with questions. "When did I say that?"

"In Cologne. You said he was an industrial spy." I clutched the blanket around me with fingers that were white with strain. "What was I to think but you were one, too? You knew all that stuff about spies, and Laura agreed with me—oh! That was because you knew what a spy would do, wasn't it? You used me to follow Elliott!"

"We were just trying to discover if he was worth pursuing or not," Laura answered, not looking the least bit contrite.

I couldn't help but look at Deidre, who made a face. "Don't worry your little head about me, darling. I have no interest in Elliott other than what he'll bring us in terms of reward. I prefer the other team, as a matter of fact."

"Well, hell," I said, feeling extremely jaded, among other things. "So let me get this straight—you're not a spy?" I asked Elliott.

"No. You really thought I was?" He moved slightly to the right, once again blocking Laura. This time, I didn't move aside.

"I did. But you have to admit that you helped it along by being mysterious, and saying what you did about Gunner."

"I was joking. He's a photographer, not a spy."

"Oh, Elliott," I said, and moved toward him.

Laura protested, but I said, as I clutched him, "If you're going to kill me and take Elliott to god knows what horrible foreign place to be tortured, then you can at least give me a minute to kiss him."

His eyes were worried as I leaned in to kiss him, whispering as I did so, "You take Laura. I'll go for Deidre."

He didn't even get a chance to protest. Just as our lips touched, Laura stepped forward to break us up. I threw myself to the side, whipping the blanket from around me, and flinging it and me onto Deidre, sending her stumbling backward into the heavy wardrobe. I had taken her sufficiently by surprise that I caught her off guard, but she recovered quickly, at least quickly enough to fire her gun. It bucked beneath the blanket as we fell to the ground. Pain burned along my rib cage, but I didn't pay it any mind. I had to get that gun away from her no matter what, and I wasn't going to let a little thing like being shot stop me.

"Ah, I see I'm a little late for the evening's activities."

The voice that spoke was male, coolly arrogant, and so familiar it had not only me stopping just as I was going to tackle Deidre, but everyone else in the room whirling around to look at the door.

Anthony stood there, a large gun in his hand, and a little smile that did not at all match the glint in his eyes.

"Drop the gun, please, Deidre." He lifted his own. It had a long extension on it that I recognized from TV as being a silencer. "I deplore violence, but that doesn't mean I won't hesitate to shoot you if I have to."

"What the—," Laura started to say. She looked in confusion at Deidre, who was glaring at Anthony, but as the latter leveled his gun at her, she snarled something rude and tossed her weapon onto the floor.

"And you," Anthony said, looking at Laura. "On the floor, please."

Laura said something very rude, but also tossed her gun onto the floor.

"OK, now I'm lost," I said, hobbling over to Elliott. "Why is Anthony standing in your bedroom with a gun on two women who are supposed to be travel agents but are really spies?"

"I suspect that is because there is more to comrade Anthony than appears," Elliott said, giving him a speculative glance. "MI5 or 6?"

"I work for a branch of the latter, one concerned with tracking domestic espionage," Anthony said, nodding toward the sisters. "We've had our collective eye on these two for some time. Now, my dears, if you will just lie down on the floor with your hands behind you . . ."

Elliott, clearly intending on helping Anthony, started toward him, but the blanket that was covering me got caught on Elliott's foot, and sent him stumbling forward between Deidre and Anthony before falling to his knees in a tangle of legs and blanket.

That's when all hell broke loose.

Laura lunged for Anthony, doing an odd sort of cartwheel toward him that ended with her kicking him in the face, which in turn sent him reeling backward until he slammed into the wall, and slid to the floor in a dazed heap. Meanwhile Deidre, grabbing the gun from the floor, turned back toward me.

I jerked enough of my blanket from under Elliott so that it caught Deidre behind her ankles. She fell forward, and I leaped on her, using the fact that she was immobile to grab her head and bash it against the wardrobe a couple of times until she lay still. I spun around, intent on helping Elliott.

He was dealing with Laura, attempting to get the gun that was pointed at his head out of her hands. I grabbed the chair next to the door, and lunged over toward them, slamming it into the backs of her legs. She fell forward, allowing Elliott to knock the gun out of her hands. She struggled against him, fighting and kicking, sending the gun skittering under the bed. Elliott pinned her down, snarling at her to stop fighting.

"Deck her!" I told him, moving over to see how badly hurt Anthony was. "Did you see that move she made on Anthony? She clearly knows all sorts of martial arts, so just knock her out!"

"I've never struck a woman!"

"Now is not the time to be chivalrous!" Anthony was out cold, but breathing, and hopefully not injured too seriously. I got to my feet, dancing around Elliott and Laura, the chair clutched in my hands while I waited for an opportunity to smash it down over Laura's head.

Elliott looked up at me. His eyes widened, then narrowed when he turned back to Laura. With great precision, he captured her arms, and pressed one hand against her neck. She fought him tooth and nail for the count of ten, then suddenly went limp.

"I knew that Vulcan death grip would come in useful one day," he said with satisfaction as he got to his feet. "Old MI5 agent once taught it to me. I had no idea it was a real thing. Alice, my love, how bad is it?"

"How bad is what?" I looked down at myself. I was still naked, but now my entire left side was covered in blood. In a rush, the burning pain I'd felt earlier returned to me, leaving me breathless and wobbly. "Holy crapballs, I really was shot."

The world seemed to tilt to the side, then got very dark and scary. At least it was until I heard Elliott's voice calling from a long way away, and felt his warm arms around me, keeping me from sliding into nothingness.

"So Anthony had been following Laura and Deidre all along? That whole business with the socioeconomic impact of tourists was bull?" I asked Elliott some three hours later. He held out a sweater for me, which I carefully put on.

"Evidently his cover is quite valid, but it is a cover." Elliott helped me get settled in a wheelchair. "He was suspicious when they started becoming interested in me—and we have to talk about that at a later time—so he used that cover to account for the river trip."

"But why did he leave to go back to England?" I shook my head when Elliott wheeled me out of the cubicle I'd been given. "Laura and Deidre were still on the boat."

"Evidently he left Dahl on board the ship to watch them. He felt that if they were that interested in me, one or both would go back to England to find me, and he wanted to be a step ahead of them in that situation."

"So Dahl was in it, too?"

"Yes."

"Huh. I would have never guessed that they are anti-spy dudes. I mean, they're so eccentric! Or at least Anthony is."

Elliott smiled as we emerged into the waiting room, one I knew very well. "I think you're going to have to reform your idea of what a covert agent is, my love. Ah, there is everyone."

We spent a few minutes being greeted, and reassuring the family that we were both fine.

"Well," Gunner said, holding the door open for Elliott to wheel me out of the emergency room. "At least you had a wedding night. I hope it was good enough to hold you for—how long did the doctor say you would need, Alice?"

"A couple of weeks," I said sadly. I wanted to slump in the wheelchair, but the bandages around my side were too tight.

"We must all be thankful that you weren't hurt seriously," Rosalyn said. She was on the other side of Elliott, Patrick and Jane at her heels. "I can't imagine what those evil women thought they were going to do with you, but I'm just glad that your friend was there to save you."

Elliott and I exchanged a look. We'd decided to let Anthony take all the credit for the capture, since neither of us wanted more attention than we were already receiving.

And that was pretty copious considering that all of Elliott's available family had come with us to the hospital, although I hadn't remembered any of that, having fainted in the very best style of heroines who lived in castles.

"Yes, it was very timely of him," I said with a little smile at Elliott.

Rosalyn patted my shoulder. "It can't be pleasant having your ribs scratched, but since nothing was broken, and the bullet didn't hit an organ, then I'm sure that you'll be able to return to making grandchildren soon." She beamed at me. "I'm so glad that Elliott chose you to marry. You're going to make an excellent chapter in my autobiography. Come, Jane, dear. I wish to have a few words with you about what you've been up to in Paris."

Elliott helped me out of the wheelchair, and eased me into the passenger seat of his car.

"I'll catch a ride with you," Gunner said, lingering behind him.

"Like hell you will. I'd like to have some time alone with my wife."

Gunner nodded to where Jane, Patrick, and Rosalyn were getting into a Land Rover. "Don't make me have to listen to the lecture Mum is going to read Jane about the wisdom, or lack thereof, regarding her proposal to move in with Patrick. It's bound to get ugly since Patrick keeps telling Mum that he has more than enough money to buy Ainslie Castle from you, if we'd just convince you to sell."

"I'm not selling, and you're not riding with me. Go talk to that detective you seemed to like," Elliott said, nodding over to where a couple of plainclothes detectives from London emerged from the hospital. Anthony, his head swathed in a bandage, was holding his own conversation with a couple of men who Elliott had told me quietly were from MI6. As we looked over, Anthony raised his hand in acknowledgment, one that Elliott returned.

"Hmm," Gunner said, his eyes on the pretty blond detective who had been sent to help take the traitorous sisters into custody.

Elliott didn't wait for his brother to decide—he got into the car, and started it up before Gunner could say anything.

"I'm sorry," he said after ten minutes of silence.

I turned my head to look at his profile, barely visible in the darkness. I'd been watching the black shapes slide by as he drove, as the painkillers put me in a suitably dreamy state. "For what? Me getting shot? That wasn't your fault."

"I'm sorry that I didn't protect you better, yes, but I was also apologizing for being so mysterious that you thought I was a spy." The silhouette of his face shifted as he looked at me. "You really thought I took that trip in order to cover covert actions?"

"Well, it seemed to make sense at the time. Especially after you said what you did about Gunner."

"I thought you knew me better than that. Perhaps we did rush things. It might have been better if we had time to get to know each other before we were married."

"You're lucky I'm drugged out of my gourd right now, because if I wasn't, I'd punch you in your good shoulder," I said sleepily. "We may have rushed things, but that just means we have lots of time to learn all there is to know. For instance, I'm not going to tell you about the fact that I can tie a cherry stem into a knot with my tongue until our third anniversary. It'll be a wonderful surprise for you when I trot out that fact, let me tell you!"

His laughter was warm and comforting, filling the car and surrounding me in a cocoon of happiness and love. "Ah, Alice, where would I be without you?"

"Lost, unloved, and miserable," I said serenely. "Now pull over and kiss me. I have about half an hour before the painkillers wear off, and it's going to be a long three weeks."

He did as he was told, pulling me onto his lap, my body singing a happy little song about being held so close to him. "All right, but remember, it'll be my turn to be in charge when the couple of weeks are up."

"Absolutely, your right royal lordship," I said, and allowed him to kiss the breath right out of my lungs.

Read on for a a sneak peek at Katie
MacAlister's next Matchmaker in
Wonderland Romance,

A MIDSUMMER
NIGHT'S ROMP

Available from Signet Select in May 2015

We continued down another dozen steps until Gunner stopped, saying, "All right, we're at the bottom."

"Sorry," I said, releasing his shirt and giving his back a quick brush to try to relax the wrinkles I'd put into it. "You may want to iron your shirt later."

"Actually, I was going to tell you to hold on to me since the floor isn't level and I have no idea if there has been any destruction since Elliott last visited."

"So long as you don't mind a wrinkly shirt." I clutched the material again, trying to peer around him as we slowly walked forward. "There aren't any rats down here, are there?"

"I imagine there are any number of them. Why? Are you afraid of rodents?"

"Not unduly so, although I could do without the mental image of being trapped by a cave-in and consumed by a horde of hungry rats."

He laughed, but it sounded muffled and unnatural, making me all that much more aware that we were deep under the castle and far away from all signs of life. "Don't worry, I won't let that happen. I have my mobile phone. Ah, here we go." He stopped suddenly and set the lamp on the ground. "I thought I remembered something like this. Let me light the second lamp, and then I'll show you what I hope will make up for losing the premium dig site."

The passage was too narrow for me to see anything around him but the brownish gray stone walls, in some places stained black over the centuries, with various bits of roots and long-dead plant life sprouting through crevices. I rubbed my nose, which was itching with the smell of earth and decay.

Gunner got the second lamp lit. He flashed a grin over his shoulder at me. "Ready to be astounded?"

I eyed him. "You're not going to drop trou and demand I admire your gorgeous testicles, are you?"

"Not after you disparaged their beauty." His teeth flashed again, and then he lifted his arms, a lamp in each hand, and turned to the side so I could see past him. Beyond him was a whole lot of blackness . . . and dull gray shapes dotting the ground.

I gawked for a second, then dropped the shovel and toolbox and squeezed past him, taking one of the lamps in the process. "What is this, a wall? Or the road?"

"That, my sweet Lorina, is the corner of a wall of a structure. See the right angles? It's definitely a building of some sort and could possibly even be part of the second villa." Gunner carefully walked past me, then stood looking down at the exposed stone structure that lay crumbled and half-buried in the dirt of the bolt-hole, disappearing under one of the brick walls of the castle.

"And we don't even have to dig down for it. It's just a matter of uncovering it."

"OK, that is worth giving up the prime spot for," I said complacently, mentally rubbing my hands together at the thought of stealing some of Paul's thunder. Then I realized I shouldn't be relishing that since I had a plan, and, the temptation of Gunner aside, I wasn't going to forgo my vengeance. Not when there were other women like Sandy out there. "We should get Daria in here, though. She's a bit hurt because Paul swanned in and took away the cellar dig from her."

He made a face, then gave a rueful grin. "I was going to protest that I'd prefer to remain with you alone, but this isn't the ideal location for seduction, so we might as well have the help she'll be able to give us."

"Look, buster," I said when he pulled the walkie-talkie off his belt, "I realize that I fully participated in the kissing and butt groping and licking of nipples and stroking of chest and arms and back, but that doesn't mean I'm interested in you, nor am I even remotely susceptible to seduction."

Gunner cocked an eyebrow at me.

"Dammit, how do you know I'm lying?" I demanded to know.

"I'm not sure. I just know." He turned a couple of knobs on the walkie-talkie, frowned at it, and pulled out his cell phone instead.

"No reception?" I asked a couple of minutes later.

"No. The phone says I have a connection, but it doesn't seem to want to actually connect." He sighed. "One of us will have to go fetch Daria. Would you prefer to stay here with the rats, or should I fend them off while you find her?"

I shuddered. "How about we both go?"

He shook his head and eased himself down onto the ground. "It's hard enough walking with the cast on this ground that I don't want to make extra trips. I'll wait here while you bring her."

"All right, but I'll leave you a shovel so you can whack at any rats that charge you." I shifted both the toolbox and the shovel so that they were set next to him. He immediately took a trowel from the former and started scraping at the exposed stone.

"Tell Daria to bring any portable lights that she can find. And possibly a camp chair if she has one."

"I'll go for the full 'digging in a bolt-hole' kit," I promised, and, picking up one of the lamps, made my way back to the stairs.

"You might also ask the catering people if they could send us some coffee or tea in a bit. I suspect we're going to be down here for a while," Gunner called after me, his voice muffled.

"Will do." I started up the steps, holding the glass lantern carefully. I was mentally rehearsing what I was going to say to Daria when I reached the door and gave it a shove.

It didn't move.

"Well, of course you're stuck. That just figures." I set down the lamp and pushed at the door with both hands.

It still didn't move.

I sighed a sigh of the martyred and threw my full weight against the door.

Nothing happened, but my shoulder protested the action.

"Great. Now I have to go down and get Gunner, and he shouldn't be walking up and down stairs on his owie foot. I just hope you're happy," I told the door, giving it another shove.

I stomped back down the stairs to Gunner.

He looked up, surprised that I was back so quickly. "Change your mind?"

"No. The door is stuck. Can you work your manly magic on it so that I can get us coffee and Daria and chairs and more lights?"

He frowned but followed me back to the door.

Ten minutes later, I started to panic. "What do you mean it's going to take more than you to get it open? You opened it less than half an hour ago! Why can't you open it now?"

"Because I was on the other side of it then, pulling the door toward me. Now I'm on the top of a narrow stair, and I can't get a running start to throw myself into it. And even if I could, I wouldn't, since I'd likely fall and break several more bones." Gunner was silent a moment, rubbing his shoulder where he'd repeatedly attempted to force the door open. "I'm afraid we're stuck here until someone notices we're gone."

I stared at him in horror. "You have got to be kidding!"

"Unfortunately, I'm not." He tried his cell phone again, shaking his head. "Still not connecting even though it displays the network. Do you have a mobile phone?"

"Not one that is set up to work in England. Maybe if you get right next to the door, you can get the walkie-talkie to work."

"I'll try." He sat on the top step and spoke into the radio, but there was no reply.

"Well, that's it," I said dramatically, taking a lamp and marching down the stairs. "We're doomed."

"Careful," he warned, following me at a slower pace. "Those steps are uneven. You could fall and hurt yourself."

"What does it matter? We're going to die down here anyway! I'd rather have a swift death due to a plummet down ancient steps than I would a slow, lingering death where I sit in the dark and wonder if I should try to eat your corpse or use it to catch rats and eat them."

"What makes you think I am going to be the one to die first?" He limped past me back to the part of the passageway where the stone ruins jutted out of the earth. "I've got more body mass than you do, so if we're going to starve to death, then logically you will be the one to go first and I'll have to decide whether to begin by eating your legs or going for your arms."

I wrapped my arms around myself and sank less than gracefully down onto a bit of stone wall. "Oh, I like that! You wouldn't even have a dilemma about whether you should eat me over the rats, where I'd be in all sorts of mental hell trying to justify cannibalizing you. Well, fine. If you want to be that way, then I won't even consider the rats—I'll just start in on you. Happy now?"

"Not very, no, but it's not because of your desire to eat me."

I glanced sharply at him, but there wasn't even the least little bit of a leer about him. That made me sad and oddly irritated. "If you're going to have that attitude, then you're going to be lucky if I wait until you're dead before I start chomping on you."

He surveyed the area for a few minutes, then, with a half shrug, got down onto his butt and started working with a brush and a trowel on the nearest stretch of archaeological interest. "I wouldn't eat your legs unless you were almost dead and were paralyzed."

I gasped. "Oh my god, do you mean you'd seriously eat me while I was still alive?"

"You just said you'd do the same to me."

"I said you'd be lucky if I waited!" I threw a clod of dirt at him. "I never said I'd actually do it. My god, you're a monster, do you know that? You're just a cannibalizing monster!"

"How is it being a monster when you'd be paralyzed and near death?" he asked, brushing the dirt off his leg—my aim sucks. "It's not like you'd feel it. You probably wouldn't even know if I waited until you drifted into a coma."

"I am speechless with appallingness," I said, heedless of grammar, and stood up. "So speechless that I'm going to leave you to your horrible, foul thoughts and take my very nonparalyzed legs and try to find a way out of this hellhole."

"Bolt-hole," he corrected, and other than raising an eyebrow at me, didn't say anything when I shuffled my way past him, carrying one of the lamps.

Almost an hour later, I admitted defeat.

"Back so soon?" he asked, looking up.

"I had to." I held out the lamp. "It ran out of oil."

"Ah. Yes, that was bound to happen. Luckily, this one seems to be all right."

"Gunner," I said, and slumped down next to him, "hold me."

He set down the tools he was still using. "Are you still angry with me?"

"No. I can't do anything about the fact that you don't have the moral compass to leave my legs alone even if I wasn't dead yet. We're trapped in here, Gunner, really trapped. There's nothing farther down the passage other than a big wall of nothing."

He nodded. "That would be the cave-in my father mentioned when Elliott and I were little. There is no more to the bolt-hole."

I scooted over so that he could put his arms around me properly, and leaned into him, breathing in the now slightly musty scent of him. "What are we going to do? I wasn't serious about eating you, you know. I don't want to die down here."

"You won't," he said in a calm, matter-of-fact voice that did much to ease the panic quickly growing inside me.

"You don't know that for certain." I swallowed back a lump of what was most likely tears waiting to be shed. "I don't see how we're going to get out of here. Why aren't you doing something?"

"I am doing something. I'm holding the most desirable woman in the world."

"Yes, you are, if by that you consider that your world is limited to this passageway, but that also means I'm the *only* desirable woman in the world, so I'm not too ecstatic over the title."

He chuckled into my hair, then slid a finger beneath my chin and tipped my head upward so his lips brushed mine when he spoke. "If I told you that at this moment the only thing concerning me is whether I'm going to be able to keep my hands off you, would you think I was sex obsessed?"

"No, but that's only because I've been trying all morning not to slide my hands into your shirt."

"Why would you stop an urge like that?" He kissed me before I could answer, his mouth warm and wonderful and so exciting that it almost made me forget the fact that we were more or less buried in a tomb beneath the castle.

I swear that every nerve in my body was alight at that moment. I simultaneously didn't want the kiss to end and wanted to fling Gunner to the ground, strip off his clothes, and rub myself all over him.

"Lorina?" He ran his thumb over my lip.

I quivered like a plucked bowstring. "Hmm?"

"If you want to put your hands under my shirt, you can. I'd even take it off for you, if you like. My shirt, not your hands. Evidently I've lost the ability to grammar."

"I think that's just my mouth being infectious," I told him, and started to reach for his chest. I stopped when my brain finally recovered enough from the kiss to remind me of several things.

His eyes narrowed on me. "What are you doing? You're thinking, aren't you? I can see you are. You were about to torment my chest again, and then you thought of something and stopped. Stop thinking. There's no reason you shouldn't touch my chest. And for that matter, any other part of me that happens to tempt you."

I sat on my hands. "You know, there are times when I really wish I could stop thinking. But unfortunately, my brain is annoying and it picks weird moments to remind me of things, and it just reminded me of something important."

Also available from
New York Times bestselling author

KATIE MACALISTER

The Dark Ones Novels

Even Vampires Get the Blues
The Last of the Red-Hot Vampires
Zen and the Art of Vampires
Crouching Vampire, Hidden Fang
In the Company of Vampires
Much Ado About Vampires
A Tale of Two Vampires

"Her world-building is excellent."
—*USA Today*

Available wherever books are sold or at
penguin.com

facebook.com/ProjectParanormalBooks